# READERS LOV
# JACKIE K

## JOB HUNT

*Job Hunt is a very well-written, fast-paced, action-packed, thrilling piece of entertainment that kept me glued to the pages.* — Prism Book Alliance

*This book was fun to read and damn hot. Just reading it set my sheets on fire.* — MM Good Book Reviews

## GHOSTS

*...a mellower, slightly introspective read with a beauty all of its own.* — Boy Meets Boy Book Reviews

*This book was a different kind of wonderful than the first, quieter, slower, more down to earth and less cyberspace-high. I read it with a wistful smile and closed it with a happy sigh.* — Prism Book Alliance

## HOUSE HUNT

*This next part of Jack's journey to finding a man to love and a real home remains thriller-level exciting, emotionally engaging, and has more twists and turns than I thought possible.* — Rainbow Book Reviews

*House Hunt is another double thriller from Jackie Keswick. It's suspenseful, fast paced and action packed, and keeps you on the edge of your seat.* — The Novel Approach

# More From Jackie Keswick

## Zero Rising
The Power of Zero
Two Divided by Zero
Zero Tolerance (Coming Soon)

## The Power of Zero
Job Hunt
Ghosts
House Hunt
Swings & Roundabouts
Dating Games
A Simple Mistake (Coming Soon)

## Rock & Art Theft
Undercover Star
Here for You
Starstruck (coming soon)

## Shades
Sword Oath
Shadow Realm
Soulbound

## Standalone Stories
Leap of Faith
Crossfire
Repeat Offence
Healing Glass
Murder for the Greater Good
Baubles

# Job Hunt

## THE POWER OF ZERO: BOOK ONE

## JACKIE KESWICK

This is a work of fiction. Names, characters, places, and incidents either are the product of author imagination or are used fictitiously, and any resemblance to actual persons, living or dead, business establishments, events, or locales is entirely coincidental.

Job Hunt
© 2015 Jackie Keswick.
Second Edition: © 2020 Jackie Keswick.

Cover Art
© 2020 Pavelle Art
Cover content is for illustrative purposes only and any person depicted on the cover is a model.

Warning
This book contains references to the sexual exploitation of children.

ISBN: 9798668178315

*For Steve.*

*For rocks and kite strings and too many cups of tea to count. None of this could have happened without your high tolerance for disjointed conversation and random music.*

*And for the real Jack.*
*I heard you.*

# INTERVIEW

**M**idmorning traffic on the Strand was steady. Jack Horwood drifted with the flow of pedestrians—mostly tourists and visitors to the capital with the odd office worker out on an errand—past the Savoy Hotel and on towards Simpson's in the Strand. The buzz and bustle reminded him of the morning after his viva exam when he and Tom had decided to treat themselves to a proper breakfast after a night out celebrating. And how that simple decision had turned into the grandest and most magnificent breakfast the two had ever seen. Or eaten.

*The Ten Deadly Sins? Was that what they called it?*

He stopped outside the restaurant's ornate entrance and snuck a peek at the menu. Yes, he'd remembered that right: everything you ever thought of eating for breakfast and then some. And they were still serving it.

Maybe, if this job interview worked out, he'd do it

again. Heaven knew he needed it. He'd shed a lot of weight in the last nine months—his usual reaction to stress—and his suit sat a little too loosely on his waist. Though trying Simpson's again without Tom might be only half the fun.

The last he'd heard, Tom Walken was off somewhere arid and rocky in the company of a hammer, preferring the life of a freelance mineral prospector to drawing a regular salary on the staff of a big mining company. Meeting for lunch at Simpson's might be tricky, but just the memories made Jack wonder if his friend would consider working for the company Jack hoped to make his next home.

Compared to the elegance of Somerset House, the Victorian red brick and white trim edifice that housed Nancarrow Mining looked ostentatious, but Jack knew that the inside of the building had a very different feel. A bit like his redheaded friend, who resembled a model pretending to be a hoodlum but had his very own brand of loyalty and integrity. Jack thought that Tom would approve of Jack's plans.

Jack Horwood had never had a job, before or after university, that did not involve the government in some capacity. He'd freelanced on projects for the secret service since he'd turned fourteen, so joining MI6 after leaving the army and gaining his doctorate had seemed the logical next step on his career path. It had taken the last couple of years, and especially his last assignment, for him to decide that it wasn't the life he wanted. He wasn't content to be written off as collateral damage. He didn't aspire to be a pawn in someone's power game. Nor did he want to be seen as a liability.

So, he quit.

And now here he was, looking for another job to fill his days. Something to pay the bills, if someone was asking. Another crusade to fight, if he was honest.

Jack slid out of the stream of pedestrian traffic and stopped in front of a store display. He had a few minutes to kill before his interview. He was also desperate for more caffeine, but that particular craving would have to wait until later. He wasn't on duty, hadn't been on duty for four months, yet he automatically scanned the crowd for conflict points, the traffic for threats, the surrounding buildings for cover and hideouts. When he checked his reflection in the glass before him, though, only his professional façade was visible: a light grey suit, the jacket fitted to his wide shoulders and slim hips, and a shirt the exact same eucalyptus leaf shade as his eyes accented by a deep green tie. His face, schooled into a calm mask, showed none of his thoughts, and the tattoo on his left temple was almost hidden by his mop of dark spikes.

Pretending interest in the store's merchandise, Jack ran a fingertip over the tattoo. Though the choice to leave the army had been his and his only, he'd struggled with guilt and heartache, had felt lost and adrift and alone. For a time back there, he'd rarely ever been sober, but when he came home with that tattoo, Tom had finally flipped and kicked his arse into the next week, not realising until much later that the tattoo had been Jack's way of grounding himself.

It seemed inconceivable that anyone so conspicuously marked would be good at undercover work, but Jack had a knack for it. Despite the tattoo, he could blend—better than most of his peers, who didn't stand out to begin with. He never bothered pointing out that just having the tat was akin to wearing a sign saying *this guy could never be a cop*.

Undercover work wasn't all Jack did or what he'd been recruited to do in the first place. He was a systems security specialist. An excellent one, if you read his appraisals. A damned hacker, if you talked to people at the receiving end of his skills. Analysing and sequencing data was second nature to him. He didn't wait for loopholes. Neither did he go out of his way to find compromised systems—he simply created them when needed. Whether or not he was tattooed hadn't entered into the equation until much, much later.

Jobs for his kind of skills simply were not

advertised.

He'd taken time out after resigning from MI6, spent a couple of weeks on a beach, three weeks in a retreat practising kendo, and when he returned to England, he'd been ready for a new challenge.

With nobody but himself to answer to, he'd thrown himself into research, creating a list of companies that were under attack from their competitors. He even pulled a few all-nighters sneaking into networks to prove how vulnerable his targets really were. Just to refine his list.

Then he'd started his real job hunt. One by one he dissected each company: their books, leaders, projects, cash flow, customers, and values until only a handful were left. Five corporations that Jack wanted to work for. Five corporations with the mindset, projects, policies, and ethics to attract him. Nancarrow Mining was at the top of that list.

His watch buzzed a ten-minute alert, and Jack turned from his contemplation of what he now saw were women's shoes. He took a breath and then a second, deeper one. The hint of pressure across his throat reminded him of the narrow strip of embossed leather that caressed his skin just under the edge of his tie, offering comfort and reassurance. Ahead of him loomed the huge metal-banded mahogany gates that guarded Nancarrow Mining's headquarters. Beside the ostentatious entrance was a more sensibly sized door—for people without megalomania—and Jack smiled, at ease with the world and with himself.

———— ◆ ◆ ◆ ————

Two hours later the world was still the right way up, and Jack got to see it through floor-to-ceiling windows from the executive floor.

The London Eye spun serenely.

The Thames flowed as it had since the last ice age.

And if he squinted and craned his neck a little, he could just make out red, open-topped buses between rows of trees, ferrying tourists along Victoria Embankment.

It didn't bother him that he did all this while civilly answering questions and discussing security issues common to most larger corporations. If anything, the sightseeing kept him calm. His mind ran on at least two tracks for most of the time, and that wasn't a habit he wanted to break.

He had hoped to find a kindred spirit in Donald Frazer, Nancarrow Mining's own systems security specialist, and he wasn't disappointed. The Scot was young for the job, but he was good. And fun to tease. Within moments of meeting, their discussion turned technical, and banter and insults followed shortly after. Jack deliberately played on his reputation, but Frazer wasn't the least bit awed. He knew his stuff, and he wasn't scared to call Jack out when he suspected bullshit.

"That's about as logical as a first-generation Pentium," Frazer commented on one of Jack's assertions, making Jack laugh.

"I can prove it," he baited, just as the room's door opened behind him. Jack didn't turn around to see who had entered. Not until his world flipped upside down and ground to a screeching stop at the sound of a voice he'd not heard in almost eight years.

"Horwood."

―――――＋◆＋――――――

Jack stared at a man he'd never thought to meet again, praying that his mouth was closed. Then a part of him remembered old times and old habits. He shot out of his seat, back straight, hands by his sides.

"Captain Flynn, sir!"

It confused him that his body acted without his mind giving directions, but the confusion fled when Gareth laughed. Jack remembered the sound of that laugh from his army days. The deep rumble had once had the power to turn an ambush into a training exercise. No wonder it sent shivers down Jack's spine.

"Stand down, Horwood." Gareth Flynn smoothed a hand over the lapel of his charcoal pinstriped suit. "No uniform, see?"

"Yes, sir." Jack's brain refused to process the facts. If this was a test, if Gareth wanted to see how Jack reacted under sudden extreme stress… then he'd just failed spectacularly.

"Are you about done, Frazer?" Gareth asked and turned to Jack when Donald Frazer nodded. "I'd like to discuss a few other issues with you. Would you care for lunch?"

Jack couldn't have answered coherently had he tried, so he merely shook hands with Frazer before he followed Gareth from the room and into the nearest elevator.

Physically his former commanding officer hadn't changed much. He'd had white hair in his twenties, and time had only added a few lines to his forehead and the corners of his amber eyes. Gareth Flynn stood tall, moved smoothly, and his presence had the solidity Jack had always loved. The silver hair was a little longer than Jack remembered, and it tried to stand up in spikes to rival Jack's. It didn't really suit Gareth Flynn's chiselled features and tough image, but Jack found it adorable.

He watched the man from the corner of his eye while they braved the bustle of the Strand at lunchtime and dodged people carrying sandwiches and coffee to go. His memories were of Gareth in fatigues, sleeves rolled up and muscular forearms on display, but Gareth Flynn in a pinstriped suit that fitted like a second skin across his broad shoulders and was tailored to hug his narrow hips just as closely… well, that was downright hot.

"You've made a right name for yourself," Gareth rumbled, voice raised a notch to be heard over the rattle and chug of a red Routemaster bus that passed only a few feet from the edge of the pavement. "But did you have to become a bloody spook? I had to pull in favours to find you, only to learn that you'd just quit your job and disappeared again."

"You were looking for me?" Jack couldn't quite wrap his head around that.

"For the better part of a year, I'll have you know," Gareth growled, sounding almost offended at the length of time it had taken. He slid out of the stream of pedestrians, leading them up the steps and through the entrance to Simpson's in the Strand. The burnished copper sign saying simply "Simpson's" looked as imposing as Jack remembered it. Entering the iconic restaurant's hallowed halls felt like stepping back in time. Now as then, huge chandeliers lit the foyer and brightened the dimness of the wood-panelled dining room, their light dancing over crystal and china and adding a soft gleam to the table linens. The mouth-watering scent of roasting meat enveloped them like a welcoming hug, and Jack's stomach reminded him that he'd skipped breakfast.

Gareth Flynn didn't seem to need a reservation. He merely nodded a greeting to the maître d' before the man conducted them to a quiet booth at the far end of the room.

Jack followed in silence. The world around him felt like a beautiful island paradise littered with land mines, a pleasant dream that could turn into a nightmare at any moment. It urged him to caution, to move with care, to listen rather than speak.

They settled into the soft cushions, and Jack's brain unscrambled enough to let him ask a question. "Do you come here a lot?"

"Often enough for the staff to know that I want peace and privacy when I do."

The answer was just this side of caustic, and Jack met Gareth's eyes for the first time since the man's surprise appearance at his interview. It wasn't the smartest move in the book. The amber eyes burned with an intensity that snared Jack's mind and took his breath. And that was before Gareth smiled.

A real, genuine smile curved the full lips into a tempting bow and crinkled the corners of Gareth's eyes into spider webs of mirth. Jack felt the warmth of that gaze like a physical touch, and he let himself drown in the sensation, painfully aware of how much he had missed seeing that smile.

"What are you drinking?"

Gareth's amused tone drew Jack from his abstraction. He blinked, noted the waiter by his side—*where did he spring from? And how long has he been standing there?*—and registered Gareth's words.

"Just water, thanks," Jack answered. He really wanted something a little more potent, but that would have to wait until he made it home. For now, he had to pull himself together and act like the professional he was. Hiding behind the menu while he chose his lunch helped him settle, and after the waiter had brought their drinks and taken their orders, he felt a tad more ready to deal with Gareth Flynn.

"When did you leave the army?" he asked, pleased when his voice came out level.

"Eighteen months ago," Gareth replied, raising his gin and tonic in a brief salute before taking a sip.

"Why?" The question slipped out before Jack could censor, and he fought not to flinch. He wanted to know, but... "Sorry. Bad form to quiz the boss—I remember." His brain stuttered over the old, familiar phrase. He hadn't heard or used it in too many years, yet here it was. Out of the mouths of babes and idiots….

"Jack."

Gareth's tone, commanding and hesitant at once, made him lift his head. Gareth wasn't smiling this time, and his gaze was unforgiving.

*What did I say?*

Their food arrived, distracting them both, and Jack was content to let the issue drop. He didn't doubt that Gareth would revisit this if it bothered him. Leaving things unfinished had never been Gareth's way. Jack concentrated on his lunch—the devilled kidneys served with his Barnsley chop were just the way he liked them, with a nice kick at the end—and wondered if Gareth's habit of neatly tying loose ends was the reason for this meeting.

"Have you really been looking for me?"

"Yes," Gareth confirmed around a mouthful of roast beef.

"Why?" This time, Jack didn't flinch when he asked. This wasn't quizzing the boss. He was… gathering intel.

"At first, I just wanted to catch up," Gareth mused. "Then I joined Nancarrow Mining and thought you might enjoy working there." He pinned Jack with a direct stare. "And I wasn't wrong, was I?"

"No." The stab of disappointment was swift and sharp, but Jack kept his face blank and his answer to a single syllable. He *had* approached Nancarrow Mining about a job, so he couldn't very well argue with Gareth's assessment. "Is that the problem?" he asked instead. "You no longer think so now that you've seen my CV and watched the interview?"

"What do you mean?"

Jack raised an eyebrow. "If you're trying to tell me that there isn't a camera in that monstrous gilt frame behind the group of armchairs—"

*… you can save your breath.*

"I'm not," Gareth interrupted. "And I'd appreciate it if you'd stop second-guessing me. If you possess half the brain everyone says you do, you must remember that I really hate being told what I'm thinking." He set his knife down with a little too much force and clenched his fingers around the almost empty crystal tumbler. "I thought I'd beaten that out of you years ago," he added under his breath.

Jack couldn't stop the grin that spread across his face. This was vintage Gareth, from the bite in the tone to the stilted language, right down to the hand reaching for a convenient missile. Not that the crystal tumbler would come screaming at his head any time soon, but the reminder was… nice. Another little piece of history verified, shifted from the realms of wishful thinking into the box marked "real and true."

Jack relaxed against his seat's cushioned backrest.

"Tell me what it is, then," he demanded with something close to his usual aplomb. "Why did you gate-crash the interview? If you think I fit so well, why not let bureaucracy run its course and surprise me on my first day?"

"Because I haven't seen you in years," Gareth replied, voice harsh. "Because you walked out without giving a single good reason. Because you've been avoiding all of us ever since." He drew a deep breath and calmed himself with an effort. "Because I wanted to see if you'd avoid me if I stood right there."

Heat washed across Jack's neck and face. He'd known that Gareth would see his actions as a kind of desertion, but hearing the pain in the man's voice as he recounted it hurt Jack on a level he didn't think he could hurt anymore.

"I had a reason," he told the linen-draped tabletop.

"I never disputed that. I just wish you'd trusted me enough to explain it to me." Like Jack had done earlier, Gareth leaned back from the table and tried to relax. "Tell me one thing," he said. "Was it PTSD?"

Jack drew a deep breath, grateful that Gareth didn't pry. Grateful, too, that this was a question he could answer. He looked up, straight into a pair of intent amber eyes. "No."

Gareth nodded, and his shoulders relaxed a fraction. "Fine," he growled, before he pointed a finger at Jack's face. "Now, what's with that tat?"

"Don't ask," Jack groaned, wishing for a place to hide. Of course, there wasn't one. Short of draping a napkin over his head or stripping off his jacket, there was little cover to be had while facing Gareth across a dining table. Just as there was no way in hell he'd admit his real reason for getting that tattoo. "It was an idiocy committed on the back of too much booze, okay?"

"Should have known," Gareth snorted. "How could you be a spook looking like that?"

"It's a gift."

"No doubt. Do you use makeup?"

"Don't be ridiculous." Jack had been trained to change his appearance—and hide the tattoo—using both cosmetic and theatrical makeup, but Gareth didn't need to know that. Or what Jack looked like while he hunted pimps through nightclubs.

The banter cleared the air, and both men stayed away from serious topics while they finished their meal and drank their coffee. Only when the grand entrance of Simpson's closed behind them and they re-joined the throng of pedestrians on the Strand, did Gareth return to their earlier conversation.

"I want you to work for me." Gareth's voice was low and serious. "We're more than busy. There's plenty of competition, and the fight gets dirty at times. Provided you're careful, you wouldn't even have to stick to one side of the law only." Gareth ran a hand through his hair and sighed. "Listen to me. I sound like a used car salesman."

He did, in an endearing way, but Jack was too tense to be entertained. "Gareth, I… I'll think about it."

"Yes, you do. Think. Usually too much." Gareth waved a hand in the air, an odd aura of defeat surrounding him. "Go and think. But watch that you don't think yourself out of something you actually want."

⬥ ⬥ ⬥

Time sped and slowed in odd patterns when there were no means to estimate how late or early it might be. Being stuck in the dark made it worse, but Ricky had long given up asking for a light to be left on. Nobody cared enough to listen, and Ricky would rather not reveal another weakness for his keepers to taunt him with. Curled into a tight, tense ball, he huddled into his blankets. He buried his head under the lumpy pillow and tried to block out the sobs and pained shouts filtering through the thin walls from Nico and Daniel's room next door.

The scent of patchouli hung in the locked,

windowless room, so thick that he gagged if he breathed too deeply. His father used to wear it, and Ricky's memories were full of insults, shouts, and pain, always accompanied by the sickly sweet, invasive scent. It made sense that Goran Mitrovic reeked of patchouli. The pimp got off on pain. He got off even more on inflicting it on others, though he tortured with more deliberation than Ricky's late and unlamented father.

Ricky found no pleasure in being hurt, but he'd long since learned that being caned was sometimes better than the alternative: streams of strangers through his room at all hours, hard hands and rough mouths on his body, and nothing but threats and insults in his ears. Ricky barely heard the words anymore. Being apostrophised as a filthy, dirty whore didn't bother him.

He was better than that.

He had choices.

Being caned was the easy way out sometimes.

Daniel didn't agree, but the slender, blond teen didn't deal well with pain or violence. Daniel could hide inside his mind—something Ricky had never learned to do—and it seemed to help get the younger boy through the days and nights.

*Please, don't do anything stupid! Just give him what he wants,* Ricky begged silently. He knew that prayers served no purpose, but the sounds coming through the thin walls made him screw his eyes shut and address any higher powers that might perchance be listening. Or maybe he was simply hoping to connect with the youngest member of their little group, who refused to scream even though it might end the beating sooner.

The wall blocked the hiss of the whip, but it did little to muffle the sounds of harsh, rough laughter from the adjoining room. Daniel's screams made Ricky bite his knuckles, made him flinch and shudder and drag the thin pillow tighter over his head, while Nico's bitten off groans tore at his soul.

Ricky knew that Nico would rather take a beating than watch his friend being hurt and abused, that he frequently offered himself in Daniel's place, to clients as well as their jailer. It had worked often enough that Nico had grown just a little too sure. He'd tried to spare Daniel when Goran was in a foul mood, and now both boys were reaping the fruits of his failure.

Ricky was wiser in the ways of their world. He had learned to pick his battles.

It hurt, but he swallowed the urge to hammer on the walls to stop the torture. Getting in the way of Goran's entertainment would accomplish nothing; might even prolong the violence if he misjudged. At sixteen, he was the eldest of Goran's boys and had been in the man's clutches the longest. That didn't mean that Goran listened to anything Ricky said. Just like the other boys, Ricky was caged. The doors to his prison opened when Goran saw fit and not a moment sooner.

Ricky pulled the thin blanket tighter over his head and buried his face deeper in the pillow. The rough laughs, Nico's broken sobs, and Daniel's screams continued for some time. Ricky huddled under his covers, muscles tight, and kept his eyes wide open in the dark long after the screams had turned to silence.

# BAIT

———◆◆◆———

Jack didn't talk to dead people. Not when sober, not when drunk. He wasn't often plagued by nightmares, either. The ghosts that haunted Jack Horwood were all among the living. And no nightmare matched the tortures his mind could inflict upon itself.

He hadn't bothered to change when he came home, merely shed his tie and the coat of his suit before reaching for a bottle of his namesake. Soul-searching didn't require fine Islay malt. Neat Jack D. was plenty to get him good and drunk. Not quite sozzled enough to muzzle his brain, but close.

It was as good as it was going to get. Any more whisky and he'd be throwing up his guts for the next six hours—a prospect that just didn't appeal, not even for the sake of nothing but white noise between his ears.

This morning's interview had rattled him, had

upset the equilibrium he had worked so hard to attain. Now his world teetered out of balance. Reality and want clashed with options he'd not realised he had.

Should he continue down his chosen road or take a turn towards something new? Confront familiar dangers or face unknown risks?

He had to decide before the alcohol-induced fog thinned and his mind went down six tracks at once again.

He stood by his bedroom window and looked out over the sleeping neighbourhood of well-kept Victorian terraces and tree-lined streets. He lived in a decent part of town these days, where people had few reasons to break the law. At this time of night, the streets lay empty, quiet, and seemingly peaceful.

Jack knew better. He had seen the living nightmares that hid in dark corners come out and prey on the unsuspecting when the sun went down. He had run from them as a kid, dodged them as a teen, and now he fought them with all his strength.

His army career had been the first thing that Jack had chosen purely for himself. He'd felt accepted there. Safe. Which was ironic, given what they did for a living. Walking away had been torture, had derailed Jack more than he'd expected it would. And it had taken a long time for him to settle and to find a measure of equilibrium. But he'd done it.

Jack was proud of his hard-won peace. He wasn't happy, but he hadn't expected to be happy. He kept busy, and he was useful—that was enough.

He stepped back from the window and closed the blinds. Then he fell onto his bed, still half-clothed but with his decision made.

⬥ ⬥ ⬥

The ringing phone brought Jack awake. Pearly grey light filtered around the blinds—too bright for his migraine-grade headache. *Too much thought and not enough water,* his subconscious mind supplied helpfully as memories of the previous day and night returned. They explained the headache and queasy stomach, explained why he sprawled across his bed in shirt and trousers… didn't explain why he had woken.

The phone. Right.

He rolled across the expanse of deep green quilt, wincing at the hammer blows inside his head, and snatched the phone from the bedside table.

"Horwood."

"Good morning, Dr. Horwood," said a voice that was too chipper for early morning. "This is Alexandra Marston, calling from Nancarrow Mining. We would like to offer you a position with our corporate security team. Can you visit the Strand office this morning to discuss your contract?"

Jack stared into the dimness of his bedroom, noting his keys on the dresser where he'd tossed them on coming home. The mostly empty whisky bottle lay on the carpet beside his shoes. His suit jacket and tie hung on the wardrobe door.

"Dr. Horwood?"

Jack roused himself a little. Answers. Decisions. A job he would love. A place to belong. Home.

"Sorry, Ms. Marston," he said slowly into the handset. "I am flattered that you think me a suitable candidate, but I have to decline your offer. I will not be able to work for Nancarrow Mining. Thank you for your time."

He disconnected the call before he changed his mind, or she tried to do it for him.

The phone dropped to the bedspread.

Jack knew that he should get out of his suit trousers and shirt, should find some aspirin and a bottle of water, should get some more sleep or go take a shower. The knowledge didn't translate into movement. He continued to stare at nothing until the early autumn sun burned off the morning mist and bathed his bedroom in a light so bright it left no room for shadows.

At close to eight o'clock in the evening, traffic around Wimbledon was dying down. Gareth Flynn slid his Range Rover into a parking space close to Jack's house, a little surprised to find himself on a street lined by trees and meticulously restored Victorian redbrick terraces. Given his penchant for petrol-powered crotch rockets and high-tech computer equipment, he hadn't expected Jack's taste in homes to run to Victorian splendour. Neither could he have guessed that Jack's house would be one of the best kept on the street.

The deep red front door sported stained glass inserts set aglow by the hallway lights. The bow windows and porch trim were painted white, while black cast-iron railings edged the steps down to the basement, surrounded the small parking space for Jack's motorbike, and marked the path to his front door. And the matching black and red tiles that covered the whole area looked like something out of a TV makeover show.

The house proved just as unexpected as he remembered Jack to be. Gareth had never been able to determine if the about-turns, false trails, and surprises had been deliberately crafted to confuse, or if they were… simply Jack. Gareth turned off the engine and sat in silence for a time, eyes narrowed in thought.

*Am I an idiot for going after the brat like this?*

He had been disappointed but not surprised when Jack turned down the offer of a position with Nancarrow Mining's CorpSec team. Jack could argue himself out of a lottery win given enough incentive, so rationalising why he didn't want to work with Gareth again wouldn't be a difficult task.

Alexandra's comment that Jack had sounded as if he was suffering from a gargantuan hangover had made Gareth wonder if there was still a chance to change the younger man's mind. Determined to try, Gareth crossed the road to Jack's front door and leaned on the bell.

"For fuck's sake don't you own a watch?" came Jack's voice from inside the house. "You said I had two hours, and that wasn't nearly enough time. I'm not a miracle worker!" The door opened, and the rant came to a sudden halt as Jack saw who stood on his doorstep. "Gareth?" he asked, voice uncertain. "Are you moonlighting for the Met now?"

"Holy Mother of...!" Gareth's mouth fell open. Jack looked barely legal and was dressed like.... Words failed him, and even swearing would only get him so far. So he stared. At leather, tanned skin, and hard muscle. At what had to be one of the hottest sights he'd ever seen.

Jack Horwood was a mirage of smooth flowing lines and sharp angles. From long legs that looked even longer encased in sinfully tight black leather and knee-high boots, to the high collar on the sleeveless green shirt, the man looked simply edible. Bare arms showed off tanned skin and muscled biceps, and the waistband of the trousers sat so low, the tips of Jack's hipbones peeked out. And the ridges of his toned abs…

Jack Horwood was a vision. Shocking, jarring, and utterly and totally wrong.

Jack had never looked his age. Not at seventeen when he'd joined Gareth's unit, not at twenty-two when he'd left it. He'd grown up since then, had added more muscle and acquired that stupid tattoo, but very few people would guess his real age on meeting him.

Gareth knew that. Had memories enough. But he'd never seen Jack look so vulnerable. Or so innocent. His cheekbones were sharp enough to cut glass, and not even a hint of shadow darkened his jaw. Liner and mascara had turned his eyes into pools of the deepest green, ready to snare and trap anyone foolish enough to look into them too long.

"Maybe you'd better come in, and I'll explain," Jack muttered and stepped away from the door.

Jack's living room was cluttered with duffel bags

that spilled their guts across the carpet. Two of the large bags held clothes, a third one smelled strongly of leather, and the fourth one—a large foldout case like the ones used by plumbers, travelling mechanics, or makeup artists—qualified for its own defence budget. It appeared to hold a specimen of almost every edged and pointed weapon ever invented.

Jack opened his mouth to speak, but Gareth stopped him. "If you're going to say that it isn't what I think it is, I'll hit you."

Jack closed his mouth, then his eyes, and took a deep breath.

Whatever else had happened over the years, Jack's tried and trusted remedy for keeping his temper on a leash hadn't changed. It looked just as adorable as it always had. "Are *you* moonlighting for the Met?" Gareth asked softly, and more for confirmation. The quantity of weapons in the room almost made it a foregone conclusion.

"I just help out now and then," Jack replied, gaze level.

"By playing bait."

"I'm good at it."

"I can see that." Gareth's blood had caught alight the moment Jack had opened the door. Even irritated and distracted, Jack was devastating. Gareth didn't want to imagine what Jack would be like once he focussed on his role. He might spontaneously combust if he did.

Gareth sought for a distraction. Asking whether Jack's work for the police was the reason that he'd refused the job at Nancarrow Mining seemed unwise. And it wasn't in Gareth's nature to push when it wouldn't get him anywhere.

"Is it legit?" he enquired finally.

Jack's lips quirked up at the corners. "They can't take exception to what they don't know…."

"I see. Whom are you baiting, anyway?"

The doorbell rang before Jack could answer. "It's open," he yelled in the direction of the hallway, and a moment later, a lanky blond man stepped into the room. He wore dark blue tailored trousers and a shirt of light blue silk that matched the colour of his eyes and carried a black leather jacket draped over one arm.

"We're late," he said before Jack could greet him.

"*You* may be late," Jack shot back, rummaging in the smallest duffel bag. "I've told you before that I need three hours. Not two. Not one. Three. If you have a problem with that—"

"You can't take any weapons," the man interrupted. "They're frisking."

Jack sat back on his heels. "You have *got* to be fucking kidding me."

"I'm not. No patrons through the door without a search—not even the kids."

"Call it off," Jack ordered, and his voice didn't waver.

"Jack, I can't." The man's bravado evaporated until he sounded desperate. "It's the only lead I have."

Jack shook his head, and Gareth was proud of him. His visitor pushed all the right buttons, making Gareth wonder how well he knew Jack, but Jack didn't give in.

"I'll not set one foot in that fucking place without a weapon! Not after the lousy intel you gave me last time," Jack said. "Can you call for backup?"

"I've only rumours. Nothing that will convince a magistrate to give me a warrant."

"Then I go armed or we call it off. You have two choices."

"Three," Gareth said and grinned when two startled faces turned his way. It was comical to see Jack recall his presence with a snap, while the stranger stared at him with clear suspicion in his eyes. "There are three choices."

"What's the third?" the man asked, but Gareth kept his eyes on Jack, not wanting to miss his reaction.

"What if I tag along and watch your back?"

# Hard Facts

———————— ◆ ◆ ◆ ————————

"**Y**ou'd do that?"

Jack's wide-eyed stare was a balm for Gareth's doubts. Jack wasn't shying away from the idea of working with Gareth. Rather the opposite, if the gratitude in the green eyes was anything to go by.

"Fill me in, and I'll keep you out of trouble," he said, expecting a typical Jack briefing—where, what, and how in six sentences. Instead, he found the blond man planted in front of him, hands on hips and glaring.

"You can't be armed, either."

"I heard you the first time." Gareth kept his face blank and his temper even, and he got a co-conspirator's smile from Jack as his reward. Just a tiny tilt of lip, but it acknowledged a truth neither needed to voice.

"Clive, relax," Jack counselled. "By the way, this is

Gareth Flynn. Gareth, Detective Inspector Clive Baxter from the Met. Why don't you get acquainted while I finish getting ready?"

"Skin trade?" Gareth asked as Jack turned and disappeared through the door and up the stairs. Given the way Jack was dressed, it was the most likely option. Baxter nodded, and Gareth wanted to ask how well the detective knew Jack, but he pushed the thought aside. "You do this a lot?" he asked instead.

"Not really, no. I was a liaison on one of Jack's cases when he was…," Baxter hesitated, and Gareth just waved for him to continue. He already had chapter and verse of Jack's official activities. "We kept on working… together… afterwards, I mean."

Jack came back into the room to grab yet another bag. The tattoo on his temple now looked like a clumsily applied sticker. He'd also changed from his green, sleeveless shirt into a long-sleeved, mustard-coloured one that was just slightly too big across the shoulders. Just that tiny change made Jack look younger, skinnier, and somehow even more vulnerable.

"What he means to say is that we both want to get the rats off the street, so we keep sweeping," Jack explained.

"Don't mix your metaphors. To catch rats you need a piper not a sweep."

"Not if they're dead rats." Jack paused on his way back upstairs to watch the detective stare at the clock for the umpteenth time. "Clive, stop fidgeting."

"I don't want to miss him."

"Then go ahead and set up. We'll catch up with you."

Baxter hesitated for just a moment. Then he nodded and turned towards the door. "Don't be too long," he admonished before he went out.

"Or all the ice cream will be gone," Jack grumbled and turned to Gareth. His smile held an apology. "You don't have to do this, sir."

"I know." Gareth hesitated but then forged ahead. "I saw your face when you told him to call it off."

"It was the right decision, but…" Jack started over. "I would have hated it," he admitted. "Word on the street is that this fucker goes after the youngest and most vulnerable boys. He's a gorilla… uses violence to keep the kids in line. And Clive has nothing to…."

"What's your objective tonight?" Gareth's calm tone fought Jack's rising agitation. It worked, just as it always had in the past.

"We have nothing on the man. And I mean nothing. So, ID. Photos, fingerprints… any evidence." Jack's eyes locked with Gareth's. "And you still don't have to do this."

"Oh, I don't know. After the day I've had, a spot of

violence sounds appealing." Gareth pulled out his scariest grin and laughed when Jack rolled his eyes. "Tell me this isn't why you quit your job."

"This isn't why I quit my job," Jack parroted and inspected his reflection in the hallway mirror. "It's not always like this, either," he said and waved for Gareth to follow him upstairs. "Most of the time, I don't even leave the house."

Gareth leaned against the doorframe and watched Jack use both hands and a tub of product to turn his dark hair into a spiky mop. He had no trouble believing Jack's words. Jack and computers went way back. He'd had a reputation for being hell on a keyboard before he was old enough to vote—a reputation that had grown steadily over the years. Even without the data he had offered to support his application to Nancarrow Mining, it was obvious that he now played in a different league.

"I hope you're taking precautions," he said in a gruff voice, feeling like a parent giving *the talk* to their wayward offspring.

Jack didn't pretend to misunderstand. "Clive's the one who wants to put perverts behind bars," he said. "I just want them stopped. I don't care how we go about it, but I do not plant or manufacture evidence. Ever." He threw Gareth a look over his shoulder. "Just so we're clear, sir."

"So what do you do?"

Jack reached for a small bottle and uncapped it. He tipped his head back and dribbled clear liquid into each eye. When he turned to look at Gareth, his pupils were blown so wide and dark that Gareth had to swallow. Hard.

"Belladonna," Jack explained and dropped the bottle onto the dresser. He slung a belt around his hips and cinched it. "I find men who use children for sex and make sure they're taken out," he said in answer to Gareth's question. "I don't much care about a few dirty pictures here or there, but the bastards who are buying… their choices have consequences. I make it easy for Clive and chums to find the evidence they need to prosecute. And if they're told not to look…."

"I see." And Gareth did see. He saw the evidence of Jack's crusade, the quiet fury that made his movements quick and sharp. The resolve and determination that were evident in the multitude of supplies and guises, in the careful preparation, and in the way Jack turned himself into a weapon that would never be recognised or suspected as such.

"So I'll be a pimp?"

"No," came the swift reply. "No competition. I'll draw his attention. You collect evidence."

"What if someone propositions you?" Gareth would never know where Jack found that smile, but it

34

was a valiant effort. It was even almost a smile.

"I'll deal. Or we get out."

"I vote we get out." Jack wasn't a helpless victim, but Gareth didn't know if he could watch him having to deal with unwanted attention. Not when a fight would blow Jack's cover, and he'd be catching hell from his boss the next morning for starting shit in public. "You have anything for a diversion?"

"Lollipops." Jack pushed past Gareth and pointed to a blue cloth roll that lay open on his bed. "Remember those?"

Gareth remembered the ridiculous smoke bombs disguised as sweets they'd used on one of their training exercises. Whoever had come up with the things had clearly read too much James Bond and was channelling Q. "Really?" he complained. "Do you have to make me look like Kojak?"

"Who?"

"Never mind. Be grateful you're not old enough." He picked up a couple of the cellophane wrapped sweets—military issue, every last one—and pushed them into his pocket. "What does the target look like?"

"Caucasian male. Medium height and build, pale blue eyes, and light blond hair in a bob or a low tail."

"That sounds like the guy who was just here. Baxter?"

"Don't even. Clive may act like an arse, but he's one of the good guys."

"If you say so. Are we ready?"

"What do you think?"

Jack sashayed towards him like a model on a catwalk, and Gareth struggled for air just watching. "I'd better not tell you what I think of that getup," he managed through half-clenched teeth. "Professionally speaking? Hot and not legal."

"Good. Let's hope the pimp thinks so." Jack hesitated in the hallway. "Where did you park?"

"Across the road. Why?"

Jack grabbed a trench coat and slung it around his shoulders. "Don't want to get you arrested."

Gareth imagined himself being hauled before a magistrate for soliciting a minor. And Julian Nancarrow's reaction when he found out. "You have a dirty mind, brat," he groaned as they got into the Ranger.

"Sure," Jack agreed. "But I was the one who thought of bringing the coat."

⬗ ◆ ◆ ◆ ⬖

Jack kept his eyes closed during the drive, but he was far from relaxed. Gareth shot glances in Jack's direction as he drove, noting the tight fists, the frown, and the shoulders that almost touched his ears.

"You okay?" he asked as they neared the address Jack had given him.

A sweep of long lashes, a half turn of a head, and Jack's gaze locked with Gareth's. "Belladonna's making me queasy."

"Then why do you use that shit?"

"Gets the look. Stop here."

"Hm," Gareth grunted and pulled the Range Rover alongside the kerb when Jack pointed out Baxter's Vauxhall parked up ahead. "So, you're going into this tense and feeling queasy. Any other important intel you want to share?"

"Watch what you drink." Jack got out of the car and shed his coat, throwing it into the backseat without another look. "Stick to bottled and keep it close."

"What about you?"

Jack flashed a quick grin. "I'm broke. And clumsy."

"As long as you're careful."

"I'm always careful." Jack waved a hand to the detective in the car. Then he turned, took a couple of deep breaths, and started to walk down the street towards his destination as if he had no thought in his head beyond a good night out.

Gareth watched him go, sure that Jack's queasiness, whether caused by nerves or belladonna, would make no difference to the outcome of the evening. Jack would get the job done, whatever he needed to do. This, in Gareth's estimation, didn't make it right. He watched until Jack had rounded the corner before he crossed the square to the waiting detective and climbed into the car.

"Are you two friends?" he asked as soon as he'd closed the door.

"Yes."

"Then why d'you do this to him?" Gareth didn't bother to hide the snarl in his voice. "You're sending him into that club without backup… since when's that in the playbook?"

"You said that you would back him up." Baxter sounded confused, which only pushed Gareth's ire up a notch.

"I *will* back him up. The point is that I just happened to be with Jack when you showed up. And you were pushing him into going alone and unarmed."

"Jack can handle himself."

"Again, not the point." Gareth was growling now. "If you ask someone to risk their life, the least you do is provide backup. Don't they teach that anymore, or do you just not care?"

The confusion on the Baxter's face sent icy shivers down Gareth's spine. Who was this guy that he ignored basic security protocol without batting an eyelash? That he was prepared to risk a friend's life for a crusade?

All of a sudden, Gareth Flynn was afraid. Not for himself, but for a courageous man with a crusade of his own. He couldn't bear the thought of Jack being manipulated into risking his life for a cause. Even if that cause was just.

"If there were another way to get this done…." Baxter hesitated over his words. "I don't often ask for Jack's help. I know it's dangerous, and I only seek him out when he's the only option left."

The careful words did nothing to ease Gareth's disquiet, and he resolved to keep an eye on Jack's interaction with the detective, whether Jack decided to join Nancarrow Mining or not. But that was for tomorrow. Right now, watching Jack's back was more important.

"Detective, I don't know you." Gareth forced calm into his voice. "Jack trusts you, so I'll give you the benefit of the doubt. I won't assume that you risk a friend's life for brownie points. Or worse, a personal vendetta. But if I ever find out that you do…." *I'll nail your damned arse to the fence.* He let the words sink in for a few seconds, then turned on his scary grin. "Now. Did you bring an evidence kit?"

"Yes, what do you need?"

It seemed that Detective Inspector Baxter was more comfortable with practical matters than questions of ethics. Gareth didn't find that at all amusing.

"A couple of bags and tape."

Baxter numbered the items and handed them over. Gareth stowed the supplies in the inside pockets of his jacket and nodded his thanks. "Make sure there are units in the area, just in case we get lucky. You never know, you might have your perp behind bars sooner than you thought."

Gareth was reaching for the door handle when Baxter stopped him with a question.

"What's Jack to you, Mr. Flynn?"

The answer came easy to Gareth. "Family. Jack Horwood is family."

# OFFERS

S natches of synth and bass beat spilled across the street, along with flashes of coloured lights, an everchanging mix of red and green, of purple and bright white. A queue of gaudily dressed people snaked towards the club's large metal doors where two towering figures stood guard. Those two were the harmless ones. Two slighter men beside the bouncers had control over who entered the club and who was turned away. One by one, they pushed waiting patrons against the wall and patted them down before allowing them inside.

*At least Clive has better intel this time*, Jack thought, approaching the end of the queue. *The pimp's here. And as paranoid as reported.*

Arriving obviously armed would have ended the night early. Not that Jack ever went unarmed, of course. Anywhere. Though that wasn't a fact he advertised.

Next in the queue was a woman in a leather miniskirt and knee-high boots. She giggled and batted her lashes as she was told to lean on the wall. Hands roamed, and the giggle became an indignant squeak when fingers slipped under her skirt.

"Watch your hands, mate!" The woman spun away from the wall and glowered.

"If you want in, you follow the rules," the man retorted, and Jack wasn't the only one who heard the unspoken *bitch* at the end of that sentence. A young couple in front of him slipped out of the queue and turned back down the street, muttering about better places for a fun night out.

Jack couldn't agree more, but he wasn't here for fun, not when a good quarter of the kids in the queue didn't look old enough to drink, or when the bouncers didn't turn even one of them away.

When he reached the front of the queue, Jack leaned against the wall, hands beside his head as instructed. He flinched when rough hands slid up his legs and along his arse, but he kept his eyes open. The bastard was doing more than checking for weapons, but unless he wanted to break his cover, all Jack could do was fume about it.

Footsteps and laughter sounded from down the road, and Jack turned his head towards the noise to distract himself. Of the three approaching men, two were strangers, but they laughed and joked with Gareth as if they'd known one another for ages. The tight coil of tension between Jack's shoulder blades unravelled a notch. Gareth had always had a knack for meshing with crowds, and some things, like the sun and the moon and Gareth Flynn, just never changed.

It warmed Jack that his former CO hadn't been thrown by his disguise. It warmed him even more that Gareth hadn't tried to talk him out of the job. Gareth Flynn might call him by the nickname he had bestowed on a snot-nosed seventeen-year-old, but he trusted Jack's instincts and decisions enough to back him up without question. Unconditional support like that was worth more than Jack could adequately explain.

A sharp swat on his arse drew Jack from his thoughts. Without looking at the man—he had the face memorised already—Jack stepped away from the wall, his stash of weapons undiscovered. He entered the club when the bouncer waved him through and stopped just inside the doors to get his bearings.

The place was dark, which was a blessing given Jack's light-sensitive eyes, and much larger than the outside suggested. Once upon a time, it had served as a workshop or a small warehouse. Most of the internal walls had been removed, leaving a wide rectangular space with two rows of floor-to-ceiling brick columns dividing two narrower aisles from the main part of the room.

Raw red bricks formed the walls and scuffed, heavy-duty vinyl covered the floor and the lower half of the columns. Racks of spotlights made a grid pattern overhead, and a bar ran along the far side of the room, the chrome top reflecting the light.

Tables and benches took up the aisle to Jack's left. The dance floor occupied the centre. Emergency exit doors were to his right, between the kitchen entrance and the DJ booth.

The club was just starting to get busy. About half the tables were taken, and a few couples busied themselves on the dance floor while the DJ warmed up. Jack turned left and followed the line of columns, intent to confirm the layout of the place while he could still move unimpeded.

On the far left-hand side of the room, next to the bar, Jack marked a second emergency exit. And another door which, given the fact that it was guarded, could be an escape route or a way to private rooms deeper in the building. With the pimp's paranoia and Baxter's information that the man liked to sample the merchandise before he put it on display, either option was feasible.

The guard didn't look as if he stood there just for decoration, and though Jack would have liked to take a closer look to confirm where the door led, he kept moving, heading in the direction of the brightly lit bar. He felt the man's eyes on his back and resisted the urge to check his weapons. There was no need. The knives, wires, CS gas and Taser were exactly where he'd stowed them before leaving home. Besides, it was just a nervous habit he'd picked up after Gareth got shot. A habit he'd been too stubborn to do anything about.

Gareth was already in position when Jack drew level with the bar. He held a bottle of Stella in one hand and juggled a scrunched-up cellophane wrapper with the other while he watched the dancers.

With their emergency exit taken care of and their target not yet in sight, Jack relaxed enough to settle into his role. Leaning on the far end of the bar, he ordered bottled water and surreptitiously popped a couple of pills. They were just painkillers, needed to help with the headache caused by the flashing lights aggravating his belladonna-enhanced eyes, but people saw what they wanted to see, and Jack didn't mind the covert looks he attracted. It all helped him blend.

He hit the dance floor a few minutes later, trying to ignore the knowledge that the man he'd fallen for when he was just seventeen was watching him. Thoughts like that would get him precisely nowhere. Much safer if he didn't consider Gareth Flynn at all and concentrated on the kids swaying and bopping around him. Some were there for the music and a good time, some—wide-eyed and hesitant—were clearly there on a dare.

Two teenage boys, one blond, one dark, huddling at the far end of the bar, caught Jack's eye. They clung together in a way teenagers never do, and both had their arms hidden in long sleeves despite the heat in the club. Dark-circled eyes darted around the room without pause or consideration, and when Gareth, alerted by a couple of quick hand signs and a look, brushed close past the two on his way to the men's room, both flinched and shrank back further into their corner.

Likely candidates, those two. Underfed, scared as all get-out, and probably hooked too. At least the two had the sense to stick together. Another body close by to combat loneliness; a voice to chase away the nightmares…. Jack knew how little comfort this was, but it was better than no comfort at all. The fine line between giving in and keeping going, between a sliver of hope and total despair.

Jack wanted to hit something… somebody, but he kept his face expressionless and his body moving to the music. He pushed the memories down, put the rage back in its box, and buried it under layers of purpose and discipline. He thought he'd masked his fury well enough, but when he looked up, there was open concern on Gareth's face and a question in the man's eyes.

*Out?* Gareth's fingers queried, and he meant it. The thought steadied Jack and he shook his head, grateful that their target chose that moment to make his entrance. He needed the distraction.

Clive's description of the pimp—medium everything and white-blond hair—didn't mesh with the reputation the man was supposed to have in the clubs. Jack had met a few gorillas in his time, and at first glance, his current target didn't make the grade. The man was neither very tall, nor very broad and had no discernible fashion sense. He looked washed-out and forgettable despite the black leather trousers and vest he wore.

His sneer told a different story. One that convinced Jack that Clive had the correct man in his sights. The sneer and the way he swaggered in, arm around the shoulders of another teenage boy. This one had brown hair that flopped loosely around his head and brown eyes that seemed too big for his thin face. He walked docilely enough beside the pimp, but his eyes looked anywhere but at the man, and when the arm around his shoulder tightened, he turned his head away.

The small signs of defiance heartened Jack even as they made bile rise in his throat, and as the music got louder and the beat picked up, he decided that now was as good a time as any to make his play.

The pimp had settled on a bar stool close to Gareth and idly scanned the crowd while nursing a beer, the brown-haired boy close by his side.

Jack moved from the dance floor to one of the columns in the man's line of sight. He leaned against it, one knee bent so the sole of his boot rested on the black vinyl and the tight leather trousers showed off his long legs and the line of his arse. He draped himself against the column as if lost to the music and whatever chemicals he enjoyed for recreation, head back, throat bared, eyes closed, and dark spikes of hair falling every which way. The hem of his shirt rode up another inch to show off his abs, and a spotlight hit the tattoo on his face, making it stand out stark black against his skin.

The pose was an invitation. Jack knew exactly how he looked and what he offered. He'd practiced the move in front of a mirror over and over, and if he tilted his head just right and squinted through his lashes, he could usually watch his target lose their cool.

The pimp was better than most. He leaned forwards, clearly interested, but he didn't get up or take his eyes off Jack. Instead, he waved to one of his men and pointed. And Jack dropped his lashes and waited.

"Hey, you!"

Jack ignored the rough voice close to his ear until the man prodded him. Then he lifted his head—slowly, as if it weighed a ton—and opened his eyes. "Yeah?" he slurred.

"The boss wants to talk to you."

"Huh?" Closing his eyes completely hadn't been a good idea. The sudden influx of light started fireworks in Jack's head. He bit the inside of his cheek to stifle a pained groan before it could slip out and concentrated on breathing until his eyes adjusted.

"Guy at the bar wants to talk to you," the rough voice repeated, barely patient. "Move your arse. He doesn't wait well."

Jack pushed himself upright and stepped away from the column with a small provocative sway to his hips. The pale-haired pimp was a little to his left, Gareth right in front of him. Both men were leaning forwards on their barstools, and both wore almost identical looks of eager interest.

Jack might have found that gratifying, embarrassing, or even faintly amusing, had Gareth not reached back towards the bar right then and snatched the pimp's beer bottle from the counter. The bottle disappeared into the inside of Gareth's jacket before anyone had noticed the man had even moved—and

Jack felt a stab of disappointment swiftly followed by irritation.

They were on a job. That meant blending with the crowd and acting like those around him. And if Jack had known how distracting it would be to have Gareth Flynn watch his back, he would have chosen to call this off. Or declined Gareth's offer. Maybe.

He drew close to the pimp, swayed a bit on his feet, and wasn't surprised when the hand reaching out to steady him landed on his hip and slid over his arse. From the corner of his eye, he saw Gareth jerk and bare his teeth before the mission face slid back into place.

Jack put his arms behind his back and kept his eyes down. This was the hardest part of his act. Submission didn't come easy to him, and he was far too old to still be bashful. He felt hungry eyes trawl over his skin, assessing, imagining, plotting… and he wanted to look up and memorise the faces of the men surrounding him. Just in case he ever found one of them alone.

"Look at me."

Jack raised his head with apparent reluctance and focussed his gaze on the bar behind the pimp, watching the man from the corner of his eye. The pale hair was stringy and curled damply around the man's neck. Something dark—blood? sweat?—stained the black leather vest in places. But right in Jack's line of sight, the man's grin lifted a cheek.

"I have work for someone like you," the pimp offered. "What do you say?"

Jack swivelled his head as if he'd just woken in a strange place and looked around. "Here?"

"Here, or any other club I send you to. We also run an escort service." He chuckled, and the sound trickled down Jack's spine like a trail of ice water. "I can see clients going crazy over you. Especially when you're bragging." He let his eyes trail from the tattoo on Jack's face all the way down his long legs to his boots and back up again. His gaze snagged on the stylised sixty-nine that adorned Jack's temple. "Yeah." He leered. "Especially when you're bragging."

The man threw his arm around the shoulders of the brown-haired boy beside him—not caring about the obvious way the boy flinched—and pulled him close. "Hey, Ricky, why don't you give Bambi the tour? Explain how things work. Do it right, and I let you have the rest of the night off."

He pushed the boy in Jack's direction, and Jack had to fight not to reach out and steady the kid, pull him away from the bleach-haired pimp. It was a close-run thing, but he managed it, tilting his head in invitation instead. The youngster pointed towards a quieter corner of the club, and Jack fell into step beside him.

"You're Ricky?"

"And you're Bambi?"

The kid's soft voice barely carried over the music, but the sarcasm in it was thick enough to spread on toast.

Jack offered a real smile. "I'm Jack."

Ricky stopped next to a bench and waved for Jack to sit. They were still in the pimp's line of sight—and Gareth's—so Jack straddled the bench. Just in case the man read lips. If he had instructed Ricky to stay within sight, he might be paranoid enough.

When he'd first seen Ricky, Jack had thought that a bath, sleep, and a few square meals would do wonders for perking up the kid's looks, but now that he could observe from up close, he felt uneasy. Ricky's face wasn't just spending-too-much-time-in-nightclubs pale. He was grey, and a thin sheen of sweat covered his skin, even though now and then, he shivered.

"You hurting?"

"None of your business."

Jack backed off immediately. "Worked for the guy long?"

"Some."

"Worth it?"

"Hell, no!"

The emphatic reply was so unexpected Jack recoiled, remembering at the last moment to mask his response and lean against the wall to hide it. And Ricky wasn't done.

"Why would you even consider working for a bastard like that?"

"I need the money," Jack said.

"There are other ways to earn money."

"If I have to get groped at work, I might as well get paid for it."

Ricky shook his head and mumbled something under his breath that looked suspiciously like *idiot*. When he looked up, his gaze held a large dose of pity. He leaned forwards, turned his head so his mouth was close to Jack's jaw, and waved a finger at Jack's tattoo. "You know what's funny about this picture?"

"No?"

"You thinking that you'll get off somewhere in all this." Ricky shook his head once. "You couldn't be more wrong. Oh sure, he'll work you till you're raw, and there are always johns willing to pay extra. But if you know what's good for you, you won't dare take any money… or pleasure."

"I just want to save up enough," Jack said, sticking to his role despite his growing concern. Ricky's shivers grew more frequent, and his colour ebbed and flowed in a way that wasn't normal. Jack reached forwards and placed an arm around Ricky. Only to feel Ricky flinch as soon as the soft touch brushed his back.

"You *are* hurt."

"And you're beyond stupid. Listen, if you don't believe shit, believe me. You don't want to get into this. Not with him. Once you're in, nobody will help you get back out. No matter how loud you scream."

Jack was grateful for Gareth's presence only a few meters away. He met the man's gaze, flicked his fingers as quickly and unobtrusively as he could through their old army shorthand signs for *witness* and *out*, before he returned his eyes to the boy opposite him.

"What if I… could?" Jack's voice was a breath against Ricky's cheek.

"Get me out of here?" Nobody could say that the kid was slow. "I *knew* you weren't fried." He rested his head on Jack's shoulder, and Jack felt the tension in the slim body pressed to his. "What'll I have to pay you for that?"

Jack didn't flinch at the suspicion in the low tone. He blipped a brief look in Gareth's direction, knowing the man would understand, be ready if the whole thing went south. "I'm here to take him down. I take any help I can get. But it's not a trade. You want out. I'll get you out."

"Why?"

"Been there. Got out. Returning the favour." Jack didn't care that he was blunt. Ricky was smart enough to recognise lies when he heard them, and soft soap wouldn't do him any good. So what if Jack's words opened old wounds? They'd healed before. They'd heal again. Far more important was the teen slumped against him, all ragged breath and clammy skin.

Ricky was hurt, and the devil of it was that Jack couldn't tell how badly. He guessed that Ricky had been caned or flogged since every touch to his back made him flinch, but even a hard beating would not cause the symptoms Jack was faced with.

The boy was showing signs of shock... and that wasn't good.

Not good at all.

He raised his eyes and found Gareth leering at the two of them. The look didn't suit Gareth, but it got them what they needed. In no time at all Jack saw him talking to the pimp. Negotiating, if Gareth's sudden studied disinterest was any indication. It was an obvious tactic, so obvious that the odds of someone falling for it were minuscule, but Gareth didn't care about the odds. He just played. And won.

Relief washed through Jack when the pimp leaned back against the bar and waved at Gareth to proceed. He didn't feel guilty about pulling out so early. They had the man's fingerprints. Knowing Gareth, they probably had pictures. They even had a witness. But that witness needed a hospital. Fast.

Gareth didn't hesitate. He rose and took the few steps across the room to where Jack and Ricky sat huddled together.

"Hey, boys, what'd you say to a little playtime?"

Ricky pressed himself closer to Jack as Gareth's shadow loomed over them both, and Jack soothed him with a quiet sound. His nod, once he met Gareth's gaze, was little more than a sweep of lashes, but its effect was instant.

Black smoke.

Wailing alarms.

And chaos.

# THE BILL

T he black smoke was a nice touch. It billowed from behind the kitchen door and wafted around the DJ booth, adding authenticity and a touch of menace to the alarms wailing through the club. Gareth mentally saluted whoever had crafted Jack's *distractions*. Dorky look aside, once operational the things were damned effective.

A cacophony of sound—a mix of thrumming beat, shouts, and blaring alarms—turned the dance club into an inferno. Patrons milled without aim in the gloom of flashing strobes, pushing this way and that while others rushed towards exits, losing their way and their reason in the billowing black smoke and growing terror.

Gareth blocked Jack and Ricky from the pimp's view. His shoulder blades itched as if he had a target painted across his back. Their masquerade would be over as soon as they moved from their position, and it irked Gareth that he couldn't predict the man's reaction to having his assets abstracted. He felt beyond stupid for making the attempt without knowing if and how the pimp and his men were armed, but then, his plans for the evening had not included nightclubs, pimps, or impromptu rescue missions. He'd just wanted to convince Jack to take the offered job.

Instead, Jack Horwood had revealed a side that Gareth couldn't have cooked up in a fevered dream. It wasn't the crusade that had surprised him—Jack and crusades had always had an affinity—but the way Jack went about it, using himself as bait and weapon both. Not to mention the fact that Jack put himself in harm's way without a moment's thought even when his allies let him down.

The memory lit a spark of anger, and Gareth pushed it aside.

He couldn't afford the distraction right now.

Despite the growing pandemonium, Jack kept to his role, held his body as if he was conversing with Gareth while he waited for his cue, and comforted the boy by his side. This close, Ricky's waning colour and the shivers that wracked his body were as obvious as Jack's concerned frown.

Gareth kept his impatience on a leash despite the need to hurry, kept his stance casual and a sharp eye on the main entrance. Once the bouncers had roughly established a little order and cleared a path in the wall of panicked patrons blocking the double door, he caught Jack's gaze.

"Go."

Jack moved like a striking snake. He shot forwards, grabbed Ricky around the middle, and slung him over his shoulder, holding him in place with an arm across the back of the kid's knees. His other hand pulled a knife from his boot. Then he was up and sprinting towards the doors, dodging the milling throng.

Gareth was right behind Jack. A part of him kept an eye on the crowd and potential threats while another part of him observed Jack's work, the way he used to do back when Jack was one of his.

And Jack did him proud.

He soothed the boy's startled shout with a brief comment and steadied him while he ran. He didn't look over his shoulder to check on the man he needed to avoid. He didn't confirm that Gareth was with him. Jack stayed focussed on his task. He wove through the surging crowd, aiming straight for the small gap of clear air the bouncers had created, trusting Gareth to watch his back.

Unlike Jack, Gareth didn't have a knife up against his wrist when they reached the club's entrance and the bouncers stationed there. It mattered little. They owed him for laying hands on Jack, and Gareth was determined to collect. Given the chaos around them, it wouldn't even be tricky.

Behind him, shouts grew louder as if someone had finally noticed that this was more than a panicked escape. The tone changed from surprised to determined to demanding. One of the bouncers straightened, just as Jack drew level with him.

"What the fuck you think you—"

Gareth's fist landed with a wet thud, and the man's head smacked into the wall behind him.

Jack was clear and sprinting up the street, the boy still slung over his shoulder. Barely anyone took notice of the two while the sounds of approaching sirens rent the air, attracting clubbers and spectators, the way disasters often do. They milled aimlessly in the night, faces and clothes bleached of colour in the light of the streetlamps, only intent on the scene before them.

The second bouncer loomed, fist moving back to strike as Gareth turned.

Gareth danced to the side, grabbed the flying fist, and yanked.

The man went sailing into the crowd of spectators.

Gareth didn't wait around to see him land. He was past the bouncer nursing a headache and back inside the club in a heartbeat.

Strobe lights still flashed around the dance floor, guiding his steps through the smoke. The crowd had thinned, and Gareth made it to the bar without incident.

The pimp was gone.

But the pimp wasn't Gareth's target.

He found the two boys Jack had pointed out to him earlier still huddled in their corner on the far side of the bar. How they could ignore the wailing alarms eluded Gareth—nobody could be *that* oblivious! He watched them, seeing nothing but misery in the way the two clung to each other. Misery, confusion—and a hefty dose of fear.

He stepped close, opened his mouth to speak… and had to move fast to restrain them as both jumped up and tried to run.

"Cut it out!" he snapped as the blond tried to bite his hand. "I'm here to get you out."

Two pairs of startled, suspicious eyes met his gaze. "You were buying. You talked to Ricky and the new guy."

Not as oblivious as he'd thought. Was that what Jack had seen? Why he had pointed the two out? Gareth heaved a frustrated sigh, wishing once more that there had been time to prepare this impromptu mission properly. As it was, Jack knew what he was doing while Gareth only wished he did.

"I was *pretending* to buy," Gareth disagreed, voice as calm as he could make it. "The new guy's my friend. He works with the police. He got Ricky out. I came back for you two."

"Why?"

A good question. Shame that Gareth was lost for an answer.

He'd come back because he thought the boys needed help.

Because they reminded him too much of Jack in his disguise.

Because they clung to each other with so much despair that something deep inside him burned.

Because Gareth rescued people who needed it.

In the end, none of his reasons mattered in this dark, smoke-filled club. None of his answers mattered.

"Don't you *want* to get away from that guy?"

The two looked at each other, and that's when he saw it: crippling fear, confusion, mistrust… and a tiny spark of hope. Jack might hit him if he ever found out, but Gareth flashed his biggest grin and leaned closer.

"I can knock you both out and carry you," he offered. "It will look good, I promise."

"Where?"

"Across the square. Jack's there with Ricky and the police."

They didn't like the idea of the police, but after a moment, Gareth got a tiny nod. "You can really carry us both? At the same time?"

Without another word Gareth grabbed both boys and hoisted them to his shoulders, much as Jack had done with Ricky earlier. "Don't worry about falling. I've got you," he said as he adjusted the slight weights. "Pretend to be unconscious. Just let your hands hang down."

He felt two bodies relax against his and nodded. "That's it."

Three long strides took him to the kitchen door, four more through the empty room. He pushed the back door open with a foot and scrutinised the small delivery area beside the club. It was empty, though a couple of fresh oil stains on the concrete suggested that a car had parked there earlier.

Gareth let the door swing open and closed a couple of times.

Then he eased outside and jogged to the mouth of the alley.

More spectators had accumulated outside the club, intent on watching black smoke billow out the doors and drooling over the firefighters who got ready to enter the building. Gareth and his two charges were soundly ignored. He skirted the back of the largest group of rubberneckers, turned the corner, and ran towards Baxter's car.

"Inside, quick!" he instructed as he set the boys on their feet and opened the back door.

They balked, eyes wide with fear. "You lied. This isn't a police car!"

Gareth bodily stopped the boys from running. "Detective—your badge, please."

He praised creation that Baxter didn't need an explanation. The detective held his warrant card out to the two boys, who examined it before finally getting into the unmarked car.

"Keep your heads down, and nobody will know where you are," Gareth said, taking the front seat.

Baxter watched the boys watch him replace his warrant card in the inside of his jacket. "I'll stay with you until our protection team gets here," he said in a much calmer voice than Gareth could muster even on a good day. "Is that okay?"

"Where is Ricky?"

That's what Gareth wanted to know too. He'd been craning his head in every direction looking for Jack and the brown-haired youngster he'd rescued. There were a few official-looking cars in the small square now, and a number of unmarked ones. Maybe Baxter had pulled in a few favours.

"Did Jack go with the ambulance?"

Baxter turned a confused gaze his way. "I haven't

seen Jack yet."

"But—" Gareth bit off what he meant to say and shoved the door open. "Call for an ambulance," he instructed. "The kid with him is injured. Possibly in shock."

Then he was out of the car and running up the street.

———— ✦ ✦ ✦ ————

"Set me down!"

A weak fist pounded on his back to enforce the demand. Jack turned into a driveway and carefully lifted Ricky from his shoulder. The boy swayed, clutching at the wall for support.

"Sorry about that," Jack steadied Ricky, careful to avoid touching his injured back. "It would have taken too long to explain what I wanted you to do."

"But you carried me!"

"So?" He flashed a smile at the incredulous youngster. "You weigh less than the packs I carry while training."

"You train carrying things?"

"I train running, too." Another shiver wracked Ricky's slim frame, and Jack frowned. "You need a hospital. Come on."

Ricky stretched out a hand to hold him back. The

65

fingers shook. "Can we just… stop a bit?" he asked in a small voice. "I haven't been outside in weeks. I'm not allowed. I just wanna…. Please?"

The sudden pause was painful. Jack couldn't catch his breath fast enough to stop Ricky from ducking his head and flinching away from him, expecting reprisals.

"Sure. There's a garden the next street over. With benches. We can wait for the doctor there." Jack kept his voice calm and his body relaxed, though there was a fist-sized lump in his throat, and his insides boiled with fury at the thought of what had been done to the boy.

There would be time for fury later. For now, he closed his eyes and drew a deep breath, then another. And if his vision was a bit blurry when he opened his eyes, he blamed it on the belladonna.

He recalled Clive Baxter's near desperation when Jack suggested they call off the job and wondered if this was the reason that the pimp kept his string of boys locked up. But why was Clive keeping this a secret? It wasn't as if Jack was reluctant to help when asked. If the detective had shared what he knew beyond calling the pimp a gorilla…

Sirens wailed, close by now, and Jack wanted to scoop Ricky up and drag him into the nearest ambulance, but he just… couldn't. Not after hearing that Ricky had been held prisoner. "Do you want to walk the last bit, or do you want me to carry—"

"I thought you were too fucking good to be true," a rough voice interrupted.

"You clearly know jack shit about it." Jack stepped in front of Ricky, using his body to shield him from the man standing in the mouth of the driveway. One of the pimp's men, but not the one with the wandering hands who'd made such a poor job of searching him for weapons. "I could be waiting for a client." Jack folded his arms across his chest. "Or maybe I wanted a bit of playtime of my own."

"And maybe you're full of shit. Hand the little whore over, and *maybe* I'll leave you in one piece."

Jack didn't waste his breath on an answer. Bullies never listened. They were too drunk on the rubbish they spouted. This one was practically legless. The question was could he back it up? He was about Jack's height, but broader and heavier, and all that swagger could be an act.

Jack watched the man's feet, noted that he had his weight on the heels, and launched himself forwards.

An arm came up in defence—Jack grabbed the wrist and spun.

A crack followed by a groan and a slew of curses.

A quick chop to the neck.

A thud.

Jack bent and placed two fingers under the downed man's jaw, satisfied when he found a pulse. Killing the bastard would have been too easy. Not to mention frowned upon.

The boot to his ribs knocked him sideways. He curled, hit the road with a grunt, and rolled. Breath left his body in a rush. *That's what you get for your Samaritan attitude*, his subconscious mind admonished helpfully. He recovered his footing but was taken off guard when—

"No!"

Like a small blur, Ricky appeared right in front of Jack.

He saw the knife an instant later—saw the move in slow motion—a straight stab aimed at his gut. Before Jack could raise a hand to push him aside, Ricky cried out and fell to his knees, knife embedded in his shoulder. Jack reached and missed, and Ricky pitched forwards to lie motionless in a slowly spreading puddle of blood.

"You fucking son of a bitch!"

Jack forgot where he was. He forgot that police and paramedics and God knew who else were just a few hundred yards away. He even forgot that he was armed. He only remembered Ricky's face, the shape of the man who'd stabbed the boy, and endless hours of training hand-to-hand combat.

Rage turned him into a blur of kicks and punches, a wall of flying fists and feet, intent on inflicting as much pain and damage as possible.

He could have knocked the man unconscious more than once, but he was careful. Despite the rage, his attacks were precise. They raised bruises and welts. They broke bones and split skin.

But they never allowed oblivion.

"That's enough!"

Strong arms wrapped around Jack's torso, immobilising his fists. He squirmed and kicked until he registered a scent he'd noted earlier that evening. Gareth's cologne. His body reacted to Gareth's warmth, the command in his voice. Jack's struggling slowed, but he wasn't done.

"Let me go! He killed the kid."

"Did not."

Jack twisted, saw Ricky slumped on his knees on the pavement, swaying in place and using a wall for support.

He tore himself from Gareth's grasp.

Three steps took him to Ricky's side. The shivering teen was even paler now and held a hand to the wound in his shoulder. Blood seeped through his fingers and trickled down his wrist, the colour vivid against his pale skin.

"Let me see." Jack pushed Ricky's hand aside. The

knife had pierced the upper part of Ricky's shoulder. The gash wasn't long but seemed deep and was still bleeding.

"Gods, you're a mess," Jack sighed, his habitual calm slowly returning. "Has nobody ever taught you not to run in on a fight?"

A tiny smile curved the corners of Ricky's bloodless lips. It made Jack's insides churn with dread, made him lean down and place a gentle kiss on the boy's forehead. "Thank you for saving my life." He rose and held out a hand. "Let's get you patched up before you pass out."

Ricky's hand was ice-cold, the skin clammy. Once upright, he swayed like a blade of grass in a hurricane. But when Gareth reached to lift the boy, Jack's hand stopped him. With the injuries to his back, carrying Ricky bridal-style was out. The shoulder wound was still bleeding. And Ricky clearly needed to walk.

They settled for Jack keeping pressure on the bleeding shoulder and supporting one side, while Gareth took most of Ricky's weight on the other. They made it to the corner of the square before Ricky lost consciousness.

The dash to the waiting ambulance took a bare moment.

"Fresh stab wound to the shoulder," Jack said as he climbed into the ambulance and placed Ricky's still form on the waiting gurney. "But he was already hurt. Wouldn't let me touch his back. Weak pulse, clammy skin. He was lucid until he passed out a minute ago."

The two paramedics set to work, and Jack hesitated in the doorway until Gareth pulled him from the vehicle.

"Give the men some room. They'll let us know when there's news." Gareth steered him to where Clive Baxter was waiting beside his car, bottle of water and pack of wet wipes in hand.

"Here," the detective said as he handed the bottle over. "Do you want something for the headache?"

Jack accepted, noting that the innocent comment painted a deep scowl across Gareth's face. He swallowed the pills and drained the water bottle, surprised at how dehydrated he felt after such a short time in the club. Baxter produced a second bottle of water and set it on the car's roof in easy reach, not asking questions or demanding answers while Jack cleaned the blood and dirt from his hands and arms.

"Why didn't you tell me he kept his boys locked up?" Jack queried when the violence of the evening had been reduced to raw knuckles and a pile of blood-and-dirt-stained cleaning wipes.

"Because I wasn't sure."

"But you had an idea?"

"I had rumours. And you know what they teach us

about those." Baxter looked towards the ambulance. "This boy you brought out… is he one of them?"

"Yes. Enough pluck for several of his size. Goes by Ricky." Jack finished the second bottle of water and tossed the container into the backseat of Baxter's car. "Sorry about the messy exit. I suppose he got away?"

The detective nodded. "By the time the teams showed up, he was gone."

Jack had no idea why he felt the need to apologise. Clive knew as well as he did that there was a price to pay for working outside the rules. "We have fingerprints. We may have DNA. And we have a witness." He leaned his back against the car, mimicking the other man's stance. "And talking of witnesses… there were two other boys at the club tonight. One blond, one dark. They looked likely."

To Jack's surprise, Clive simply nodded. "Daniel and Nico. Your Gareth snatched them on the way out. Social Services just picked them up."

"Just anyone? Or do you know who's taking the case?"

"Gillian Kent came to collect them, so I'm assuming she'll keep hold of it."

Jack opened his mouth to reply when the back of the ambulance opened, and one of the paramedics climbed out. He walked across the buzzing square, shoulders hunched and steps dragging, and stopped beside them.

"I'm sorry… the kid didn't make it."

Jack had known the news would be bad before the paramedic announced it, but that didn't make hearing it any easier. He barely noticed Gareth draping a blanket around him and not withdrawing his arm from Jack's shoulders when he was done. All he could see were deep brown eyes; old eyes that had seen far too much.

"It wasn't the knife," the paramedic said, his face a grimace of distaste. "There's internal bleeding, open lash marks. Looks like he'd been beaten and…."

"… raped," Jack finished in a low voice when the man couldn't go on.

"Yes. The knife wound just sent him more deeply into shock. He had no fight left in him."

Jack straightened his spine with a snap. "That's where you're wrong," he said. "Ricky didn't know who or what I was. He knew what would happen to him if he didn't do as he was told. And he tried to save me… and others like him. He had courage."

"'S not what I was saying," the paramedic placated. "I'm saying that that boy's body had no strength left. Not after so much abuse. He was probably starved too."

"Leave no witnesses," Baxter said softly.

"Oh, I wouldn't say *that*." A calm voice spoke from

behind them. "Good evening, gentlemen."

The slim, dark-haired woman who stepped between them wasn't anyone Jack had met before. She was dressed casually in skinny jeans, a dark blue T-shirt, and a loose plaid shirt that almost reached her knees. That late in the day, her long braid was on the messy side, but her eyes were alert, and her voice held a determination that Jack took comfort in.

"Dr. Tyrrell?" A deep blush stained Clive Baxter's ears. "You are working this case?"

"Looks like. Want to fill me in?" She nodded towards the ambulance and waited until Baxter and the paramedic were on their way before she held out a hand to Jack. "Lisa Tyrrell, Special Projects Unit," she introduced herself. "Ricky may no longer be able to testify against the men who hurt him, but he *will* make sure they're buried under the jail. I promise." She rose to her toes and pecked Gareth on the cheek. "Good to see you again, Colonel."

"You too." Gareth smiled a tiny smile. "Thanks for coming out. There's too much red tape in this mess."

Lisa shrugged. "Not to worry. I'm good with a knife. I will need the two of you for statements, but I'll call when I'm ready for that. Best go home before the press gets here." She didn't wait for a reply from either man, just spun on her heels and followed Baxter and the paramedic to the waiting ambulance.

Gareth watched her leave, then tightened his arm around Jack. "Come on, brat. I'm taking you home."

# GLIMPSES

J ack obeyed the pressure of Gareth's arm. He walked the few steps to the parked Range Rover and slid into the passenger seat, glad that nothing more was demanded of him for a time. He knew that this was far from over. There would be questions and reconstructions and—maybe—repercussions, but all that could wait until morning. Right now, he needed a quiet space to draw breath and reflect. And he was grateful that Gareth understood that.

The car purred to life. Gareth waited until Jack was settled in his seat, turned the heating up and the seat heaters on, and peeled away from the kerb. The kaleidoscope of flashing lights vanished behind them, lingering black smoke drifted away, and soon the familiar sights and sounds of London by night soothed Jack's jangling nerves. The ever-present traffic had thinned. Taxis cruised almost unimpeded, and every now and again the Range Rover slipped past a brightly lit night bus taking clubbers home the long way. Pedestrian traffic fizzled out the further they moved from the West End, and Jack noted with surprise that it was half past the witching hour.

No wonder he was beat. Since Baxter's call earlier that evening, events had raced to overtake each other. Usually he knew in advance when Baxter needed help and had time to prepare and plan his involvement. This time, Clive's call had come out of the blue, and only Jack's experience playing bait and their history of working together had made their attempt at all feasible.

Then Gareth had turned up. Just as out of the blue as Baxter's call.

Gareth Flynn hadn't featured in Jack's life in years—much as he would have wished otherwise. Gareth's sudden appearance at his interview had played enough havoc with Jack's mind that he'd turned down a job he actually wanted.

He should have known that Gareth would see through his flimsy excuse and not let the matter go. The man was like a Rottweiler with a whorl of Cumberland sausage when he wanted something, so Gareth turning up on his doorstep should have been a foregone conclusion.

What hadn't been a foregone conclusion was the

way Gareth had backed Jack. The way he'd challenged Clive. The way he'd ditched what he'd come for and joined in Jack's hunt, no questions asked.

Jack wrapped fingers in his hair and yanked until his eyes watered. The effortless fluency with which he and Gareth worked together after all these years should amaze him or at the very least comfort him. It did neither. Instead, it left him downright irritated.

He'd worked so hard to stand on his own feet after he left the army that interacting with Gareth as if they'd never been apart upset his equilibrium.

As did the fact that Gareth had watched him screw up.

Again.

Jack wasn't proud about losing his temper, though he was honest enough to admit that it had felt damn good to let rip. He might have gone one better if his opponent had been the guard with the wandering hands. But maybe then the repercussions for his actions would be impossible to avoid.

"Thanks for going after the two boys," Jack said, voice gruff. "At least one of us didn't screw up."

"I couldn't let you mash that idiot into the road," Gareth answered as if he'd spent the last ten minutes listening to Jack's thoughts rather than the car's engine.

"S'pose not," Jack mumbled, turning his face to

hide his sudden flush. "I bet you'd have done the same had you been in my shoes."

"No doubt. But I was in a hurry, so the other bouncer got off with a broken jaw and a sore head."

Jack's head snapped around, and he gaped while his mind played catch-up.

"That kid really got to you, didn't he?"

Gareth's voice was soft and laced with concern. It loosened the tight knot in Jack's chest and sent a wave of warmth through him. Gareth didn't just understand his need for violence; he also remembered Jack's need to analyse the events to see what he'd missed. Jack leaned against the headrest and exhaled slowly.

"I should have rushed him to the ambulance."

"Why didn't you?"

"Because he asked to walk."

"You could have ignored that."

"After what he'd been through?"

"Right. So how did you screw up if you did exactly what Ricky needed?"

"Because he needed an ambulance more!" Jack couldn't keep the frustration from his voice. He remembered similar discussions—Gareth providing the voice of reason until Jack's mind accepted what was—and marvelled at how well Gareth still knew him, even after all this time. The thought scared him… and comforted like a warm blanket, or the smell of baking bread.

"You can't know that," Gareth replied, and Jack believed him, clung to the words as if they were a lifeline. "All *you* know is that Ricky asked you to let him walk. You could have ignored what he wanted—just like everyone else—and he still might have died. You based your decision on Ricky's choices and needs—and that's *not* wrong."

Silence reigned in the car for a time. Jack watched streetlights twinkle on dark water while they crossed the river. He counted the seconds between oncoming cars, then switched to counting cars parked illegally on the pavement and calculated an accumulating total of parking fines. His breathing slowed and deepened, and the pain in the back of his head eased to a mere memory.

"Now let it go, and tell me something else," Gareth ordered in the calm, deep tone that could carry through mortar fire.

"What do you want to know?"

"Why this particular crusade?"

Jack wondered how to phrase his answer. The words he'd said to Ricky came back to him, and he spoke them aloud before he could filter. "Been there. Got out. Returning the favour."

"I thought so," Gareth said after another long

silence.

Jack frowned. He'd never told the whole story to anyone. A few people knew snatches. Rio Palmer, the dreadlocked hacker who had offered him a home when Jack had had nowhere to go, might know more than most, but even while living with Rio, Jack had kept the details well under wraps. The sudden urge to confide in Gareth made him squirm in his seat, and he clamped his teeth together.

"I wish I could kill whoever did that to you."

"Too late," Jack said, voice very soft. "My mother's been dead for years."

Time froze, traffic lights winked, and Gareth stared through the windshield as if he'd seen a ghost. Jack thought of castles, of walls and battlements and moats, and the idea of anything being able to shock Gareth Flynn into immobility lightened his mood with a tint of amusement.

"Green, Gareth," he said, as the car behind them suggested that they should do more than block the middle of the road.

"She sold me to her pimp one day, when she needed a fix," Jack continued his story once they were underway again. "I didn't like the idea, so I ran away." It wasn't that simple. It had *never* been that simple. But Jack felt too comfortable there in the dark, with the car's warmth and Gareth's scent surrounding him, to step back into that cold and scary place.

"How old were you?"

"'Leven, I think."

Gareth didn't comment, but even over the sound of the engine, Jack heard him grind his teeth. The fury expressed on his behalf warmed Jack's mind and drew him another step closer to letting the events of the night slide away.

"I had nothing to do with her death," he added as Gareth pulled the Ranger into a parking space across the road from his house, feeling that it might be beneficial to clarify that fact. Especially after his outburst earlier.

"Didn't think you had." Gareth turned the engine off and got out of the car.

Jack followed suit, confused when Gareth blipped the locks and started to move towards Jack's home. "Gareth?"

"You want me to leave you alone without making sure you're okay? Think again." Gareth stopped in the middle of the road, waiting until Jack joined him. The frown on his face was impressive but nothing Jack hadn't seen before.

"Mother-henning doesn't suit you, Gareth. I'm fine."

"You're not *fine*," Gareth shot back and reached for Jack, peering closely at his face. "Look at yourself!

You're shaking with excess adrenaline. You may have a broken rib that needs taping. And when was the last time you ate something?"

That question caught Jack out. He had to think about it. "Lunch, with you," he decided in the end, the defiance in his tone dying a swift death.

"Jesus!" Gareth shook his head and gripped Jack's elbow a little more firmly. "I'm sure it helps you pull off that look, but I'd rather you didn't starve yourself to death just for the sake of catching pimps."

"It's not that," Jack disagreed. "Stress makes me sick." He flushed crimson admitting as much, and Gareth snorted.

"I really should have remembered that."

"Yeah... because you force-feeding me on that Welsh exercise worked so well."

"It got you home."

"I would have got home anyway."

"Says you," Gareth said and handed Jack his front door key. When and how Gareth had taken possession of it, Jack had no idea. And that told him a lot.

"Fine. Have it your way," he submitted and reached to unlock the door.

❖ ❖ ❖

Besting Jack's quick mind in an argument wasn't easy.

Gareth breathed a sigh of relief when Jack stopped fighting. It got them off the street and inside the house. It had worried him that Jack didn't seem to notice how badly he was shivering. But after hearing that Jack had consumed nothing but whisky, water, and chemicals since Wednesday lunchtime when it was now very early Friday morning, Gareth wasn't too surprised.

He slipped out of his shoes and watched as Jack sank down on the dark oak blanket box that took up the space below the mirror. He yanked on his boots to remove them, but the leather was stiff, and the angle was awkward. Gareth took pity when Jack started swearing. He reached over and pulled on the heel until he held Jack's right boot in his hand.

"That your idea of going armed?" He pointed to the stitched pocket in the inside of the boot, and Jack nodded.

"Can't hide stuff very well the way I'm dressed," he said, a dull blush staining his cheekbones. "The boots are my armoury." He pulled off the other one and turned it around until the heel faced Gareth. "Stiletto," he said as he ran his thumb up the broad leather strip at the back of the boot. "CS gas and a Taser in the heels. Another knife in each sole."

"No range weapons?" Gareth was pleased his voice came out level. The sight of Jack in bare feet and skin-tight leather did things to his mind and body he didn't want to contemplate right then.

"As if." Jack rubbed his fingers over the leather cuff on his wrist. "You taught me better than that."

"I damn well hope so," Gareth growled and set the boot down. "Go grab a shower. I'll fix you some food."

Jack flushed bright red in less than a heartbeat. "You don't have to do that!"

"I know." Gareth rose, took Jack's shoulders in a firm grip, and turned the man around until he faced the stairs. "Shower. Now."

Jack went, with only a half-hearted complaint mumbled under his breath. Moments later Gareth heard the sound of rushing water from upstairs and hastily retreated towards the kitchen. Bare feet and leather were quite enough to rattle his cage. There was really no need to tempt his control with images of a dripping Jack clad only in a towel.

While Jack showered, Gareth surveyed the kitchen. The replica Victorian stove was stunning, as were the period tiles and the restored cast-iron fireplace, but that's where the impressive display ended. Having seen Jack in tight black leather, Gareth wasn't surprised when he didn't find an awful lot of food to choose from. He located bread, butter, sugar, cinnamon and milk and was pleased as Punch when he could add cream and top-quality cocoa powder to his small stash. He would feed Jack cinnamon toast and cinnamon-laced hot chocolate, sweet enough to calm Jack's jangling nerves and rich enough to help put a bit of padding back on the lean frame.

Decision made and linear plan established, Gareth set a frying pan on the stove to heat while he cut two slices of bread into fingers. He added a hefty chunk of butter to the frying pan and while he waited for it to melt, he mixed the ingredients for the hot chocolate in another saucepan and placed that on the stove too.

It took just a few minutes to soak the toast in melted butter and dredge it in sugar and cinnamon before placing it under the grill. And only a few moments more before he had a plate of hot toast and a huge mug of warm, spicy cocoa all ready.

"God, that smell!" Jack groaned as he stepped into the kitchen. "I've just died and gone to heaven."

He had changed into jogging bottoms and a deep green rugby shirt. His hair was damp, his feet were bare, and Gareth made a determined effort not to drool.

"Like?"

"Definitely," Jack settled himself at the kitchen table. "I'd forgotten how handy you are in the kitchen."

"And around a campfire, don't forget that."

"How could I? We used to be the envy of the whole brigade. All we had to do was *find* food, and dinner was taken care of. Nobody else had it that easy!"

Gareth watched the toast disappear at light speed and wondered if he should make more. "Maybe I should have taught you how to cook it too. But what's the benefit of being in charge if I can't do what I like best?"

"That I can find me a mountain of food, but then still starve to death?"

There was a twinkle in Jack's eyes that Gareth was glad to see. "That is a handicap," he agreed. "And one I need to take responsibility for. Maybe a few cookery lessons are in order."

"Tried that," Jack said around a mouthful of crunchy toast, washing it down with a large swallow of hot chocolate. "Our local curry house did a cookery evening, and I went along to learn how to make their lamb phall." He set the mug on the table and leaned back in the chair. "Let's just say... it didn't end well."

"How so?" The blush on Jack's face intrigued Gareth enough to keep at it.

"Well...." Jack picked up the mug again and hid his face. "I set the ingredients on fire."

Gareth bit his lip in a valiant effort not to laugh, but it was useless. "That's one way to get a hot curry."

"It's not funny!"

"Yes, it is," Gareth disagreed. "I didn't think I'd almost have a curry house on my conscience. They still serve you?"

"With great enthusiasm," Jack admitted. "They don't want to see the neighbourhood go up in flames any more than I do."

"Never thought I'd screw up that badly," Gareth admitted. "But I'll make up for it. I promise. I'll teach you how to cook without starting the next Great Fire of London."

"Good luck with that," Jack grumbled, draining his mug and holding it up. "Is there any more?"

"Sure." Gareth reheated the remaining chocolate and refilled Jack's mug. "Can't believe that your police friends don't look after you better," he mused. "What do you usually do after one of these stunts? Just go home and dine on takeaway and beer?"

Jack managed a lopsided grin. "That. And put my memory to use."

"Missing persons?"

"Yes," Jack sighed over his next sip of hot chocolate. "Clive always wants me to look through his database of perverts, but if I've spotted any likely kids—like those two boys tonight—I'd rather find out about them."

Their earlier banter had eased the tension in Jack's frame, but now his shoulders crept towards his ears once more. Without a word Gareth rose and stepped behind Jack's chair.

"Do you think they can be helped?" he asked as he dropped his hands to Jack's shoulders and started to rub the tight muscles.

"If they're strong enough." Jack relaxed into Gareth's touch with a soft exhale. "You don't ever get out of hell undamaged. It tends to spit you out in jagged pieces. Sometimes it takes just too much effort to put yourself back together."

"I've always wondered how you knew that."

"Now you know."

"No, I don't," Gareth disagreed. He slid his fingers down to Jack's shoulder blades, feeling the tightness in the trim frame and wanting to ease it. "I have a very faint idea. At most."

The rugby shirt's collar hampered Gareth's fingertips on the upwards stroke, and he slipped his hand around to Jack's chest to undo the top button. The fabric loosened, and Gareth's fingers slid inside to push it wide… when Jack shot out of the chair and away from Gareth as if he'd been burned.

"Don't!"

# Coming Home

— ✦ ✦ ✦ —

**J**ack turned away at the same time as Gareth reached for him and yanked him back. His shirt tore open, revealing a thin strip of leather embossed with an intricate Celtic pattern around his neck. Jack flushed a dull red and stood rigid under Gareth's scrutiny, staring anywhere but at the man before him.

Gareth brushed his fingertips over the soft leather, tracing long-gone bloodstains. "I remember this," he said, awed as the past came calling in the most unexpected way.

His closest brush with death was a fractured memory of heat and sand, shouting voices, and the metallic scent and taste of blood. He'd drifted in and out of consciousness a good deal, especially towards the end, but he remembered Jack tearing the battered leather strip from Gareth's arm and using it to fashion a tourniquet.

He had never considered the whereabouts of this particular strip of leather, and the fact that Jack *wore* it staggered and enlightened Gareth as much as Jack's rigid stance and flushed face. Memories and old observations aligned like the tumblers in a complicated lock, offering chances he'd not even dared to dream about. The choice was easy. A heartbeat later, he pinned Jack against the wall and pushed their lips together. For a small eternity—no more than a breath or two—Jack stood frozen. Then he melted into the kiss with a soft moan that went straight to Gareth's groin.

"You blithering idiot! Why didn't you say something?" Gareth demanded when he drew back from the kiss, his breathing ragged. It was so easy to get lost in Jack, all cinnamon, chocolate, and heat, as if Jack was a treat designed specifically for Gareth's senses.

"Yeah, like you did?" Jack sounded peeved.

"That's different. Back then, I couldn't make the first move."

"Same reason," Jack shot back. "I didn't want to jeopardise your career, either."

"My career? What the fuck are you talking about?"

"Then why?"

"Your age, moron!" Gareth snarled. "Never been one for cradle snatching."

"My age?" Jack's wide-eyed stare would have been comical, but for the outrage in the grey-green depths. "That's your excuse?" he demanded. "I was old enough to go out and get shot, for Christ's sake!"

They stared at each other until Gareth reached out and cupped Jack's cheek. "True," he acknowledged, voice wry. "Only thing I can say is that—at the time— it felt all wrong. And given what I've learnt tonight…."

Jack turned his head and let his lips brush Gareth's palm. "That's not the same, and you know it," he said, the fire in his eyes replaced with certainty. "With you, I would've had a choice."

"You still do."

"Then stay here?"

Gareth hesitated a heartbeat too long. Hurt bloomed across Jack's face.

"If you don't want…."

The rest was cut off as Gareth crushed Jack back against the wall. "What *I* want?" He breathed across Jack's ear and relished the shiver that ran through the lithe form in his arms. "I'll tell you what *I* want, brat. Rip every piece of fabric off you. Taste every inch of you. Screw you into the nearest available surface until you scream my name. And then do it again." He bit down on an earlobe until Jack arched helplessly against him. "Been wanting that for years. Just so we're clear."

He drew away, far enough to pull Jack's chin up and meet the wide eucalyptus-coloured eyes. "Doesn't mean that staying's a good idea. You're strung out and tired, Jack. And tense as a bow."

"Help me relax?"

"Yeah, I could," Gareth sighed. "But I don't want you to regret this tomorrow morning."

"Regret it?" Jack touched the strip of leather around his throat. "Does this look like I'll regret… anything?"

Gareth sighed. He was doing a lot of that lately, and it wasn't doing him any good. Why was he fighting anyway? He didn't want to leave. And Jack…. Jack wanted him to stay. "My rules," he growled before his brain noticed he'd opened his mouth. "I stay, but we play by my rules."

Gareth expected dissent, but if anything, Jack looked relieved. "Just… stay," he pleaded. "I don't need another hangover, but…."

"I remember." Gareth nuzzled a line from Jack's ear down his neck, tasting skin as he went and loving it. "Massage oil?"

"Bathroom." Jack's answer was breathy.

Gareth pushed away from the wall and the warm body he'd pinned against it, grinning when Jack swallowed a protesting whine. "Strip and get on the bed," he ordered and went to find himself some massage oil.

Compared to the muted chaos of Jack's bedroom, where makeup, club clothes, and weapons warred for space on floor and dresser, the bathroom was neat and well supplied. Besides various massage oils, Gareth spotted bath bombs, bath salts, and a few waterproof toys that set his mind racing, but he shelved the wayward thoughts. Tonight's objective was getting Jack to relax. Fun and games could wait.

He repeated that to himself a few more times for emphasis as he returned to the bedroom and found Jack stretched out on the deep green sheets. He had his head on a pillow and his gaze on the bathroom door. The sheer want in the grey-green eyes did amazing things to Gareth's insides. It also made him question the sanity of his decision to stay. Again.

"You're a beautiful sight, brat." His gaze slid appreciatively over the endless legs, firm arse, and finely muscled back and arms. He knelt beside the bed, so his face was level with Jack's. "Beautiful… and tempting… and far too tense." He punctuated each word with a soft brush of lips, pulling back when Jack reached for more contact.

"Take a deep breath in. Let it out slowly. Good. Again." The fingers of Gareth's right hand slid into Jack's hair and rubbed soothing circles over his scalp.

"I want you completely relaxed," he breathed against Jack's ear. "Release all tension, and let me work, okay?"

He waited for the nod before he traced the shell of Jack's ear with his tongue, his fingers pressing more firmly on Jack's scalp. With an explosive exhale, Jack tried to lean into one touch and away from the other, unable to do either.

"There's a reward if you do as I say," Gareth tempted, voice low and seductive. He relished the shudder that rippled through Jack's frame. He loved it even more when Jack closed his eyes and forced his muscles to soften.

"Just like that," Gareth praised. He shed his shirt, reached for the lavender-scented oil and climbed up on the bed to straddle Jack's hips. "Hands under your head," he instructed as he poured oil into his palms to warm it. "I'll start on your shoulders and work my way across your back. I want you to stay relaxed at all times. Got it?"

Another small nod and Gareth set his hands to Jack's back. For a heady moment, he just held still and savoured the contact.

His hands on warm, soft skin.

The slow rise and fall of the ribs under his palms.

The beautiful golden tan, still fresh, that highlighted the pale lines of old scars.

The trust from a man who had more reason to be wary than Gareth would ever know.

Jack was amazing. And Gareth wanted to keep it that way.

The thought calmed and steadied him. With careful movements he spread the oil over Jack's skin, finding continent-sized knots in Jack's neck and upper back in the process. No wonder Jack went about with his shoulders around his ears.

"You need a more ergonomic workstation," Gareth decided as he ran his thumbs along the edge of Jack's shoulder blades. "And fewer hours in front of a screen."

Jack's breathing hitched, and he tried to stifle a low moan. "My workstation's just fine," he mumbled.

"Not if you're this tense." Gareth rubbed soothing circles, determined to loosen all the knots even if it took him until sunrise.

"I skipped my workouts while I was job hunting," Jack admitted.

"And more than a few meals," Gareth opined. "You really haven't changed much, have you?"

That had Jack tensing and pushing up onto his elbows. "That's not true," he said with a surprising amount of heat in his voice. "I'm nowhere near as stupid as I was back when."

"You were *never* stupid." Gareth planted his palm

in the middle of Jack's back and pushed him onto the sheets before setting his hands either side of his head. He leaned forwards so he could speak in Jack's ear. "You've always been mad with skills and exceptional at your job. You tend to overanalyse and beat yourself up over things outside your control. And you get so caught up in what you're doing that you neglect your own needs." He nuzzled Jack's ear until Jack's eyes slid closed, and the taut frame beneath him relaxed. "Now, which of these assessments do you want to argue over?"

Jack remained silent. He exhaled small gasps through half-opened lips when Gareth explored the area behind his ear with the tip of his tongue. Jack had such an addictive taste that Gareth wanted nothing more than to stay right where he was to explore and get lost.

But that wasn't on the menu. Not yet.

Gareth brushed a soft kiss on the corner of Jack's mouth and then pushed himself upright. He poured more oil into his hands, warmed it, and traced Jack's ribcage with careful strokes. The outline of a forming bruise marred Jack's right side, and Jack hissed a breath through clenched lips as Gareth traced his fingertips softly across it.

"Bruised but nothing broken," he decided. "You wanna tell me how he got that one in?"

A deep breath was his answer and a soft dusting of pink across Jack's neck and ears. Gareth held himself still and waited until Jack relented. "I was checking his pulse to make sure he was alive."

"Jesus, brat! You're unreal." Gareth dropped a quick kiss between Jack's shoulder blades to show how he meant that, then continued working the muscles in Jack's back and neck until the tightness eased and knots loosened, allowing Gareth to work his fingers deeper.

Jack's breaths grew into soft appreciative moans, and he melted into the sheets as Gareth worked his way south. Jack held most of his tension in his neck and shoulders. The state of his upper back reflected the endless hours spent in front of computer screens with fingers busy on keyboards. His lower back, glutes, hamstrings, and calves were in much better shape, and Gareth eased back on the pressure he applied but still diligently teased out even the smallest knot while enjoying the feel of soft skin over firm muscle. Arousal added a pleasant buzz to his blood, but Gareth kept a lid on his needs. This night was for Jack, and Gareth had plans.

Still, those plans didn't prevent him from taking pleasure in his work. He could appreciate Jack's perfect arse and long shapely legs as much as the scandalous sounds Jack produced when Gareth's touch changed from massaging hamstrings to long caressing strokes up the inside of Jack's thighs and over the swell of his butt.

"Like?" he asked, repeating the move just to hear that low moan again.

"God, yes," Jack groaned, shifting on the bed in search of friction.

Gareth pinned Jack's hips, hands pressing down firmly as he explored the perfect combination of firm muscle and yielding flesh that was Jack's arse. The skin under his fingers was silky soft. Even the silver lines of old scars didn't detract from the sensation. Gareth was reminded of items that were so wonderful men deliberately added flaws to them so that the gods would not be jealous.

A deep, ragged breath shuddered its way out of Gareth's throat. Straightening up and moving his hands took effort. Damn! He was becoming addicted to that perfect arse, and they hadn't even started anything yet.

Jack's fingers curled around his in a silent entreaty when Gareth slipped off the bed, and Gareth made no move to free himself. "Just need to wash the oil off my hands," he explained. "Get under the quilt. I'm not going anywhere."

He made his escape when Jack let go, fully aware that he needed a few moments. That was unusual.

Gareth loved to play, and he *never* lost control. So why was it suddenly so hard to focus even after a liberal application of cold water?

It was the brat, of course. Gareth had been attracted to Jack Horwood almost from the day he first met him after Jack's basic training, but as he'd tried to point out to Jack earlier, cradle snatching wasn't a pastime of his. Neither did he like to take advantage of people under his care. That didn't mean he wasn't aware of how he'd felt or that he hadn't been hoping Jack might return the sentiment.

Jack's leaving the army—and on the exact day he'd saved Gareth's life only a year before—had torn a hole into Gareth's world. For a long time, he'd wondered whether the fault had been his. Whether he'd been too obvious in his regard and had scared Jack away. It was only after he himself had left the army and found out that Jack was serving in MI6 that he'd stopped blaming himself and instead tried to find Jack again.

And now he had, only to learn that he'd been right on both counts. Jack's leaving the army had been his fault, but not because he'd been too obvious. Rather, he hadn't been obvious enough.

Gareth splashed more cold water in his face and ran his wet hands through his hair. He wouldn't make that mistake again. From now on he'd make doubly sure that Jack knew how much he was appreciated and how much Gareth wanted him. And he would start right now.

Only a single small lamp shed its soft yellow glow across the bed when Gareth closed the bathroom door. Jack had hidden that delectable body under the quilt, but he was awake and watching from dark, intent eyes, not yet convinced that Gareth would stay the night.

"Has anyone ever given you reason to believe they'd turn you down?" Gareth queried as he shucked his jeans and climbed under the quilt.

"I don't care about *anyone*," Jack replied, eyes careful. "Just you. And you *would* turn me down if you thought it was the right thing to do."

"Oh, you underestimate yourself, brat." Gareth settled onto his side and gave Jack a heated look. "C'mere."

Jack shifted, and Gareth pulled Jack's back flush with his chest. He had to swallow a groan when Jack's tight butt made contact with his groin, doubly grateful now for keeping his briefs on. Skin on skin in *that* area would evaporate his control at an even faster rate, and that wasn't how the rest of this night was meant to go.

He slipped his arm under Jack's pillow and curled himself around Jack in a full-body hug. "I'd have to be out of my mind to turn down something I've wanted for so long. And I assure you, I'm quite sane."

Startled, Jack turned his head, and Gareth wasted not a single second. He kept the kiss slow and sweet, kept Jack wrapped tightly in his embrace, and relished it when Jack relaxed into his hold and opened his lips.

"Ready for your reward?" Gareth breathed over kiss-swollen lips a while later, grinning when his only reply was a heartfelt moan.

"Okay then, here's what we do. You stay where you are, totally relaxed… and I'll do my best to make you feel good." Gareth nipped on Jack's earlobe, causing him to flinch. "Remember, I said *totally relaxed*. You tense up on me, I'll feel it… and I stop what I'm doing."

"Gareth, no—you can't…."

"Shhhh," Gareth soothed, lips ghosting over the shell of an ear. "It will be so worth it. Trust me."

"I do trust you," Jack argued. "But I need—"

"I know what you need, Jack. Trust me. Relax. Every muscle. Completely." Gareth kept his voice low and hypnotic, and after a long, tense moment, Jack shuddered and let go. The body in Gareth's hold softened and relaxed.

"That's it. Stay just like that," Gareth singsonged and wrapped his arms tighter around Jack. The fingers of his left hand traced the column of Jack's neck and explored his collarbones while his other hand stroked upwards from Jack's firm, flat stomach to brush softly over his nipples.

Every time Jack tensed Gareth stopped moving until he gave up trying to direct Gareth's actions.

"Make all the noise you want," Gareth whispered in Jack's ear. "Swear at me if you feel like it. Just make sure your muscles stay relaxed. It's worth it. Believe me." Gareth's mouth roamed over Jack's ear and along the soft skin of his neck until his lips landed on the pulse point at the base of Jack's throat. There he rested while his hands played, while Jack's breaths turned to moans, and the occasional curse crept through Jack's control.

The fingers tracing Jack's collarbones slipped down to toy with his nipples while Gareth's other hand began to explore ridged abs and dip into Jack's navel.

Jack's hips rocked forwards, enticing the playing fingers, and Gareth froze.

"Relax, Jack," he instructed. "You're doing well. Just stay relaxed… totally relaxed…."

Jack ground his teeth. And produced some highly creative language that had Gareth grinning. Oh, yeah—here was the man he remembered, temper and all. The years hadn't impeded Jack's ability to outswear a regiment of dragoons, but he still trusted Gareth enough to give in… eventually.

A heady mix of emotions washed through Gareth.

That Jack would trust him that much was... an unexpected gift. And as Jack resigned himself to Gareth taking the lead in their play and followed instructions, Gareth kept his lips over Jack's pulse.

His hands roamed over the enticing body he was wrapped around: teasing nipples, stroking Jack's balls, wrapping fingers around his length for long, slow strokes... only to stop and retreat when they'd driven Jack close to the edge. To let him recover his breath, let his heartbeat even out, before starting the pleasurable torture once more.

"I could do this for hours," Gareth whispered while his fingertips teased Jack's painfully hard length with soft little flicks. "Just to listen to the sounds you're making."

"Never... took you for a... tease." Jack panted with the effort to keep still.

"Shows how much you don't know." Gareth smiled and sank his teeth into Jack's neck to a yelp of surprise.

Jack's breaths had turned into toned sobs, and the sky outside the bedroom window showed the first hints of grey when Gareth finally relented. He shifted his knee over Jack's legs to pin him more firmly in place while his left hand turned Jack's face up so he could claim his mouth.

A brutally hard grip on Jack's length and a vicious

twist-pinch-pull to a nipple had Jack's body bucking and writhing in sudden shock. In no time at all he flew over the edge Gareth had kept him on for so long, his shout muffled by Gareth's kiss.

Gareth kept hold of Jack as his body shuddered through an intense orgasm, as Jack slowly came down from the high and melted into boneless bliss against the body wrapped around him.

"That was…." Jack's voice was but a thread of sound.

"Worth it?" Gareth inquired as he reached for tissues to clean up the mess.

"You're not kidding." Jack sounded drowsy, content, and already half asleep. Gareth shifted to his back and pulled him close, pillowing Jack's head on his shoulder. His body throbbed and burned, but Gareth found that compared to seeing Jack's face relax into sleep, body soft against Gareth's side, the burn meant little. He rested his chin on Jack's head, grateful for the chance to hold Jack so peacefully after all the time he'd spent chasing him.

<hr />

Jack came awake on a wave of contentment, with warmth and solidity surrounding him and his mind blissfully at peace. Stretching a little, he nuzzled his face into Gareth's neck. His lips dragged over soft skin, and his tongue slipped out to catch a taste.

"Good morning to you too," Gareth chuckled, and the roughness in his voice sent blood straight to Jack's groin.

He wasn't an innocent by any stretch of the imagination, but he'd never experienced anything like the previous night. He couldn't explain how Gareth had done it; he just knew that he'd never hung on the edge of release for such a long time. And he'd never come so hard that his release left his body thrumming *and* boneless all at once. He didn't even remember falling asleep—and that had never happened before. All he wanted now was to make Gareth feel as out of control and desperate and *needy* as he had been hours earlier.

Jack slid his hand across Gareth's chest, delighted to find a small nipple ring to play with. His lips teased the soft skin of Gareth's neck, nibbling and sucking in long meandering lines. The arms around him tightened, and Jack chose to take that as an invitation. His lips moved to play with the other, unpierced, nipple, and when he felt the little nub harden under his ministrations, he slipped his hand down Gareth's torso to trace the edge of his briefs. He was just about to slide his fingers under the elastic, when one of Gareth's hands flew down and stopped him.

"You don't want me to return the favour?" Jack hoped he didn't sound as confused as he felt. He would have sworn that Gareth was enjoying his caresses.

"Oh, I do. Just not right now," Gareth told him. He wrapped Jack into a bear hug and pushed himself upright until he leaned against the headboard, and their eyes met. "I wanna savour you for something special… go slow and explore, spend hours teasing you." Gareth's hand came up, and Jack bit back a groan when Gareth started dragging blunt nails over his scalp. "What would you say to spending the weekend with me?"

"After last night? I'd have to be stupid to miss out on a repeat performance." The expression of relief that crossed Gareth's face was unexpected. "You thought I wouldn't want to?"

"You've always been a law unto yourself, Jack." Gareth shrugged. "I can read you, but I find it damn difficult to predict your actions."

"Ditto." Jack smiled, unwilling to let go of his blissful mood. "I've never had something so…." He searched for a word that would adequately describe his experience. "Intense." He finally decided. "And we didn't really do anything." He straightened in Gareth's lap and brought their faces close. "Just make sure you have a fire extinguisher handy," he said before he claimed Gareth's lips.

Time passed in heated exploration until Gareth drew away. "We'd better get up. You have an appointment with HR this morning to sign your contract."

Jack struggled to remember what day it was, not to mention what was on his agenda. "Not such a good idea, since we've just compromised our working relationship with a one-night stand," he muttered and pushed himself upright.

"I really can't flatter myself, can I?" Gareth grumbled and pinned Jack with a lightning move. "I swear to God if you don't stop spouting bullshit I'll tie you to something sturdy, find my belt, and explain *in detail* why I spent favours and my employer's resources to find you."

For a long moment Jack stared, then he started to laugh like he hadn't laughed in years. When the helpless chuckles threatened to turn into something far more embarrassing, he reached up and pulled Gareth close. "Gods, Gareth, I love you," he mumbled against a shoulder when he finally relaxed.

Gareth held him until his breathing evened out. "Does this mean you'll come work for me and stop giving me trouble?" he queried as Jack sat up.

"I'll work for you," Jack agreed, excitement starting to thread through his mind as he began to contemplate new challenges ahead. "Not sure about not giving you trouble."

The way they moved through their morning routine made Jack think of the well-trained staff behind a busy cocktail bar. It felt like a closely choreographed dance routine that allowed them to share space without one impeding the other.

Jack never spent nights with lovers, and he'd expected a level of awkwardness. But nothing further from the truth. With Gareth, everything seemed easy, everything they did just... worked. And while Jack didn't believe that things would stay that way, he wanted to take advantage while the going was good.

"What do you say we go out for breakfast?" Gareth's shout came from the kitchen as if he'd remembered from his previous foray how limited Jack's culinary resources were.

"Great idea. Think you can handle the Ten Deadly Sins?" The look on Gareth's face was worth recording for posterity, but Jack didn't reach for his phone to snap a picture. Instead, he grabbed Gareth's hand and dragged him out the door, content to let matters explain themselves in due course.

# TEASE AND CHALLENGE

━━━◆◆◆━━━

"**I** can't *believe* I've eaten all that!" Jack groaned and rubbed his stomach. He felt stuffed. Content, sort of happy, but definitely stuffed. Breakfast had been magnificent, Simpson's kitchen doing full justice to the famous meal they called The Ten Deadly Sins. Jack had devoured Cumberland sausage and baked tomatoes, indulged in liver and bacon, black pudding, and mushrooms, and followed that up with bubble and squeak, fried bread, scrambled eggs, and baked beans. When toast, jam, and various pastries appeared on the table, Jack was convinced he wouldn't need to eat for the rest of the weekend. Now, the table in front of him was a splendid ruin, with Gareth—looking like a sleek, well-fed cat—presiding over the teapot.

"I can't believe it either," Gareth replied in a deep, amused rumble. He had opted for a more reasonably sized full English breakfast, but his plate was just as bare as Jack's. "But since you do need more meat on your bones, I'm perfectly willing to indulge your appetite."

*Hmmm*. Jack hid his face in his fourth cup of coffee. *Too easy*. He slipped a foot out of the soft suede loafers he wore and slid it up the inside of Gareth's leg. Voluminous white tablecloths had their advantages, after all.

"Jack!" The faintest hint of pink dusted Gareth's cheekbones. He slid as far back into the seat as he could, trying—and failing—to avoid Jack's questing toes.

"Yes?"

"This is one of London's oldest, most respectable restaurants," Gareth said. "I come here a lot."

"Yes?"

"So I wouldn't relish being thrown out."

Jack made puppy-dog eyes. "You just said you'd be willing to indulge my appetite," he purred.

"Food, Jack!" Gareth spluttered. "I was talking about food."

"Of course." Jack kept his face blank and his eyes down as he slipped his foot back into the loafer. He finished his coffee and started to arrange the used china into neat piles. Opposite him, Gareth fidgeted. He opened his mouth a few times as if to make a comment, then gave up and called for the bill instead.

When that was settled, Jack stood without a word and turned towards the exit, amused when Gareth stayed close. Too close.

"Gareth…." Jack drew out the name on a sigh, heard the hitch in Gareth's breath, and spun around with a huge grin splitting his face. "You don't need to step on my hems. I wasn't planning on running in the other direction."

"Why you little…."

Jack ducked out of the way of a fist trying to connect with the back of his head and laughed. "You should have seen that guilty look on your face… undercover work is not for you."

"You are a manipulative little…."

"Gareth!" Jack wanted to grab the man by the front of his polo shirt and push him against the nearest wall, but he refrained. Simpson's hallowed halls were not the place for horseplay. Not for Gareth Flynn, at any rate. "Keep calling me names and I *will* run," he declared in his most ominous voice. "Just… FYI."

And with that he was out the door and down the steps before Gareth could reply.

Jack slipped into the thick pedestrian traffic, walking just a bit faster than most of the people heading to work. He had never quite understood the buzz of working a crowd, but right then, dodging and weaving around human-shaped obstacles, aware that

Gareth was trying to catch up without creating an obvious scene, Jack suddenly felt insanely happy.

The unexpected surge of emotion stopped him in his tracks. He was… happy. And it had little to do with the fact that it was Friday or that the sun was shining. The excitement of a new job was a contributor, but most of his elation was tied to the man who was drawing level with him, eyes narrowed to angry slits and face like a thundercloud.

A broad hand closed around his bicep, holding him in place. "You deserve an arse whipping for that stunt."

"Promise?" Giddiness flooded Jack as he rendered Gareth speechless for a second time that morning.

It didn't last long.

"For Christ's sake, Horwood, get a grip!"

"Sorry." Jack drew a deep breath and slowly let it out. He was standing on the Strand during the morning rush, pedestrian traffic surging around him, and wondered why feeling happy reminded him of crazy nights drinking and laughing with Tom. It couldn't have been that long since he felt like this, could it? He smiled into irate amber eyes. "I was just teasing."

"Well, don't. It's irritating."

The growl was more bark than bite, and the smile that crinkled the corners of Gareth's eyes made Jack's insides crinkle right back. With a little effort, he managed a wink and a half-hearted salute.

"Yes, sir."

———— ◆ ◆ ◆ ————

"I suppose I have you to thank for my rearranged schedule and this…." A slender hand waved at a thick concertina file on the corner of the desk, and Gareth tried not to flinch.

"Guilty as charged," he admitted and stepped into the one room in the building that never failed to calm him. The space suited the quiet psychologist. The walls were painted a pale amethyst grey that complemented her eyes, the furniture was dark autumn-leaf oak, and a deep red sofa and two armchairs invited visitors to take their ease. With her delicate build, expressive eyes, and neat mahogany bob, Alexandra Marston looked positively regal surrounded by hibiscus trees in dark red ceramic pots, like a female Buddha or something equally Zen.

Gareth's office faced the city and his desk offered views over London's skyline and the River Thames, while Marston had opted for an office with windows onto the inner, glass-roofed courtyard of the Nancarrow Mining HQ and the graceful tall birch that took up the courtyard's centre.

Gareth liked his view out over London, but he could appreciate the serenity of Marston's domain, a place to relax tight controls for just a moment.

"You really managed to convince him," Alexandra Marston said, thoughtful, inviting her visitor to take a seat and reaching for the teapot on her desk. "I'm impressed."

"Don't be," Gareth huffed in mild irritation. "It didn't go as planned."

"Because of the police operation?" Alexandra poured tea and held out a cup. "Close your mouth, Gareth. I'm still not clairvoyant. Lisa called earlier, so I know you didn't have the most restful of nights, and neither did your Jack."

Gareth considered scoffing at Marston's description of his night, or taking umbrage at having Jack apostrophised as his, but in the end he did neither. Knowing Alexandra, each word had been chosen with the utmost deliberation, and it was far safer to let her say what she felt she needed to say.

"How is he handling the death of that child?"

"Professionally," Gareth replied, wondering if Jack was even better at hiding than he gave him credit for. "A little uneven when something catches him off guard, maybe."

"Lisa wants his help with the investigation," Marston informed him.

"I'm not surprised. He's good." Gareth's mind filled with images of Jack moving about the dim club assessing targets, exits, and potential victims, missing nothing despite a belladonna-induced headache, impaired vision, and the obvious disadvantages of using himself as bait. He'd had to run that op with minimal intel and no backup, but once there, Jack had owned the space and had done everything he needed to do to achieve his objective. "Damn good, actually."

"So you approve?"

"Not my place to approve or disapprove," Gareth said. "Not my place to stop him if he wants to help, either. Don't think I could."

There had been a time, years ago, when he had been able to control the dangers Jack faced. Now Gareth could watch and advise, but control was outside his remit. The fact stuck in his craw, though he was honest enough to admit that Jack grown up and making his own decisions was enticing for entirely different reasons.

The beautiful woman facing him across the tea table smiled ever so slightly. "You didn't answer my question," she said.

"Alex, it's not my place to make his choices. Do I want him to stick his head into a hornet's nest and rip open wounds from his past? Hell no! Do I want him to do what he needs to be at peace? Yes, I do. Does *that* answer your question?"

"More than you realise, perhaps."

His teacup rattled in the saucer, and Gareth growled in frustration. It was Friday—and yes, people were a little more relaxed on Fridays—but that shouldn't have translated into everyone thinking that teasing him would be a good idea.

Jack had almost driven him insane that morning and—within minutes of stepping into his new office—had promptly recruited Frazer to join in the mayhem.

For two specialists of their calibre, defining the spec for Jack's workstation should have been the work of moments. Or at least that's what Gareth had thought.

Instead, the two started drooling over processors, memory, and various esoteric components as if they were pictures in a dirty magazine, arguing in high, excited voices and trading insults as if they'd been married for twenty years. And the way Jack, in his tight black jeans, kept bending over the desk to point at stuff in the catalogue Frazer was holding….

Gareth had left them to it in the end and had holed up in his office, intent on burying himself in work.

Only to end up watching Jack on the security feed instead.

Grainy images of Jack smiling and arguing blended with images of Jack barefoot and in tight leather trousers, of soft skin under his hands, of Jack writhing and shuddering in his arms until Gareth could barely contain himself.

Yeah, he'd sure gotten it bad in a hurry.

◆ ◆ ◆

"Your application was most impressive."

"Thank you." Jack leaned deeper into the comfortable armchair and kept his hands loosely in his lap. He wondered if the chairs were deep red for a reason, an imaginary hot seat designed to make the occupants squirm and spill secrets they'd rather keep hidden. It was a fanciful notion but not easily dismissed given the company. The woman sitting opposite him, Alexandra Marston, might look unassuming with her neat figure and neater bob, but she had a stare like a power drill.

Fortunately, Jack was years past getting flustered by stares. Even ones as intent as hers.

"You provided an extremely detailed analysis of the shortcomings of the company's network as part of your approach to us." Marston began their conversation, her voice soft and melodious. "Why?"

"Network security is one of my specialties. You

could say I was showing off my talents."

"I could also draw a very different conclusion."

*Hot seat, definitely,* Jack decided. At least she wasn't beating around the bush. "I don't list blackmail or extortion amongst my specialties."

Alexandra Marston's smile lit her face from within, like the glow of a candle lights a stained-glass window on a dark night. Jack loved the expression, and it drew a smile from him in return. "It's part of my preparation," he offered. "I see no point in applying to a company that doesn't need my skills."

"You made your decision where to apply based on whether the company needed your skills?"

Jack nodded. "It was one of my criteria, yes."

"May I ask what other criteria you applied?"

"Integrity, cash flow, reputation, ethics, corporate policies, type and nature of competition, short- and long-term threat level," Jack recited in an almost bored voice. Then he sat back and waited for it.

Marston busied herself making notes on a pad. She used a type of shorthand Jack couldn't decipher from his position, but then she listed the criteria he had just recited in plain script. "You've already broken one of those corporate policies."

"I'm not an employee of Nancarrow Mining… yet."

Jack pushed his back more securely into the

armchair and relaxed his posture on a breath. This was the second time Marston had tried to rile him. A hint of accusation followed by a veiled threat. No doubt the third attack would be the charm.

He stopped himself from folding his arms across his chest as if he needed protection. His fingers wanted to tap on the arms of the chair to distract his mind, but he kept them in his lap, unmoving. He waited, breathing slowly and taking comfort from the silence as he had been trained to do.

"Do you frequently break the law, Dr. Horwood?"

An unexpected moment of respite. *Very smart.* Jack was tempted to let his sense of mischief take over. Just for a moment or two, to see if he could shock this woman with the gorgeous smile and mind like a spymaster into losing her footing on that tightrope they both balanced on.

It was an appealing thought, but prudence won in the end. Prudence and a sense of duty.

"You're aware of my employment history, ma'am. Which means you have to know that I am not at liberty to discuss any of it."

Not that he would have wanted to discuss his past even if he'd been at liberty to do so. The few people who knew did so because they'd seen him at work.

Talking about himself wasn't Jack's way. Though why that thought produced an image of Gareth standing on his doorstep, staring at Jack from wide amber eyes in which shock and heat mixed most effectively….

Returning his focus to the conversation took effort. Marston was smiling at him, nothing more than a tiny curl of lip, and Jack braced himself.

"What is your association with Gareth Flynn?"

Bingo.

"He was my commanding officer while I served in the army."

More illegible notes blossomed on Marston's pad. The woman wrote and wrote as if Jack's succinct answer demanded a lengthy commentary. Jack was sure his voice and body language were perfect. She was baiting him. She had to be.

"Does he know you well?"

"Yes." *Maybe not well enough if he thinks I need an impromptu psych eval.*

"Were you aware that Gareth headed our corporate security division when you applied to Nancarrow Mining?"

Jack let himself smile as he remembered the moment Gareth had walked back into his life. Three days ago, that had been. And now everything had changed. "I had no idea."

A knock on the door announced a tray of coffee. Jack accepted a cup with a grateful bow of his head, understanding that the preliminary skirmish was done. What came next was serious business, and Marston wasn't hanging around.

"I would like to understand the reasons for your initial refusal to accept this position. And how your involvement in an ongoing police investigation will affect your work for Nancarrow Mining."

# SECURITY LEAKS

———————◆◆◆———————

J ack made his way to Gareth's office two hours later. Activity in the building had died down while he evaded Alexandra Marston's carefully chosen personal questions and answered all work-related ones. Most employees had taken advantage of the fine weather and the chance to leave early on a Friday afternoon, and the almost empty corridors and open-plan offices breathed calm and tranquillity.

The low hum of electronics on standby, of processor cooling fans and air conditioning, reminded Jack of long, quiet nights huddled over screens and keyboard, chasing trails too faint to follow in the daytime.

It was work he loved and work he looked forwards to spending time doing once more.

He passed his new desk, fingers caressing the smooth wood. Four screens now lined the top edge of the solid oak board, ready to form a near seamless wall of images, and a low-profile keyboard and graphics tablet with stylus took up the space in the centre. Only the heart of the setup was missing and, seeing how quickly Frazer had started implementing the plans they'd made this morning, Jack was certain that he'd have most of the requested gear by Monday.

Donald Frazer was as much fun to work with as Jack had thought he'd be when they met during his interview. They held similar views on technology, and before Jack had been dragged off to his meeting with the HR manager, he'd watched Frazer deal with an attempted break-in in a way that commanded his admiration.

The Scot was quick, decisive, and did neat work.

"Come in and grab a seat," Gareth instructed when Jack popped his head around the door of Gareth's office. "I'm almost done."

Gareth had his nose buried in a stack of financial-looking forms, pen moving swiftly across the page. It was a side of Gareth that Jack hadn't seen before, and the fact that the man sat meekly filling forms, and looked like an accountant doing so, only added to Jack's good mood.

He closed the door and wandered across the expanse of pale carpet.

"Wow," he huffed as he fell into one of the armchairs and stretched his long legs towards the lemon tree growing in a deep blue metal container. "That last one had claws and teeth and a mind that wouldn't be out of place over there." He waved a hand in the general direction of the MI6 building along the river.

Gareth looked up from the form he was filling out. "Marston? She's ex-MI6, just like you. I think she still consults at times."

"Right." Jack swivelled his head and contemplated the view. He shuddered at the idea of consulting for his old firm and wondered where in the huge organisation Alex Marston would have worked.

And whether she still did.

Their little battle of wills had been entertaining. Jack guessed that Marston had been trained in interrogation, but he knew from experience that not everyone who'd had the training was actually good at the job. Marston had that steel-trap mind that characterised the best interrogators, and she'd shown enough flexibility to make Jack think she might be truly outstanding.

She also had access to classified information, even while employed at Nancarrow Mining. She wasn't even hiding it. *You are currently involved in a police investigation.*

She'd been profiling him during their discussion. Her cryptic writings hinted as much, as did the abrupt switches in topic. The schema she used to question him hadn't been familiar, but Jack didn't tend to stick to the standard ones when he worked either. And despite all the games and challenges, Marston's had been a comforting presence, a vibe that something in Jack responded to however much she pushed him out of his comfort zone.

"I like her," he decided, startled from his contemplation when Gareth barked a laugh.

"You'd better. Alexandra Marston is someone you want to keep on your side in a fight. Just like Julian Nancarrow." He rose and shuffled the papers into a neat stack. "Are you ready to sign your life away?"

"If that's what you want? Sure." Jack stretched suggestively as he stood just to yank Gareth's chain. "I had no idea you'd let me spec my own equipment, so the way I see it—I owe you."

"Had I known how much you were going to spend I would have set a budget."

"Ah." Jack waved the complaint away. "Frazer's a Scot, so he'll haggle. And when he's done, my setup is gonna be epic!"

"It better be." And with that Gareth was right there in Jack's space.

Jack shivered at the sudden warm touch to his nape. Calluses dragged on the sensitive skin, sending sparks down his spine. Then Gareth's mouth closed over Jack's, hard and hungry and all too brief.

"Let's get this done," Gareth ordered before Jack had a chance to complain about the unexpected attack or its brevity. "We have a weekend starting straight after."

<hr />

After years of barracks, student digs, and plain, utilitarian office furniture in various shades of Whitehall Ugly, the stylish interior design of the Nancarrow Mining HQ had attracted Jack's attention long before he ever thought of applying to the company. He liked the idea of working in a building where grandiose Victorian architecture blended with glass and muted shades, with real wood and flowering plants, with specimen minerals and well-chosen art.

His introductory tour that morning, courtesy of Gareth, had confirmed that the whole building was as impressive as the lobby and visitor area.

Each floor had its own distinctive style, from colours and carpets to the type of art that was on display on the walls and in glass cabinets in the corridors.

To crown it all, a ground floor cafeteria that didn't just serve home-cooked food and freshly baked pastries, but hand-roasted Arabica coffee in proper china cups augmented a basement equipped with dojo, gym, sauna and core store packed full of rock samples.

Earlier in the week, during his interview, Jack had thought the coffee machine in the corporate security office dispensed liquid gold compared to the sludge produced by the office vending machines he was accustomed to, but this... coffee that smelled and tasted as if someone had taken care and time to make it... this was a workaholic's dream of heaven.

The enticing smell of freshly roasted coffee beans also permeated the executive floor as Jack followed Gareth out of the stairwell and through the double doors towards Julian Nancarrow's corner office. Judging by the empty desks, the CEO's support staff had already left, but the door at the far end of the room stood open and a rich baritone invited them to enter.

Jack felt a sudden need to apologise for his presence as the CEO of Nancarrow Mining stepped around his desk and moved towards the centre of the room to greet them. He'd seen photographs of Julian Nancarrow, of course he had, but none of them conveyed the fact that the mining tycoon looked like he'd be at home on a catwalk.

Since it was Friday, Julian Nancarrow wore fitted black trousers and an open-necked cobalt shirt, but he looked more formal than Jack would in a three-piece. Fortunately, there wasn't much formality about his greeting.

"I'm Julian Nancarrow," he introduced himself as he held out a hand.

"Jack Horwood," Jack replied, cheered by the firm handshake and lack of posturing. It was plain refreshing.

They moved to the group of armchairs by the window, and Jack had a moment to look around the executive office, take in the pale blue-grey walls complemented by carpets that were the shade of a thunderstorm.

Nancarrow Mining's CEO appeared to prefer traditional materials—the top of his desk was a slab of solid oak, at least an inch and a half thick and stained the deep Georgian brown Jack had used on the wooden beams of his first home.

The styling of the room was entirely modern, though, the dark wood tempered by smoky, chrome-framed glass and a huge collection of rocks. They were simply everywhere: on Julian Nancarrow's desk, under bright spotlights in glass cases, on the low coffee table… samples and specimens both.

During the day, Jack had begun to classify parts of the building by greenery. Flowers in Marston's domain, bamboo arrangements in HR, citrus trees and herbs in the corporate security division… so it struck him as curious that Julian Nancarrow's spacious office didn't hold a single plant. Jack was reminded of his best friend and the rooms they'd shared as postgrads.

*I'm away so often, plants'll only die*, Tom used to say. *I'd rather admire them in situ.*

Jack wondered if Julian Nancarrow, who had staff to tend his plants when he could not, would express similar sentiments if asked.

"What made you suspect our network security needed improving?" Julian queried once they were seated, and Jack felt his lips turn up at the corners.

"Rumours, mostly."

"Expand on that, please. What kind of rumours?"

The request came smoothly, and Jack thought about his answer, considering facts he could reveal and details he couldn't. "I noticed commonalities in takeover bids that have been made for Nancarrow Mining and other companies in a variety of sectors," he said. "Eventually, I came up with a list of… likely targets, if you will."

"And we were on that list?"

"Yes, sir."

Eyebrows twitched, so slightly that Jack would have missed the tiny movement if he hadn't watched for it. Lips tightened by a fraction, and the expressive grey eyes darkened in an emotion Jack took for frustration.

"I will let Gareth explain the particulars of our situation," Julian said after a moment. "I will not bother you for information you are not at liberty to provide, but I expect you to make sure we are as protected from attacks as we can be. I want to be kept informed about your progress and any threats you discover from here on out."

The last instruction was clearly directed at both of them, and Jack watched Gareth nod in agreement. "Jack's first job will be to isolate that leak."

"You said it is no longer hurting us."

"It's not, but I still want it shut down, and I want to know who's behind it."

Gareth's tone made something in Jack sit up and take notice. His mind seethed with conjecture, but true to form and training he considered it prudent to wait to confirm Gareth's statement, only turning to Gareth once they'd left the CEO's office. "Which leak?" he demanded.

Gareth pulled a face. "Financial information is leaking out of the company."

"Oh, *that* leak."

"What do you mean, *that* leak?"

Jack held back on his answer a moment longer than necessary, expecting a trap or an attempt on Gareth's part to get him back for his earlier teasing.

But when Gareth's face showed nothing but intent expectation, he shrugged and sighed. "You don't *know* we have another one?"

"You're not joking."

"No."

"Can you show me?"

"Sure."

Gareth turned and stalked down the corridor. He ignored the elevator, opting to take the stairs again and Jack followed, not even a little bit surprised that the start of their weekend would be delayed.

———◆◆◆———

"Help yourself."

Gareth indicated the workstations lining the back wall of his office, and Jack slid into the chair in front of one and keyed the system.

"Login?" he requested, having spent the day in so many induction meetings, they hadn't had time to set up access protocols to the company network yet.

Gareth came to stand behind him. "You can't break in?"

"Sure." Jack slid down in the chair and tipped his head back so he could observe his boss. Gareth upside down was just as breathtaking a sight as Gareth right way up, even in this tense and irritated incarnation.

He smiled at the strange easiness of their interaction, at how he wasn't at all embarrassed to be thinking such things even though Gareth stood right there. "Just didn't think you'd want me to waste the weekend doing it. Frazer isn't witless, you know?"

Gareth leaned forwards until he could claim Jack's lips in a soft, upside-down kiss. His hands reached for the keyboard and started typing.

"You're right, of course." He straightened while hitting return. "There you go."

"I hope that wasn't your idea of preserving network security," Jack chided while his hands went to work. "Go change your password."

"You mean to tell me you weren't distracted?" There was a pout in Gareth's voice, right alongside the grin. "I swear you had your eyes closed."

"My ears worked just fine. Go. Change. The password."

The keyboard keys rattled staccato as Jack connected to the laptop he used at home and found the relevant links and codes. Ten minutes later he'd located his secret stash of data on the far side of the Internet and requested access.

"And now we wait."

"For?"

"The back door to open." Jack leaned back in the chair and watched Gareth fidget. Memories of splintered wooden chairs, wrecked by muscles so tense they misjudged their own strength, washed through his mind. Nights full of maps and banter and caffeine. Fingers in his hair, rubbing gently to keep him awake for a little while longer. The crunch of sand underfoot—

Jack hit keys at random. He so wasn't going there, even if he had to rerun the security protocol on his stash.

Lucky for his state of mind, the sequence had completed before he'd interrupted. The back door opened, and he snuck in, quickly locating the library and directories he needed. Green lines of text filled his screen a moment later.

"That's not very fancy."

"I don't need fancy," Jack replied absently. "I need secure." He selected a file and copied it before retracing his steps, one keystroke at a time. "Now tell me that's public domain, and we can all go home," he said as he opened the map and report he'd copied and made space for Gareth in front of his screen.

Gareth stared at the report, brows drawn together over narrowed eyes as he read. "Hell no!"

Jack smirked. "That's what I thought."

"I should have come by bike," Gareth groused. The A316 was bumper-to-bumper, and the powerful Range Rover barely managed a crawl. Six o'clock had been and gone, and why everyone was still out on the road when they could be firing up the barbecue or eating pizza in front of the television was a mystery to Gareth.

The confirmation of the second leak had thrown an unexpected spanner into his weekend plans.

He got to work on an initial threat assessment and instigated lockdown procedures, pleased when Jack turned to locating leaked documents and tracing their paths without question or complaint. Information passed smoothly between them as if they'd never stopped working together.

Gareth hadn't suggested they call it a day until he'd made his report to Julian and had seen Jack set programs in place to run over the weekend. By which time most of the rush hour traffic should have cleared. Instead he was reduced to doing two miles an hour barely two miles from his destination.

"I *really* should have come by bike!"

Jack stretched in the passenger seat, arching his body until Gareth had to avert his gaze. Though not before he noted the teasing crinkles at the corners of Jack's eyes.

Jack was back to playing his games, and damned if

Gareth didn't enjoy the show. At the very least, it took his mind off the traffic.

"Whatcha got?" Jack asked a moment later, voice soft with idle curiosity.

"Triumph Tiger."

"Nice."

"Very. You?" Jack had owned a bike ever since Gareth had known him. There was no doubt in his mind that he owned one now.

"Gixxer."

"Speed merchant."

"Yeah, and? A guy's allowed to have a little fun, right?" The morning's mischievous mood had returned with a vengeance. Without warning Jack leaned over the centre console and buried his face in Gareth's lap, rubbing his cheek against the rapidly forming bulge.

"Jack!" Gareth tightened his grip on the steering wheel and pressed his back deeper into the seat to stop himself from pushing his hips up. No need to encourage the brat. He was doing a fine job of driving Gareth crazy as it was.

"What?" Jack's long lashes rose, and his gaze slanted up to look at him in innocent confusion. "Thought I owe you an apology for getting us stuck in… that." A swish of dark spikes indicated the mass of crawling traffic in front of the Range Rover.

"And that traffic jam is your fault… how?"

"Not the jam. Just the fact we're in it. I could have told you about the other leak on Monday."

"Says the man who goes pimp hunting on an empty stomach and with a hangover just because someone's asking."

Jack shot upright, a flush burning its way across his face.

*Way to go, idiot!* The back of Gareth's hand grazed Jack's hot cheek in a soft apology. "Being conscientious is nothing to be ashamed of."

"I know." Jack's voice was soft, the flush slow in fading. "Then, if I'd worked faster, we wouldn't be here."

"Now you're slipping," Gareth said in a mock-sympathetic voice while the traffic around him began to shift. "I was expecting you to sting me for a superfast fibre optic broadband installation or satellite uplinks or some such crap. Are you tired or something?"

"Just hungry," came the reply, and heat was back in Jack's eyes.

Gareth ignored a few speed limits once he had extricated them from the traffic snarl. He took every back road and rat run he knew and breathed a sigh of relief when he finally pulled the Range Rover into his driveway.

Jack had made a much better job of hiding his impatience, but his arms wrapped around Gareth as soon as the front door closed behind them, and he rested his cheek on Gareth's shoulder.

"Wanted to do that all day."

The words came on a soft exhale, barely there, and Gareth curved his palm around Jack's neck, sliding his fingers up into the silky, dark hair. Their first kiss was but a taste, a gossamer brush of lips but growing in urgency as the tip of Gareth's tongue grazed Jack's lower lip, and Jack slid his hands up Gareth's chest to tug and tease the nipple ring through the fabric of Gareth's shirt.

Electricity spiked up Gareth's spine at the touch, and he tightened his other arm around Jack, pulling them flush together in a single hard move.

That's when his phone started to ring.

And Jack's followed only a few seconds later.

# HALO OR NOOSE?

———— ◆ ◆ ◆ ————

G areth dug for his phone while he moved a step further towards the middle of the hallway to give Jack room to do the same. He fumbled the buttons, but at least he had his breathing under control when he answered.

"Tyrrell," came the reply. "I know it's Friday and all, but I need you for statements."

Gareth sighed, knowing that there was no way he could put her off until Monday. Or even until morning. The very fact that Lisa was still at work—and didn't bother to observe the common courtesies—made that abundantly clear.

"Where am I meeting you?"

"At the Yard. You're cleared to drive in."

"Thanks." Gareth's tone was only mildly sarcastic. Parking in Whitehall was tricky, especially around the Metropolitan Police's headquarters at New Scotland Yard, and he didn't fancy having to hunt for a parking space and spare change on a Friday evening. "I just got home, and traffic was a bitch, so give me a few."

"Double-time it," Lisa ordered. "I need your help, and we can order takeaway if it gets late."

"Lisa, it's late already," Gareth pointed out. "Just make sure there's food."

"I know what you like. What about Horwood?"

"Anything edible," he replied, realising only after the fact that he was smiling, and that Lisa would be able to hear it. "He hoofed down the Ten Deadly Sins for breakfast without breaking a sweat. Oh, and he likes hot curries." He ended the call on Lisa's appreciative whistle, hoping that she had something tastier than cold pizza or coffee and doughnuts on offer by the time they made it back to Whitehall.

"I'll be there," Jack said into his phone, as Gareth turned to him, his voice quiet.

The change in Jack was startling. Gone were the boyish enthusiasm, the teasing smiles and heated looks, the crinkles around his green eyes. Jack's stance had shifted from its earlier loose slouch. His shoulders now formed a tense, tight line, and he hid his thoughts behind his sweep of lashes.

Deeper than mere frustration over a ruined Friday evening, the transformation indicated a type of dread that Gareth couldn't fathom. As far as he knew, Jack had never backed away from anything, especially not a path he'd chosen to walk.

"Statements?"

"Statements," Jack confirmed. "A break would have been nice. And dinner." He reached for the duffel bag he had dropped by the door on coming in and slung it over his shoulder. "Between Baxter's shit and the leaks at Nancarrow, my brain's gonna get whiplash," he said, voice tight. "And that's before they throw the book at me." He straightened his shoulders with an effort and found a crooked smile. "Wonder if they'll let me post bail."

"What *are* you talking about?"

"Spending the night in a cell, dumbass!" Jack shot back, sounding strangely petulant. "I fucked up—with honours."

"That's hardly a jailing offence."

"No? Just wait 'til you see 'em drooling over the chance to score a few points on the vigilante who usually shows them up for the morons they are. I scared off the perp, lost a major witness, caused a public panic, and forced the deployment of emergency services. If they're feeling vindictive, they can add GBH and carrying a concealed weapon with intent to the rap sheet. And now that I'm with Nancarrow Mining, I don't have the option to pretend I'm working."

"You weren't in that club by choice," Gareth

interrupted. "Are you telling me that Baxter won't back you up?"

"The way that one went south, he may be joining me in the clink."

"That's bullshit," Gareth declared. "Lisa wants your help with that case. She said so."

"I know." Jack sighed. He sank back against the wall with a soft thud and stayed there as if the plaster was the only thing holding him up. "And I'll owe her for the rest of forever. Might be easier to serve time."

"You believe that?"

Jack shrugged, and that small indication of defeat rattled Gareth's cage like little else had done in a long time. He couldn't imagine what Jack had seen to lose faith like that.

"C'mere." Gareth wrapped Jack in a hug, ignoring his reluctance, and let the duffel slide to the floor. "We won't let that happen," he said while rubbing fingertips across Jack's neck until he relaxed his tight stance by a fraction.

"Right," Jack breathed and settled his forehead on Gareth's shoulder as if he was making a concession.

"Lisa's not that bad."

"She's not bad at all. But she didn't get to be where she is by pussyfooting around. I read her file. She's excellent at trading favours."

"When did you read her file? How did you even *get*

her file?"

"Over lunch," Jack said, failing to answer the second half of the question. "There had to be a reason you called her—as opposed to a dozen other equally likely people in your address book, I mean," Jack explained. "Marston knew about her too. She implied that I'd be working the case with Dr. Tyrrell."

"That should tell you something."

"It tells me I'm being sold, Gareth," Jack snarled, pushing Gareth away and straightening up. "Bartered, at the very least. And I hate it."

"It's not like that!" Gareth had called Lisa because she was the most efficient person he knew for cutting through red tape and bullshit. She was sharp, admittedly, but Lisa was fair, and she fought the good fight, just like Jack.

"Then tell me what it *is* like, because I can't see it. Is she on a crusade? Do I follow orders? Can I argue, or do I end up in jail if I disagree with her?" Jack's voice echoed in the hallway, and the hands on his hips were in tight fists.

"She's not on a power trip," Gareth growled. "Lisa's honest. She wants justice for Ricky as much as you do."

All the fight went out of Jack in a long single breath, and a resigned smile replaced the frown. His fingers uncurled, his shoulders relaxed, and he straightened his arms by his sides. "Then we have us a problem, Gareth," he said softly. "After everything I heard from Ricky, I don't give a shit about justice. I want revenge."

<hr />

Gareth stopped the Range Rover in front of the barrier at New Scotland Yard and wound the window down. Jack stirred from his doze in the passenger seat, straightening and opening his eyes. He had not spoken a word during the whole drive back into London and—despite Gareth's protests—his bag rested between his feet in the Ranger's passenger foot well.

"If they choose to go postal on my arse, I want at least a change of clothes," he'd grumbled, and dodged Gareth's attempts to keep the bag at his house.

Jack clearly expected to spend the night in a cell, and the thought made Gareth shudder. He had once tried to detain a rookie Jack for returning from leave late and drunk to boot. The fallout had been spectacular, and nobody was surprised when Jack later outscored his entire team in evasion and escape skills.

Jack used to have issues with being physically restrained—held down, cuffed, tied up—even after he'd attended counseling and training sessions, and

Gareth didn't know if those issues had eased in the intervening years or if mayhem would ensue if anyone came near him bearing handcuffs.

"You're cleared to drive in, sir." The uniformed guard behind the barrier concluded his checks and caught Gareth's attention. "An officer will escort you to your interview. Please do not leave the vehicle until he is with you."

Gareth was familiar with the procedure. It had been a while, but he had been here before. "Do you have a solicitor looking after you, or do you want me to warn mine that he may be needed?" he asked as he drove down the ramp into the garage.

"I thought nothing is going to happen?"

"I don't think anything will. But I'm all for putting your mind at rest before you snap."

Jack snorted. "Good luck with that. I usually need at least a bottle of Scotch to shut up my mind and you think you can do it with a phone call?"

"You forget I'm made of awesome," Gareth said, a touch caustic, just as their escort materialised beside the Range Rover.

⬤▬▬◆ ◆ ◆▬▬⬤

The conference room on the twelfth floor smelled like a curry house. A damn good one, where the chef blended his own spices until the atmosphere swam with mouthwatering aromas and enticed people who hadn't even planned on eating curry when they left their homes. Late as it was, Jack's stomach growled at the inviting scent despite the dread that sat like a tight coil in his gut.

In Jack's experience, giving statements to the police involved smartass comments and defensive posturing, endless hours of mindless waiting, and almost unpalatable coffee—never good food.

Dr. Lisa Tyrrell liked to do things differently, if the table to the right of the conference room's door was any indication. It was covered with a white cloth and set with poppadoms and naan, rice, chutney, and an unexpected array of freshly cooked curries. There were also bottles of Kingfisher, tins of Red Bull, and plenty of bottled water.

"I must have lost the friggin' keys again!"

Gareth barked a laugh and pushed past Jack, patting his head condescendingly.

"Well, Toto, I really think this isn't Kansas." He made his way to the conference table, where Lisa and three other people were already busy eating. He claimed a seat, shrugged out of his jacket, and slung it over the back of the plush chair. "Come on, Jack, stop gaping at the munchkins. We have stuff to do here."

Lisa snorted in amusement, and Jack thought the

look suited her. It brought out lights in her eyes and even a dimple in her cheek. Most of all, though, it made her look approachable. More like a person and less like the hardass her file said she was.

From across the table, she waved her fork at Jack and Gareth. "We had no idea how long you'd need to get here, so we've started. Help yourself to dinner. I'm told the curries get hotter the further you move from the middle of the table." She pointed at her plate. "I can vouch for the korma. It's excellent."

Jack dumped his bag beside a chair and turned towards the food, picking up a plate as he went. Korma, however excellent, held little interest for him. He aimed for the dish right at the edge of the table: beef in a deep red gravy with lots of visible slices of chili. He smelled cinnamon and cloves in the steam and happily loaded his plate. A few spoonfuls of channa dhal and a couple of poppadoms later, Jack was content to settle down at the table and enjoy a belated dinner, barely noticing when Gareth replaced the tin of Red Bull by his plate with a bottle of Kingfisher.

"The gentleman opposite you is Rafael Gallant from the firearms unit," Lisa introduced. "And I believe you already know Walshaw and Nell."

Jack managed terse nods to the men.

The burly firearms officer dressed in fatigues

seemed a steady sort, but Jack and DI Walshaw had history, and not the kind rehashed fondly over a beer.

The statuesque woman on the other side of the table, though, merited a wide smile. "Hey, Nell, it's been a while."

"Still fighting the good fight without any sense of self-preservation, eh?" She smiled back, albeit wryly. "You look good, Jack."

"And you need your eyes tested. Unless sleep deprivation looks good on me."

"Sarcasm sure doesn't," Gareth grumbled from his side.

"It's not sarcasm if I'm right."

"Quit with the cryptic and enlighten us," Rafael growled. He sounded grumpy, as if he'd been dragged from his normal Friday evening activities at short notice.

"Jack expects to spend the night in a cell." Gareth cackled, clearly delighted at a chance to tease.

"Jesus! Do we really look that stupid?"

Rafael barked a laugh at Walshaw's exclamation, and Jack kept his eyes on his plate. Walshaw was a pompous arse with a conveniently selective memory. Jack would have loved to remind him of the score of times the man had tried to get him and Clive Baxter into trouble. Shame Baxter wasn't here to enjoy the irony. He would have appreciated it.

"Your skills would be wasted in a cell," Lisa said a moment later. "Really, Horwood—have you read your file lately?"

"He was too busy reading yours," Gareth informed her, gleeful as Puck, when Jack kept quiet and his head down.

"He… what?"

"Don't tell me you wouldn't want to know who you're dealing with," Jack defended himself.

"Sure," Nell retorted. "But none of us would break into protected storage to do it."

"You would if you knew how," Jack disagreed. "And if you could be sure not to be caught."

"I heard that Gatting was heartbroken when you quit," Lisa said from her side of the table. "I'm starting to understand why he was so desperately hunting around for an incentive he could offer you to change your mind."

Jack leaned his head against the edge of the seat and closed his eyes. He didn't need to see Lisa's face to hear the wheels turning in her mind or see her eyes to know that she was studying him as if Jack was some newly discovered species in the zoo. People tended to see his skills rather than him, and many a time he had allowed himself to be used to further someone else's goals. Until he'd grown tired of the game.

Sitting there, surrounded by the comforting scents

of curry and with his thoughts safely hidden behind his lashes, Jack allowed himself a few moments to mourn. Four months of freedom were gone in a flash. He'd managed to extricate himself from the service, had gotten away clean… and now he was right back in the mire because he had gone to help a friend. The relief of not having to face an investigation and possible time in jail paled in comparison.

Gareth's amber gaze was the first thing he saw when he opened his eyes. Realisation mixed with concern in that gaze and knowing that Gareth understood and cared eased the tight knot of regret in Jack's chest. He managed a minuscule nod, a thank-you as much as an acknowledgement. Then Jack straightened and placed his hands on the table in front of him.

"Let's quit with the bullshit," he said to the room at large. "It's late, and I'm tired. Ask what you want to know. Then tell me what you want me to do so I can go home and sleep."

⬛◆◆◆⬛

All six settled down to work, going over every detail of Jack and Gareth's foray into the dance club. The detectives made extensive notes, asking question after question. Jack described the layout along with his observations and impressions, and Gareth added his own thoughts and opinions.

Rafael asked more questions than the other three put together. Not a single one was about the man they hunted. Neither did he speculate about motivations or outcomes. He asked about flooring, lights, doorways, and even the positioning of the columns to a level of detail that neither Jack nor Gareth had a chance to provide.

"Why don't you go in daylight and check it out? You could always pose as someone from the Health and Safety Executive," Jack suggested when Rafael asked for the third time about the rooms in the back of the club that Jack hadn't been able to explore.

"I could at that, but I'd imagine they'd grow suspicious if I asked about air vents and loft space and drains."

"How about the architectural drawings for the place? That has to be a better start."

"Might need a lengthy explanation or even a warrant to get those. Can't wait that long."

"Don't wait, then."

Rafael caught on and cocked his head. "Think you can find them? Now?"

Lisa called a recess and pushed her laptop across the conference table towards Jack with a wry smile. "Leave me a little privacy… if you're able."

"Your dirty pictures are completely without interest to me, Doctor," Jack deadpanned as he pulled up a browser, followed by a command prompt. His fingers started dancing over the keys, and moments later he was lost in reams of data.

Gareth watched him quietly, noting the tired slump to Jack's shoulders and the tiny creases between his brows that meshed oddly with the intent focus and the swift dance of his fingers. Once he had resigned himself to the situation, Jack had focussed on the job at hand. He had answered every question, including Walshaw's personal, insinuating ones, promptly and in detail, but with as much emotion as he would expend on reciting a shopping list.

Gareth hadn't been as sanguine. Walshaw really was a first-class arse, one whom even his much more sensible partner couldn't keep in check. Gareth had fought the repeated urge to bash the idiot's face into a new shape. Not on his own account, but on Jack's, who somehow managed to ignore the clumsy digs and snide remarks. Gareth didn't even care that Lisa noticed his ire. He was just grateful that she shut down Walshaw's idiotic lines of questioning without having to be asked.

Fortunately for Gareth's peace of mind, Walshaw soon grew bored with the games, and Rafael Gallant was as pragmatic as Gareth was himself. He appeared to be planning a mission of some sort and openly appreciated Jack's help. The two sat close together, heads bent over the screen of Lisa's laptop while Lisa dismissed Nell and Walshaw for the evening. Gareth was glad for that small favour and waved to Nell as she left.

"You have no idea how close I was to hitting that oaf," he said a moment later as he joined Lisa by the coffeemaker.

"I could tell." Lisa passed him a mug. "He wasn't having digs at you."

"Doesn't matter." Gareth poured milk until the mug almost overflowed. If he had to drink coffee to stay awake, at least he could make it somewhat palatable.

"I don't suppose it does," Lisa agreed. "Nell is trying to straighten him out."

"She's not having much luck."

"Give her time."

"Keep him out of my hair, then," Gareth growled. "I detest men like that. It wouldn't even occur to him to do what Jack does, but he has the gall to taunt and judge and…."

"Gareth."

He closed his eyes and breathed, clutching the mug of hot coffee with both hands until he got his temper under control. It took some doing. "Sorry," he said as he set the mug down.

"He really got to you, didn't he?"

Gareth nodded once, not caring whether Lisa was referring to Walshaw or Jack. Her words were true for either man. Walshaw's comments had been aimed at Jack, but Gareth was the one who'd felt the sting.

Walshaw would never understand how much courage a man needed to use himself as bait. Gareth wished he could ram that knowledge down his throat.

"Tell me about the pimp," he said instead. "We have a profile yet?"

"Not even ID."

"He doesn't have form?"

Lisa shook her head and grabbed a clean mug from the table. "And the forensics guys are struggling with that beer bottle."

"Why?"

"The bottle was dewy when the pimp first picked it up. The prints are layered and smudged. Wet glass is one of the worst surfaces to lift prints from... did you know?"

"I had no idea," Gareth grumbled. "Next time I'll ask for six beers, a packet of peanuts, and a towel."

Lisa laughed and patted his shoulder. "Glum doesn't suit you, Gareth."

Gareth shot a look across the room to where Jack and Rafael were still huddled over Lisa's laptop. The two looked cosy, intent on their work, and Gareth bit back a sigh. "Glum's all that's left tonight," he said, feeling cranky. "Really, what have I ever done to deserve getting cockblocked by you?"

"Um… let's see… left me?"

"How come I remember that the other way around?"

Lisa smiled a little. She leaned her back against the counter next to the coffeemaker, watching it gurgle and hiss as it poured steaming black liquid into her mug. "Probably because it's true," she quipped. "Let a girl repent in peace."

"By ruining my weekend?"

"If you call in the wind, be prepared to reap storm," she smirked as if he needed reminding. "I did cut you a lot of slack."

She had. Gareth knew that she could have ordered them to the nearest police station last night to give their statements there and then. Instead, Lisa had suggested he take Jack home before most of her team had even arrived. The option was a win for them both, giving Jack a little time to recover and Lisa the chance to familiarise herself with the case before she started asking questions. So he nodded and tried for a grateful smile. "You're right, of course."

"Planning ops would be so much easier if I had someone like you on my team." Rafael rose and stretched before stacking his notes in a careful pile, ready to call it a night. His voice was wistful, and he watched Jack as if he was trying to think of ways to spirit him away.

Jack had enjoyed the brief trawl for data. It was different from the work he did every day, and Rafael's requirements had been very precise. Hacking was fun when he knew what he was after.

"Give me a yell if you need a hand," he offered, ignoring Gareth's groan from across the conference room. "I'll be happy to help out if I have the time." Then he added a smirk. "Provided you take the heat, of course."

Rafael smirked right back. "You're on," he agreed. "Taking heat's what I do."

"I'll wait for your call then."

"You do that."

They swapped mobile numbers, and as Rafael left Jack saw calls for extracurricular activities in his future. He didn't mind. The sort of information Rafael Gallant needed was easily, and in many cases totally legally, obtained. He had no issues helping out, not when he knew how much of a difference an accurate map could make to the success or failure of an operation.

"You really can't leave well enough alone, can you?" Gareth asked, resigned, and Jack shrugged.

"He shouldn't even have to ask. Fucking bureaucrats."

"You can't help everyone."

"I can help those who ask." Jack cleared history and any traces of his activity from Lisa's laptop, taking his time and making sure he got every tiny footprint. He didn't feel the need to offer even more ammunition to a woman who was going to own his arse.

The thought annoyed him, but he pushed it aside. His skills and training made him a valuable commodity. He had accepted that a long time ago. It was his own fault that he'd forgotten that truth in a brief bid for freedom. The sooner he resigned himself to the cage again, the safer it would be for all concerned.

An almighty yawn overtook him, and he stood, trying to shake off the fatigue. "Can I ask a question?" he queried, turning towards Lisa.

"Shoot."

"The two boys Gareth rescued from the club—how are they?"

Not knowing what had happened to the two had bugged him all day, but he'd kept from snooping. Though his first day at Nancarrow Mining had been busy, he could have found time and opportunity if he'd really put his mind to it. Lisa seemed to know that too.

"Still in hospital and fully sedated," she replied. "They weren't as far gone as Ricky, but he'd started to hook them on blow besides the... other damage. Baxter is watching over them, but they're not expected to talk to anyone until tomorrow at the earliest."

That explained why Jack had had to put up with Walshaw. He didn't mind Nell. The woman had a brain and knew how to use it, but Jack had worried about Baxter's absence. It was unlike the detective to start something and not see it through to the end.

"What's on your mind?"

The question drew him from his thoughts in surprise, and he rubbed a hand across his face. He really needed sleep if he started zoning out in the middle of a conversation. A mug of steaming hot coffee slid into his field of vision, and he accepted it with a rueful chuckle.

"Should have bought Kenco shares years ago," he muttered as he took a sip, grateful that just the three of them were left. "Whatever you do, don't separate the two boys," he continued, hoping Lisa realised how seriously he meant his words. "Not even for treatments or baths or stuff. They are each other's strength." And comfort and nightmare guard, but he didn't feel the need to point that out. Better that his mind didn't go there.

"Gillian Kent from social services is in charge of the boys," Lisa replied. "I believe you've met?"

Jack nodded. "She's good. Really knows what she's doing, even though…."

"What?"

"She's great with the younger children, especially the girls," Jack answered. "These two boys, though… I'm not sure they'll respond that easily."

"Right now, they're drugged and out of it. Let's wait and see."

Lisa's voice was comforting, and Jack relaxed. The endless week was finally ending. All he wanted now was a chance to sleep.

He was grateful for the quiet time while Gareth drove through a city on the cusp of waking. His thoughts moved at a sluggish crawl as if the coffee he had drunk to stay awake was sloshing around his brain instead of his stomach. There was much to ponder, and he needed to get a grip on the details if he was to contribute anything useful to the investigation.

Walshaw was an annoyance, and Jack would have preferred Baxter in his place. Having Gareth beside him helped, as did the fact that Walshaw's threats were without substance. On the plus side, it had been nice to see Nell again. And Rafael Gallant's attitude was just plain refreshing.

Jack wasn't aware he'd nodded off until Gareth pulled the Range Rover into his driveway and called his name, startling him awake. They looked at each other in the pale grey light, tired and a little unsure, and Jack felt a curl of anticipation in his gut as Scotland Yard, the investigation, and even his annoyance with Walshaw faded into the background.

Their feet crunched on the driveway gravel, the sound echoing dully in the early morning silence. The front door closed with a soft jangle of keys, locking them in and the world out. Jack's breath washed out in a long sigh, and relief hit him so hard his knees went weak.

"You wanna share, or shall I get the spare bed ready for you?"

Gareth's voice was muffled as he bent to take his shoes off. Jack waited until he straightened, then he hooked a finger through a loop on Gareth's belt and pulled him closer until their chests almost touched.

"You wanted me to spend the weekend so I could check out your spare bedroom?" he teased, head tilted to one side to appreciate Gareth's expression. "That's one hell of a pickup line."

"Jackass." Gareth made no move to get away. He watched Jack, brows drawn together in something that looked like concern and maybe a little trepidation. "You need to sleep."

"So have you started to snore or do you hog the covers?"

"Neither."

"Then I don't see the problem." Jack remembered that a tired Gareth was invariably a cranky one. He'd never seen the man so adorably unsure. It really wasn't as if they'd never shared a bed or floor before, even if it had been years ago. He leaned close to speak in Gareth's ear. "Let's go to bed. I promise faithfully that I won't bite. Or try to jump you."

# SHUTDOWN

——————◆◆◆——————

**B**etween shoppers, sightseers, and anyone actually living there, Richmond was a busy place. This was especially noticeable on Saturdays, when traffic wound in an endless snarl from the Thames to the park and from Clapham to Twickenham. Very little of all that activity could be heard in Gareth's bedroom, and Jack was fine with that. He'd been awake for a while now and felt well rested, but he was far too comfortable to move.

He hadn't minded at all, when he woke, to find himself draped over his bed partner as if Gareth were an extra pillow. Neither did he see a reason to change his position. His nose was buried in Gareth's neck, his arm clasped Gareth's waist, and their legs tangled in ways Jack found pleasantly suggestive. He breathed as softly and evenly as he knew how and enjoyed the moment.

There was a hint of roughness to Gareth's jaw, and

despite the previous night's shower, Gareth's skin held a trace of scent that Jack found irresistible. If asked to define it, he'd call it spicy, even though that didn't quite do it justice.

It was a dark, rich scent, more alluring than cinnamon and chili spiced chocolate, but somehow containing both these aromas, along with a bitter edge and something that reminded him of well-worn leather.

Jack preferred clean citrus notes for everyday wear, but his stomach muscles clenched every time he caught a hint of that dark spice. He turned his head just slightly and nuzzled his way deeper into the silver hair, for once content to lie in bed and dream.

He was so lost in quiet bliss that he disregarded the warning signs: the slide of a foot along his calf, the tensing of the muscles in Gareth's abdomen, and the hand that suddenly cupped the back of his head. So when he found himself flipped over and pinned to the mattress with Gareth's face above his own, he could do little more than gape.

"You sure have the patience of a saint," Gareth huffed. "How long were you going to pretend that you were asleep?"

"I wasn't pretending," Jack protested. "Just enjoying myself."

He stretched, testing Gareth's hold. It was firm but

not really restrictive. He could get away if he needed to. That realisation soothed the small spike of panic in his chest and turned it into a well of heat. He let a teasing smile curl the corners of his mouth, and he stretched again, more deliberately this time, brushing skin against skin. "I couldn't make a move, anyway," he announced on the heels of Gareth's soft gasp at the contact. "I promised I wouldn't jump you."

"See, I would never promise something as stupid as that," Gareth rumbled before he leaned in to brush their lips together.

"Good for you," Jack whispered back and concentrated on tracing Gareth's lips with the tip of his tongue until Gareth pressed in more firmly.

Their kiss was like the entree to an exquisite meal: sweet, promising, and with just enough fire to whet the appetite. Jack soon wanted more. He buried one hand in Gareth's hair and slid the other across Gareth's broad back until he felt the muscles shift under warm skin as Gareth moved. Teeth clashed, and tongues tangled as both grew more serious, and Jack didn't give a damn when a deep moan escaped his throat. Gareth deserved some credit. He'd managed to turn him on to an almost painful degree in no time flat. With barely more than a kiss.

Jack arched up to bring their bodies firmly together and felt Gareth's arousal press into his hip.

Glad for the assurance that this was a two-way street, he shifted and pushed up, rolling them over, thrilled to hear Gareth growl at the sudden separation of their mouths. His teeth grazed a trail along Gareth's jaw and down his neck.

"Dammit, Jack!"

Gareth gasped and squirmed but didn't try to get away from Jack's ministrations. His hands found skin, slipped to Jack's arse, and pulled him down. Hard. Heat flared through Jack, and he retaliated by nipping on Gareth's collarbone before moving his attentions to the hollow of Gareth's throat. Gareth's fingers painted trails of fire on his skin, and every time he caught a whiff of that spicy scent, something like an electric shock spiked through him.

He raised his head and went for Gareth's lips again, adding teeth and fire and clear intent. The kiss turned messy, Gareth's hand tangled in his hair, and Jack was on the verge of losing his train of thought when Tohoshinki's "I Think U Know" interrupted their heated exchange.

Jack froze. Then he swore. Then he bent over the side of the bed to fish his phone from his trouser pocket, swearing some more when he came up empty on the first couple of tries. Finally, he found the phone and answered.

"Horwood."

"Jack, are you okay? You sound strange."

*No shit.* If Jack sounded even half as murderous as he felt at the untimely interruption, Baxter would have already dropped dead. "You woke me up."

"Oh. Sorry."

"Yeah, whatever." Jack listened to Baxter's breathing. "Was there something you wanted?"

"Sorry," Baxter repeated. "We need your help. Daniel and Nico—the two boys from the club? They're awake, but they're just sitting huddled together, not acknowledging anyone. Gillian was hoping that you might be able to...."

"Where are they?" Jack knew that he sounded more like a robot than a human being at that moment. He didn't care. He squeezed his eyes shut and breathed through his nose, willing the sudden nausea to go take a running jump.

"St. Thomas's Hospital," Baxter replied, cautious now and undoubtedly realising which door to hell he'd just cracked open. "I'll text you the details and meet you there?"

"Yeah, okay." The connection cut off, and Jack sat frozen, staring at nothing. "I must have done something truly horrendous in my previous life to deserve *that*!" Jack threw his phone onto the nearest chair before he hunched over and rested his forehead on his knees.

Baxter's call had done a fine job of ruining the mood.

Jack's heart still beat up a storm. He had Gareth's taste on his lips and could feel the traces of fire that Gareth's fingers had left on his skin, but deep inside he felt like ice. He remembered fear and recalled fury, and combined they burned all other thoughts from his mind.

"C'mere." Gareth's arm snaked around his shoulders, pulled him up against a warm chest, and wrapped him in a hug. "Guy's got crap timing, but we'll get it sorted." Gareth's voice rumbled against Jack's ear once Jack had relayed Baxter's message. "Will they need to stick to hospital food, or can we bring cake?"

"Cake?" Jack huffed a confused laugh. "Does it really bother you so little? Baxter's interruption, I mean."

"I know what you meant, and it bothers me a lot." The arms around Jack tightened. "Seeing what it did to you bothers me a lot more. Do you want to talk about any of it?"

"No. Actually, make that hell no!"

"Well, then. Let's get this done. Cold showers, cake, and then we'll turn up at St. Thom's like Father Christmas."

Deeds followed words, and in no time at all Jack

found himself shoved under a torrent of chilly water. He yanked Gareth into the shower with him, and the warm body at his back made the cold water almost bearable. By the time they stepped out of the shower, Jack had found ground again.

"Now, cake?" he asked as he finished buttoning his jeans and rummaged in the holdall for his favourite deep green Henley. Given their plans for the afternoon, he needed all the comfort he could devise. And the thing looked good on him.

◆ ◆ ◆

"Hey, look at you—you're awake!" Jack smiled as he stepped past two uniformed police officers and into Daniel and Nico's hospital room. "And you know what? We brought cake."

The room wasn't large, just big enough for two beds, a small coffee table, and four moderately comfortable chairs, but it did have an attached bathroom and a great view over Big Ben and the Thames.

Not that the view seemed to impress Daniel and Nico. The two boys huddled close together on the bed furthest from the door, their arms around each other and their eyes on the brightly coloured hospital quilt. Baxter had implied that the boys weren't acknowledging anyone, but Jack's instincts told him otherwise the moment he stepped into the room.

Daniel and Nico, one blond, one dark, and both maybe fourteen years old, were well aware of their surroundings. They kept their eyes down, the better to watch the room and everyone in it from their peripheral vision. And both were strung so tight, a mere breath might snap their control.

"*You* brought cake? That's rich," Gareth's voice teased as he placed two large shopping bags on the low coffee table by the window. "You wouldn't have thought of bringing sandwiches, let alone sweet-talk Richmond's best baker out of some of her specials."

Gareth was right, of course. Left to his own devices, Jack would have grabbed a mug of coffee on the run to the hospital and wouldn't have remembered food until his stomach reminded him. Repeatedly. He shot Gareth a grin and shrugged a shoulder. "Same difference," he said and reached for a bag. "Look, we've got Richmond Maids of Honour, custard tarts, choux buns, cream horns and… whatever are these things?" He held up a bag of sugar-crusted puff pastry treats until Gareth took it from him and looked.

"Pig's Ears."

"Gross," Jack commented, delighted to see Nico's lips move as he silently repeated the words. "What do pig's ears have to do with cake? Shouldn't they be sausage or something?"

"You're a kitchen menace, Horwood." Gareth picked up the thread and ran with it. "You haven't got the first clue what's tasty." He turned towards the bed and shook the bag. "What's it gonna be, boys? I suggest you decide quickly, or the hungry hordes over there"—he threw a pointed look at Jack and Baxter—"will polish off the lot before you know it."

"Well, I haven't had breakfast yet," Jack said into the sudden silence. He watched Daniel give a tiny shake of his head and saw Nico hug his friend tighter in reply, giving him a little squeeze as he did so. The silent argument was riveting, but he couldn't let on that he'd seen it. "Or lunch. I haven't had lunch, either. Did you get enough so I can have one of each?" he asked with half an eye on Gareth. "Then I won't need dinner."

"I know you for a glutton," Gareth said, and Jack laughed.

"That's a yes, then. Bring it!"

"Is it true?"

Nico's voice was so quiet that Jack wouldn't have heard it if he hadn't been watching and waiting for it. He half turned and raised an eyebrow. "Is what true?"

"That Ricky is dead."

For one long, crazy moment, Jack wanted to kill

someone. Baxter, Gillian, the fuckwit who hadn't kept his trap shut… he didn't care. The urge was so strong he almost reached for the knife in his boot. Then he caught Nico's gaze, and the rage disappeared under a flood of regrets.

"Yes, it's true," he said, turning to face the two boys. "But maybe not the way you think. You know that Ricky was badly hurt?"

He waited while the two locked eyes, communicated as silently as only prisoners know how until Nico looked back up at him.

"Yes."

"When I met him at the club, he was drugged. He had internal injuries. And you probably know that he'd been caned. I've no idea how he managed to move so easily, let alone sit down on that bench with me."

From his peripheral vision, Jack saw Gillian take a step forwards, her face perturbed. Jack didn't pay her any heed. He knew that his words sounded brutal, but Nico and Daniel deserved to know the truth. They needed it.

"When I was talking to him, I could see that his body had started to go into shock," he continued, relieved when Gareth stepped into the woman's path and headed her off. "That happens when you're badly injured. It's dangerous and if nothing is done, you can die. So, I offered to get Ricky out of the club and away from the pimp. And he agreed."

"Then why is he dead?" It was the first time Daniel had spoken, and Jack was so grateful to hear rage in between the fear and pain, he had to take a few deep breaths to make sure he kept his composure.

"One of the bouncers came after us. Ricky took a knife in the shoulder for me." Jack made sure he had both boys' full attention. "He saved my life."

It hurt to watch the two boys with their arms around each other, the tight embrace growing more desperate by the moment. Jack knew he had to let them work it out for themselves, but it was hard. Harder this time, because of Ricky's sacrifice and Jack's failure.

"He said that he would kill anyone who broke the rules. He'll come after us."

"Of course not," Gillian tried to assure, but Jack was having none of that.

"Yes, he will." Jack cut across Gillian's softly voiced protest. He took the last few steps and dropped to one knee in front of Nico and Daniel, careful to leave space so that his proximity wouldn't feel like a threat. "He considers you his property, to do with as he chooses. You make him a lot of money. Of course, he wants you back."

Blue and brown eyes widened in fear. Daniel's arm

tightened around Nico's waist, and the dark-haired boy held tight to Daniel's hand.

"He's also shit-scared of you two right now," Jack continued, his calm voice at odds with the subject and the tightness in his chest that made it hard to breathe. "What you know about him and his operation can put him in jail for forever and a day—and he's well aware of that. I admire Ricky for what he tried to do. I was going to help him. I'm sorry I screwed up. I'm sorry I could not save his life."

Jack didn't bow his head, however much he wished to have somewhere to hide. He let Nico and Daniel see his anger and his anguish, laid himself open as he rarely did in the hope to make them believe him.

"Will you be there?"

It was Daniel asking the question, and Jack had a first inkling of the dynamic between the two: Nico, bolder and less patient; Daniel more tentative with, maybe, more experience.

"If you need me, I'll be here," Jack promised. "This part of your life can be over. You will never have to go back. But you need to make an effort to get well again. For me, that's part of the deal. And you owe that to yourselves."

"What if he sends someone for us?"

Jack settled himself cross-legged at the foot end of the bed, pleased when the two stayed were they were.

"Starting over isn't easy," he said. "While he's free, you're both in danger. And you're most in danger when he knows where you are. *Your* first priority is to get well and out of here. Our first priority is to catch him and put him away. After that, you'll have a chance at a new life."

"What if he comes before we're well?"

"You'll never be alone until he's behind bars," Jack said with quiet authority, glad when Gillian Kent stepped up beside him and nodded to confirm his words.

"While you're here there'll be a police guard outside your door at all times," she said.

"Really?"

Jack half turned his head, and Gareth opened the door for one of the uniformed officers to come in and introduce himself.

"When you're ready to leave here, Gillian and her colleagues will take you to a safe place." Jack continued. "When we've caught him, you may be asked to help us put him away, but nobody will force you to do anything. We have enough on the guy to bury him under the jail. Ricky's made sure of that. And now I want cake." Jack rolled off the bed to his feet and turned towards Gareth, deliberately ending the conversation and giving the two boys time to process the reams of information he'd just flooded them with.

Gareth was busy laying out cakes on the small table, and Jack stepped up beside him.

Memories crowded so close his vision started to tunnel with his efforts to hold them at bay. He was so tightly wound he feared he might throw up if he even looked at food. But he was determined to keep it together while he was in the room. He owed the boys at least that much.

"Are you okay?"

Caught between Baxter on his right and Gareth on his left, the soft query caught him off guard. As did the looks both men directed at him. Irritation bubbled swiftly. He had no idea what he looked like, though he did his best to keep his expression bland. But really, how did they think he'd feel?

"I'll live," he muttered, turned his back to the room, and fixed his eyes on the view. The peace and contentment of the early afternoon had fled, but peace and contentment had been rare visitors in his life to begin with. No wonder their sticking qualities were fleeting at best.

He focussed on details to ground himself, counted pedestrians crossing Westminster Bridge, watched the reflections of clouds on the grey waters of the Thames, and let himself be cheered by hearing Nico's voice in answer to a question from Gillian and by the fact that

Clive Baxter and Gareth actually seemed to be having a conversation of sorts.

When the nurse came in to tell them that visiting hours were over and Clive asked them to stop in at the Yard and see Lisa before they headed home, his stoic facade was almost back in place.

# WATCHING BRIEF

———————✦ ✦ ✦————————

I n Gareth's opinion, watching Jack fidget was the best Saturday night entertainment ever devised. Jack had a mind like a shunting yard and being asked to do just one thing at a time clearly confused him. Nor was he used to sitting in front of a computer he wasn't supposed to touch.

"Lisa has had words with the magistrate. We have a warrant and three days to move," Rafael had told them as soon as he saw them, without bothering with greetings. "We've selected the three most likely clubs from the work you and Clive did previously. Now all we need is someone to tell us where he shows up." He nodded to the array of TV screens in the neighbouring room.

"You put eyes in already? Nice."

"Why waste the plans you found for me?" Rafael shrugged, and Jack beamed. A real smile instead of the grimace he'd been wearing since Baxter's call.

For the first twenty minutes of their surveillance stint, Jack had watched the feed intently. Every now and then his fingers flashed up to the keyboard, ready to do… something, until he remembered that there wasn't anything *to do*. And he'd settle back in his chair with a sigh.

Twenty minutes seemed to be the limit of his endurance, though, and soon he was prowling the room looking for things with which to distract himself while he monitored the feed. Another twenty minutes later, and Jack had scrounged a stack of clean paper from the printer and a handful of whiteboard markers, a box of paper clips, and three erasers from a drawer that needed its lock picking before Jack could even see what was in it. Jack's gleeful grin when he'd finally gotten the drawer open and found the pens and erasers had made Gareth's night.

"Should I wonder why you even carry lock picks?"

"They're useful." Jack settled back into his chair and set out the pens and erasers in a neat line on the desk.

"Carrying them is also illegal."

"We're in Scotland Yard, Gareth. I'm sure they can deal."

"With you breaking into their cupboards?"

Jack rolled his eyes and waved his hand, unaffected by the criticism. He pulled a Leatherman from the back pocket of his jeans and cut the erasers in half. Then he spread out six sheets of printer paper on the desk and placed an eraser half in the centre of each. He pulled the caps from six whiteboard markers and added those to the erasers before picking up the box of paper clips.

"Wanna explain what you're doing there?"

"Making juggling balls," Jack replied as if that was obvious, and then he chuckled. "Close your mouth, boss."

"You're kidding me."

"Am not." A light flush spread over Jack's cheekbones. He waved a hand at the wall of screens in front of him. "The thing's looking at me as if it knows I can't touch it. That's just… wrong."

As Gareth watched, Jack first folded the sheets carefully, then scrunched them up until he had six evenly sized little balls. And then he started juggling.

<hr />

The rhythm was broken, uneven. More than once, Jack had to reach to snag one of the improvised juggling balls and return it to the pattern. These were the first moments of downtime he'd had since Gareth Flynn's surprise appearance at his interview had turned Jack's life upside down, so a few boring hours of surveillance should have been welcome. It was just his luck that his mind had other ideas. Juggling usually calmed him, allowed him to think while the sounds of the juggling balls hitting his palms kept time. He hadn't expected his trusted remedy to fail just because Gareth Flynn sat an arm's length away.

The man was a picture of ease, hands folded behind his head and legs stretched out and crossed at the ankles. He had settled in for the night and diligently watched the feed, but every so often his gaze flicked sideways to Jack with a tiny smile that curled one corner of the full lips and creased the skin beside his amber eyes.

Jack's body flushed with heat every time he caught that gaze. His heart picked up speed, butterflies crowded his stomach, and juggling, pimps, and surveillance were as far from his mind as the moon.

*God, I really need to get laid.*

Jack's mind stutter-stepped over that thought, irritated by its inaccuracy. He knew that he could get laid any time he wanted to, but cruising nightclubs for meaningless hook-ups had long grown stale. He could just as easily relax with a bottle of his namesake in the comfort of his home.

No, it wasn't the idea of getting laid that made his heart race and his breath catch in his throat. It was the combination of *Gareth* and images of getting laid that destroyed his focus and made shivers of want wash over his skin.

Gareth Flynn shouldn't be allowed out. At the very least, he shouldn't have been allowed to cross Jack's path again.

The man defied all Jack's logic. Always had, from the time Jack had been a scrawny seventeen-year-old with a cocky attitude and a crush the size of Everest, to the moment Gareth stepped out of his office and back into Jack's life.

The odds of that happening had to have been minuscule, but no… not only was Gareth Flynn right there, he was showing a distinct interest in Jack. There were just no odds big enough for that.

Jack was as enthralled by the man now as he'd been years earlier. Gareth had been an excellent CO: decisive, empathic, and with eyes in the back of his head. Jack had taken to him immediately, had cared about his captain's approval when he'd never needed approval from anyone. Other feelings had come later, and time had done little to change those. Gareth was supportive without being judgmental. And… of course… he just had to be the biggest tease alive.

That tiny amused smirk on Gareth's face used to send Jack straight to the gym to beat the stuffing out of a heavy bag. In the beginning, because he didn't understand how an expression that small could cause so much confusion. Later, because he needed to work off his frustration. He'd been decent at hand to hand, even then—quick and unexpected and dirty enough so that he occasionally managed to surprise his instructors. Never Gareth, though, apart from one memorable occasion when he got in a stunning hit. Gareth had handed him his arse moments later, but the thin scar where Jack's fist had split his brow still told that story. Jack had seen it just that morning.

Jack caught the juggling balls one by one and dropped them into his lap. He was right back where he'd started, thinking about sex and Gareth and feeling hot and uncomfortable and rattled.

Swearing wouldn't help.

Complaining wouldn't help.

Being mad at himself for being an idiot might help for a little while.

Jack was telling himself firmly to get a grip when something on the screen in front of him caught his attention.

Stealth was not a skill that men were born with. It had to be learned and practiced. The blond man who leaned on the bar, pretending to chat up the bartender while casually spiking drinks, was far too obvious. The only reason he hadn't been caught yet was because the people crowding around him had their minds on other things.

Jack reached for his phone and dialled Clive Baxter's number.

"Can you see the feed?" he asked without preamble. "The Woolwich one. Blond guy at the bar."

"What am I supposed to be looking at?" The detective sounded confused.

"He's dealing," Jack replied. "And spiking people's drinks."

"Not my brief, Jack."

"You're a fucking detective. You don't choose what to investigate!"

"Like you do?"

That was patently unfair. Jack had never turned down a job, whether it was his brief or not. He still didn't, even though his employer was now Nancarrow Mining. "If that's what you believe, then what the fuck am I doing, sitting here on a Saturday night?" he asked, voice tight. "If you think that—"

Gareth leaned into his line of sight and made a quit motion with his hand. A command, not a request. Jack ended the call without another word and tossed the phone onto the table, not ready to let it go but too drained to fight over it. He'd not thought so before, but Clive Baxter seemed no different from the last lot he'd worked for, blinkered by his own pet projects and only willing to move if something advanced his cause.

"Can you pull off the images for me?"

"What?"

Gareth held up the USB stick he carried on his key chain with one hand and waved at the surveillance monitor with the other. "The pictures of the dealer. Can you copy them for me?"

Before he knew it, Jack sat at the computer and bypassed the login. Gareth's tone, the don't-think-just-do voice he hadn't heard in too long, cut through the anger and the fatigue. Gareth's hands on his shoulders helped to ground him further. Jack worked the feed, using the controls to zoom in, to find the clearest images, and transferred them out.

"It's not conclusive enough to take him to court," he said while he worked. "That's why I wanted Clive to…."

"The dealer is not tonight's objective," Gareth counselled.

"Doesn't mean we have to let him get away."

"We're not going to."

Jack leaned into Gareth's touch and sighed. "You're telling me to focus, aren't you?"

"You're plenty focussed." Gareth pressed a light kiss to Jack's temple, right over the tattoo. "I'm telling you that you don't need to solve all the world's problems at once."

"Even if I trip over them?"

"Even then." Skilled fingers worked the tight muscles in Jack's neck, loosening the knots. "You don't need to solve all the world's problems all by yourself, either."

"Do you really think me that conceited?"

"I think you're a sucker for punishment." Fingers tightened on Jack's hair and pulled his head back until he stared straight up into Gareth's eyes. The look he got was serious and searching. Jack felt stripped bare and squirmed without knowing why. "When did you start trading people for crusades?" Gareth asked.

"I... what?"

"All you seem to do is find a cause and fight," Gareth said and let go of Jack's hair, smoothing the mussed spikes back into a semblance of order. "You don't trust people. I get that. But you don't ask for help when you need it, either. And that's just stupid." The hands on Jack's shoulders spun him around, chair and all, and Gareth seated himself so Jack could see him without craning his neck.

"You used to know the difference," Gareth said. "Now.... What happened?"

Jack shrugged, unsure how to explain why he felt safer working alone. "Too much time undercover," he settled on after a silence. Which wasn't an answer.

Gareth knew it, too. He didn't comment. He sat and watched Jack, the video feed forgotten.

Jack returned to New Scotland Yard late Sunday afternoon. He'd had a busy day, crisscrossing London by bike on various errands, like ordering two pairs of shoes in an unassuming little pub near Elephant & Castle and stopping at St. Thomas's hospital to check on Daniel and Nico. He wanted dinner and a night off, but he recognised that for the pipe dream it was. The clubs would be buzzing in another hour, and he had promised to help look for the pimp.

The officer manning the gate nodded a greeting as Jack parked his bike, which was odd, though not as disconcerting as stepping up to the reception desk and being handed a pass along with an order to report to the twelfth floor. He wasn't sent through the security scanner. He wasn't searched. Instead, one of the guards paged the elevator for him and gave him a nod as he stepped in.

The elevator's walls were mirrored, and he frowned at the dark shadows under his eyes that strove to match the dark shadow on his jaw. There was no hiding the week he'd had.

Seven days earlier, he'd been eating takeaway curry on his couch while dreaming up ideas to improve data security at Nancarrow Mining.

His old life had been behind him.

Done with.

Over.

He barely thought of the case that had made his choice for him. He was in shape, at ease, and pleased that he'd finally managed to cut himself a tiny slice of contentment.

So how was it that only a few days later he was fixing security leaks for his new employer, owed favours to one of Scotland Yard's finest, and was chasing yet another pimp while trying to help two traumatised teenage boys? All that while suddenly working for the one man he had fought so hard to forget.

It was just his luck that the years hadn't changed his former CO. Not in any of the ways that mattered. True to form, Gareth Flynn was not just on his radar but right on his case. The Post-it Gareth had left under his phone that morning—*Julian's called a meeting to discuss the second leak. Remember that there's more to breakfast than coffee*—had made him smile. The text a few hours later reminding him that it was lunchtime had not.

Jack had spent a large part of his career in darkened back rooms full of computer equipment or on solo assignments, which suited him just fine. He'd been trained to look the other way and let bad things happen to good people if the job demanded it. And while he didn't find it easy, he had never let anybody else make that call for him.

Jack trusted himself, his instincts, and his reasoning. Gareth's mile-wide protective streak, while useful when Jack needed a break, wasn't something he would handle well on a normal day.

"I thought you'd ditched me, Horwood." Lisa caught him as soon as the elevator doors opened, and Jack blinked twice.

"Just a few errands," he answered. "Gareth is meeting with our boss."

"Yeah, he called me." She nodded and guided him towards her office, where the coffee table was set with food. "He also told me to make sure you're fed. What's with that?"

Jack shrugged and hid his scowl. He loaded his plate when Lisa told him to get stuck in, chewed and swallowed. If anyone had asked him what he'd been eating, he couldn't have answered.

"How did you meet Gareth?"

Lisa's question pulled him from his abstraction. She held a mug of black coffee out to him, and Jack took it, grateful for the chance to duck out from under her scrutiny. Whatever it was she wanted, he wasn't going to like it.

"I thought you read my file?" he queried. Then added without needing another prompt, "He was my

CO."

"I didn't know that. Your file isn't exactly easy to read."

"Yours doesn't look any different," he assured her. It was sort of true. To anyone else her file would look like Jack's: pages of redacted script with the odd titbit of information left readable. Not to Jack, though. He knew that Lisa Tyrrell was thirty-six and had spent plenty of time on clandestine assignments. She'd been excellent at it… until she had sacrificed her cover to save a man's life. It was something Jack could respect.

Ever since he'd found out, the fact that he owed her a favour didn't bother him nearly as much.

"Clive told me about your… discussion last night," Lisa said as he set his mug down. "He asked me to tell you that what he said wasn't meant the way it sounded."

"I know."

"He should have asked you to collate the details and passed them on."

"I know."

"We'll make that standard procedure from here on out."

"I know."

"Horwood!"

Jack flinched at the sudden increase in decibels and looked up. Lisa was pissed. Jack didn't care. They had wasted a chance at catching a dealer red-handed. That was the only thing he cared about right then. "Why the hell don't you use facial recognition software?" he queried instead.

"Because we'd first need a face to recognise."

It took Jack only moments to catch on. "The strobe lights. Shit!"

"You said it."

"Man needs a decent phone," he grumbled. "What about a photo fit? Give the software at least something to go on."

"Will that be enough?"

"It's better than nothing. We can improve the hit rate if you let me play with it."

She reached for her phone. "I'll call in an artist for you to work with."

She didn't mention anything about computer access, and Jack shrugged and went back to his coffee. If she was happy to be oblivious, he wasn't going to tell her that he wouldn't need it.

# Private Investigations

———— ✦ ◆ ✦ ————

"**F**razer, get your arse in here!"

Donald waved a hand over his head to indicate he'd heard. He dropped screwdrivers and wires onto the desk next to Jack's hand, picked up his tablet, and trotted across the room.

"Oh my God, boss, I love you!" he groaned the minute he smelled the freshly brewed coffee and saw the mugs on Gareth's desk.

"Knock yourself out, kid." Gareth waved him into a chair and handed over a mug of blond, sugar-laced coffee, made just the way Frazer liked.

"Is Horwood always such a menace?"

"How do you mean?" The question was rhetorical. The first thing Gareth had seen when entering the corporate security office that morning had been Jack Horwood in tight black jeans, bent over his desk. The image had done nothing for his peace of mind.

Neither had Jack's smirk and the way he deliberately hadn't moved from his position across the desk as he greeted Gareth.

"Security logs say he's been here since before six this morning," Frazer reported, surfacing from his coffee mug and settling into the visitor's chair. "When I got in, he already had stuff running on the servers, and I finally tracked him down in the gym lifting weights. He hasn't stopped since."

"That sounds about right." Gareth wondered if Jack had come to work straight from his surveillance gig at Scotland Yard or if he'd managed a few hours of rest. Jack curled on the narrow cot in Scotland Yard's ready room the night before had been an adorable sight. He'd had his back tight to the wall and a pillow tucked against his chest. Sleep-darkened eyes had opened for a moment when Gareth had moved, only to fall shut again when he'd signalled an all clear. "He can get carried away when he gets his teeth stuck in a problem."

"And we have a problem."

"Did Jack talk to you about the leak?"

"He said that something went down Friday night but that he didn't have a green light from you to give me details."

"I have *got* to beat that out of him," Gareth muttered.

"Good luck with that. He was a spook."

"He was mine before he was a spook. There's gotta be hope for him." Gareth leaned back in his chair and toyed with the files on his desk. He used a computer, tablet, and his phone to keep track of information like everyone else, but every now and then he needed the physical reminder, needed to print results and analyses and sit somewhere peaceful and read. Fortunately, Julian Nancarrow's mind worked in a similar way, and they had sifted through pages and pages of financial information the previous day. Not to mention the maps and mineral deposit analyses Jack had handed him on Friday night.

"Jack mentioned during his interview that we had a data leak," he said when Frazer was working on his second mug of coffee.

"We knew that."

"We thought we knew that," Gareth corrected wryly. "I found out Friday night that Jack hadn't been talking about the finance leak. He had turned up some highly confidential prospecting data."

"Shit. I just assumed there was an issue with the containment we put in place. Or that he'd caught on to the leak before we did."

"Nope." He picked up a file and tapped it on the edge of the desk before sliding it across to the younger man. "Julian's put together fake finance stats for the next month. He's enjoying this a lot more than he should."

"You think the family has something to do with the second leak?" Frazer had been briefed on the numerous attempts by members of Julian Nancarrow's extended family to wrest control of the company from him. And being Scottish, he'd taken the threat seriously.

"I don't, but the boss is twitchy. So take it under consideration."

"Why don't you think so?" Frazer scanned the contents of the file.

"Historically they've always been after money or control. They don't have the tech know-how to evaluate the prospecting data. The finance leak is more their style."

"They could have bought the skills."

"True." Gareth slid another folder across the desk. "These are all the details on the mineral deposits. Deal with it."

"Wouldn't Horwood be the better choice?" Frazer's tone was careful. "It is his area of expertise."

"He's moonlighting for the Met for the next couple of weeks, and he's not up to speed on the family. So, you take this one. But keep him informed and let him help."

Frazer nodded, mind already miles away assessing

the task. Gareth watched him go, sure that the matter was taken care of. Donald Frazer was only twenty-five, but he already had an industry reputation as a safe pair of hands. It was telling that Jack hadn't applied to Nancarrow Mining HR but had contacted Donald Frazer about a job. The Scot, instead of feeling threatened, had come directly to him, buzzing with the news that Jack Horwood wanted to work with Nancarrow Mining. Gareth hadn't been surprised when the two had hit it off within minutes of meeting.

It was obvious to anyone watching how instinctively the two men worked together. It was in the way Jack looked up from his cabling work when Frazer returned to his desk and caught the folder the younger man tossed to him. He flipped through it while Frazer snagged his keyboard, pointed at one or two items in the file and went back to wiring his workstation. Frazer nodded and kept talking while he typed, and when Jack's head came up, eyes scanning the desk for something, Frazer tossed him the tool he needed without having to be asked. If Jack hadn't been one of the proponents, Gareth could have enjoyed watching their interaction like a movie.

He closed the distracting security feed, and when lunchtime rolled around, he had caught up with his inbox and reviewed the actions from the emergency meeting Julian Nancarrow had called the previous day to discuss the security breaches at the company.

The finance leak was the first real threat since he had joined Nancarrow Mining. He had devised a way to make use of the leak to their advantage, but he was no closer to finding the culprit than he'd been the day they'd found out they had a leak.

Jack's application had come as a stroke of good luck, admittedly one that left him staring in shock at the polished wood of his desk. Only for Jack to arrive with another puzzle in tow—one he had found before anyone else at Nancarrow Mining had even been aware of it.

This, Gareth concluded as he ordered a stack of pizzas and called a lunchtime team meeting to bring everyone up to speed and plan strategy, was how he remembered Jack.

Back when they served together, Jack used to spend his spare hours doing… stuff… on a computer and turning up the most unexpected information in the process. Gareth had been left fielding calls from the police, civil servants, or various agencies demanding confirmation of data Jack had provided out of the blue. Jack never bothered to reply. He didn't discuss his sources, and he never argued his data's veracity. He just continued doing what he did, whether the recipients of the information he'd unearthed were grateful for it or not.

--------◆◆◆--------

"Horwood." Gareth stopped Jack from leaving the conference room with a word and a wave, watching as Jack set his tablet back on the table while everyone else filed out.

The team meeting had been a noisy affair. As usual, Gareth neither interfered nor directed the discussions. He made sure everyone ate, brewed coffee, and listened as Frazer explained the nature of the leaks and the decoy they had put in place for the financial data.

Donald Frazer went through each bit of leaked information, tracing the path it had taken—and everyone around the table scribbled furiously. The leaked finance data would be scrutinised from a myriad of additional angles as early as this afternoon.

Gareth liked that about his team, the way they all pitched their strength and expertise without feeling they had anything to prove.

Jack fit right in, though it hadn't escaped Gareth's notice that Jack had barely paid attention to the food, or that he clung to his coffee mug as if it was a lifeline. The years had made no difference. Gareth knew that Jack was running on caffeine fumes and attitude, that the tilt of his head—forwards and a little to the right—screamed killer headache. And that Jack would start a fight rather than admit any of it.

"Hey," Jack smirked—playing the "offence is the best defence" card, just as Gareth had expected—as soon as they were alone in the conference room. "You shouldn't be allowed to wear suits."

"I'm not the one draped over my desk showing off my arse."

"You didn't enjoy the view?"

"How'd the surveillance go?"

Jack shrugged. The collar of his polo shirt slid sideways with the movement, and Gareth caught a brief flash of something dark along Jack's throat. That damn strip of leather! His chest grew tight at the sight, and it took some effort to process Jack's reply.

"Washout. We built a composite, and I'm using that to pre-screen the feeds."

"Prints?"

"None on file. So either he's new, which I doubt, or he's careful." Another shrug. "Doesn't matter either way. He'll trip."

Jack shoved his hands into the back pockets of his jeans and leaned against the conference table. He looked awake enough, but the tone of his voice gave him away.

"I want you to go home and get some rest before

you go in tonight," Gareth said carefully.

The green eyes narrowed. "I'm fine."

"You don't look it. Go home. Sleep. I bet you came here straight from the Yard this morning."

"I have a leak to find," Jack argued, and Gareth knew he'd been right.

"You don't have to solve all the world's problems all at once," he reiterated. He'd pointed that out to Jack Saturday night. Clearly, Jack hadn't heard him. "Frazer's got this for the moment. Focus on finding the pimp."

"You didn't hire me to find a pimp."

"I didn't know you had a pimp to find when I hired you."

"Yeah, well. Neither did I." Jack crossed his arms and kept his gaze on the floor. "Look," he said, "let me finish setting up that trace I'm working on. Then I'll go home. It's not fair to bring me in and then make Frazer do all the work."

"If I find you here after three, I'll kick your arse, got it?"

"Sure."

Jack pushed away from the table and was out of the conference room in a few long strides. Gareth watched him leave, ready to bet that Jack wouldn't be gone by three.

Jack had become a familiar figure in this quiet corner of the hospital. This was his third visit since Clive had called him in on Saturday, and the two uniformed officers keeping watch didn't bother to check his credentials anymore. They didn't check the small backpack he brought with him, either, and when he popped his head around the doorframe, both Nico and Daniel were awake.

"You came." Nico, always the more forward of the two, sat up and swung his feet off the bed.

"Hey! I promised." Jack pretended to be hurt as he dropped the backpack and shrugged out of his jacket. "How are you two?"

"Bored," Nico declared, just as Daniel mouthed *scared* without a sound.

Jack sat between the boys on the bed, pleased when neither Nico nor Daniel flinched away from him. He was careful how he moved around the two, but they were growing more comfortable having him close even after only a couple of days.

"Did you find your thief?"

For a moment Jack regretted talking about his job. It had seemed a good idea when he needed to establish an identity that distinguished him from the police and social services. The sudden burst of interest in Nico and Daniel's faces had encouraged him, and he'd spent some time talking about the data thief and what he was doing to catch him. He didn't yet know how long the boys had been with the pimp—only that Daniel had been there longer than Nico, and that Ricky had been with the man when both of the younger boys had arrived—but he couldn't imagine that the bastard had cared any more about the boys' education than the man who'd had Jack. Talking about his job and making it sound fun had been a lure. Still was a lure. What he hadn't planned on was making himself look like a failure. Again.

"Not yet," he admitted. His voice was tight, and Daniel caught it.

"Your boss isn't pleased about that?"

"Gareth isn't pleased about a lot of things right now," Jack groused, forgetting for just an instant whom he was speaking to. "What about you guys? Any news?"

Daniel and Nico rarely spoke without checking with each other first, but Jack's sitting between them made eye contact difficult. He leaned back a little and waited.

"We don't have any horrid diseases."

"That's great, right?"

"Only if it means you'll still come see us," Daniel muttered.

"Hey, now I'm insulted. It's my choice to be here, and I don't care what your medical report says." Jack turned his head to consider first Daniel, who was red with embarrassment, and then Nico, whose lips were clamped tightly together.

"What happened?"

The two were silent for the longest time. Jack didn't fidget. He could outwait two scared teenagers any day of the week.

"Inspector Baxter came to see us this afternoon. He wants us to help him find…." Nico trailed off, and Jack nodded.

Of course, Clive would be pushing for information now that the boys were at least stable. He wanted the monster off the street. While Jack agreed with Clive's goal, he could only shake his head at his flatfooted ways. It was an argument Jack hadn't managed to win yet. Clive Baxter simply didn't get the level of terror just the thought of their pimp could inspire in the two boys. Neither did he understand denial.

"It's the quickest way to get him off the street before he hides." Jack kept his voice soft and his hands still. The fear in the children's faces always broke his heart, made him wonder if Rio had seen that looking at him. Or if there had been something else, some emotion that made him different, less of a victim.

After seventeen years, Jack's memories had started

to blur. Occasionally some of them surfaced, bright and sharp and as unexpected as a hailstorm in June, but the triggers were few these days. More recent memories had overlaid and changed things he used to know were true.

"Nobody will think badly of you if you don't wanna help."

"Will you?"

Jack held Daniel's gaze, not flinching from the boy's emotions and not denying his own. "Think badly of you? No, I won't. But I'll not stop hunting that man. I promised Ricky." Ricky's death was a memory that stung and burned, something Jack needed to deal with in his own time.

"You take promises seriously."

"I do. I also promised to teach you how to defend yourself." Jack reached for his backpack, pulling out two pairs of hi-top Converse. "I had to guesstimate your shoe sizes, but these should do until you're out of here. Then I'll get you proper ones."

"Why do we need shoes?"

Jack quirked a smile at Daniel's suspicious tone and parked chin on fist. "Because I want you to have somewhere safe to hide your knives."

"We don't have knives."

Jack handed them the gaudily coloured shoes. "You do now."

Jack would be first to admit that he had a thing for crisp, clean sheets. They were a sign that he was safe and settled, reminded him of comforts that were there when he felt the need for comfort. More than once, after a long undercover op or a difficult case, had he wrapped himself in clean, citrus-scented linen and buried his face in the fragrant steam of freshly brewed coffee.

Right now, at 3:00 a.m. on a Tuesday morning, Jack was more in need of sleep than comfort. He stumbled bleary-eyed into his bedroom, shedding his jacket and sweatshirt as he went, only to stop dead in the doorway.

The room looked like he had left it on Friday morning. He had locked away his case of weapons, shoved his bags of disguises back into the blanket box they'd come from, and piled his club clothes on top of the wash basket. But that was as far as he'd gotten after Gareth had driven him home. The makeup bag lay open on the dresser, a stack of handwritten notes he'd made while being briefed by Clive over the phone on the corner beside it.

He'd barely been home to change and shower since then, his time spent at the Yard, the hospital, Gareth's bed, or his new desk.

He crossed the room, steps dragging, and pulled a pillow from the bed. He brought it to his face, and warmth bloomed in his chest as he caught a hint of Gareth's spicy cologne on the pillowcase.

His life had gone crazy in a handful of days. Right then, he didn't care that two scared kids trusted him to keep them safe. He didn't care that he owed favours to people he never wanted to owe favours to again. And he deliberately ignored the fact that Gareth Flynn seemed intent to run his life for him.

All he cared about was the spark of warmth in his chest and a faint trace of spice on his pillow.

⸺◆◆◆⸺

The buzz of a text message woke Jack just before seven. He fumbled for his phone and rolled his eyes. Gareth Flynn took mother-henning to stratospheric levels. But he was right, Jack admitted with a sigh. Jack's bike was still parked at Nancarrow Mining and accepting a lift from his boss meant not having to hunt up a taxi during rush hour or, heaven forbid, take the train to Waterloo Station.

By the time Gareth arrived, Jack was showered and dressed and working on his second mug of coffee.

"I'm older than five, you know," he greeted as he opened the door.

"Sometimes I wonder about that."

The little half smile on Gareth's face made Jack's insides clench. It just wasn't fair how the man affected him, even when he said things Jack wanted to slap him for.

"I have coffee," he offered and held the door wide.

"Of course you do."

Gareth Flynn looked good standing in Jack's kitchen.

Actually, no.

In a closely tailored charcoal suit that emphasised that perfect *V* he had going on, Gareth looked like a walking wet dream. His amber shirt brought out the gold in his eyes, and the top two shirt buttons, left undone, bared the hollow of his throat. Formal and casual combined like this should have looked jarring, but Gareth made it work.

Jack couldn't take his eyes off the man and only just kept his hands to himself.

"Lisa said that last night was a washout too," Gareth commented as he took the brimming mug Jack offered.

"That surveillance gig was always a long shot." Jack placed his tablet on top of his laptop case and went looking for his phone and keys. "We called it early," he said as he returned, loving the way Gareth leaned against the fridge as if he belonged there.

"When did you get home?"

"Threeish. And before you start: I did sleep. I feel fine. I'm going to get breakfast, and then I'll help Frazer trace those leaks."

Gareth's eyebrows shot up. He stepped away from the fridge, set his mug down, and got right in Jack's space. "I love it when you get all snarly," he said and wrapped a palm around Jack's nape.

Jack melted at the touch. Gareth bossing him around when it wasn't needed was an issue. Gareth this close to him was fine. More than fine.

"So you're being bossy just to wind me up?" He was pleased about how steady he sounded.

"I'm not bossy."

"And I'm not six."

"I'm so glad we got that settled."

The spark of warmth in Gareth's eyes lit an answering fire in Jack's chest. They tasted the coffee on each other's lips, the exploration oddly gentle and slow.

"You have excellent taste in coffee," Gareth purred when he drew away.

"You just want—"

"Oh yeah, I want."

Their second kiss was much less careful. Gareth's hands came up to frame Jack's face and hold him still. Jack let his eyes slip closed and concentrated on feeling: the brush of warm, calloused fingers on his cheekbones, the tug on his hair, the slip and slide of lips and tongue, the heat slowly rising in his gut.

Jack wasn't a passive lover, but right then—after a long, stressful weekend and with only four hours of sleep to his name—he was happy to relax and let Gareth kiss him senseless.

"God, I could eat you right now."

The deep growl sent a shiver through Jack's frame.

He wanted that, wanted Gareth's hands on his skin, Gareth's lips on his. He brought his hands up, and as his fingers closed over smooth, brushed wool and the edge of linen cuffs, a tiny sane corner of his mind reminded him that it was Tuesday morning.

And that he was standing in his kitchen, getting ready to head off to work.

A chuckle bubbled up his throat. "Strange, that."

"What is?" Gareth drew back far enough to send a confused scowl Jack's way.

"I've done a lot of stupid shit in my time," Jack confided while he stepped out of Gareth's hold and around the table to grab his laptop case. "But I've never kissed a guy wearing a suit before."

"How's it compare?"

"It's hot."

"Wanna make sure you got that right?"

Jack smiled. When Gareth was like this, stuff was

so easy. "We could experiment with different suits," he suggested. "Come on, boss, rush hour beckons."

Gareth grumbled, but he followed Jack out.

"Call the cafeteria, and ask them to send up breakfast for three," Gareth told him once they were on the road. "Frazer forgets to eat almost as often as you do, so I can feed you both while you brief me."

Jack complied, only just not rolling his eyes.

———— ◆ ◆ ◆ ————

Tuesday passed faster than a lightning strike, with little time for Jack to focus on anything but work. He'd been speaking to a very apologetic Clive Baxter late in the afternoon when he'd suddenly remembered his plans for a trip to Clapham.

Jack's phone rang just as he stepped from the train onto the crowded platform. Negotiating the zoo that was Clapham Junction during early evening rush hour, he pulled it out and answered it without checking the caller ID.

"Where did you disappear to?"

"Hi, boss." He smiled at the grumpy tone in Gareth's voice. "What's up?"

"You left."

"Hm." Jack fished in his jacket pocket for the ticket to make it through the turnstile.

"Jack."

"Yes, sorry. What?"

"I was asking you where you are."

"Clapham. Running errands."

"You said you wanted to go to the hospital. I thought we'd have dinner after."

"I've been to the hospital," Jack said. "And you didn't mention dinner."

"No, I know. Any idea when you'll be back?"

"Not really, no. So, I'll see you tomorrow morning?"

Silence at the other end of the line.

Jack was out of the station and a way down the road when Gareth finally answered.

"Jack, what are you up to?"

"Just... talking to people."

"That's what phones are for."

"If I wanna read about it in the *Sun* tomorrow morning," Jack scoffed. "Privacy, Flynn. Ever heard of it?"

"Fine." Gareth wasn't happy. He couldn't hide his growl, but he recognised a lost battle when he faced one. "Don't get into trouble."

"As if." Jack grinned wide as he ended the call and continued on his way.

Sending Frazer—tired, disgruntled, and with a very cute pout—to do the end-of-day briefing had been a stroke of genius on his part. The Scot didn't mind being fussed over. He'd told Jack he came from a huge family, had a mum and older sisters who were champion fusspots. Jack had sacrificed him to facilitate his getaway without a hint of regret.

Getting away had been vital.

It was scary how much Jack wanted Gareth Flynn. He felt vulnerable, and that never worked out well. Better to put some distance between them.

Tomorrow, Gareth would be tied up with the monthly operations review, Frazer would work with Jack on plugging the leaks, and in the afternoon, Jack was due to meet with Raf Gallant at Scotland Yard.

It was good to be busy.

And out from under Gareth's scrutiny.

———————◆◆◆————————

Time stood still in Clapham. At least in the small corner of Clapham that Rio Palmer called home.

The black Citroen DS was parked in the driveway, roof up to protect the red leather interior from the forecast rain. It had been this very car that had drawn Jack to the house with the bright red door seventeen years ago. That and the vintage Triumph motorcycle parked beside it.

He hadn't known then that Rio was an odd

dichotomy, a lover of vintage vehicles and collector of vinyl records whose house was brimming with the latest high-tech electronics and who owned a computer system that cost more than the whole house and everything in it.

The doorbell still played Santana's "She's Not There" as Jack leaned against it, letting him know that Rio was home and not off somewhere on assignment. Just as always, whole minutes passed before Rio answered the door, barefoot and with his shirt open, the mahogany dreadlocks drifting like a cape around his shoulders.

"Jack!" The grin was wide and inviting.

"Got a minute?"

"Sure, come in. What brings you?"

"I… may need a favour."

"Okay. Wanna sit down?"

Jack looked around the familiar room with a smile. "Thanks."

He sank into the soft sofa cushions, remembering the last time he'd been here.

They'd spent four days tracing a drugs shipment halfway around the world, living off pizza and beer, working their way through Rio's extensive music collection, and napping where they sat. They'd kept the heavy drapes shut against the light of day and had lived in a cave of their own devising, where time passed differently from the rest of the world. It had been a fun few days. And a job well done.

Today, Rio's living room looked merely civilised, and the heavy green velvet drape covered the doorway to Rio's inner sanctum.

"They tol' me you quit," Rio said as he sat down and handed Jack a bottle of Coke.

"That particular madhouse, yes." Jack nodded.

"Bored?"

"That too."

Rio knew him well enough to stop digging after a mere moment or two. "So wha' favour do you need?" he asked and took the chair opposite.

"I may need to get two boys off the grid."

"Since when's tha' an issue for you?"

"I already owe a favour," Jack said gruffly. "I don't want to offer more ammunition."

"Tell me about it."

Jack explained about Clive Baxter's call, Ricky's death, the favours he now owed, and the two boys in the hospital. Rio listened attentively, his eyes never leaving Jack.

"Nico lost his sister when they were sent to separate children's homes after their mother died. If there's even a hint of social services planning to separate the two boys…."

"I hear you."

"Yeah." Jack grinned suddenly. "But will you help?"

Rio didn't flinch, and his gaze was steady on Jack's. "Always. You know tha'."

"He's exceptional," Alexandra Marston's soft voice came from the curtained doorway as Rio returned to the room after seeing Jack out. He carried a china tea service and set the tray on the low table by the sofa.

"Always has been. Come sit an' ask your questions," he invited, taking one armchair and leaning forwards to pour tea.

"Do you think he knew I was here?"

"He knew someone was."

"Then I'm surprised he spoke so freely."

Rio's smile was wide as he handed Alex her cup. "I don' believe you," he said. "An' Jack only told me what was already public knowledge."

"Jack trusted you to warn him off if there was need."

"So he did."

They drank their tea in silence for a while. Alexandra's gaze was turned inward, and Rio took the opportunity to study her more closely.

Time was being kind to her. Her dark bob was shot

through with auburn highlights, and there were but a few small laugh lines at the corners of her eyes. Serene and calm, she had changed from the ardent young spitfire she'd been when they'd first worked together.

Alexandra Marston had set out wanting to save the world. Time had taught her to save people.

"I wish I'd been here when Jack decided to quit the service," Rio admitted after a time, and his regret was genuine. For all his knowledge and convictions, Jack without a touchstone was a scary proposition, and Rio still felt guilty about that. "I might have been able to stop him."

"I've seen the notes of the last case he worked," Alexandra replied. "I'm not sure anyone could have stopped him. I was glad when he applied to Nancarrow Mining. The company needs his help and…."

"You think you can bring him back in."

"Maybe not that," she conceded. "But I'm hoping to keep him close and cooperative."

Rio considered that. Alex Marston had earned her spurs as a profiler, quickly garnering a reputation as one of the best in the business. But the woman was far more than just a skilled psychologist.

"So why come to me? Lookin' at that stack"—Rio waved a hand towards the thick folder Alex had brought with her—"you know everythin' there is to know about Jack Horwood."

Alexandra's response was a very delicate snort. "If we were talking about anyone *but* Jack Horwood, I'd agree, but this is the blandest, most information-free personnel file I've ever come across. I'm amazed he left his shoe size for me to find."

"Hm." Rio stretched, uncomfortable under her scrutiny but trying to make it look as if he was merely working the kinks from his neck. He knew Alex and what she could do. It shouldn't affect him like it did. "Jack's never been one for sharin', and I'll not betray his confidence," he said.

Alex nodded. "I'm grateful for anything that will help me understand him so I can be there when he needs it. I promise not to push beyond what you're ready to tell me."

"You're worried about Jack," Rio said, incredulous. Alexandra didn't bother to deny it, and that just opened a wholly different can of worms. "What has he got himself into?"

"A new job, a police investigation, and a shed load of old ghosts, if I'm not missing my mark."

Rio would have sworn blind that the investigation didn't bother Jack in the slightest. "He hates owin' favours," he said. "As for the two boys he saved an' the one he couldn't, it's bound to remind him of stuff he worked years to forget."

"How long have you known Jack?" Alexandra asked, sipping her tea.

"I think he was twelve when I found him squattin' in my basement."

"He… what?"

"Have you never wondered why there are no school reports in tha'?" Rio pointed at the thick blue folder in Marston's lap. "Jack's a street kid."

"He has two degrees!"

"Didn' say he wasn' smart. Or that he was lazy. When he was thirteen, he ordered a daily pizza delivery for the homeless shelter two streets over. Hacked a pimp's account to pay for it. He ran that for two years, and the arse never noticed."

"And he started to work with you when he was fourteen."

"He helped catch his mother's killer even though he had no earthly reason to. I knew then that I could trust him."

Alexandra's blank face made Rio sigh. "Really?" he asked and left the room, only to return a moment later with a bottle of Morgan's and two glasses. "If you don't even know this much, how can you hope to understand him?"

Alex took the glass and tossed back the deep brown liquid with a deft hand before setting it back on the table. "Educate me?"

Rio contemplated that for a long time while he emptied and refilled his glass. Alex didn't move beyond shifting the thick file to rest beside her on the sofa, and Rio was grateful for her patience. He had seen Jack grow from a fierce, defiant twelve-year-old, ready to die rather than let someone touch him, into a confident, skilled fighter who cared too much for those around him.

Jack didn't trust easily.

Most of the time, he didn't trust at all.

And Rio would rather disappoint Alexandra Marston than lose the fragile trust Jack had offered him. Because when it came right down to it, Alexandra Marston might be scary. Jack Horwood was a lot more dangerous than that.

"I'll tell you three things about Jack," he decided after another long moment. "No questions. 'Kay?"

Alex straightened in her seat and focussed. "Thank you."

"Don' thank me yet," Rio grumbled, still not sure if he was making the right choice. Finally, he took a deep breath. "First, when it comes to Jack, treat anythin' electronic as suspect," he said. "Especially data that is in any possible way connected to him."

Alex made a face. "I already knew that pile of stuff was useless," she said. "But I had no idea it was as useless as all that."

"Yeah, righ'. Next. Jack's mother sold him to her pimp. He escaped when he was twelve." Rio spoke faster now, trying to ward off memories and failing. "An' last, Jack can never not offer help when it is needed. He's jus' not built that way."

Like the consummate professional she was, Alex didn't react to any of Rio's revelations. Her face showed neither rage nor pity, and Rio didn't try to explain that—for him—it was Jack's capacity for crusades that turned him into the most valuable ally and asset.

# LOVE IN THE MIRROR

"**M**y office, two o'clock."

Jack shook his head. "Can't. I have a meeting with—"

"No, you don't. I've called Raf Gallant to let him know."

Jack scowled at the calendar on his tablet, where his lunchtime meeting at Scotland Yard was no longer listed. Rage zinged through him so swiftly he had to catch his breath and snap his mouth shut before he boiled over. Owning his choices was a matter of survival. He couldn't let anyone take that away from him. Not even Gareth. Not even for something as trivial as a meeting at Scotland Yard.

Jack turned on his heel without another word and caught the elevator down to the basement. Once in the empty, quiet dojo he changed into his gi, wrapped his hands, and went to beat the blue bejeezus out of the heavy tethered bag, kicking and punching until his body slipped into the familiar rhythm, and his mind took a break.

He didn't stop until his skin was slick with sweat and his muscles burned. Hands on knees, he gulped air as if it was rationed.

To his surprise the anger lingered, jabbing at his mind like a rusty nail. Stuck in his mind, it was only when he straightened that Jack noticed he wasn't alone in the room.

A dark-haired man leaned against the door that led to the changing rooms. At a shade over six feet, Jack had never considered himself short, but the man had at least four inches on him. And he was built to match.

"Horwood, right?" he asked in a voice that was all gravel and waited for Jack's curt nod before he pushed away from the door. "If he pisses you off that much you really should tell him. He's crap at the mind-reading stuff."

That was probably the best advice Jack'd been given all week. Not that it helped solve his problem. He was wiping sweat from his forehead when the man spoke again.

"You done with your warm-up? I need a sparring partner."

Jack's eyebrows shot up in surprise. He let his gaze trail from bare feet to shoulder-length hair and back down, before he shrugged. "Why the hell not?"

They stepped onto the mat.

They bowed.

A moment later Jack no longer had time for anger or distraction. He was simply busy.

"You got some nice moves there, Horwood," his adversary praised twenty minutes later as he rolled to his feet, breath slowly evening out. He held out a hand to haul Jack upright. "Aidan Conrad," he introduced himself.

Jack smirked. "I'm aware."

Aidan Conrad might not look the part—certainly not right then with his hair dishevelled and a bruise blooming on his jaw—but the man was Nancarrow Mining's company solicitor and legal counsel. He sat on the board of directors and had chambers in Lincoln's Inn. Aidan Conrad had other interests too, but Jack kept that knowledge in reserve. He had a dossier on the man, just as he had dossiers on the other directors and department heads. All of them… except for one Gareth Flynn.

Jack knew that he would never have missed someone as obvious as a company director. He wouldn't have missed the man whose department he was planning to join. If he'd had his head in the game that day, rather than staring in shock at Gareth Flynn in a suit, he would have realised that the moment

Gareth had stepped out of his office.

His customary smirk turned into a scowl. "Why are you keeping Flynn off the books?"

"How d'you mean?"

"I had no idea he even worked here when I came for my interview."

"And?"

The lawyer had a smirk to match Jack's. And wasn't that annoying?

"That doesn't happen."

"You're that good, eh?"

"Ah, fuck you, Conrad!" Jack was done. Right now, his head might be in six places at once, but he'd been focussed when he researched Nancarrow Mining in preparation for his interview. He wouldn't have missed the fact that Gareth Flynn worked for the company. Hell, he wouldn't have applied had he known.

And that was an interesting conclusion, but one that wouldn't calm him down any time soon. Jack filed it for later, much later, and turned towards the changing rooms. He had a meeting to reschedule.

"Just one more thing." Aidan stopped him before he could close the door. "Running doesn't solve arguments. Just makes you fight tired."

Jack dropped the paper bag on the kitchen table. The spicy scent of his favourite curry should have been soothing, should have made him look forwards to a bit of R & R. But not even the idea of a beer or two could soothe him tonight.

He had kept a lid on his ire while he met with Raf and Lisa at Scotland Yard to strategise.

Spending time with Daniel and Nico in the hospital had taxed his mind and his emotions enough to keep his anger at bay.

But now that he was home, he was clean out of distractions. All he could think about was Gareth treating him as if Jack was… what? Four?

Raf had laughed his arse off when Jack had called him, seething, to reinstate their meeting. He'd still been laughing when Jack had turned up at the Yard before advising Jack to let it go.

Jack couldn't. Trivial, but not, harmless, but not, Jack felt unsure of his footing, felt the steady base he needed to function slip and slide beneath him.

He went into his bedroom to change into tracksuit bottoms and a T-shirt, and the bed caught his gaze; the pillow that had offered comfort only a couple of days ago was now a mockery.

"He's shit at the mind-reading stuff," Jack muttered as he stripped the bedclothes, his movements savage. Aidan Conrad had been right about that. And Jack was used to seeing Gareth as his CO, to treating Gareth with the respect that position deserved. Calling him on his bullshit was so close to out of the question, it was laughable.

Jack had no idea where that left them.

———————— ♦ ♦ ♦ ————————

Briefing. 10.30. Julian's office. And turn your fucking phone on!

Jack frowned at the terse message. He had ten minutes to get his notes together and his arse upstairs to meet with Julian Nancarrow. And a very pissed-off Gareth, judging by the way the exclamation mark had nearly ripped through the paper.

This clearly wasn't working.

Jack hadn't slept a wink; the fresh, lemon-scented sheets neither comforted nor relaxed him. When he wasn't mad at Gareth for treating him like a child, his mind dwelt on images his body found far too enticing.

Like Gareth in a suit.

Or Gareth wrapped around him in Jack's bed, hands warm and firm on Jack's skin.

At 2:00 a.m. Jack had given up on sleep. He'd taken a quick shower and dealt with his most pressing problem before he had packed his bag and ridden to work looking for distractions.

The corporate security office was the haven of peace Jack hadn't been able to find at home, and he worked at a steady pace surrounded by the soft hum of electronics and lights turned low, escaping to the roof when the sky outside the windows brightened, and the office was no longer his alone.

Jack was avoiding Gareth Flynn. A childish and temporary measure, sure, but Jack just couldn't help himself.

He didn't deny that he was attracted to the man.

He accepted that he was stubborn, independent, tricky to work with, and a dozen other epithets that superiors and shrinks had bestowed on him over the years.

What he had deluded himself about was his ability to work with Gareth outside of a chain of command.

Jack's past had never impeded his work.

Nothing had ever been more important to him than his crusade.

Until Gareth had reappeared and made a mess of Jack's carefully constructed life with his need to feed him and protect him and boss him around as if Jack was six and away from home for the first time. Nobody had ever tried to run Jack's life… and he knew he wasn't handling it well.

He could deal with attempts to order him

around—his long-suffering handler would testify that he'd done it for years—but Gareth wasn't just bossy. He was fun to be with, loyal, protective, infuriating... and damned hot.

Jack's watch alarm interrupted his musings. *Meeting, right.* He shoved a stylus behind his ear, grabbed his tablet, and headed for the stairs.

Could he be mistaking physical need for attraction?

It had been a while—a long while—since he'd bothered to hook up with anyone. Maybe all he needed was a night of hot, sweaty sex to get rid of the tension that had been simmering all week, to make him realise that there was nothing else left when they were done.

Caught between wanting to strangle Gareth Flynn and wanting to tie him down and kiss him all over, it seemed as good a plan as any.

Jack took the stairs two at a time and stepped into the executive office a moment later, back straight and face blank.

◆ ◆ ◆

Gareth's eyes strayed from the stack of documents before him to the security feed running on a monitor off to one side.

The feed showed Jack's desk. Without a sign of

Jack, who had been the epitome of professional while briefing Julian Nancarrow, only to disappear at the end of the meeting without giving Gareth a chance to apologise.

"Got a minute?" Aidan Conrad leaned in the doorway, dressed in a light grey shirt and an immaculate charcoal grey suit that screamed Savile Row.

"Sure." Gareth pushed the papers aside and straightened in his seat. "I'm hardly making headway with this stuff. And you sound as if you could use a drink."

"Thanks." Aidan settled in the visitor's chair and accepted the teacup Gareth held out. "Thought I'd come tell you that Horwood's caught on."

"Told you he'd be quick."

"So what d'you do to piss him off?"

"He told you?"

"If he'd told me, I wouldn't have to ask," Aidan lectured, fingers trailing over a faint bruise on his jaw.

"It's this fucking crusade of his," Gareth groused. "He works all hours, doesn't sleep, doesn't eat, runs himself ragged. I just tried to give him a break."

"How?"

Embarrassment heated Gareth's neck and the tips of his ears. "I may have rescheduled some of his meetings," he mumbled, palm coming up to rub his neck and stopping in mid-air. He thought he'd cured himself of that giveaway gesture but add one Jack Horwood and all bets were off.

"Without telling him."

"Obviously."

"You blindsided a spook." Aidan shook his head. "No wonder he's a barrel of laughs."

"Jack's damn good at what he does."

"Never argued that. But there's more to him. Hell, you just have to look at that fucking tattoo to know that." Aidan scrubbed a broad hand through his hair and pulled out the tie that secured it at the base of his skull. He didn't look any softer with his hair loose. "Problem is, he could be too good. We have no idea why he really quit. Why he's here."

Gareth opened his mouth to argue, not surprised when Aidan stopped him.

"Don't get me wrong, Flynn. I want him here. I want him to become part of the team. But what if…."

"Jack is loyal. I know it."

"You knew that eight years ago. Now? You don't have a clue."

"I'm thinking with my dick. That what I'm hearing?"

Aidan didn't bat an eyelash at the growl in Gareth's voice. Fucker was always as steady as a rock, even when Gareth's temper got the better of him. No doubt that's why they made such a good team.

"I imagined you think you owe him. That's not what I'm talking about, anyway. I've asked Alex to dig up some background."

"A right bright idea." Gareth nodded, sarcasm thick as a blanket. "He goes apeshit when I cancel one of his meetings, and you think he'll take kindly to us poking around where we're not wanted?"

"He'll never know."

"That'll be the day."

Aidan looked deeply offended. "Wash your mouth out. That's Alex you're bitching about."

"You've really got it bad, huh?"

"Hello pot, I'm kettle. Have we met?"

Gareth's rueful chuckle drew an answering grin from the lawyer, one that grew serious a moment later.

"Wanna hear a bit of friendly advice?"

Gareth slumped into his chair. "Ah, why the fuck not? You're going to tell me whether I want to hear it or not."

Aidan made himself comfortable on the other side of the desk and crossed his legs. "You are out of uniform."

"What?"

"You," Aidan repeated, "are out of uniform. Back in the day, you could have rearranged all of

Horwood's schedules, and he wouldn't have batted an eyelash. But that was a long time ago. Give him room," Aidan counselled. "Introvert, remember? If you force him to fit in, you only exhaust him."

"And make him resent me, I know." Gareth sighed. "I hate to see him work all hours just because someone asked for his help, or working with a migraine, just because he's forgotten to eat. Again."

"Then surround him with food. He knows how to eat. And while you're at it, you'd best accept that you'll never be able to stop him from offering help. That's who he is."

Gareth acknowledged that truth with another sigh. "Frazer is just as bad."

"Nah. Frazer grew up the youngest of a huge family. He's used to being bossed around and fussed over. Horwood isn't. He had no family at all growing up from what I'm hearing. He's independent to a fault and stuck in his own head for too much of the time."

"I've got it, thanks. I'm not that slow."

"You're not usually so inept, either," Aidan said. "I thought I'd better make sure you don't piss the kid off so much he ups sticks and leaves."

"Oh, screw you, Conrad. You just want him."

"Hell yes, I do. But not until we're sure of his motives. And not until he asks." The lawyer set his empty cup down and stood. "Now go and talk to him. I'm sure Frazer knows where he's hiding."

————◆◆◆————

The trickle of rain down the windscreen and the steady movement of the wipers lulled Jack to sleep despite the traffic noise, Gareth's proximity, and the arousal simmering in his blood. A hint of Gareth's aftershave drifted on the air, warm and spicy like a secret promise of pleasures to come.

Accepting Gareth's apology—and his invitation to have dinner and talk things out—had required no soul-searching.

Leaving the bike at Nancarrow Mining and driving home in Gareth's Range Rover had been a good call as well.

Getting wet riding home was off the agenda.

"Did you come to an agreement with Lisa?" Gareth's voice interrupted his languorous musings, and Jack snapped awake.

"She's running down leads from the club, and we'll keep an eye on the video feed. I doubt we'll get a name. Unless we catch him right at it or someone has an axe to grind and shops him, the breakthrough has to come from the boys."

"And Lisa wants you to drive that since the two

won't talk to anyone else," Gareth surmised.

"Yep."

"Are you going to?"

Jack leaned his head against the backrest and closed his eyes. He wanted to get his hands on the bastard who'd imprisoned the boys and killed Ricky. He wanted that so badly he could taste it. But hell would freeze over before he forced Daniel and Nico to relive their ordeal when they were not ready to deal with the fallout. They first needed to feel safe, and both were still a long way from that.

"I'm in your corner, Jack," Gareth reminded him. "You don't need to hide."

Jack grunted, not planning on sharing his thoughts. "I need to take a look at the feed," he said. "The algorithm isn't tight enough."

"Do it while I make dinner. You can use my computer."

"You're hilarious." As far as Jack was concerned, the PC in Gareth's study was ancient, decrepit, and barely powerful enough to order takeaway. "Don't worry. I brought tools."

"Don't you need a face to run facial recog?"

"I had no idea you thought so highly of me."

"What?"

Jack smirked at the snap in Gareth's voice. He'd forgotten how much fun he used to have baiting his

CO. "Facial recognition needs fairly sophisticated programming. It's not something you knock up in a couple of hours," he explained. "I'm just picking patterns. Hair colour, face shape, height… that sort of thing."

"So what's the problem?"

"Too many blonds. Under strobe lights even brown hair can look blond, so I need to narrow it down."

"Perfectionism, thy name is Horwood."

"Sure. You look at hundreds of blonds a night and tell me you still remember the face of one man you saw a week ago."

It was a good thing that the Range Rover was stopped at a traffic light or there would have been carnage.

"*You're* stripping the feed?"

Jack managed not to roll his eyes. "Along with Baxter and Walshaw," he agreed. "If you wanna pick a perp out of a video feed you need someone who actually knows what the guy looks like."

"I know what he looks like."

"You're busy."

"And you're not? Jesus!"

Jack didn't bother with a reply. He closed his eyes again and was soon stuck in that twilight zone between awake and asleep while Gareth fought traffic and weather on the way home to Richmond.

———————◆◆◆———————

Soft jazz drifted through the kitchen, the notes of the saxophone soothing as Gareth chopped and stirred and mentally kicked himself.

He had checked on Jack earlier and had found Jack's laptop propped open on the coffee table, flashing through grainy images at mindboggling speeds while Jack was otherwise occupied.

Arms neatly folded against his chest, he lay curled on his side on the couch, feet still on the floor as if he'd just tipped over sideways and gone to sleep.

The sounds of Gareth moving around the room did not wake him, and that fact alone told Gareth how much Jack had changed.

Sleep and Jack Horwood used to have only a nodding acquaintance. Whether in the barracks or in the field, he didn't sleep unless he was alone or barricaded and the softest noise would find him awake and ready to defend himself.

Finding Jack asleep like this made Gareth feel like a fool.

He had seen the outside and had found it as enticing as it had ever been.

He'd seen Jack's eyes, where competence and determination warred with vulnerability and doubt.

He'd touched the leather Jack wore around his throat, and he'd ignored the fact that eight years had passed, that even all those years ago Jack had been strong enough to walk away when he felt he needed to.

Gareth had tried to pick up the pieces of their relationship from a point they'd never actually been at. And it had needed Aidan Conrad to point that out.

Gareth set the table before he returned to the lounge, dropped to his knees beside the sofa, and ran fingers through Jack's hair until the long lashes fluttered, and Jack opened sleep-darkened green eyes.

"You need to eat."

"I need to sleep." Jack's voice was an attractive, husky rumble. "Feed me breakfast?"

Gareth ghosted his lips over Jack's. "I'm feeding you dinner," he declared before he leaned in for another soft kiss. "And then we're gonna talk. That bullshit we've been running all week… it's ludicrous."

Jack blinked himself awake. He didn't argue when Gareth rose from his knees and held out a hand to haul him upright. He just rolled off the couch and followed Gareth to the kitchen.

"You really love to cook," he said, surveying the dinner Gareth had put together while he slept.

"I do. Especially for an appreciative audience," Gareth agreed. He watched Jack demolish pork chops and green beans, making careful note that the cheese and garlic mash seemed a particular favourite.

"So… talk?" Jack suggested when Gareth topped up their wineglasses, sounding as if he'd rather do anything else.

Gareth wasn't looking forward to this conversation either.

"Eight years have changed things," he said, not taking his gaze from Jack. "I keep forgetting that we're different people now, and I think you do too. We're second-guessing each other and keep getting it wrong. And we don't need that kind of shit, right?"

"So it bugs you that I'm too focussed—"

"I think the term is obsessive." Gareth grinned at Jack's flushing cheeks, loving that he'd been the cause of that.

"Okay, fine, so I get a little obsessive when I work. There's nothing wrong with that."

"No, there isn't. And I'm happy to give you the space you need to obsess."

"You are?"

"Provided you look after yourself. Or let me do it."

"How?"

The suspicious look on Jack's face came as a surprise. He couldn't have fucked up matters that badly, could he? He chose his next words with care.

"Well… when I think you're overdoing it, I'll tell you, and you will listen." He held up a hand before Jack had his mouth fully open. "I didn't say you had to stop working. All I said was that I'd tell you. If you feel you want to keep going, that's your choice. I'm just alerting you to the fact that you've maybe lost yourself in your work."

"Okay?" Jack sounded adorably unsure. "That's reasonable, I suppose. Anything else?"

"I hate seeing you work with a migraine, just because you've forgotten to eat and overdosed on caffeine. So when I put food in front of you, you'll eat."

"I'm not six, Gareth. I can look after myself."

"I know you can."

"Then why?"

"Because," Gareth started. And stopped, caught between history and need. *Take care of your mum while I'm gone.* Was that how it had started? Maybe.

For as long as Gareth could remember he'd looked after others, made sure that anyone around him was safe and cared for. A habit he'd cultivated, a need that had been easy to feed given his career choices. Jack just brought all that out in full force.

"Because?" Jack prompted when the silence grew too long.

"It's something I do," Gareth explained. "Like you never say no when someone asks for your help."

Jack's scowl smoothed out. "Fair enough."

"So when I put food in front of you, you'll eat it?"

Jack's eyes sparkled with mischief. "Not if it's something I hate."

"Then you tell me, and I'll get you something else." Gareth smiled and mentally tipped his hat to Aidan Conrad. "Now you."

"I know you're bossy. And I know you get off on it," Jack said in a serious tone, though the smirk was out in full force. "But I can't have you making decisions for me."

"Cancelling your meeting with Gallant was an error in judgment. I already apologised for that."

"I know. But it's important to me. Especially as I can't always tell you what I'm doing or why. Maybe it's too much to take on faith."

"That would be my decision."

"Yes."

"But?"

"I'd… maybe I'd want to know."

Jack's fingertips traced patterns on the tabletop. He didn't look up, so he missed Gareth's smile. "You can't break protocol," Gareth argued. "You're not built that way, and neither am I."

"I don't have to break protocol. But if I know it

bugs you, I can make allowances for you acting like an arse."

"As if I ever…."

"Deluded too. Great."

Gareth loved seeing the smile on Jack's face. His eyes lightened when he smiled, and his dark lashes added lustre to his gaze. Without thought, Gareth reached across the table and smoothed his fingers over Jack's tattoo. "So I won't boss you around, and you'll let me take care of you. Agreed?"

"Sure."

They touched glasses to seal their accord, and Gareth didn't believe for a single moment that it would be that easy.

<hr />

Jack stood in front of the mirror in Gareth's bedroom and rubbed at his damp hair with a towel. The thin strip of leather around his neck and the towel he'd wrapped around his waist only emphasised the fact that he was otherwise naked. Bathed in the golden glow from the bedside lamp, he was a vision of tan skin and sleek, rippling muscle.

Gareth's breath caught at the sight. He'd offered Jack the option to sleep in his guest room, but Jack had scoffed at the idea, and Gareth blamed the heat in

Jack's gaze for the short circuit in his brain. Why else, after that comment, would he have let Jack shower alone?

Gareth closed the bathroom door, and their eyes met in the mirror. Jack's expression was soft around the edges—not a real smile yet, more a wry invitation—and Gareth couldn't let that go. He stepped into Jack's space, and his hands slid over shower-warm skin and tight stomach muscles to pull Jack's back to his chest. They were almost the same height, so it was easy for Gareth to rest his chin on Jack's shoulder and press their cheeks together. Jack watched him, eyes never leaving the mirror, and Gareth turned his head and ran his lips over the tattoo at Jack's temple.

"You can't even tell it's there," he murmured, and he heard, felt, and saw Jack huff a laugh.

"Not by touch, no. But I know. Always."

"Why did you get it?"

"'Cause I was drunk."

"Not what I asked." Gareth tightened his arms around Jack's waist, and his fingertips skimmed the edge of the towel, teasing until Jack squirmed.

"As a reminder," he offered finally with a shit-eating grin that Gareth could do nothing but return.

Jack was not going to explain either the remark or the reasons for the unusual adornment, at least not tonight, and Gareth shelved the inquiry. It was just one thing among many that he wanted to know about Jack, and there were more pressing concerns on his mind right then.

Like the skin under his hands, soft and hot, that Gareth couldn't get close enough to. He skimmed his palms up and down Jack's chest, traced the ridged abs with calloused fingertips, and teased Jack's nipples until Jack arched and hooked one arm around the back of Gareth's neck, his head thudding against Gareth's shoulder.

"Do you have any idea how much I want you, brat?"

"I'm right here."

Jack tightened his grip and ground his towel-clad arse against Gareth's hardness until Gareth struggled to breathe. He wanted Jack like he'd never wanted anyone before. But despite the heat between them, this wasn't what he'd had in mind when he'd invited Jack to dinner.

What they had was too fragile.

Jack… was too fragile.

They were trying to establish boundaries, find ways to work together, and Jack was so tired he could barely see straight. A night of hot sex, while certainly high on his bucket list, had not figured in Gareth's immediate plans.

"What do *you* want, Jack?"

"You," Jack answered on a soft exhale. "Hands, mouth, cock… I don't care. Don't care who does what, either. Wanna see you. Feel you. Just… you."

Jack was hiding again. Gareth had noticed during their after dinner conversation, but had been more intent on reaching an agreement. Now, though….

"Jack, you're tired."

"And your memory's for shit." Jack tried to pull away, but Gareth's arms around his middle didn't budge.

"Not true."

"Then kiss me."

Their lips met softly, more breath than touch, and Jack melted into Gareth's hold. A long while passed before they separated.

"See, that's what I'm talking about." Jack smiled, lips only a thought away from Gareth's mouth. "Just… you."

"Us," Gareth whispered back as chills raced down his spine. "Just us."

It wasn't the best way to resolve the issues between them. Maybe it would turn out to be Gareth's worst decision ever. But giving Jack what Jack wanted had become an imperative.

Stumbling steps and heated kisses ate up the

distance from the mirror to the bed. A good tug had Jack's towel sliding to the floor. Then Gareth's lips were on the leather around Jack's throat and the racing pulse beneath.

Jack tumbled them to the sheets and flipped them, keeping one hand on the back of Gareth's neck and the other on his hip. His form was perfect, and Gareth laughed when long-forgotten memories of training sessions at the break of dawn flashed through his mind.

"You taught me all sorts of useful things, see?" Jack teased, before he stretched out alongside Gareth and claimed another kiss.

Gareth didn't mind. He enjoyed Jack hot and hungry, the slip and slide of lips and tongues, the taut, straining muscles under his palms. Jack's taste was addicting too, all heat and wine and spice like a rich casserole at the end of a long day spent in frosty air. Gareth tilted his head to deepen the kiss while his hands grabbed hold and pulled Jack's hips down. Jack's loud gasp and louder moan shot fire down Gareth's spine. He did it again, laughing when Jack broke their kiss to swear at him.

"What?"

"You're a bloody tease."

"And?"

Being on the receiving end of Jack's green glare

sent more heat into Gareth's blood. He dug his fingers into Jack's hips and held him still. Just before he bucked his hips up. Jack's glare turned dark, and Gareth had a single moment to marvel at the sight before Jack's fingers found Gareth's nipple ring and yanked in retaliation.

Time slowed and sped in strange patterns after that. Kisses grew voracious, hands went everywhere, and Gareth relished every gasp and moan he could wring from Jack's throat.

Most of all he loved Jack's purr, deep and throaty and so heartfelt that Gareth would have bet money Jack wasn't even aware of making the sound. Jack was losing himself in their increasingly frantic mutual exploration, and Gareth thought that the hottest thing he'd ever experienced... until Jack flinched when Gareth slid his fingers over Jack's arse and between his cheeks.

"Jack?"

"Fine." Jack's face was buried against Gareth's neck, but Gareth would have sworn the words were grated through clenched teeth. "Just... caught by surprise."

Gareth threaded his fingers into Jack's soft hair and held on. "You *have* done this before, right?"

Jack relaxed enough to lift his head and roll his eyes. "Just not in a long while," he admitted.

"How long a while?"

"Years."

A new wave of heat swamped Gareth at the breathless admission. He eased his grip from Jack's hip and rubbed gentle circles across the small of Jack's back.

"Do you want—"

"No!" Jack's tone was sharp, the kiss that followed short and brutal. "I want *this*. Now."

He dipped his head down for another kiss, and Gareth didn't fight the urgency and need. He didn't resist the questing hands, the feverish clutches, or the whispered demands. His body was on fire, and he'd already decided that whatever Jack needed….

But their paths diverged right there. Jack was tense and heedless, no longer in a mood to enjoy their night. When Jack all but snarled an impatient, "Get on with it, Flynn!" Gareth snapped.

In a move straight out of the close combat manual, he put Jack on his back and pinned him. Jack squirmed and bucked, but Gareth's fingers found a nipple and pinched. Hard. Shock made Jack arch up, and Gareth took his mouth, all tongue and teeth and hunger while he held Jack's body captive.

"If you're looking for a quick fuck you're in the wrong bed, brat," he said, adding a twist to the pinch that had Jack groaning and shivering in his hold.

Gareth didn't ease his grip. Jack would climax as soon as Gareth's fingers released him. And that was just the way he wanted it.

"You haven't changed so much that I can't see what you're doing," Gareth continued. "You're one step away from walking out again…." Gareth stared into Jack's wide eyes, and he knew he was right. He leaned down to kiss Jack again. A soft brush of lips this time, at odds with his earlier ferocity and the brutally tight grip he had on Jack's nipple. "If you choose to walk out," he said, voice quiet and serious despite the heat between them, "if you'd rather have strangers in your life than people who know you… then I want you to remember this. I want you to know—really know this time—what you walked away from."

The soft kiss he placed on Jack's lips heated, turned hungry in an instant. Gareth's nail caught the top of the trapped nipple. He pressed down until Jack gasped, and when he let go, Jack's body convulsed.

"That's it," Gareth whispered into yet another kiss as Jack shuddered beneath him. "Gonna make you come until all that fury's gone and you're so relaxed you're begging me…."

"Was begging before," Jack retorted, but he stopped fighting.

Jack Horwood, spread out on Gareth's bed, all

tousled hair and swollen lips and hooded eyes, made Gareth's mouth water. He wasn't going to let Jack's impatience or his need to run get in the way of their enjoyment. Not when he had Jack right where he wanted him. Gareth took a few deep breaths to bring his racing heart under control. Then he stretched out on top of Jack.

"Now, let's see how much I can relax you before I fuck you through the mattress," Gareth suggested.

"I'm sure relaxed is exactly what you want me to be," Jack grumbled. There was a smile in his gaze, though, and he wriggled suggestively until Gareth's teeth found an earlobe and bit down.

With Jack less frantic, Gareth set about exploring. Lips and fingers roamed to find all of Jack's most sensitive places. Gasps, groans, and shivers guided him, along with the curses Jack resorted to when sensations overwhelmed him. Sharp nips to Jack's triceps produced the most creative language Gareth had heard in a while, yet those words were tame compared to the sounds Jack made when Gareth scraped teeth over Jack's hipbone or when he bit and sucked a trail of hickeys into the soft skin of Jack's inner thigh.

Jack was writhing by then and clutching at the sheets with white-knuckled fists. He didn't react when Gareth reached past him under the pillow to find lube and condoms, didn't flinch when well-slicked fingers breached his entrance, only demanding that Gareth put his mouth where it could do some good.

Gareth watched Jack come apart under his hands. He mouthed Jack's balls and teased along his thigh again before finally leaning to suckle the tip of Jack's cock into his mouth.

"Gods…. Gareth!" Jack howled at the heat and suction. His eyes were wide open, and his head thrashed from side to side. He was leaking, and Gareth let his tongue tease the slit and enjoy the taste of Jack's arousal before bobbing his head and taking Jack to the back of his throat. Jack's deep, gravelly groan rattled through Gareth like a minor earthquake, trying to undermine his control.

"You're hot, brat, you know that?" Gareth rasped, drawing back and sitting up.

"Then will you fucking do something about—shit!" The last word was a yell, a complaint and a heartfelt moan wrapped into one as Gareth's fingers disappeared.

"Gareth, please…." Jack's voice was soft all of a sudden, and Gareth leaned in for a kiss that was hot, demanding, and promising at once.

"You have no idea how much I want you," Gareth huffed, his vaunted control suddenly tenuous. His hands shook as he rolled on a condom and coated himself in lube. He couldn't look away from Jack's bitten, quivering lips and the intent eyes that showed almost no green at all.

"Wrap your legs around me," he directed as he positioned himself and leaned over Jack. Never taking his gaze from Jack, Gareth laced their fingers and brushed their lips together. He rocked against his lover, sliding in inch by slow inch. Jack's eyes dilated even more. His breathing grew erratic, and his fingers clenched around Gareth's.

When he was buried to the hilt, Gareth stilled. They stared at each other across an ocean of memories and time apart until Jack let out a long, slow breath, and smiled.

"Move already, Flynn!"

Gareth kissed him instead, long and slow and—for once—not to make a point. He needed to know they were okay, needed to know that Jack was with him, that this was about the two of them… together.

And Jack got the message. He didn't snark, and he curbed his impatience. He kept his fingers wrapped tightly around Gareth's, clenched his muscles around Gareth's cock, and let the other man kiss him until they ran out of air.

━━━◆◆◆━━━

"Shower?"

Jack's lashes barely moved. Gareth revelled in the blissed-out expression that their lovemaking had put on Jack's face. The marks that bloomed low on his throat, right along the lower edge of the decorated strip of leather, sparked a wave of possessive pride. Jack was his. Whether he knew it yet or not.

"Come on," he coaxed, "a shower will make you feel better."

"Not possible," Jack mumbled, not even opening his eyes this time.

Gareth chuckled and gave up. He grabbed a damp washcloth from the bathroom for a quick clean up before settling into bed and dragging the quilt over them both.

He pulled Jack close, tucked the younger man's head under his chin, and then lay awake listening to Jack's deep breaths.

Given the way the night had started, he'd not expected Jack to cede control so easily. Hell, he hadn't expected Jack to stay after he'd told him to stop fighting.

Jack Horwood was made of a medal-winning brand of stubborn, but he'd stayed, and he'd not objected to Gareth taking charge.

The display of trust from someone who didn't trust anyone on a normal day was breathtaking. As were the soft, surprised sounds Jack made deep in his throat every time Gareth found yet another sensitive spot, almost as if Jack had never been touched before.

And being with Jack like this… face to face, close enough to kiss and breathe him in, their fingers woven together and Jack holding on for dear life until their climax hit them almost simultaneously…. Gareth would swear that he'd never experienced anything so intense before.

He already wanted this again. Wanted more. Wanted….

Body relaxed and sated, Gareth's mind refused to shut down. He lay in the dark, Jack's warmth on his skin, wondering if Jack would disappear from his life come morning to continue his crusade, or if—by some miracle—he might decide to stay and fight his crusade with Gareth and Aidan and all their resources at his back.

The darkness offered no answers and neither did Jack's sleeping form, nestled warm and close against Gareth's side. The quiet regular breaths Gareth felt on his chest were soothing, though, and Gareth counted each soft inhale and exhale until he finally drifted off to sleep.

# THE POWER OF ZERO

———— ◆ ◆ ◆ ————

Jack woke in an empty bed. Gareth wasn't far given that the sheets still held some warmth, so Jack snatched Gareth's pillow and pulled it close, cherishing the silence in his mind like the gift it was. He didn't recall falling asleep, but he remembered waking up in the small hours wrapped around Gareth Flynn.

Jack never spent the night with any of his casual hook-ups.

He never brought lovers home.

He never shared his bed, but three times in the last week he'd woken beside Gareth, and not once had he panicked or felt the need to run. Gareth touching him, holding him, felt so right that each time it had happened he'd gone back to sleep in moments.

He'd been running on too little sleep all week, he knew that. But being behind on his sleep quota had never before resulted in him sharing his bed. Usually when Jack got that tired, all he wanted was enough booze to make his mind take a break and let him rest.

Jack stretched languidly in the huge bed, the vague ache in his lower back a pleasant reminder of the night's activities.

Gareth's ministrations had stopped his busy mind most effectively, even if Jack could not explain what had prompted him to so relax his guard.

Jack hadn't bottomed in years; seventeen years to be exact.

For a long time after his escape, sex—or rather his memories of what had happened—had forced him to carry a knife wherever he went. Once he'd learned to defend himself and gotten over his aversion to feeling someone else's hands on his skin, he'd never had the inclination to cede control to his bed partners.

Until last night, when he'd wanted nothing more urgently.

Jack buried his face in Gareth's pillow, and the spicy scent of Gareth's cologne sent a curl of arousal through his gut. So much for using sex to get the man out of his system. Great.

He growled into the soft cotton, irritated by his inability to just let it go. Life would be so much easier if he could just be done with this crush... this attraction... this... thing that made him wish for Gareth's hands on his skin right now.

He wasn't that needy. Not ever.

"Head out of that pillow or the coffee goes down the drain," a cheerful voice interrupted his self-flagellation.

"Don't you dare," Jack threatened. He rolled onto his back, reluctant to lose Gareth's enticing scent, only to find the man himself close enough to touch. "Hi," he managed.

"Hi." Gareth grinned. He was shaved, freshly showered, and already half-dressed. "Breakfast's almost done," he said, sitting down on the side of the bed, hands going to Jack's shoulders. "I thought I'd let you sleep for as long as possible."

The touch of Gareth's palms on his skin kicked Jack's libido into overdrive. He swallowed and took a deep breath before he tried his voice again. "Much appreciated."

"Really?" Gareth's hands slipped down to rub over his nipples, and Jack shivered. "Maybe you'd have liked being woken." The silver head dipped to nuzzle along Jack's jaw to his ear. A flash of heat raced across Jack's skin, and he dug his teeth into his lower lip to stifle a groan. When had he ever been that easy?

Truth was, he hadn't been. He'd only ever carried a torch for one man, and he should have remembered that.

Using sex to get Gareth Flynn out of his system was

about as logical as using a lit match to find a gas leak.

Jack blamed sleep deprivation.

Cross with himself, he pushed the enticing hands away and struggled upright. "Did I hear you mention coffee?" he asked, voice gruff.

"Sure." Gareth's playful mood vanished. He reached for the mug he'd set on the bedside table and held it out. "I've put fresh towels and stuff in the bathroom. Come down when you're ready."

And just like that, he was gone, leaving Jack to scowl at his coffee and feel uncomfortably as if he should go after Gareth and apologise.

———— ✦ ✦ ✦ ————

In the week since their reunion, Gareth had gotten a good measure of Jack's monstrous appetite. So when Jack arrived downstairs shaved, showered, and—regrettably—fully dressed, the kitchen table groaned under a load of breakfast dishes.

Jack nodded in appreciation as he took a seat, but then he kept his head bent over his plate and avoided Gareth's gaze. He didn't respond to attempts at conversation, and Gareth wasn't sure what to make of Jack's mood. Jack wasn't a morning person, but the black scowl on his face hinted at other issues besides waking up in instalments.

"Do you want to stop by your house on the way in?" Gareth asked as he collected the empty plates and loaded the dishwasher.

"No need. I brought my go bag, remember?"

Jack sounded like a stranger, and Gareth wanted to shake him. Would have done if he hadn't known that intimidation didn't work on Jack; it would only make him clam up more. He topped up Jack's mug with the last of the coffee.

"Last night…." He struggled to find words that would erase the wary look from Jack's face. A deep breath steadied him. "Last night… wasn't an apology."

"Good to know."

Jack's tight shoulders relaxed a little. He leaned his head against the wall and closed his eyes, not objecting to Gareth's scrutiny.

Jack looked more rested than Gareth had seen him in the last few days. The shadows under his eyes had lightened, but the crease between his brows had not, and Gareth was reminded of their discussion the night before.

*I can't always tell you what I'm doing or why.*

Gareth didn't believe that Jack had let this slip by accident. Even too tired to see straight he wouldn't make such a rookie mistake.

This could only mean that Jack wasn't as *out* of the

service as Gareth had thought, that there were ties and obligations that held him still. Whether the ties were too close for comfort or whether Jack was trying to keep Gareth and his new colleagues out of the line of fire didn't really matter. Jack felt bound, and Gareth wasn't happy about that.

He considered telling Jack about Aidan and Alex's attempts to learn more about Jack's past, but then he decided against it. He wasn't going to ruin their fragile accord by quizzing Jack the morning after they'd reached it.

"Do you want me to brew another pot?" he asked instead, waving the empty glass carafe to emphasise his point.

"Do we have time?"

Gareth couldn't resist the hopeful note in Jack's voice. He set the carafe on the table, reached for Jack's chin, and leaned down to kiss him slowly and sweetly. "Just this once, I'll let you have a pass," he said.

---

"Do you have a moment?"

Gareth looked up from his study of the most recent threat assessments to find Jack standing in the open office door.

"Come in." Gareth set his keyboard aside, noting

Jack's tense stance and the uncertain look on his face.

Despite their slightly slower start to the morning, they hadn't been that late arriving at the office, and Jack and Frazer had immediately buried themselves in the results of their overnight searches. Neither had come up for air since, but they had both accepted the brimming mugs Gareth had set on a corner of their desks halfway through the morning with grateful nods. It was close to lunchtime now and, as far as Gareth was aware, nothing of note had happened.

Jack stepped into the room and carefully closed the door. "Frazer's onto something," he said before he had even taken a seat.

"Yes?"

"Yes." Jack didn't meet Gareth's eyes. He crossed and uncrossed his legs, tapped the arms of the chair, and rubbed at his face until—

"Jack. Just spit it out."

Jack squared his shoulders and braced as if for a blow. Just as suddenly, he relaxed back into the chair and crossed his arms. "Fuck it!" he said succinctly and took a breath. "I can catch the fucker. With the stuff Frazer found last night, I can catch the fucker."

"But?" Gareth could hear the "but" as if it was a black shadow looming over Jack.

"It could take all night. And tomorrow. And the day after." He shrugged. "I just don't know. It's like…

259

like—" He waved his hands around vaguely. "—like looking for a needle in a haystack? I could get lucky and find something right away, or I won't. I don't want you pitching another shit fit and…. Hell, I *hate* asking permission to do my work!"

The last words came out as a shout, and Gareth flinched. He supposed he deserved that one. "You don't have to ask permission," he reminded. "We cleared that up last night, remember?"

"As long as you do. Remember, I mean. You know I get a little…." Jack sighed before he stood and stretched until his back popped. "It was easier while we served. Do you wish you were back?"

"No. And it wasn't easier. You were just resigned to having fewer choices." Gareth couldn't hide the smile that came with the memories. "I used to be on your case all the time. I lost count of the number of times I had the spooks 'round wanting your help…."

Jack huffed. "And you never once pushed me where I didn't want to go."

"I told you that I would not on the day you first reported to me. It's not my fault you weren't listening."

"I was listening," Jack disagreed. "I just didn't believe it would work out that way."

"Well, believe me now. We'll make this work. We'll find an MO that suits all of us." Gareth had no idea where the sudden bout of certainty came from, but he welcomed it just as he welcomed the glimmer of a smile that lightened the colour of Jack's eyes. "You haven't been here a week, and a lot of shit's blown up out of nowhere. Give us time to find our feet, okay?"

He waited for Jack's nod before he reached for his keyboard and mouse. "Now get out and catch that fucker."

———— ✦ ✦ ✦ ————

"Don't mess with me, you little cunt."

The backhanded blow sent Nico's head into the wall with a crack. Stars danced through his vision, and his teeth came together with a snap so hard a flare of pain shot down his spine.

A part of him wanted to let go, let his unsteady knees fold and sink to the floor. He wanted to pass out from the pain and nausea and pretend the coming torture was already over.

Despite being in the hospital, despite the police guard outside their door, Goran's man had found them. He would drag them back to Goran now, and Goran wasn't merciful.

Nico had seen him deal with boys who had tried to run. He carried scars aplenty to know how brutal the punishment would be, and the next breath seemed one effort too far.

Another backhand.

Another impact rattling his teeth until a wave of nausea forced him to clamp them tightly together. Coffee and garlic scented breath blew in his face, and a harsh voice rasped in his ear.

"You're nothing, you hear? You're a zero. Nothing. There's nowhere you can go I won't find you. And you have nowhere to run."

The moment the enforcer reached for Daniel, Nico's vision cleared with a snap. Daniel was his sanity, his lifeline. Without Daniel the world would be scary, without comfort, smiles, or jokes shared in quiet whispers. There would only be fear and pain and helpless loathing. And while Nico shivered in terror at the ordeal in store for them, he also knew that Daniel might not survive it.

Daniel didn't deal well with pain and struggled with the increasingly brutal abuse. After each one of Goran's punishments, he withdrew a little more into himself: not speaking, not eating, and sometimes barely breathing.

If the man who'd come for them—Nico had no name for him, had never seen him around Goran before, and thought he might be a tracker working for a fee—returned them to Goran, neither one of them would make it out alive.

The idea of losing Daniel scared Nico more than Goran's enforcer.

Ricky was gone.

If he lost Daniel, he'd be… alone.

*You're not alone. You are not helpless.*

The words Jack had spoken over and over during the last week penetrated the clamour in Nico's mind. He remembered Jack's green gaze—calm eyes that never judged, never pitied, or demanded. Steady hands and slow, deliberate movements.

Jack knew.

He… understood in a way nobody else did.

Detective Inspector Baxter wanted justice, or perhaps revenge. The social workers wanted to… make him and Daniel forget what happened, maybe?

Jack dressed like a boy for hire and stepped into nightclubs where pimps hung out. He used himself as bait to rescue boys like Daniel and Ricky and Nico, even though his wrists bore faded scars, and his eyes burned with pain and shame when he failed.

Jack brought weapons and food, stood guard while they slept, and taught them how to fight.

Jack never judged, never pushed, and never expected… anything.

Nico slid down the wall as if his legs couldn't hold him. His fingers shook as he pulled the knife from his shoe and gripped it the way Jack had shown him.

He wasn't a zero.

He wasn't helpless.

Having the knife in his fist helped him focus. His grip on the handle was white-knuckled, but he was no longer scared. Jack's words came back to him as if they'd been branded into his mind:

*Work as a team.*

*Go down when hit.*

*Get the knife.*

*Wait until he turns away from you to deal with Daniel.*

*Push up from the floor. Hard.*

*Lead with the knife in your fist.*

And Nico did just that.

———— ✦ ✦ ✦ ————

"Thank you." Clive Baxter smiled at the tired-looking girl behind the refreshment counter. Judging by the queue of people behind him, she wouldn't catch a break for a while yet. He took the last of the plastic mugs from her, slipped it into a protective cardboard sleeve, and set it into the carrier she'd provided as soon as he'd rattled off his order.

Clive had never trained as a waiter, so weaving through crowded hospital corridors with three coffees and two hot chocolates on a tray hadn't sounded appealing. This was easier.

It was early afternoon, and there should have been a lull in normal hospital activity. It was Friday, though, and Fridays seemed to march to a different beat.

Clutches of people thronged the hallways, hospital personnel in their vary-hued garb hurried this way and that, and the short walk to the elevator turned into an obstacle course dotted with children, wheelchairs, and rushing nurses.

The small gift shop's customers, browsing for paperbacks and sweets and waiting to pay for their purchases, spilled out into the concourse, and Clive pushed his way through the queue, smiling in apology and nodding in thanks at the same time.

The area in front of the bank of elevators felt like a haven of peace in the melee, with only a few orderlies and two women waiting for the next car. All three elevators hit the ground floor in short order, and by the time he was past the fourth floor, Clive was alone in the car.

He slumped against the wall and sucked in a deep breath. Babysitting two barely responsive teenagers when he wanted to be out pulling in the pimp who had hurt them was a darn sight harder than it looked.

He took a sip from his cup and decided that

hospital coffee wasn't the worst thing he'd ever tasted. It came close, though, especially after a week such as he was having.

He settled the cup back into the tray and prayed for patience. He didn't expect Nico and Daniel to throw the hot chocolate in his face when he offered it, but he could already picture how they would scrutinise the cups for the longest time, wordlessly debating whether what he'd brought them was safe to drink.

He'd been watching over them for a week, and the two boys still didn't trust him.

Not enough to accept anything he offered without scrutiny.

Not enough to talk to him.

None of his explanations and assurances had convinced Nico and Daniel to help him find the man who'd incarcerated and abused them. Hell, he didn't even have a name to add to the wanted list!

Not for the first time that day did he consider calling Jack Horwood.

Not for the first time that day did he decide against it.

Jack had never actually worked for the Metropolitan Police, but while still at MI6 he'd been at least nominally a colleague. Now he was a civilian hard at work at his new job. Disturbing him for nothing more than a status check wouldn't be wise.

Bugging him to speed up his interrogations and produce a name would be worse.

Jack had a way of dealing with traumatised children that neither Clive nor Gillian Kent could match or even explain. There was no doubt that it worked like a charm every time Jack chose to get involved.

Right now, Jack was the only person the two boys let close. However much Clive wanted to move this investigation forwards, he couldn't jeopardise the rapport Jack was building with Nico and Daniel.

The elevator doors opened on the eighth floor, and Clive froze, half in and half out of the cabin.

At the far end of the corridor, two men traded blows and punches.

Right outside the door to Nico and Daniel's hospital room!

Clive dropped the drinks and covered the distance at a dead run. The uniformed officer looked like an experienced fighter, but his attacker was simply huge. As Clive skidded into range, the officer crumpled to the ground, unconscious or dazed Clive had no way of knowing.

Clive jumped over the prone form and landed a hard kick to the attacker's knee.

The man merely grunted.

His fist flew straight at Clive's face.

Clive avoided the blow and saw the kick to his ribs at the last moment. He didn't have quite enough momentum to block, so he hit the wall, breath leaving his lungs in a rush.

The attacker's fist thudded into the wall beside him. Clive wrapped both hands around the man's wrist and yanked as hard as he could, pulling the man off his feet. His head slammed into the wall, and he slumped forwards, dazed.

Clive tried to get his knee in place to do damage when a hoarse shout from inside the boys' room had him spinning around in alarm.

There were two of them?

The door flew open, and Clive saw the second man. Bent over, one arm clamped around his middle, he tried to grasp Daniel with his free hand and drag him along.

"Police," Clive yelled, and the man let go of Daniel's arm as if it had grown red hot. To Clive's everlasting relief—tempered by a good dose of confusion—the two would-be abductors considered him enough of a threat to turn and make a run for the stairs, leaving Clive in the hallway with two semiconscious police officers, breathing hard and clutching his bruised ribs.

━━━━◆◆◆━━━━

Clive ushered the boys back inside their room, helped the two police officers in after them, and locked the door.

It was yet another miracle that nobody had heard the commotion and come running. And that nobody had been passing anywhere close by.

Granted, Nico and Daniel's room was as out of the way as it could be in a hospital that size, but nurses checked on the two at intervals or just stopped by to chat with the officers. For the whole incident to pass unnoticed was as strange as two bullyboys turning tail and running at his mere presence.

Clive made sure the two officers were not seriously hurt before he turned to Daniel and Nico.

"Are you okay?"

His question received no audible answer. The two boys huddled close together on the bed furthest from the door. All that was visible of Daniel was the shock of honey-blond hair. The boy had darted from the door to the bed while Baxter's back had been turned, suggesting that he wasn't injured. Though judging by the bruise on Nico's jaw, their would-be abductor hadn't been gentle.

Neither boy was looking his way, but as soon as Baxter took a step towards them, both shrank back against the wall, eyes wide and bodies shaking.

Frustration boiled hot in Clive's gut. After taking

that kick to his side, he had trouble breathing, though that discomfort paled compared to the terror in the two boys' faces. He had promised them all week that they were safe. And he hadn't delivered.

He stayed in the middle of the room, making sure both his hands were out by his sides, the way he had seen Jack approach children. He kept his voice low and tried for a gentle tone.

"Nico, he hit you. I need to know you're okay. Do you need a doctor?"

Neither boy reacted.

Clive's hands curled into fists. He was a detective, not a babysitter or a counsellor. He had no idea what to do to get through to the two. "I'm calling Jack," he decided, digging for his phone.

"Jack gave me my knife," Nico whispered. He raised his right fist a couple of inches off the bed. The fingers were clenched tight around the handle of a thin blade. "I cut him."

"Good work," Baxter replied without hesitation. "Did you draw blood? That can help us find and identify him."

"Do I need to give you my knife?"

"No. Just get a clean rag and wipe the blood off."

There were enough blood spatters on the linoleum for forensics to work on, but Clive was too grateful that Nico had spoken to him to point that out.

He pulled an evidence bag out of the inside pocket of his suit jacket and placed it on the table before moving towards the window, creating a safe, empty space in the centre of the room the way Jack had taught him to do. "Put the rag into the bag. Only touch the outside of the bag."

He breathed a sigh of relief when he saw Daniel's head move, looking for a clean tissue. Nico didn't shift from his place on the bed. He had one arm around Daniel's waist and half shielded the smaller boy with his body, braced for another attack.

Baxter turned his back and pressed buttons on his phone. Jack answered on the second ring.

"I'm at the hospital," Baxter said without preamble. "He sent someone to get the boys back."

"Did he succeed?"

"No. But...," Baxter hesitated over what to say next. Gareth's comment the other night had stung because the man had been right. Clive asked a lot of Jack. Always had, since the very first case they had worked together. Jack got things done. He was smart enough to make the law work to his advantage and able to bend the rules without getting caught.

"What happened to the uniforms?"

The snap in Jack's voice brought Baxter back to the conversation. "Got knocked out. I'm with them and the boys in their room."

"Wait for me," Jack instructed. "Don't call it in yet."

"You think it's an inside job?"

"It's possible."

Baxter nodded, though Jack wouldn't be able to see. All the little things that were niggling at him fit the pattern if someone had orchestrated the abduction. "I'll wait for you."

＊＊＊

Jack dropped the phone into his lap and stared into the drizzle that draped the capital like a dreary blanket.

One week.

It had taken the pimp just one week to find the two boys and send someone to the hospital to retrieve them.

Jack had no need to imagine how scared Nico and Daniel must be. They'd had no reason to trust the system to begin with, and what little hope he'd managed to instil over the last days was bound to be gone. At least Baxter had been close enough to stop the planned abduction.

He had to get Nico and Daniel out of the hospital to a place he could guard, a place nobody would find. Given his and Baxter's suspicions, that was not an easy task.

The two boys still needed medical attention, so going on the run with them was out. Not to mention that his new boss expected to see him at this desk on a regular basis.

Most of all, though, Daniel and Nico needed stability, a solid foundation they could lean on. Rushing around the country hoping to avoid their former pimp and the police wasn't going to do them any good.

*You don't have to solve all the world's problems by yourself.*

Jack knew that. It didn't change the fact that he didn't ask for help. For a large part of his past, there hadn't been anybody to ask. And the few times when he'd really had no choice, appearing weak or placing his trust in others had only made matters worse. Now, though....

Jack thought about the previous night's dinner conversation, the compromise he and Gareth had agreed on. It was hard to ignore a lifetime's worth of lessons, but he owed it to Gareth to at least give this a try.

"Don?" Jack waited until the Scot looked up. "Some... shit... just happened."

Frazer's eyes went wide for an instant. He was smart enough not to ask. Instead he waved his tablet at the trace flashing on Jack's screen. "Shoot it here. I'll carry on while you go fix your shit."

Gareth sat where Jack had left him an hour before, scrutinising a set of blueprints. He looked up as soon as Jack darkened his doorway. "What happened to today, tomorrow, and the day after that?" he queried with a smile.

Jack shook his head once. All levity vanished from Gareth's mien, and he waved for Jack to come in and shut the door.

"I may need some—" Jack drew a deep breath and, soldiered on stubbornly. "—help. Somebody just tried to abduct the boys."

"Tried."

"Yeah. Baxter got there. He wants me."

"'Course he does," Gareth growled and ignored the eyebrow Jack raised for clarification.

"I need a safe place to stash the boys until they're stable. Then they need to disappear."

Gareth's brows drew together. "Call Lisa?"

Jack hesitated on yet another choice. He shook his head. "Not safe." He stepped closer to the desk and dropped his voice a notch. "He found them within a week, Gareth."

"London only has so many hospitals."

"It's… not the first time," Jack elaborated.

*Oh.*

Having a lover with a military background saved time and lengthy explanations. As soon as he realised what Jack implied, Gareth was coiled for action, and his mind was racing. When he made a decision, it showed in his eyes, the deep amber lightening to molten gold.

"Let me make a call. Get what you need, and meet me at the car?"

Jack took a deep breath and—once more—decided to give trusting Gareth (and not insisting on all the details up front) a try. He nodded, turned, and strode to the door.

"And, Jack?"

"Yes?"

"Thank you."

———— ♦ ♦ ♦ ————

"Baxter. It's Jack."

It was Jack's voice, and the patterned knock came a moment later. Clive heaved a sigh as he pushed out of the seat by the window. To his surprise Jack was not alone. Gareth Flynn slipped into the room behind Jack and promptly turned to lock the door.

"You okay?" Jack barely waited for Clive's nod before he strode across the room and stopped in front of the bed that was Daniel and Nico's refuge.

"Are you two hurt?" he asked urgently.

Clive had hoped the two boys would talk to Jack. He'd not expected Nico to launch himself at Jack as soon as Jack stepped close to the high bed, wrap his arms around Jack's waist, and bury his face in Jack's chest.

This was new.

He'd watched the boys cling to each other, but they shied away from all other physical contact. Even the nurses explained first and then asked permission before touching either boy.

Nico's throwing himself at Jack with such abandon was a shocking sight. He was the more stoic of the duo, and he was coming apart in front of Clive's eyes.

"I stabbed him," Nico whispered over and over, his body shaking. "He was going to hurt Daniel, and I stabbed him."

Jack put an arm around Nico's shoulders and held him. He bowed his head and murmured words too low for Clive to make out. A moment later Daniel touched Jack's other arm and, without letting go of Nico, Jack joined the two boys on the bed.

"You with me?" Gareth Flynn waved a hand in front of Clive's face. "What happened?"

"Two men," Clive summed up. "Came up while I was getting drinks and attacked the officers standing guard. One made it inside to Nico and Daniel. Looks like Nico had a knife and stabbed him. They both hightailed it out of here when I yelled."

Baxter scrubbed a hand through his blond hair until it stood up in a worried shock. "This isn't making sense," he said, frustrated. "There was no way I could have taken them both."

"Jack intimated that something like this has... happened before?"

Gareth's voice was pitched low enough not to carry to the uniformed officers sitting against the wall. They'd gone along with Baxter's claim that he'd called in the assault, but they wouldn't be too cooperative if left out.

Clive considered Gareth Flynn before moving his gaze towards the officers. Without a word they both turned and reformed as a foursome on the other side of the room.

"I think this was too easy," Baxter said, feeling awkward. To his total surprise, the older of the uniformed officers nodded.

"Can't agree more. Reminds me of that case last year."

Baxter stared. "You were on that one?"

"On the team that found the other children once Horwood provided the details. I've been on the force for a long time, but I've never seen anyone so pissed off." He turned his head and watched Jack from the corner of his eyes. "He looks better today."

That couldn't be argued. Jack's voice was soft as he focussed on calming Nico and Daniel, his body loose and his movements gentle. The image was far removed from the tight-faced, blood-spattered agent who'd come barging into the deserted club yelling directions into a phone before going on to smash every bottle in the place.

Clive considered the broad-shouldered man who seemed to be guarding Jack's back. Was he the reason Jack was different? Or had Jack become a different person months earlier, with the kidnap case that prompted his career change?

"Don't look at me as if I know what you're all talking about," Gareth said when Baxter raised an eyebrow in question. "I served with him. Now he's working for me. I have no idea what he did in between."

"You're full of shit," Baxter decided after one look at the tiny smirk that curved Gareth Flynn's full lips.

"If you say so."

━━━━◆◆◆━━━━

Jack had seen the disbelief on Baxter's face when Nico lunged at him, but he ignored it. He had tried to explain, in the past, why teenagers like Nico and

Daniel responded to him while ignoring Baxter or even Gillian Kent, who was one of the gentlest, most emphatic women he'd ever known.

Clive had listened to Jack's careful words, but he'd never gotten it. He continued to question and demand responses. He let his frustration show, both in his face and his movements. Worst of all, though, Clive Baxter showed his disgust. The children had no way of knowing that Clive's disgust was directed at the perpetrators—or maybe himself for having been unable to remove the threat in time. They only saw disgust, and since they'd been told they were *filth* and *worthless* and *nothing*, they believed that Clive was disgusted with them.

Clive Baxter would never understand that.

Jack tightened his arms around Nico, who was shaking so hard his teeth rattled.

"I stabbed him," Nico repeated over and over. "He tried to take Daniel, and I stabbed him."

"Nico, listen to me." Jack's soft voice cut across Nico's litany. The boy wasn't hearing him right now, but hopefully some of his words would sink in, to resurface later when the nightmares came calling. "If you hadn't stabbed him, then Daniel would be gone. You wouldn't ever see him again."

He smiled at Daniel, who rubbed Nico's back with one hand and held on to Jack's sleeve with the other.

"Remember what I told you. The first rule of survival is sticking together. Holding on to each other doesn't make you weak. You can't put your arms around a memory, remember?"

He said it over and over, voice quiet and gentle and full of conviction. He'd repeat it all night if needed, the reassuring tone never slipping while his mind processed at a million miles an hour.

He made lists of people who had known where the boys were, lists of people who might have connections to the pimp… and he planned how to chase them.

Every now and then he thought about Gareth's promise to find a safe place for Nico and Daniel. Whenever his thoughts strayed that way, he pulled them back.

He'd made his choice.

He was trusting Gareth with the arrangements.

It was almost an hour later when Jack's phone buzzed. The caller display was blank, and Jack put the phone to his ear with a frown. "Horwood."

"Hey," Rafael Gallant greeted before Jack was able to draw breath to ask who was calling. "Your boss called my boss for help with hiding the boys."

"Lisa?"

Gallant scoffed. "No. The other one. We have a safe house set up, and I've handpicked the guards. You and Baxter can move in if you want, but I'd not recommend it, just in case someone's keeping tabs on you."

Jack wrapped his arm tighter around the shivering boy in his lap. Nico's breath came fast and shallow. He clutched his knife and clung to Jack like a drowning man clings to a lifeline.

No way would Jack be able to leave him with strangers right now.

"Yeah, no," Jack said into his phone. "Baxter and the two uniforms need to see a doctor. The four of us are ready to move."

"I'm right on that." Raf's cheerful growl reached his ear a moment later. "See you in five."

# SAFE HOUSE

———◆◆◆———

The house Raf Gallant took them to was in no way remarkable. Like hundreds of other properties in Golders Green, it sat on a small plot composed of a driveway and patch of grass out front and a small garden in the rear.

Jack noted bricks, tile, a double garage, and a few late roses around the front door and guessed at four bedrooms, maybe five if the developers had been greedy.

At first glance it looked as if they had been. All the properties were detached but crammed so close to one another that Jack could have jumped from roof to roof without straining himself. The small back garden was no doubt overlooked by the neighbours.

He had to keep that in mind. He had plans for the boys that included fresh air and sunshine, but not at the cost of their safety.

He slid forwards on the seat as Raf opened the rear

passenger door.

"Come on, guys, we're here," he coaxed, keeping his arm around Nico and a hand on Daniel's elbow as the boys climbed out of the car.

The worst of the shivers had passed during the journey, but Nico had yet to let go of Jack. They settled on the large double bed in the master bedroom, Jack's back to the headboard and Nico's head in his lap. Daniel slid close on Jack's other side and pulled Jack's arm around himself.

Jack gazed down at the two teenagers in something close to wonder. That the two were willing to come to him for comfort when he wasn't just a stranger but also a man who could easily overpower them….

He wrapped his arms around the two and sighed, anticipating that the next few days would be harder than he'd expected. Much harder.

"What happened to you?"

For a heartbeat or two, Jack's thoughts turned to the intercom. They hadn't discussed it, but Raf wasn't a newbie at this game. He and his team would be recording every word the boys spoke in the hope of learning details of their ordeal without having to ask.

They would hear what Jack had to say too, and Jack was suddenly very aware of Gareth's presence only a few rooms away.

But then Daniel looked up at him from deep blue

eyes full of fear, and all thoughts of embarrassment faded.

"What happened to me? My mother." He hugged the boys closer. "She turned tricks for drugs. One day she sold me to her pimp for a fix."

Nico's gasp was loud in the quiet room, but it was Daniel's response that caught Jack's attention. The blond boy merely nodded and burrowed closer against Jack's side.

"Daniel's dad did almost the same when he found out Daniel wasn't his," Nico confided.

"He wasn't… kind, was he?" Daniel asked, voice muffled by Jack's sleeve.

"He was a rat bastard," Jack replied. He did not intend to share the details of his months of imprisonment, but Daniel surprised him once more.

"Were you caned to make you submit?"

The medical report had noted extensive scarring on the boys' backs and thighs. Even stripes, laid deliberately by a man with skill, with control and precision—who was a dead man walking if Jack had any say in the matter.

Jack had been luckier, in that way at least. The pimp who had owned him liked to hit, but he hadn't wanted to mark his youngest and prettiest toy too badly or damage him permanently.

"Yeah. Sometimes, that was the easy way out."

Nico nodded, and his grip on Jack grew painfully tight.

Of the two, Nico had taken more of the beatings. The boy's lower back was a fearsome mess of scars upon scars, and the doctors were worried that his back would give him trouble as he grew. Jack rubbed softly over the rough skin on Nico's wrists and felt the shudder that ran through the teenager.

Jack wasn't that worried about Nico's recovery. Nico had drawn strength from Daniel and comfort from his ability to protect the other teen. He'd fought when it counted while Daniel disappeared into his mind when he couldn't handle reality. Daniel would be the one battling nightmares and flashbacks, the one who woke up screaming.

"Did he rent you out to other men?" It wasn't a question as such, merely a confirmation of facts.

"Yes. One of the men carried a knife. I'm not sure why, but I took it. And I got away," he said, skimping on the details. His fingers tunnelled through Nico's dark curls, moved to soothe. "I know you were scared today, Nico, but you did good. Really good. Clive wouldn't have got to you in time if you hadn't stood up to the bastard."

"I hurt him."

"Yes."

"Will I get in trouble?"

"No, but he will." Jack didn't mind that both boys could hear the promise in his voice.

"What happened after you got away? Did you go home?"

It had never occurred to Jack to go back to live with his mother, odd as that seemed. "I lived on the streets for a while. Then I met a man called Rio. I was squatting in his basement, and he caught me."

"Was he angry?"

"No. Rio was the best thing that could have happened to me. He let me stay at his house, he taught me about computers… and he never once asked me questions I had no answers to."

"The pimp who had you… where is he now?"

"Dead. Just like my mother."

"Did you kill him?"

Jack huffed a laugh and shook his head, the familiar feeling of regret in his heart. "I only helped to put him away. He died in prison."

━━━━◆◆◆━━━━

Gareth lounged on the sofa in the living room, head against the cushions. The intercom Raf had installed was top-of-the-line. Every sound from the master bedroom came through with utter clarity including Jack's voice, soft and at odds with the horrors he discussed with Nico and Daniel.

Gareth closed his eyes against a sudden burn and swallowed hard to dislodge the lump in his throat. He'd learned more about Jack in the last ten days than he had in the ten years before, and it scared the shit out of him.

He'd had Jack under his command for five years, and he'd barely caught a glimpse of what lay beneath that enticing surface.

The more he found out about Jack's past, the more he wondered how Jack had grown up even remotely sane, though some of Jack's more unexpected reactions now made sense. How he wouldn't sleep unless he was in a defensible position. His issues with restraints of any kind. The stubborn need to do everything himself and the need to help everyone who asked—and those who didn't. The long silences, and the way he lost himself in his work to the exclusion of even food and sleep.

Just hearing Jack fight to give Daniel and Nico new hope changed everything Gareth thought he knew about Jack Horwood.

A soft touch on his arm startled him from his reverie. Gareth opened his eyes and took the mug of tea his mother held out to him with a grateful sigh.

"He's the one," she stated as she settled into the nearest armchair with her own mug of tea. "Jack

Horwood. He's the one. Right?"

Gareth answered with a half nod, half shrug and a tiny smile. "It's complicated."

"It will get worse. He'll feel fifty shades of awkward tomorrow, knowing you've heard all that."

"You don't even know him."

"I've been listening," his mother disagreed, relaxing as if she'd spent the last twenty-five years in this house, rather than the last two hours. "He's cutting his heart out to help those boys, and he didn't strike me as the sort who likes to show off his scars."

"Definitely not," Gareth scoffed. "I had him for five years, and I had no idea."

"And that bothers you."

"Yes, it bothers me. A lot."

He'd always thought that Jack was special. Now he was sure. Jack had not only gotten out of a hell not of his devising, he had then turned himself into someone who cared for others, almost to the exclusion of his own safety.

Alex Marston had briefed him about the last case Jack had been involved in, where a diplomat and his family had been kidnapped. Jack had hated the political manoeuvring and deal making that had gone on behind the scenes while the victims' lives hung in the balance. He'd shown remarkable patience with all the shifting and meddling around him, but in the end, he'd ignored protocols and policies in favour of freeing the kidnapped family. Then he'd tendered his resignation, right there in the hospital corridor.

The style of narrative had made it clear that Alexandra didn't just condone Jack's actions. She approved. Knowing how hard it was to gain her approval told him that he'd heard maybe a third of the whole story. If that.

"He's bound to want to stay here, isn't he?" Gareth mused, work schedules, leaks, and missing data bouncing around in his mind.

His mother's smile was soft. She'd fostered troubled teens for years and always stepped in to help when there was need. Strange to think that Jack Horwood would find a kindred spirit in his mother.

"I would imagine so. He makes those two feel safe. It's important that he keeps his promises, at least until they're settled."

"I'd better go and get him his laptop. That way we can talk, and he has the option to work if he wants to."

"He has lots of work to do?"

Gareth nodded, thinking of the conversation he'd had with Jack just before lunch. "An awful lot," he admitted. "Time-sensitive stuff, and tasks I can't farm out."

He knew he sounded plaintive and frustrated. It

was a good thing that his mother knew him too well to tease. And she always understood more than she was told.

"I'll make sure he gets time to himself," she said, before Gareth closed the door on the way out.

——————◆ ◆ ◆——————

Dinner had been a palaver with Daniel and Nico too agitated to even look at food without throwing up, and Jack starving after missing lunch.

For once he'd appreciated Gareth's need to feed and coddle him. Without the gigantic breakfast and the hot, sweet coffee the man had plied him and Frazer with during the morning, Jack would have been nursing a migraine of epic proportions. Instead, he just had to tune out a moderate headache while pondering how to get out of the room long enough to talk to Gareth.

Daniel and Nico were fast asleep, but even in sleep, they clung to him like limpets. Jack growled when he realised that he wouldn't be able to extricate himself without waking them.

He understood that he was Daniel and Nico's lifeline, that they trusted no one, and that his presence reassured them. Still, getting the two to take a shower before going to bed had been hilarious, with both boys vacillating between teenage awkwardness when using the toilet and shower and their need to keep him close at all times.

Jack had lived on the streets. He'd served in the army. He wasn't fussed by watching another guy take a piss. What bothered him was that he couldn't tease the two about it. They just weren't ready for it yet.

Neither could he hole up in this bedroom forever. He needed to talk to Gareth, so best get this done as quickly as possible.

He loosened the tight grip both boys had on his sleeves, slid down the bed, and was off the mattress before the two were properly awake.

"I need to go to the bathroom," Jack informed the two bleary-eyed kids in his calmest voice before they had a chance to scramble up and grab hold of him again. "And I need to talk to Gareth."

"Why?"

"He's my boss. He's expecting me at work tomorrow morning."

"Tomorrow is Saturday," Daniel protested, eyes wide and alarmed. "And you said you won't leave us here alone."

"Which is why I need to talk to him. Now, can you let me go for a few minutes? I'll just be on the other side of the door talking to Gareth. Rafael and his men are watching the garden, so nobody will come through the windows."

Huge frightened eyes followed him as he made his way across the room to check the locks on the window, and the only thing Jack's memory could think to torture him with in that moment was the morning he had said good-bye to Gareth as he was leaving the base for the very last time.

It had been early, bright and cold, and Gareth had been standing in a beam of sunshine, lit up in gold and silver. Despite the angry words of the night before, he'd been there at the gate, waiting to bid Jack good-bye as Jack had known he would. Gareth had wrapped him up in a bone-crushing hug and walking away from everything he'd ever wanted had hurt like a bitch.

He'd been scared back then, but that fear had been of his own choosing. He'd not been as terrified as Daniel and Nico were right now, but he understood that fear too, and he knew how to allay it.

"The windows are locked," he said, hand on the door handle. "Lock the door after me. Don't open until you hear my voice."

He stepped out and kept his hand on the door until he heard the lock engage.

"I won't be long," he said, comfortingly, before he turned around.

The light on the landing was on and, of course, Gareth waited for him. He leaned against the wall, feet planted and head back, and Jack searched in vain for any sign of tension.

"Hey," he sighed, and stepped closer.

"Hey yourself. You okay?"

Jack nodded. The warm palm that curled around his neck and pulled him close came as a surprise. For a heartbeat he stood stiff and unmoving, waiting for Gareth's voice. But there were no questions and no recriminations, and Jack relaxed. He wound his arms around Gareth's waist and let himself lean.

"Are you okay?"

Jack nodded again, not moving from where his forehead rested against Gareth's shoulder. He had buried his past so deeply that digging it up left him feeling hollow. Jack didn't give a shit what other people thought of him. But seeing pity or disgust in Gareth's face would kill him. So he did the one thing that made sense. He didn't look.

"And the boys?"

"Scared stupid," he mumbled. "Nico's fine, mostly. Daniel will wake up screaming."

"You gonna stay here with them?"

Gareth's voice was carefully neutral, but Jack

straightened anyway and stepped out of his hold, noting how bereft and cold he felt without Gareth's arms around him. He put the width of the hallway between them before he looked up, wondering what to say.

He needed to stay here. He had become the person Nico and Daniel relied on. He had to stay until the two had grown comfortable with.... Then it hit him: the one bit of information he'd heard and filed away and not paid any attention to.

"Your mother," he said in a hoarse whisper.

Gareth looked like a smug cat, his amber eyes shining gold in the reflected light. "Good to see you're with the program, Horwood."

"Oh, fuck you!" Jack's reply lacked force. He slumped against the wall and closed his eyes. Gareth was beside him in an instant, and Jack didn't resist the palm that cupped his cheek or the soft touch of lips that brushed over his eyelids, cheekbones, and jaw.

"Of course, you're gonna stay here," Gareth breathed between kisses. "I asked Frazer to send over a tablet, but he says you'll need a laptop, and apparently you own half a dozen. So which one do you need, and is there anything else he should pack?"

Jack opened his eyes and stared at Gareth. He could find nothing but concern in the intent gaze.

No anger, no frustration.

Certainly no pity.

A wave of calm washed over him. The kind of calm he would need to help two scared boys through their nightmares and interrogate them without them noticing.

"Can I have the big Dell, the tablet, and the go bag from my locker?" He reached up to the hand that still touched his face and wrapped his fingers around Gareth's wrist. The strong pulse beating there was reassuring, as was Gareth's warmth. Maybe they really had a chance to make this work. "Ask Frazer to set up high-level access protocols for the Dell. Just to be safe."

"You're expecting trouble?"

Jack shook his head once, then shrugged. "If Raf is dirty or one of his men runs his mouth."

"Or I do, or my mum does… yeah, yeah."

"You asked."

"I know." Gareth pushed away from the wall. His hand slipped from Jack's cheek. "Your stuff will be here when you wake. Try not to work around the clock, okay?" He turned to leave, but Jack held him back.

"Wait." Jack wrapped his arms around Gareth's neck and leaned close. "Thank you," he said, a moment before his lips touched Gareth's.

# SECOND TIME RIGHT

---

T hursday had rolled around by the time Jack returned to his desk at Nancarrow Mining. He didn't regret the time spent with Daniel and Nico—the two now had ways to deal with their nightmares and were learning ways to deal with attackers—and he had picked up information that brought him closer to locating the pimp.

Thanks to Gareth's foresight, Jack had been able to work on both tracing the pimp and his day job. Being out of the safe house and back at his desk was nice too. Especially when the people around him made him feel as if he'd been missed.

He'd barely made it to his desk when Aidan Conrad dragged him to the dojo for a sparring session that left his body sore all over, his muscles like jelly, and his brain humming contentedly. A big breakfast came next, and he had just settled in front of his screens with a huge mug of coffee when Frazer rolled

296

up to discuss a Trojan he'd designed to trace the leaked data. And that thing was so elegant it left Jack wondering if the Scot would be up for extra money and excitement in his life.

After that, they were busy plotting and planning until a text flashed up on his computer screen just before lunch.

*Fancy dinner at my place?*

While he'd been on babysitting duty, Gareth had taken to texting him. At first just a simple check-in every few hours, then the odd question, until they had spent the small hours in silent conversation while Jack stood guard in the sleeping house. Now it looked as if Jack's being back at work wasn't going to change that.

*Sounds good. Need to pop home first. Feed the dog.*

*You don't have a dog.*

*Same difference.*

The next message took its time coming, suggesting that Gareth was rolling his eyes. Or trying to decipher Horwood code.

*Anything you want for dinner?* Gareth asked after a time.

*I'm easy.*

*I know, but that wasn't the question.*

Jack grinned, excited by the prospect of having dinner with Gareth. They'd used the time apart to catch up and relearn each other, strange as that sounded. *Surprise me*, he texted back.

✦ ✦ ✦

Streetlights glowed through the thin mist like orange Christmas baubles strung up early, giving the quiet Richmond cul-de-sac an almost Victorian feel—if one ignored the cars lining kerbs and driveways, that was.

Jack parked his Gixxer beside Gareth's Triumph, blew warm breath on his freezing fingers, and berated himself for forgetting his gloves. He was relieved to find that Gareth was home, as if, at the very back of his mind, he'd expected the man to stand him up.

The porch light was on, and the enticing aromas of spices and roasting meat hung around the front door. It didn't smell like anything he could identify, and as Jack leaned on the bell, he wondered about the extent of Gareth's culinary skills.

While they'd served together, Gareth had mastered the art of one-pot cooking for a crowd, using whatever ingredients came his way. He'd had a well-deserved reputation, and their fire had always been good for tasty, filling stews and the very best curries. Jack also recalled large pans of softly scrambled eggs and even pancakes on the odd day when eggs, flour, and milk happened to coincide with time to cook breakfast.

Whatever Gareth was cooking tonight smelled homely and inviting, yet at the same time richer than the food Gareth's mother had cooked during the week Jack had been staying with her and the boys. More… decadent, somehow, and Jack's stomach growled in happy anticipation.

"I almost thought you weren't coming."

"Yeah, I can smell that you thought that." The smile on Gareth's face started butterflies in Jack's gut. He managed a smile of his own, held out the wine he'd brought, and then bent to take off his motorcycle boots. "What *is* this, anyway?"

"Goose."

"Goose?"

"Goose."

Jack looked up into amber eyes and considered. Gareth didn't seem to be pulling his leg. And technically goose was very much like duck or chicken, so why shouldn't it be edible?

"You said you didn't have any preferences, and I felt like it. It's a grown-up thing, sort of." Gareth sounded almost apologetic as he set the wine on the shoe cupboard and turned to lock the door. "You don't have a problem with eating goose, do you?"

"I'll tell you after dinner," Jack said. He set his boots down and shrugged out of his jacket, hanging it beside Gareth's. Freed from the restraints of damp leather, he wrapped his arms around Gareth's neck. "It smells damn nice. And I missed you."

"In that order?" Gareth wasn't slow returning the embrace. He nuzzled Jack's shirt collar out of the way to trace his lips along the strip of leather around Jack's throat.

"Maybe not," Jack allowed, tilting his head to give Gareth's lips more space to explore. The warmth and soft light, the scents of cooking, Gareth's hands and mouth on him, even the shivers running up his spine, all made Jack feel as if he was coming home—until a sudden alarm sent his hand flashing for a weapon.

"Dinner's ready." Gareth's warm breath against Jack's neck comforted and soothed, and he was unfazed by Jack's grab for the knife. "Good timing." He dropped a brief kiss on Jack's forehead and headed towards the kitchen. "Bring the wine?"

"My timing's crap," Jack groused, shoving the knife back into its sheath and picking up the bottles. He'd been hungry when he arrived, but now his body didn't want goose. It wanted Gareth. And it was anyone's guess when he was going to get that.

❖ ❖ ❖

Jack's sudden grumpy mood didn't last. Not once he stepped into the kitchen and caught sight of Gareth lifting a roasting tray from the warming oven. After the chilly grey mist outside, Gareth's kitchen was a haven of warmth, wonderful aromas, and soft music. Not a place to stay grumpy.

"We're eating in here?"

Jack waved at the large farmhouse table, where plates and silverware sat next to bottles of water and outsized wine glasses.

"Didn't feel like setting a fire. Do you mind?"

"Nope." Jack leaned his head back and took a deep breath. "That smells heavenly." His stomach agreed, loudly and insistently. "Anything I can do?"

"Wine."

Jack found the corkscrew and got busy while Gareth carved the goose and placed laden dishes on the table. In no time at all, they sat facing each other and touched glasses.

Jack hunted for words to continue the quiet discussions they'd been having all week, but his brain had called a timeout. He focussed on his plate instead, consoling himself with the thought that it was rude to talk with his mouth full, and Gareth's feast deserved to be enjoyed.

"Every time I come here, you feed me," he observed when his plate was half-empty, not needing to look up to know that Gareth's eyebrow was shooting up.

"That a complaint?"

"Nah. Is this pineapple?"

"Yes."

"And it's purple because?"

"Red cabbage bleeds when it cooks."

"So, why do you feed me every time I'm here?"

"Because it's polite. Because you need food. Because I like cooking for people. Take your pick." Gareth reached for the wine and topped up their glasses, and Jack frowned at the mashed potatoes on his plate until Gareth took pity on him and asked about Nico and Daniel.

"You'd never guess that Nico's the younger of the two," Jack said, after he'd told Gareth of his suspicion that the pimp had been keeping more than just Ricky, Daniel, and Nico locked up. "Nico deals with all that crap head-on. Daniel's the tricky one. He's scared shitless, and he hides."

"Have you noticed how unbelievably quiet those two are?"

Jack shrugged, not looking up. "Yeah."

He didn't want to remember, but the memories of Nico clinging to him in the darkness reliving his nightmare were hard to repress. Nico had confided that he'd always tried to keep silent when he was being punished, even though both Daniel and Ricky had repeatedly told him that this was the worst possible course of action. Jack had stayed out of that argument, merely hugging the youngster close and murmuring soothing nonsense. He couldn't just sympathise, though. He'd been like Nico, never giving anyone the satisfaction of hearing him scream even if he made matters worse for himself. And when reaching for a little comfort incurred painful punishment, the ability to stay silent was just another bonus. Nico understood that better than most.

"Jack?"

A hand cupped his cheek, and Jack looked up in confusion. Gareth's gaze was full of concern. "What?"

"Where did you go? You zoned out on me."

Jack blinked. "Sorry," he apologised, leaning into Gareth's palm and enjoying the warmth. "The first few days Daniel barely got any rest between his nightmares. Nico only had a single one the whole week, but I…." He shrugged and drew away, suddenly unwilling to explain.

"Will you see them tomorrow?"

Jack nodded. "It got a bit rough this afternoon," he confided, unsure of his motivation. He wasn't looking for sympathy, and he didn't need Gareth to tell him that he was doing the right thing.

"First night alone, eh?"

"They're not alone. Your mum's with them. And Raf has the night shift."

"'S not what I meant."

Jack twirled the stem of his wineglass and let himself be comforted by warmth and the ruby flashes the kitchen lights sparked in the Merlot's inky depths. "I know."

———◆◆◆———

"You're a damned tease, brat, you know that?"

The flush on Gareth's cheeks looked so inviting that Jack hunted for another incendiary comment, just to see it deepen. He wasn't accustomed to feeling at home anywhere, but he enjoyed it and let himself be reminded of the years he spent serving alongside Gareth Flynn. The crazy discussion—and Gareth pretending to take offence at his words—just fit right in.

"Don't insult me," he purred, making sure he peeked through his lashes, and the light hit the tattoo on his temple just right. "I don't tease. I put out."

"I remember," Gareth growled. "And I can't fucking wait for you to do it again."

All air left the room the moment Gareth's eyes locked with Jack's in a gaze so full of heat that Jack could no longer breathe. Never mind teasing. His mouth went dry, and he shivered, not caring what he was giving away. All he could think about was how he'd bitten his lips and held back a scream as Gareth had made him come.

There had been surprisingly little dirty talk in their late-night meanderings during the previous week, though they had discussed, briefly, the night they'd spent together. Long enough for Jack to understand how much Gareth relished calling the shots… and for Jack to admit how surprised he still was that he'd handed over control so easily.

Gareth hadn't asked any questions. He'd just listened to Jack's halting words until Jack had got it all out and moved on to other topics.

The man was good at that, waiting for others to sort out what they wanted to share or didn't, and Jack appreciated it just as he used to back when. Gareth had never pushed for answers that Jack was determined to keep to himself, so how they had arrived at playing twenty questions was a mystery to Jack.

"Come on, brat. Answer the question."

Jack stared at the dishcloth in his lap. He sat on the wide kitchen island polishing glasses while Gareth loaded the dishwasher with the other dishes. "I had no idea crystal glasses had to be washed by hand," he deflected.

"The other question," Gareth insisted.

"Stiletto," Jack admitted eventually. "Laptop," he

added when Gareth gave him a disbelieving look.

"You'd brain someone with your favourite toy?"

"Don't be an arse."

"Fine. Explain it, then. I asked for your favourite weapons. I get the stiletto, even though I think it's poncy. But what damage can you possibly do with a laptop?"

Jack reached for the last dripping glass Gareth held out. Slowly and methodically, he started rubbing cloth over crystal. "Imagine you wake up one morning to find your electricity, phone, broadband, and gas disconnected," he began after a moment. "Your mobile phone doesn't work, either. You eventually locate a phone to call your bank, but they have no records for either you or your accounts. Neither does the phone company, any of the utilities providers, or your local council. Your employer has no record of you and neither does the tax office. Someone else's name is on the title deeds to your home, and you are accused of squatting. Your car keys don't open your car. Your credit cards aren't accepted anywhere. If you manage to make it to the airport, your passport and driving license are considered forgeries that get you arrested." Jack straightened and set the glass down. "How would you prove you're you if, bureaucratically speaking, you don't exist?"

The chill in Gareth's eyes told Jack when Gareth

got it.

"You think of hacking in terms of intel, of information," he expanded. "And for much of the time, you'd be right. But tracing and redirecting information isn't the only thing I can do. Changing information—for good or evil—isn't any more difficult than finding it. And I'm in charge of a delete key too."

Gareth stared at him for a long time. Then he crossed the kitchen to retrieve a bottle of Armagnac and two snifters. "That's hypothetical, right?" he asked as he filled the glasses and handed one of them to Jack. "When you said the boys needed to disappear you didn't mean…."

"No, I wasn't talking about taking them out of the system. The opposite, actually. I was thinking of building them backgrounds so tight, not even social services will find a chink to exploit."

"Will they even try?"

"Yeah, they will. There's usually an overzealous soul or two, and they get into it right when they should leave well alone. And the pimp is bound to have contacts."

"In social services?"

Jack slid off the counter, careful of the amber liquid in his glass. "You didn't just ask me that," he accused.

"I did, though," Gareth defended himself. "My army career hasn't exactly exposed me to prostitution or trafficking. That night in the club was as close as I've ever been to a pimp."

"That you know of."

Gareth looked startled, but then he nodded in agreement. "That I know of." He picked up his glass and touched it to Jack's with a soft, musical clink. "Your turn."

Frontal assault wasn't Jack's preferred MO. He did most of his work in the shadows. But he didn't like answering questions, and his body had distinct ideas about how it wanted the rest of the evening to go, so he simply asked the question that was on his mind, hoping that Gareth would take the hint. "Favourite fantasy?"

"Besides you in nothing but a towel with that strip of leather around your throat?" Gareth made a show of considering the question seriously. "Scarlett Johansson. In heels and a towel. And red hair."

"You're a Black Widow fan, really?" Jack couldn't have explained why he found that thought amusing. He only knew that he did.

"Sorta. Halle Berry gets my vote, too."

"Okay… that's starting to make sense." Jack took another sip of the smoky, fruity Armagnac. "Your turn."

"Least favourite position?"

Jack didn't think and didn't filter. "Facedown on the bed. On anything flat, actually."

"Does that mean I can bend you over the dinner table?"

Gareth's suggestion short-circuited any and all bad memories, leaving nothing but heat. "Yeah," he said, setting the snifter down and leaning towards his lover. "I can get on board with that. What about you?"

The simple question produced a visible shiver that Jack found incredibly sexy.

"In that scenario? I actually like facedown on the bed if you're up for it, though…."

"Yes?"

"I'm very patient when I'm in control. When I'm not then… not so much."

"Figures," Jack drawled. "So what, you want me to see how quickly I can get you off or how long I can make you beg?"

"You'd better be able to back that up, brat. Or I *will* bend you over the dinner table."

"Did I say that you can't?" Jack walked backwards out of the kitchen, pulling Gareth with him towards the stairs. "But I'm not going to refuse your offer. In fact, I'm taking you up on it right now."

Gareth stopped them before they reached the bottom stair, pulled Jack close, and crushed their lips together for a brutal, hungry kiss flavoured with passion and a hint of fine, smooth alcohol. "Eager, much?" he rasped as they parted.

"You got a problem with that?" Jack slid his hands under Gareth's shirt and shoved it upwards on his way to take it off, right there in the hallway.

"Not likely."

"Shower," Jack ordered as soon as they made it upstairs. "I want that spicy soap of yours over every inch of you."

Ever since he'd woken beside Gareth for the first time, the spicy scent had been driving him crazy. By itself—as a bar of soap or an aftershave—it smelled pretty decent, but mixed with Gareth's warm male scent it was nothing short of fucking fantastic. It was different from the green citrus notes he chose for himself, reminded him of fir trees baking in late summer heat, their resinous bitterness tempered with the spice of cinnamon, orange, and leather. Jack only needed to catch a tiny whiff to imagine Gareth cooking or to think of mulled wine shared in front of a blazing log fire, of a place to hide out when the world closed in on him. And it was sexy as all get-out to boot.

Jack wrapped his arms around Gareth's waist and ground himself against his lover's soapy backside while the hot water slid down Gareth's skin. "Do you have any idea how much I just want to…."

"Am I stopping you?"

Jack didn't mind admitting how turned on he was. His other thoughts were harder to voice, and he laughed, a little embarrassed. "I wanna do you how you like it, on the bed. Still—" He drew back a little and pulled on Gareth's arms to turn him around. "Doesn't mean that I can't do this," he said as he slowly slid to his knees while his lips traced a trail from Gareth's neck to his groin.

"Jesus, Jack," Gareth growled as teeth scraped gently just below his navel, and a hard grip dug into his hip. "Are you trying to kill me?"

"You were the one who told me he wasn't patient," Jack murmured. "Just taking care of that for you."

Besides, Jack wanted this, wanted to taste his lover, drive him insane and listen to him moan. It was only fair, seeing what Gareth had done to him the last two nights they'd spent together. Not to mention that Gareth had a cock that just begged to be sucked.

Jack went to town, laving and teasing and not caring that he struggled to breathe under the incessant stream of hot water or that Gareth's hands in his hair were almost painful. Gareth was so deliciously responsive that Jack's blood heated at an alarming rate, but Jack held tightly to his control. He knew where he wanted this encounter to end, but if there was even a chance that this might not be a one-time thing, he wanted to make sure that he knew exactly how to make Gareth squirm and lose his mind.

He counted it as a victory when he took Gareth to the back of his throat and made him spill without losing his focus… or his mind, though he was sure he'd be hearing Gareth's throaty growls in his dreams for the next month at least.

When Gareth yanked him upright, he went willingly, and they kissed under the stream of hot water until the lack of air and acres of Gareth's soft skin under his palm made Jack fear for his sanity. He marshalled his last few working brain cells into marching order and pulled away.

"You ready for the facedown on the bed bit?"

# HIDDEN IN PLAIN SIGHT

◆◆◆

From his desk Jack had an exceptional view across the river. Maybe Gareth had hoped, when he chose Jack's desk, that watching boats and barges plying their trade would relax Jack and keep him focussed. Jack didn't know and hadn't bothered to ask.

He'd woken that morning with an irritating itch in his brain—the sort of distraction that would prompt him to work from home or at the very least take the train to Waterloo rather than ride his bike.

Waking up at Gareth's place had proved useful, since Gareth was delighted to give him a lift. He knew how to read Jack too, and after taking one good look at the way he buried himself in his coffee mug, Gareth hadn't asked any questions and just made breakfast before driving them both to work.

Jack had said little all morning while he chased the elusive itch, barely aware of his desk, let alone colleagues, windows, or the view. Gold and red flashed in and out of his vision as he tossed juggling balls into the air and caught them again, his hands moving by rote. The balls were soft Moroccan leather and perfectly weighted. Jack had left his old set behind, along with his old job, and had treated himself to a new stack and a smart copper bowl to hold them. He hadn't expected to put them to use so soon after his arrival.

Rio had taught him to juggle and how to categorise problems based on the number of balls he needed to spin while he thought—introducing him to the works of Arthur Conan Doyle in the process. Right now, he already had half the balls from his bowl moving in the air over his head, and he still couldn't see a pattern in the problem his mind contemplated.

*It's not hurting us anymore.*

Gareth had neutralised the finance leak by the simple expedient of issuing two sets of figures, a clean set for the CEO and a modified set for anyone else. Any information leaving the company was bogus, and Gareth used it to obfuscate and misdirect.

Gareth had always been good at throwing others off track, and Jack approved of the tactic, though in contrast to his superiors he was more inclined to assume guilt until innocence was proved. He had substantially increased the number of bogus data sets in circulation before following the trail of the leaked data halfway around the world to end on the website of a south-coast building contractor.

The company had gone to the wall three years earlier, but the website offering the company's services was still live and being updated by someone at least once a month. The story got interesting the moment Frazer—tracing the technical leak—arrived at exactly the same website.

Jack added a ninth ball to the eight spinning in the air and then a tenth. He rested his head against the edge of his chair and focussed on the flashes of colour.

Out of the corner of his eye, he was aware of Frazer studying the coding and construction of the building company's website on three of his four screens, of Gareth stopping beside him at intervals, of Julian Nancarrow's PA placing more financial information on a corner of his desk with an apologetic smile.

His focus remained on the red and gold balls. Each flash of colour connected data points: turnover linked to employee numbers, profits to tax allowances, loans to repayments to bonuses, and back to employee numbers. The various takeover bids, amicable and hostile, that Julian Nancarrow had briefed him on the previous week found a place in the pattern, as did hacking attacks, grievance procedures, and dismissals.

A large mug of steaming black coffee appeared on

the corner of his desk. Gareth didn't linger or interrupt, and Jack caught the spinning spheres one by one and dropped them into his lap. The coffee was strong and sweet enough to rot his teeth. It reminded Jack that he'd skipped lunch and that being so well known wasn't always a bad thing. At the very least, it cut out the migraines.

When he set the empty mug back on the table, he'd decided to make time to eat in the future, rather than ruin exceptionally good coffee with sugar. He had also convinced himself that the company's finances, bogus or not, weren't causing the itch in his brain.

He picked up the juggling balls and tossed them about idly while he waited for the caffeine to jumpstart his thoughts.

The technical data then: mining, prospecting, deposits, yields, concessions, exploitation costs, mineral prices, refining operations, environmental impact studies, clean up, commodities, stock prices, coffee, commodities….

Commodities.

Jack sat up straight.

One by one, the juggling balls spiked high into the air before hitting the carpet around his feet in a soft patter.

He didn't notice.

His hands found the keyboard, and all four screens in front of him flared to life. He smiled when he heard the door to Gareth's office hit the wall with a crash and looked up.

"The problem with a photographic memory," he said when Gareth stood beside him, "is that you rarely consciously compare images."

Two of the screens in front of him showed the same page from the building company's website. At first glance, they were identical. At a second glance, though….

"The text."

"Yep." Jack nodded. "I'd say there's your finance data. Hidden in plain sight." Gareth grunted something about peas in a pod that Jack tuned out. He wasn't having that discussion today. Or ever. At least the man had the sense not to push. He just sat on the edge of Jack's desk and pulled out his phone.

"What do you need?"

"Two teams."

"Fuck this!" Frazer flew into the room he'd left only minutes earlier. He skidded to a stop behind Jack and looked over his shoulder at the screen. Jack could hear the dismay in the Scot's voice as he put the facts together. "Keywords? That's just…."

"Pull analytics, Adwords, Market Samurai, Wordtracker—any of that shit," Jack said as if he'd never been interrupted. "I don't care. Just match the numbers."

"And the second team?"

"This has been updated last night," Jack informed his superior. "And just yesterday Frazer planted a little surprise on the server hosting the site."

"Don't drag me into this, Horwood. You did the sneaking and planting of stuff."

"You designed it."

"I didn't break in, though."

"Fine, fine. And only yesterday Frazer designed a little surprise, which ended up on the server hosting the site."

"I got it, thanks," Gareth said dryly. "So Frazer determines the source, and you trace the transmission. How do we find out who the data is going to?"

"We don't." Frazer sounded defeated. "It's like a billboard at Waterloo Station. No way to tell who reads it. No way to know who understood what they read."

"Maybe," Jack commented absently, already engrossed in picking up the trail of Frazer's Trojan.

"Horwood, share!" Frazer demanded.

"That'd be the day." A voice could be heard grumbling from across the office. "The famous hacker sharing his secrets. Yeah, right."

"If you have something to say, Mason, say it to my

face," Jack replied without heat before he turned to Frazer. "You're smart. You'll figure it out." After watching the Scot work for just a few days, Jack was already convinced that Frazer paid far too much heed to jealous idiots like Mason and rarely gave himself enough credit. It was time to change that.

◆ ◆ ◆

Nobody in Nancarrow Mining's corporate security division went home that evening. Frazer dished out jobs left and right, and every person in the team pored over stacks of numbers, trying to find patterns that matched the company's finance data.

Gareth felt oddly nostalgic as he turned his office into an impromptu dorm with air beds and sleeping bags and made sure that everything from sandwiches to pizza and freshly made curry was available to soak up the seas of caffeine washing through the room before he settled down with his own stack of numbers.

Jack's desk was a haven of peace in all the to-ing and fro-ing, the muttered curses, and noisy cryptography debates that sprang up when a set of figures looked as if it might fit. He didn't join in the conversations, and neither did he theorise ahead of his data.

Jack barely moved.

He kept his hands poised over his keyboard and his eyes intent on the data on his screens.

Every now and then, he would rub the tattoo on his temple as if it helped him focus. Bursts of rapid typing alternated with long periods of nothing but watching data scroll and slide into geometric shapes, and Gareth couldn't tell from Jack's expression if Jack was anywhere near achieving his objective.

He was as methodical and patient as a hunter on the trail of a large predator.

And about as silent.

It startled everyone, therefore, when Jack suddenly jumped up, grabbed his phone and tablet, and hurried towards one of the small meeting rooms in the back. He turned and met Gareth's gaze before he slipped through the doorway, and Gareth abandoned his stack of numbers, pushed to his feet, and followed.

He should have expected Jack to have a Skype session running when he entered, but the two boys who were in his mother's care had slipped his mind.

And didn't that make him feel like a heel?

"Where are you?" Nico's voice came over the loudspeaker as he stepped up behind Jack and looked down at the small screen showing Nico and Daniel in the living room of the safe house.

"Still at work," Jack replied. "We've got a major

lead on the data thief."

There must have been a grin on Jack's face when he said that because Nico immediately leaned forwards and demanded details.

"Remember what I told you about the website?"

"You both got there. You and your colleague."

"Right. And we couldn't work out how they hid the information. Now we have."

"How?" Daniel was right alongside his friend now, head almost in the screen.

"It's a code," Jack confided. "Numbers into words. The text changes every few days, but only a little, so we had trouble spotting it. Wanna see if you can crack it? I can send you a bit of it."

"What if we don't know how? Can we ask Raf?"

Gareth leaned close enough for the camera to catch him and smiled a greeting of his own, pleased about the chance to put his hands on Jack's shoulders. "My mum's good at codes," he said. "You can ask her to help."

"No way!"

"Yes, way! When you're in the army, people read your mail, so my dad used to write in code when he wrote letters home. That's how she learned."

"You're not coming over today, are you?"

Jack shook his head.

"We did the training with Raf," Nico said after a

moment. "It was different."

"That makes sense. Every person fights differently, depending on where they grew up and who taught them. It's good if you can work with Raf."

"He's okay."

"I'll come over as soon as I've caught the thief," Jack said. "If I can't make it, I call, right?"

"Can we... call you?" Daniel's voice was barely louder than a whisper, but Jack heard.

"That's why I put my number into your phone. Call when you need to, okay?" Jack was about to sign off when Daniel leaned forwards.

"Jack?"

"Hm?"

"I didn't have a nightmare last night."

Gareth felt Jack's muscles go rigid under his hands before he breathed out a long soft gust of air and melted into the seat. He didn't reply, not with words Gareth could hear. Maybe he'd made a face at the screen, because the last thing Gareth heard before Jack signed off and the connection closed was Daniel's soft giggle. It brightened the room and relaxed Jack to the point where Gareth felt safe teasing him.

"Did you really need me as backup to deal with two wayward teens?"

Jack slid down in the chair until his head leaned against the backrest, and he looked straight up at

Gareth. "Not really," he smirked. "I just wanted to have you to myself for a minute before I head back to the zoo."

"They are rather loud."

"It's called enthusiastic. And I don't mind." He drew another deep breath and let it out, dropping his shoulders on the exhale. "Did your parents really communicate in code?"

"Yep. Mum used to teach maths, so…."

"I didn't know that."

"Are you going to send them bits of code to crack?"

Jack looked maybe a little embarrassed, but he nodded anyway. "I put something together when I realised I wasn't gonna make it over to see them."

"A distraction."

"Yes. I know they're safe, and I know it can't be helped, but it still makes me feel like shit, you know?"

"They handled it well."

"They shouldn't have to handle it at all."

Frustration peeked through the fatigue, and Gareth frowned. "Maybe you should ride over."

"I left my bike at your house," Jack reminded him as he slipped out of the chair and straightened up. His lashes painted a dark shadow on his cheeks. "It's fine. Really. We'll run with this as far as it takes us, and I'll go see them after."

"Make a better job of convincing yourself." Gareth

chuffed. "That one was pathetic."

Jack grabbed his gear and waved a finger at Gareth on the way out. "Get bent, Flynn."

By 4:00 a.m., most members of their team had stopped for a nap, leaving Gareth alone with Jack in the main office. Gareth kept himself awake through sheer force of will, sifting through stack after stack of numbers.

The right encoding continued to elude them, and it looked as if Jack's attempts at tracking the source weren't any more successful. Jack was stubbornly glued to his screens, but his shoulders were up around his ears. His chin pushed forwards, and his head tipped to the right, advertising the fact that he had a headache to anyone who knew how to read him.

"Are you close to taking a break?"

Gareth gently rubbed his palms over Jack's tight shoulders while he watched a misshapen… thing… on Jack's screen twist itself into a perfect hexagonal dodecahedron.

Jack leaned back into Gareth's touch and pointed at the screen. "See that?"

"Yes?"

"That says it's time for a break."

"Right." Gareth found every ounce of scepticism

he possessed and poured it into his voice. He didn't understand the significance of the geometric shapes, but while Jack was tired and hurting, he didn't want to ask. "Go crash," he said instead. "When do you want me to wake you?"

"Seven?" Jack pulled the top drawer open and hunted around inside it without looking down. "Do you have aspirin?"

"I thought you'd never ask."

———— ◆ ◆ ◆ ————

"What? Wait." Jack rolled off the air mattress and headed out of Gareth's office-turned-crash pad. He used his phone as a torch and moved silently so as not to disturb any of the sleepers, rubbing at his gritty eyes.

The light outside was hazy, the air full of moisture that hadn't yet decided whether to turn into mist or rain. Jack had no idea what time it was. Early enough, at any rate, that he caught the orange glow of streetlights through the murk, and he'd slept at least long enough for the aspirin to kick in and take the edge off his headache.

"Can you say that again?" he asked, closing the door behind him and drawing a deep breath.

"Clive has been stabbed." It was hard to miss the

tight, angry edge in Lisa's voice. "They found him a couple of hours ago in the alley behind the club."

"Why?"

"What do you mean why?"

"Why was he in the club? Or was he?"

"I don't know," Lisa sighed. "He was in surgery when I got here, and he's too hopped up right now to make any sense. I was hoping you knew."

"Nope. Haven't spoken to him since… I dunno…. Tuesday?"

"Where are you?"

"At work. Want me to come over?"

"No. Maybe later. Why are you at work at five o'clock on a Saturday morning?"

"I have things to do?"

"Sure," Lisa snapped. "Listen, can you meet me here later? Say, lunchtime? Clive should be awake enough to talk then."

Jack heard the pain in her voice, remembered the sudden heat in Clive's face when Lisa Tyrrell had appeared outside the club on the heels of Ricky's death, and felt like a certified asshole. He and Lisa might not know each other, but he owed Clive Baxter better than that. "I'll come over now if you want me there," he offered by way of an apology.

"You sound barely awake, Horwood."

"I *am* barely awake."

"Then go sleep, and I'll see you later."

"Okay." Jack closed the phone and shoved it into the back pocket of his jeans. Clive Baxter had gone into the club they'd had under surveillance and had ended up in an alley bleeding from a knife wound. It made no sense for the detective to do that. He had no warrant. He had little chance of getting one unless....

Jack headed to his desk, staring in distaste at the dodecahedron on the screen to his left. He hadn't expected to hit pay dirt on his first try, but it would have been useful.

He woke the remaining screens and looked at a visual that resembled a bowl of spaghetti. "For a non-existent company your website gets a fuck ton of traffic," he told the display, taken aback when his voice raised an echo in the empty space. "Let's see...." He highlighted one of the spaghetti strands and fired off a trace before he even sat down.

On the remaining two screens, he pulled up the previous night's video feed from the nightclub. The club had been busy, and the dance floor was heaving. Jack kept one eye on his trace, the other on the feed monitoring the club's doors, and mentally placed bets about which of the two would get a result first.

When the traffic trace came back empty, it was close to 6:00 a.m. Jack paused the feed, stretched, and went to brew coffee. Gareth would no doubt be up shortly, and the rest of the guys would appreciate a caffeine injection just as much.

Jack was shovelling sugar into a large mug when Gareth joined him by the coffeemaker.

"Did you sleep at all?"

"Lisa woke me an hour ago." Jack took a careful sip from his mug and sighed. Sugar spoiled even the single estate Java. It was one of the sad facts of life he'd learned over the years. "Clive's got himself stabbed."

"What?"

"He might have gone to the club last night. I haven't spotted him yet, but he was found around 3:00 a.m. in the alley behind the club, bleeding from a stab wound. He had just gotten out of surgery when Lisa called me."

"Why would he do that?"

"Yeah, just what I'm wondering. Unless he had a lead, in which case I might just not kick his arse."

"He wouldn't go follow up a lead without telling anyone."

"Wouldn't he?" Jack snorted. He watched Gareth boil the kettle to make tea and rubbed his neck a little sheepishly. Tea hadn't even occurred to him. "Ask me sometime how I met Baxter," he said and turned back towards his desk.

"Did Lisa say how he was?"

"Shot full of the good drugs. She wants to meet

with me at lunchtime."

"I can go talk to her if you want."

"Why?"

"You're busy," Gareth said slowly, considering Jack over the rim of his mug. "And you're flaming mad— even though I'm not sure why."

"If he tipped off the pimp…."

"Oh."

If Jack hadn't felt so off balance, he might have found the flush on Gareth's cheeks enticing. But all he could think of right then were six boys in small dark rooms, hearts beating like crazy while they listened for footsteps outside their doors and dreaded the sound of a key turning in the lock.

It was little more than a suspicion at that point, a few whispered words overheard when Nico thought nobody else was around. But if there was even a chance that it was true….

"I'm gonna kill him if he's screwed this up, knife wound or no," he said with deadly conviction.

"Then it's *much* better that I go see them." Gareth's voice was firm. "You keep doing your stuff. Remember that there's an emergency board meeting later this afternoon. Make sure there's network access for anyone attending, but keep it contained."

"Why on a Saturday?" Jack shook his head clear of the disturbing pictures and started to take notes.

"Julian's cousins got their knickers in a twist," Gareth replied with a negligent wave. "It's crap, anyway. Most of the department heads won't make it. Niki Desmond is covering HR. Aidan is out of town, but Alex will brief him when he's back. Gavin and Lynn—that's prospecting and mining—are at a conference and won't be back in time. Not sure if Tim Gorish is coming himself, or if he's sending someone. Paul Kendall is holding the fort for refining and ops. None of the family are execs, so keep their access to the extranet. No need to borrow trouble."

"Gorish is finance, right?" Jack scribbled on a Post-it. He frowned at the list of names. "That's hardly half the board. And I can't remember what you didn't tell me in the first place, you know?"

"You're right. I told Frazer to handle that. Julian's family is… well, combative. One of his cousins is pitching a fit and making noises about wanting to remove Julian as CEO."

"What?" That was actually funny. After realising that Gareth Flynn wasn't listed as a company director in official communications, it hadn't taken Jack long to figure out that Alexandra Marston had never left MI6.

A mining and prospecting firm was a handy cover to explore far-flung places, gather intel, and open doors that would remain firmly shut to anyone remotely associated with a secret service.

Jack doubted that Julian Nancarrow himself was an operative—the man's looks were far too memorable—but he had to be aware and supportive of Alexandra Marston's work.

Knowing that, Jack wanted to be a fly on the wall when Alex found out about his cousin threatening Julian's tenure as CEO. "Is the man suicidal?"

"Just full of shit," Gareth snorted, and then he suddenly stared at Jack as if he'd grown a second head. "You're a fucking menace, you know that?"

To which Jack merely shrugged and smirked before returning to his work.

--------◆◆◆--------

Gareth wasn't prepared to see Lisa holding Baxter's hand when he walked into Clive's hospital room, but he pushed the surprise down before it could register on his face. If Lisa thought the detective was her cup of tea, who was he to argue? He didn't have to agree, after all, and it might keep the blond of Jack's way.

"Where is Jack?" Lisa's voice was a touch sharp as she posed the question, but Gareth had known Lisa long enough to put that down to embarrassment and ignore it.

"Working," he replied and held out a cardboard

carrier with Starbucks mugs in it. "Wasn't sure if they'd let you have coffee yet, but I brought some anyway."

Baxter reached for his with a grateful sigh, and Gareth could tell when he caught the scent of cinnamon and nutmeg. "Who told you how I like my coffee?"

"Jack."

"Thank him for me."

"Knock it off. You should be thanking me on bent knee that I'm keeping Jack at work. He'd be kicking your arse right about now."

"Why?"

Gareth stared at Baxter, who looked pale but otherwise awake, and wondered how drugged up the man was. And why Lisa was letting him get away with that bullshit. "You're a fucking idiot," he sighed.

"First Jack absconds with our only witnesses and won't tell anyone where he's taken them. Then he spends all his time at work," Baxter griped, and Gareth wanted to tell him that he sounded like a petulant four-year-old. "It's like he doesn't care about getting the pimp off the street," Baxter passed judgment.

"Yeah?" Gareth recalled the conversation between Jack and the two boys he'd overheard in the safe house and held on to his temper with both hands. "If that's what you think, I wonder why you keep asking for his help," he growled, not at all mollified when Baxter had the grace to blush.

"You have to admit that it looks that way," Lisa placated.

"I have to admit shit. Jack's doing his job. Only, it's not actually *his* job, you know. You should be out there trying to find those other boys, or resting your bruised ribs, but no—you go out to attract attention and piss off our quarry. If he loses those boys, Jack will kick your arse. I guarantee that." Gareth took a deep breath that did nothing to calm him. "I might even help him."

"There are other boys?"

"Yes. Six of them."

"He hasn't said anything about that."

Gareth scoffed at the offended tone in Baxter's voice. "Pot, meet kettle. Of course, he didn't tell you. He hasn't seen you since he took the boys to the safe house. Besides, you were the one who sent him into that club with only half the story, so those hurt looks don't work on me."

"I had no evidence. Only rumours."

"Well, good morning to you too. Jack is working to substantiate the information he has before he spreads it around. Now tell me you had a good and valid reason for straying into that club without a warrant or backup."

"I had a tip that the pimp would be in the club," Baxter confided after sharing a long look with Lisa.

"From a reliable source?"

"Clearly not."

"The man wasn't there?"

"He was. I saw him go in." Clive stared at his coffee as if the dark liquid held the secrets of that fuck up of a night. "I got jumped," he finished in a quiet voice, "before I could follow the pimp."

Gareth cursed himself for not spending more time talking to Jack about Baxter. Never mind that it was anyone's guess where they would have found the time to do it. What Baxter had said didn't sound… right. The direction of his thoughts must have been easy to guess, since Lisa nodded before Gareth had time to say anything.

"I was thinking the same. We've pulled in Clive's informant. Maybe that will shed some light."

━━━━◆◆◆━━━━

"Jack?" Don Frazer's voice shook so badly that Jack was out of his chair and around the desk before the Scot had finished speaking.

It was late afternoon. Gareth was meeting with Lisa and Baxter. The Nancarrow Mining HQ lay deserted except for Don Frazer and Jack in the corporate security office and a couple of directors who were late leaving after the board meeting.

Gareth had sent everyone home after lunch. Jack hadn't budged, needing a lot more time to untangle the website traffic, and Frazer was deep into keyword data and happy as a clam, so Gareth had left them to it. The two of them had worked amicably side by side until Frazer's outburst.

"What is it?"

"Tim Gorish."

"What?"

"Tim Gorish. He's the leak."

"You're sure?"

Frazer waved at the numbers on his screen, a recent P&L statement as far as Jack could tell. Hardly something to get into a tizzy about. Added to that, the Scot didn't flap easily. Jack checked the total at the bottom of the page and recalled his matrix:

*03: Finance Department, 01: The Director.*

Shit.

Frazer was so pale the freckles across his nose looked like spatters of dried blood. He nodded, the mouse pointer tracing down the columns filled with numbers.

"I didn't get what you meant, at first," he confided. "But when I saw the data we recovered, I realised that it's easy to tell. You *made* it easy."

"*We* did." Jack debated for a moment before he placed a hand on Frazer's shoulder and squeezed, unable to offer more than that tiny bit of silent comfort. "We can rerun the figures to double check if you want," he offered.

"I did before I mentioned it. Twice." Frazer drew a deep breath and looked up. "Will you sanity check me? Just…."

"Of course." Jack reached across the desk for his laptop and pulled up a chair beside Frazer. "This part of the job is never easy," he said as he logged himself in. "Why don't you back up his access logs while I verify the numbers?"

"Could you check his laptop? He's still in the building, and you're better at…." Frazer blushed crimson, and Jack couldn't hold back a chuckle.

"Sneaking around, breaking the law, sticking my nose in where it's not wanted?"

"Wasn't meant as an insult, whatever Mason said," Frazer grunted, pink from collar to ears.

"Didn't take it as one," Jack assured him cheerfully. "I've learned how to fight dirty. You never had to. 'S not a bad thing, you know."

"What if he destroys evidence as we speak?"

Jack's fingers flew over the keyboard as he accessed Tim Gorish's laptop. "Why should he? He has no idea you've caught up to him. He also knows that we can monitor his laptop while he's here, and he'd only alert us by doing that. The most likely… oooh, yeah!" Jack chuckled as the Scot jumped up and almost tripped in his haste to look over Jack's shoulder.

"What?"

"Now why would his laptop need a second level operating system?"

"We didn't install that!" Don Frazer sounded indignant, which only served to remind Jack how young Don was, not in years—after all, Jack was only four years older—and certainly not in technical expertise, but in exposure to thieves and scumbags.

"Do you think he's gonna leave the laptop here?"

"I don't know the man," Jack commented absently, exploring the programs and data files on the machine. "Is he that stupid? Do me a favour and call the boss. I'm sure he wants to know."

"But…."

"You're not accusing anyone," Jack soothed when it dawned on him what bothered Don. "This stays between us until we confirm beyond all doubt that Gorish is the leak. But Gareth needs to know. Right away."

Frazer grabbed his phone and walked towards the windows, ears red and shoulders tense. Jack spared a thought to wonder how well Don Frazer knew the company's finance director. He himself had never cared so much about a suspect that it had bothered him to take them down, but he could imagine that it might leave him feeling dirty and off-kilter if he did.

Jack turned in his chair, giving Frazer a little more privacy and returned to his work. He didn't look up again until Gorish's laptop was suddenly shut down, and it was only then that he noticed that Frazer had left the office.

"Stupid idiot!"

Jack should have known that Frazer wouldn't do this by the book. The kid was too straight, too innocent to know that he was putting himself in harm's way.

Jack flew down the stairs, not bothering with the elevator, and almost face-planted when he caught his heel on the next to last step. He pushed through the double doors onto the floor that housed the finance department just in time to hear the jarring crash of a heavy object hitting glass. A lot of glass.

"There goes the coffee table." He crossed the deserted office, not daring to hope that it was Gorish who'd taken out the glass top with his body.

The finance director was packing. His laptop sat beside several thick manila folders, and Gorish's briefcase was full of papers. Why the man couldn't use a scanner and a handful of USB keys like a normal person Jack would never understand. A second later Gorish's motivations ceased to matter entirely, because Don Frazer lay motionless in the wreckage of the coffee table. And that was just all shades of fucked up.

Jack flanked the desk in a single leap. His fist took Gorish in the jaw the moment the man turned. The punch laid him out, and Jack didn't stop to check if Gorish's head had met something hard enough to do damage, too concerned with the motionless Scot on the carpet. He slapped the intercom on the broad desk on the way past.

"Gorish's office, now!" he barked when Alexandra Marston's voice answered the call, and then he dropped to his knees beside Frazer.

"Donald, can you hear me?" The coffee table's solid glass top hadn't broken. It had shattered into hundreds of small, sharp fragments instead. Jack pushed as much of the glass aside as he could, using his sleeves to protect his hands from the shards, then carefully turned Don onto his side, making sure he had an airway. Blood darkened the ginger hair and slowly trickled down the younger man's neck.

"Frazer, talk to me!" Jack tried again, reluctant to move Frazer more than necessary. He had nothing to stop the bleeding after clearing the glass with his shirt, so he laid his hand over the wound and pressed down.

The blood was hot against his palm, and he could feel Frazer's steady pulse with his fingertips.

"Here." A wide gauze pad appeared in his field of vision, and Jack shifted to make room for Alex Marston. "Move your hand," she instructed when she was in position, neatly placing the pad over the gash in Frazer's skull. The Scot moaned softly and stirred.

"Frazer, can you hear me?"

"My teeth hurt," Donald mumbled, the words almost too slurred to make out.

"Anything else?"

"My head?"

"I would imagine so. Can you open your eyes?"

Frazer slitted his eyes open. "'S bright," he complained.

"But you can see?"

"Yes."

"How many fingers?"

"Two."

"Good. Stay there. Don't move."

Jack looked at Alex, who considered him in that grave, careful way she had. "I can take over here," she offered after a moment.

"That would be good," Jack agreed. He had work to do, and if he stayed—and Gorish returned to consciousness—he'd do damage.

When he pushed to his feet and headed for the

door, he spotted Gareth, still in his leather jacket as if he'd just come in.

"Baxter's fine," Gareth told him, and Jack needed a moment to put it all together.

"Can you get him checked out for a concussion?" he asked, tilting his head towards Don Frazer. "He was out cold when I got here."

"What are you going to do?"

Jack snagged Gorish's laptop off the desk and turned towards the door. "I have a hot lead to follow."

<hr>

The neon strips in the ceiling flickered to life when Gareth stepped into the corporate security office. It was past 8:00 p.m., and Jack sat hunched over his keyboard in a small yellow pool of light cast by his desk lamp. His fingers moved swiftly despite the tired slump to his shoulders, and he paid little heed to the suddenly bright illumination that heralded company.

Gareth had always been impressed by Jack's capacity for work and the intense level of concentration he could maintain, even when tired. Two long days and a short night were dragging on Gareth's body and mind, and he couldn't imagine that Jack felt any livelier. But there he sat, doggedly plugging away at… whatever it was he was doing.

"Let's go home," Gareth suggested when he reached Jack's desk, not at all surprised when Jack didn't react.

"Jack."

"Got stuff to do."

"You can carry on at my place. Gorish is spending the night in the clink, and Frazer is waiting downstairs in my car. Don't make me drag you out."

Jack's busy fingers stopped their dance over the keys. "Is Frazer all right?"

"Six stitches and a tetanus shot. They don't think he has a concussion, and they were happy to send him home provided someone keeps an eye on him overnight. So, he's coming home with us. I'll make dinner, and you two can geek until you pass out. Bring his kit, will you?"

Gareth's tone had drifted towards bossy there at the end, but Jack seemed content to let it slide. He froze his screens, stowed his laptop, tablet, and phone, and then went around the desk to Frazer's side to pack a similar bag of toys for Don.

"How are you getting on?"

"Gorish's a piece of work, and you won't like what I think I'm finding," he said as they made their way out of the office.

"I won't like it regardless."

"His laptop is… very nice."

Gareth huffed a surprised laugh. That statement, coming from Jack of all people, was hilarious. He'd sounded almost dreamy. "Very nice? Really? Nice as in geek speak nice?"

"Oh, yeah. He didn't do that himself."

"How do you know?"

"I've been dissecting his files, how do you think? He doesn't have the mind for devising something so neat. Hell, even the man's VBA is clunky!"

Gareth stopped halfway down the stairs. "Where *is* Gorish's laptop?"

"In your safe. If Julian wants to press charges, the police will need it. Don't worry, I have left it as I found it, and I've documented every keystroke I made to get what I needed."

"You've done this before."

Jack rolled his eyes. "You think?"

"Actually, I didn't. You were a spook, remember?"

"I was a lot of things."

Jack's shoulders brushed Gareth's as they walked, and Gareth felt a wash of warmth at the little gesture. Despite all this mess, they were making progress.

"Daniel and Nico say hi," he said as they reached the ground floor and crossed the empty lobby to the garage entrance.

Jack went still. "You went to see them?"

"After I dropped Frazer off at the hospital, and they

said it would take a couple of hours to check him out." Gareth held the door open and waited for Jack to catch up. "They were hard at work on your code, but they spared me a minute of their valuable time."

Don Frazer was waving from the passenger seat of the Range Rover, looking surprisingly chipper after his run-in with Tim Gorish, and Jack lifted the bag to show he'd brought his gear.

"They were looking much better," Gareth concluded just as they reached the car. "More… alive."

If he hadn't kept his eyes on Jack the whole time, he would have missed Jack's grateful smile and quiet word of thanks in the flood of recriminations that started as soon as Jack climbed into the Range Rover.

"I'm sorry," Frazer blurted out.

"You're a fucking idiot!" Jack snapped while he dumped the bags on the seat and belted himself in.

"I already said I was sorry!"

"Yeah, but for the wrong things, I just bet!"

Frazer turned in his seat and looked at Jack. "Gorish hired me, Jack. I still don't believe he…."

"Nobody asked you to believe it." Gareth could tell that Jack made an effort to keep his voice even and the volume down. "We just found evidence. Evidence isn't proof. All we were doing is securing what we'd found. Now, of course, you've got a broken head, Gorish's in on assault charges, and the evidence we need to clear or convict him of fraud may very well be down the drain."

"Wish I'd recorded that little speech," Gareth commented as he manoeuvred the car out of the garage and into the traffic streaming along the Strand. "Could have played it to you, next time you go off on one of your excursions."

Jack's jaw clamped shut, and Frazer turned back around so he faced forwards.

"Was he right?" the Scot asked Gareth after a half a mile.

"Yes. Now that Gorish knows we're after him he'll wiggle like an eel."

"He couldn't have destroyed any evidence. You and Dr. Marston were in the room with him the whole time until the police came."

"He was allowed to call his lawyer from the police station," Jack pointed out from the back. "What if he said, 'Get me out of here, and while you're at it... remember that envelope I gave you a few months ago? Put it through the shredder.'"

"I didn't think of that."

"Clearly not. And I'm not really mad at you, Don. I'm mad at myself for not keeping an eye on you. How's the head?"

"Hurts, but that's all. You shouldn't *have* to keep an eye on me."

"Listen, if you sent me into a ballet studio or a restaurant kitchen, you'd have to keep an eye on *me*. I didn't say you couldn't do your job. I was saying that with a fraud investigation you were out of your element."

"I wasn't—"

"Time out," Gareth cut in. "You sound like bickering six-year-olds. Why don't you get some rest while I drive and carry on arguing once we're home? Then you"—he threw a look at Jack in the rear view mirror—"won't have to yell, and you"—a sideways look at Don Frazer—"won't have to twist your neck like an owl."

It was an ego boost for Gareth that neither of the two even tried to argue.

# CHASE

━━━◆◆◆━━━

**A**fter the productive quiet of a Sunday at Gareth's house, catching up on both work and his sleep deficit, Monday morning hit Jack like a blow to the gut.

Frazer had woken grouchy and, when questioned, had admitted to a migraine-strength headache and blurry vision. Gareth wasn't taking chances. He handed Jack a key to his front door, bundled Frazer into the car, and headed straight for the hospital, leaving Jack to tidy up and take the bike to work.

The ride restored some normality, and Nancarrow Mining's underground garage was starting to feel like a familiar place. Jack parked the Gixxer and pulled off his helmet as he walked deeper into the building, anticipating the smell of freshly roasted coffee emanating from the ground floor cafeteria.

It was early enough that he didn't have to queue. Only a few minutes later, Jack mapped out the morning's work in his head while he sipped at his cup of Java on the way up the stairs. The corporate security office lay deserted; the neon strips only flickering to life as Jack pushed the door open and stepped in.

His complacent mood blew away like smoke in a gale when he caught sight of his desk and the video feed from the nightclub frozen on two of the screens.

"Bloody hell!" The need to hit something—anything—was sudden and all consuming.

Clive was in the hospital with a stab wound.

Frazer had stitches in his head.

The pimp was in the wind, nameless and almost faceless.

The data leak at Nancarrow Mining hadn't been neutralised yet….

So why the fuck had he let Gareth talk him into going home on Saturday night?

Jack knew why, of course. Scowling, he picked up his phone and dialled Gareth's number.

"Problems?" Gareth's voice came with a background of loudspeaker announcements and excited babble.

"I forgot about Clive." It needed saying, but Jack hated it. At least Gareth knew him well enough, so he didn't have to explain any further than that.

"It's being dealt with. Clive said that he saw the pimp enter the club, so Lisa has asked Walshaw to look at the feed to see if he can spot him. They'll try and get a usable image this time." Gareth's voice was maddeningly calm and reasonable. "There's also a CCTV camera that covers the area just outside the alley where Clive was stabbed, and they're looking at that too."

"When were you gonna tell me?"

"Later today, or whenever you asked. I haven't checked in with Raf or Lisa yet today, so I have no idea whether they've found anything yet."

"Right. How's Frazer?"

"No damage as far as they can tell. They've done an MRI scan, and there's no swelling or clot. Doctor in charge thinks he's just overdone it. They'll keep him in today and tomorrow to make sure he's keeping quiet."

"Okay."

"Jack. It's not your fault. None of it."

"I know. I'll speak to you later, okay?" Gareth's assurances didn't make him feel any better. Neither did knowing that Gareth had caught the ball that Jack had dropped. Jack wasn't used to anyone picking up after him, and being a liability sucked.

"Morning."

Aidan Conrad stood in the empty office, sporting a couple of fresh bruises and looking as tired and frustrated as Jack felt. Maybe here was a way to clear his head. "You wanna spar?"

"No," he growled. "I want you to brief me on all the shit that's been going down since Friday." He waved his phone at Jack in short, jerky motions as he spoke. "Thing's been burning my ear all the way from the airport just from the messages."

"Got coffee?"

"You bet, Horwood. You bet."

<hr />

Briefing Aidan was easier, in some ways, than talking to Gareth. The lawyer was just as blunt as Gareth, but their interaction lacked the baggage of shared history and the deference that Jack struggled to shake whenever he went head-to-head with Gareth Flynn. Without any expectations on Aidan's part, Jack felt more at ease admitting mistakes.

"How do you want it?" he asked, tossing his tablet onto the table in the small meeting room and reaching for the pot of coffee that had just finished brewing. The rich smell alone was heaven, and since he'd eaten breakfast before leaving Gareth's house, he didn't have to ruin the fragrant brew with sugar.

Aidan took his mug with the same clear enjoyment. "I've been out of town since Thursday night. So... chronologically from Friday morning, please. And include that police crap you've got going on. Maybe I can help."

"Didn't think you'd wanna. 'S not your crap."

"You're here, aren't you?"

Jack blinked. Stared. He was used to a world built on plausible deniability. If he screwed up, there would be no help. If he were caught, they'd throw away the key. He had informants, money, caches of gear, and safe places, but before Gareth had walked back into his life, the only person he'd ever considered backup was Rio Palmer. Aidan's intimating that Nancarrow Mining was more than a job was….

"The fuckers really hung you out to dry."

Jack didn't answer that. He drained his mug and started to walk Aidan through the events of the previous days, not leaving anything out.

Aidan Conrad stretched out his long legs and—for the most part—sat as still as a meditating cat. Occasionally he wrote a brief note on his pad, but he didn't interrupt Jack's narrative.

Jack was aware of the office getting busy as people arrived for work. He registered the curious glances that were thrown their way, but he didn't get up to close the door to the small meeting room.

"So Gorish is facing assault charges over Frazer's broken head, and you're tracing his activities to find solid evidence for fraud," Aidan summarised when

Jack stopped speaking.

"Correct."

"On top of which you're trying to find that pimp, six boys he's keeping locked up in a brothel, and the man or men who stabbed Baxter."

Jack nodded again. Another mug of coffee seemed appropriate, so he slipped from his seat to get the coffeemaker started again.

"I'll have one too, thanks." Aidan watched Jack pouring water and measuring coffee beans. "I'm thinking that the pimp is more of a priority here, especially if you want to get to those boys. So why don't I sit on Gorish while you focus on locating that sucker? You can't tell me you don't have an idea or two."

"You have scary cat ears." Jack handed over a fresh mug of coffee.

"Barrister. Comes with the territory."

"What about Gorish, though? Don't you want to know who he's in bed with?"

"Sure, but get your priorities right, kid. Gorish has nowhere to go. That pimp does. At least until you have a name and a mug shot. And if he's cocky enough to take out a cop, you must be close."

"Or he's desperate."

"Whatever. Point is you need to focus on him. If you're not sure about Lisa, work with Raf Gallant. He won't fuck you over."

A whole chandelier lit up Jack's mind at those words. "Gareth called you when I needed a safe place for the boys."

Aidan nodded, and his eyes were careful. "He didn't tell me shit, you know. He just said he needed a safe house and someone to guard it."

"And you sent Raf."

"He's good."

"Yes. He's that."

"And I trust him."

There was that word again. Jack still frowned every time he heard it. To him, trust was a sum of two parts: Rio Palmer and Gareth Flynn. And Gareth's half of that equation was so new it was still shiny.

"That's why you don't answer your phone. Either of you." Gareth breezed into the room trailing scents of rain and hospital disinfectant in his wake. "Before you ask, Frazer is fine. He's overdone the geekery is all. They actually allowed him home, but nowhere near a computer for the next three days at least."

"He'll die of boredom."

"That's what he said. Is there any more coffee in that pot?"

"Help yourself," Aidan rumbled. "I've suggested that I deal with Gorish while Jack goes after the pimp. Any problems with that?"

"I'm worried we—"

"You said something last night about a money trail?" Gareth cut in, emptying the contents of the coffeemaker's glass carafe into a mug and immediately refilling the machine to brew another batch. Coffee machines in the corporate security office led a short but busy life.

"Yeah. Frazer thought he recognised bank details. It's possible. Kid has a good visual memory."

"Bank details are easy to check. Just give me the list, and we'll flag anything that isn't part of payroll for a more detailed look."

Gareth didn't even sit down. He gulped coffee and shifted on the balls of his feet, ready to jump into action at a moment's notice. He used to be like that while they served, always buzzing until the orders came down. Then he'd grow calm and as solid as a rock, the steady centre of the maelstrom.

Seventeen-year-old Jack used to admire that ability. Now he admired the fact that some things never changed.

"Like Aidan said, nailing Gorish for fraud is not as critical as getting the pimp off the street."

"Fine." Jack knew he was being managed, but he didn't care enough to argue. He didn't waste time explaining that he didn't want to find the pimp as much as the other boys Nico and Daniel had talked about when they thought nobody was listening. Nico in particular was worried that Goran—and Jack hadn't missed that slip either, though he kept that piece of information to himself—would take their disappearance out on the other boys. Jack had racked his brain trying to remember if there had been any other boys in the club that night who could have belonged to the pimp. Nothing had come to mind then or since, and those shadowy figures nagged at him.

He could lose himself in work, in tracing communications halfway around the world, but those distractions never worked for long before the image of six trapped boys intruded once more. He was grateful to Aidan and Gareth for giving him the time and opportunity to hunt, wishing he'd not feel guilty about skipping out on a job he'd been hired to do.

"Don't issue any finance data just yet," he advised gruffly as he stood and drained his mug. "And keep in mind that we have no evidence that Gorish is behind the technical leak. We're nowhere near home and dry."

He didn't wait to hear the snarky comments that were brewing behind two pairs of lips.

Their first break came from Raf. He called Jack just before lunch, voice full of triumph. "I know who stabbed Baxter, and I know where we can find him. You in?"

"Is the pope a catholic?" Jack was already up, freezing screens and reaching for his jacket. "Where?"

"I'm almost to you."

"'Kay."

Jack sprinted for the stairs, dialling Gareth's mobile as he ran. "Raf's got a lead. Checking it out," he said when the voice mail kicked in. Let it not be said that he didn't keep his boss informed, not even when said boss was in a meeting with Julian Nancarrow and Aidan Conrad and had his phone turned off. Gallant couldn't have timed that any better.

"Who and where?" he asked as Gallant pulled his car to a stop, and he slid into the passenger seat.

It was a measure of how screwed up his life had become that Jack was spending more time in Range Rovers these days than on his bike. Raf's Ranger was forest green on the outside, the paint clean and the chrome polished to a high shine. The interior, by comparison, was a total mess. Notebooks and maps vied for space with camera equipment, crumpled sandwich and chocolate bar wrappers, and empty Starbucks mugs.

"Stakeout?"

"Yeah, ignore it. I'll get it taken care of when this is over."

"Come on, spill," Jack demanded. "Who stabbed Clive, and how do you know?"

"I recognised a face from the feed in the alley. Guy is small-time muscle for hire. Stabbing a cop is out of his league. I reckon he was threatened, or he got paid extra well."

Jack woke up his tablet. "Name?"

"Gary Downs. Hangs out at a popular boxing gym in the East End."

"That's where we're headed?"

"Yep. And by the way, Danny and Nico had another very quiet night. No idea what you did, but no more nightmares."

"For now," Jack muttered, trying to keep focussed on his search. Nightmares had lives of their own, and Jack couldn't stop them any more than he could erase the memories that triggered them. All he could do was teach Nico, and especially Daniel, ways to handle them.

A bump in the road jolted him out of his thoughts, and the tablet lost Internet access. Wi-Fi reception in the city was patchy and hot-spotting his phone didn't improve matters by much. Jack kept at it, though, trying to learn as much as he could about the man Raf thought had assaulted Clive Baxter.

"That's the place," Raf announced after half an hour. By now Jack was up to speed on Gary Downs's personal information and the contents of his rap sheet. The thing read like the Magna Carta, but as Raf had pointed out, knife crime or human trafficking hadn't yet made it into the man's skill set.

"How do you wanna play this? Does he know you?"

"I've arrested him twice, so I should imagine so." Raf pulled up on the other side of the road from the gym. "They should stop letting them back out, know what I mean?"

"Oh, I hear you." Jack nodded even as he surveyed the street. Traffic was moderate, heaviest along the small row of shops and towards the bank at the corner. Cars pulled in and out of half a dozen marked parking bays in quick succession as people stopped to grab sandwiches or run a quick errand or two in their lunch breaks. The end of the street where Raf had parked was quieter. The gym had its own parking lot with some very shiny metal in it, and Jack took a moment to memorise number plates.

"Do you want Downs, or do you just want to know who hired him?"

"We need to talk to him about the stabbing, on the face of it, at least," Raf said, and Jack smirked at the way Raf's mind worked.

"Let me go chat him up. If he has anything useful

to say, I'll bring him out. Park so you're ready to back me up?"

Raf nodded and waved for Jack to get going. "I can work with that."

━━━◆ ◆ ◆━━━

The boxing gym was larger than the outside suggested. Busier too, with a lunch crowd composed of both hopeful young talent, eager to be seen, and corporate types coming in for their workout.

Jack liked the sanded wooden boards that made the space appear like a giant stage. Individual training areas clustered together like room sets, and a row of padded sparring rings ran along the far wall.

The acrid mix of sweat, air freshener, and heavy-duty disinfectant common to gyms all over the world hung heavy in the air, but the atmosphere held a cheerful buzz, and the high ratio of trainers to trainees suggested a well-run, popular place to work out.

"Checking us out?" A man with some complicated initials embroidered on the breast pocket of his maroon polo shirt stepped up to him as Jack came through the door.

"Just moved jobs." He nodded, looking around as if curious. "Looking for a place to work out."

"Boxed before?"

Stray memories made one corner of Jack's mouth curl up in a smile. He preferred martial arts schools that used weapons, but where Gareth was in charge everyone was taught to box. Jack had the basics down even if gloves weren't his thing.

"While ago."

"Well… we run both beginners and refresher sessions every week. Once you've decided that you'd like to get into it again, you're assigned to a coach who will work with you every time you come in…."

The man rattled on, pointing out class schedules and going on about training regimes, nutrition plans, and equipment. Jack followed him around, attentive look on his face and nodding in all the appropriate places, while a separate part of his mind catalogued every face and assessed the fight capabilities of each man he saw. He'd spotted Gary Downs from the doorway and kept half an eye on the man while he followed in his guide's wake.

At the far side of the gym, Jack's guide retrieved a stack of papers for Jack to complete and return on his next visit. They were the usual stuff—personal information, health questionnaire, and banking details—and Jack nodded his thanks and stowed the forms.

He'd been watching Downs get ready for a sparring match, but when he turned away from the small desk where the forms had been, Gary Downs was no longer in his line of sight. Instead of the man suspected of stabbing a detective, Jack locked eyes with a pale-skinned, pale-eyed man with stringy blond hair and a face he had reason to remember.

The pimp—Goran?—didn't wear leather today, but the T-shirt, jeans, and jacket combo he'd chosen didn't make him look any more approachable. Or enticing.

Jack owed someone a candle.

He had just been handed the man he sought, along with a roomful of other men who knew him. Men who could be made to answer questions.

He couldn't arrest Goran, couldn't even make a move towards him, but none of that mattered now that he had a place and people that were tied to the pimp.

Jack's gaze didn't linger. He shifted his stance a fraction to keep the tattoo on his temple out of the man's direct line of sight before he scanned the room for the pimp's hired muscle and—with his heart in his throat—any of the man's boys. It was a long shot, and Jack didn't expect to get that lucky twice in quick succession, but he took the time to take a good look around regardless. At least the bodyguards were easy to spot, one close to the pimp, the other near the entrance.

He followed his guide as he continued the tour of

the gym, moving by rote, nodding, and answering questions he barely heard. The man led him towards the back of the room to inspect the sparring rings, and Jack suddenly found himself wedged into a small crowd cheering a fight, his view of the exit barred by hard, muscled bodies.

It was obvious that the pimp or his bodyguards had caused the crowd's reaction, though there was no hint of violence in the air. Had Goran recognised Jack as the man who had abducted Ricky, his reception would have been much less benign than a casual attempt to distract him from something he might have seen.

He had to get to Raf before the pimp disappeared again. Trapped in the small crowd, with only a lacklustre fight in the ring in front of him, Jack considered his options.

*Over, under, around, or through?*

Jack made his choice. He stumbled a step backwards to create space, before he used the edge of the mat and the supports of the boxing ring as stepping-stones to flip over the men standing behind him.

He landed like a cat; grinned like one too, when he saw the surprise on the faces of the turning men.

Then he was running, lunging through the gym's doors and just caught sight of the pimp as he dove into the back of a black Jaguar XJ.

The car took off in a plume of burning rubber.

Raf was too far away, but fate was still in a good mood. Two girls stood at the kerb, chatting with a biker. Jack didn't hesitate. Before he had a chance to switch off the engine or pull down the stand, Jack slipped between the man and his bike, swung a leg over the machine and gave chase.

He even begged the biker's pardon.

Raf yelled from across the street as Jack peeled away from the kerb, expletives he couldn't make out over the sounds of the engine and the rush of the wind in his hair. He'd lay good odds that a police patrol would spot him riding without a helmet, so even if Raf didn't manage to get his tank started and keep up with him, he'd have company soon enough.

The Jag had a head start, but when it came to manoeuvring through traffic, Jack had the advantage over the heavy saloon with its blingy twenty-inch rims.

He wove around cars, dodged pedestrians and bollards, all the while hoping for the sound of sirens.

The purr of the engine made his body thrum and his mind buzz.

He squinted into the wind, kept the black car in sight, and made damn sure the driver was aware he was being followed.

Somewhere behind him, Raf Gallant was tearing his hair out trying to catch up, and very soon Lisa would be gunning for his balls. Chasing after the Jag *was* unnecessarily dramatic when Raf could have run the license plate and followed the car's journey on the traffic cams. But Jack had good instincts, and he'd been taught to trust them.

Those instincts led him not into the warren of warehouses and workshops along the river, but right into the heart of the City where none of them would have even thought to look.

Jack knew the City of London well enough to follow along despite abrupt turns, sudden shortcuts, and dives down unmarked alleyways. When the Jag sped up even more, squealing around corners at a rate that threatened the occupants with seasickness, Jack could guess what the driver was planning.

He tried to get close enough, but the solid metal gate was faster, already closing as the Jaguar rounded the corner. The driver slipped between the two halves of the gate like a minnow swimming through the teeth of a shark, and Jack couldn't help but admire the man's timing. Faced with a wall of solid, brushed metal he hit the brakes and swung the bike sideways in a cloud of tyre smoke, prepared when the machine tried to slide out from under him.

The police caught up with him then.

Two patrol cars at first, followed by an unmarked car, and then Rafael pulled in right behind, blocking the mouth of the alley and the access to the underground parking lot. The uniforms got to him while he parked the bike. They didn't try to arrest him on the spot, so Jack saw no need to waste time with introductions.

"Tablet," he requested from the uniformed officer closest to him.

"What?"

"Tablet, Kindle, laptop... just get me a fucking computer!" His voice was a snarl, but Jack didn't care. He was close; he wasn't losing the trail now just because the local law couldn't follow his train of thought.

"There's no open Wi-Fi in this area," a plaintive voice said beside him, and Jack grabbed the offered laptop and flipped the lid up.

"Talk to me after we're done here," Jack muttered under his breath as the screen came to life. "I'll show you how to hot-spot your phone."

"My password is—"

"Thank you. Don't need that." Hell, he was far ahead of passwords, sliding neatly into a database he shouldn't have known about let alone have access to.

Jack hit pay dirt on the second try. The number plates he'd memorised belonged to the Jag, which was registered to one Goran Mitrovic, property developer.

*Goran wouldn't let us….*

Here was the reason Jack Horwood didn't believe in coincidences. He backed out of the database, cleared his footprints, and handed the laptop back to the officer with a nod of thanks after shutting it down.

He needed his own gear for what came next.

He needed it now.

Lucky for his temper, Raf Gallant was already headed his way, under a full head of steam.

"What the fuck, Horwood!" He threw the tablet at Jack and got right in his face. "Are you out of your fucking mind? What was that shit?"

Raf in a temper was a sight to behold. Shame he didn't have time to enjoy the show. "Goran Mitrovic," he said, booting up his tablet.

"What?" Raf stopped midtirade.

"The pimp. His name is Goran Mitrovic."

"You were chasing the pimp."

"No. I was racing around the City on a borrowed bike to get my adrenaline fix," Jack snapped, hiding an ounce of guilt for not going by the book under a mountain of irritation.

"And here I thought you were begging for attention," the man beside Rafael chimed in.

"I never beg." Jack frowned at the slim stranger he hadn't met before. "And who the fuck are you?"

"Skylar Payne."

Under normal circumstances Jack would have taken note of the man's trim build and stunning looks. He would have registered the hint of purple liner, stylish hair, and carefully chosen outfit—all black, but the textures so artfully mixed that there was a distinct illusion of colour. Then, as soon as he'd seen the man move, he would have dismissed the outside as irrelevant and focussed on the predator that resided within.

Circumstances were not normal, though, and Jack glared instead of treading softly.

"You're not invited."

"That's cold, man."

"Stop baiting him, moron," Raf cautioned, diverting his ire to a more responsive target. "He'll rip your head off."

"And play football with it, perchance? I always want—"

"This isn't a pissing contest! Shut the fuck up and let me work!" Jack sank down cross-legged, right there in the dirt in front of the metal gate. The road held some of the lunchtime sun, and if he craned his neck all the way back, he could see a small strip of sky between the towering office blocks around him.

He settled the tablet across his knees and promised more candles for a decent Wi-Fi signal so he could find out everything there was to know about Goran Mitrovic, starting with the names of anyone who had the code to the metal gates and the exit the Jag had taken from the underground garage complex.

He was peripherally aware of Raf directing the uniformed officers and of Skylar Payne keeping a clear space around him, wide enough so nobody could even guess at what he was doing. The two worked seamlessly together, and Jack filed that away for thinking about later. Right now, he was on the hunt.

# PHALANX

———— ◆◆◆ ————

D inner was at Scotland Yard that night. The amount of food on offer was almost as extensive as the first time Jack had sat in the large conference room, but this time Walshaw wasn't there to try his patience.

Clive Baxter sat beside Lisa, pale and with his left arm in a sling to immobilise his shoulder but determined to be part of the action. Raf had brought Skylar Payne, who looked even more exotic than Jack remembered him from earlier in the day, and Aidan Conrad had joined Gareth and Jack on the brief ride from Nancarrow Mining's offices in the Strand.

"Don't make us wait," Aidan admonished almost as soon as he sat down. "I'm due in court first thing tomorrow morning, and I need my beauty sleep."

Jack crammed the last of the pizza into his mouth and booted up his tablet. "The pimp's name is Goran Mitrovic," he began. "Born in Serbia, March 2, 1964.

Arrived in London October 17, 1998. Holds a British passport since 2009. He owns Metro Properties, a company that buys and renovates industrial spaces and neglected residential properties before renting them out or selling them on. Profitable since inception and—on the face of it—totally legit."

Jack flipped screens and continued: "I've mailed you all the list of properties he's turned over in the last ten years, copies of the accounts he's filed with Companies House, and all banking activity on his business and main private account for the last five years."

"You did that in *one* afternoon?"

Jack ignored the incredulous looks from Raf and Aidan. "Getting at credit cards and phone records takes longer, so yell if you feel you need them," he continued. "I've started going through the list of properties looking for the most likely places to use as a brothel. With such a mixed portfolio, there are bound to be a number of options to run down. We must find the other boys and get them out before we can shut him down. Once that's done I'll go after the buyers."

"Can I just point out that we have no warrant for any of this activity," Lisa bit out. "If we arrest Mitrovic, we'll never make it stick."

Unless they caught him red-handed, of course.

Jack didn't care whether the data he provided was

admissible in court or not. He'd spoken nothing but the truth when he'd told Gareth that the motivation for his crusades was to get men like Mitrovic off the streets. Permanently. If the law needed breaking to achieve that, then Jack would gladly break the law.

"We don't need Jack's evidence," Aidan interjected, almost as if he'd read Jack's mind. "We have witnesses."

"No, we don't. Right now, Nico and Daniel are missing or not cooperating," Lisa argued right back.

"You're wrong on both counts, there, Dr. Tyrrell," Skylar cut in. When he wasn't snarking he had a pleasant voice, soft and melodious. "Daniel and Nico are in a safe place, and they *are* cooperating. Not with as much enthusiasm as you'd like to see, but given what they've been through, I don't think we have any right to push them. Not if we want them to come out of this mess even halfway sane."

Jack hadn't known he had an ally. He shot Skylar a look; one that Skylar returned with a small nod and a curl of lip. Skylar Payne hadn't been part of the protection detail Raf had put together when Jack needed a safe place for the boys, but it seemed he was helping out when Jack wasn't spending all his free time at the safe house.

"They don't trust the system," Clive suggested.

"You don't trust the system either." Jack pushed a

box of Nurofen and a bottle of water across the table when he saw Clive shift restlessly in his chair, unable to get comfortable.

"Do you have any leads on your leak?" Gareth queried. "A list of likely suspects?"

"I have a list of all personnel directly involved in both cases," Lisa said, and some of the tension left her frame. She no longer looked as if she was on the warpath. More like dejection and worry were sapping her composure. "It's a long list. I should report it to internal affairs and let them take over, but…."

"Maybe we can help you out with that once Mitrovic is dealt with," Gareth suggested, and Jack raised his head in time to see Aidan give a decisive nod.

*What the fuck were those two on?* Granted, he wanted the backstabbing bastard caught too, but in his experience Met officers scoffed at suggestions of outside help. Jack had given up offering quite a while ago. It occurred to him that he'd been facing Walshaw… and that he and Baxter worked together just fine most days.

"Do you really think you can trace all the buyers?" Clive asked in a low tone that carried no further than Jack's ears.

"You bet. I'm not planning to let a single one of those perverts get away. All it takes is time."

"And effort."

"Work's never bothered me."

"No. Only red tape."

"Let's get this organised, then," Raf suggested before the meeting could devolve into individual conversations. "Do we split the list of properties, or do you want to narrow them down? Anyone got a hunch?"

"I followed the Jag on the traffic cams after he got away from me, and he went north towards Shoreditch."

"His offices."

"Yes, but also about a dozen properties. Some that he's had since he started the business. One is a dining club. It could be a blind—"

"Or he's running home to check on his assets," Aidan grunted.

"Either way, let's check it out. Can you flag those for me?"

Jack nodded, and if he wondered at the raft of helping hands that suddenly surrounded him, he kept that to himself.

⬥ ⬥ ⬥

"Jack? Can you spare me a few minutes?"

Jack had been a quarter of the way through the list

of properties Mitrovic's company had developed over the years when he'd answered his phone without checking the caller ID. He'd expected Raf on the other end. Or maybe Clive. Alexandra Marston's name hadn't even made it onto the list. "Sure. What do you need?"

What she needed was to see him. Ideally in her office.

Jack didn't mind a stretch and a caffeine fix, and he made his way across to Alex Marston's workspace without demur.

This time around, the large office felt peaceful. One of the hibiscus trees had opened its flowers, and even from as far away as the door the big blooms looked as soft as bloodred velvet. They matched the furniture as perfectly as the red ribbons on Alex Marston's pale blouse.

"Have you studied poisons?" Jack asked as he settled into the armchair Alex indicated.

"What makes you ask that?"

Jack sighed. At that rate, they'd never get a conversation going. He supposed that Alex couldn't help being evasive any more than he could. "You've surrounded yourself with some very potent ones." He waved at the greenery gracing the office.

"It's interesting that *poison* is the first place your mind goes to." Alex set a tea service on the low table between them and poured. "Most people see beautiful flowers."

"Most people haven't worked where we have." Jack took the tea she offered and leaned back into his chair. "But I'm sure you didn't ask me over to discuss botany. Or personal history."

"You are correct. I would like to ask for your help."

"With?"

"Gary Downs."

Jack set his cup down and considered. "He's being held for questioning about the stabbing of a police officer. But you know that."

"Yes. He's uncooperative, and Lisa's in a hurry, so she asked for my help."

Alexandra Marston didn't evade Jack's searching gaze this time. Her head was tipped a little to one side in invitation, and Jack might have found the look enticing if he had believed it genuine. He found he liked the woman, hardassery and evasion and all, as much as he'd ever liked a mental challenge. "What do you need from me?"

"Dirt."

"Well, that's an unexpectedly precise request," Jack smirked. "There's plenty of it on his rap sheet."

"I'd love to tie Mitrovic to the stabbing."

"Wouldn't we all? I'm happy to go digging for any connection between the two, but Lisa's not really fond of my way of working."

"I don't think she cares."

*Since when?* What had happened to make Lisa drop the book she'd so far adhered to so carefully? There weren't too many options, and Jack pulled the phone from his pocket and hit the speed dial keyed to Clive Baxter.

"What do you need, Jack?" came the detective's voice through the receiver a moment later.

"How are you feeling?"

"Like shit warmed over, why?"

"I was… just wondering."

"That's why you're ringing? Really? Stop that, it's creepy." Baxter sounded incredulous, and well he might. It wasn't every day that Jack called him just to ask how he was. Jack got that.

"I know. Sorry. Take it easy, will you? I'll talk to you later." Jack closed his phone on Clive's annoyed huff. Baxter would take it easy when hell froze over. He was very much like Jack that way. But if Clive was as okay as he could be after being stabbed, it made Lisa's strange request more worrisome.

"Why doesn't she care?" he enquired, not really expecting an answer.

Alex's lips curved in the faintest of smiles. "You might not know this, but Lisa also has a history of playing bait. She didn't start as early as you did with your mother's killer, but she's done it a lot in the past, and she's considered very good at it."

"I didn't get the impression that Mitrovic had any use for women," Jack posed, pragmatic.

"Maybe not."

She didn't elaborate, and since it wasn't a conversation Jack wanted to have, he didn't dig. "Fine. I'll see what I can find," he said when Alex's power drill stare started to grate on his nerves. "Give me an hour?"

"That would be excellent."

⬥ ⬥ ⬥

Gareth raised his head from the avalanche of papers on his desk and watched Jack walk in with a mug of tea in one hand and a large jug of water in the other. He took the steaming mug Jack held out to him, grateful as much for the break it signified as for the stimulus it promised, while Jack made his way around the desk to the lemon trees.

"Alex said they weren't self-sustaining," Jack explained as he watered each tree. "Apparently you forget about your plants when you're distracted."

"And I suppose she told you I am. Distracted, that is."

"Yep." Jack set the empty carafe down and crossed

his arms. "Not that I've noticed, but then maybe she knows you better."

"Better than who?"

"Dunno? Me?"

Gareth didn't know what to make of the strange tone in Jack's voice. "Jack? Whatever it is… just spit it out."

"Lisa has a thing for Clive."

"Yes, and?"

"She asked Alex to help her interrogate Gary Downs. And Alex in turn asked me to find her some dirt to work with."

"Which you did, I assume?"

"Sure."

"And now you're bothered by hypocrisy?"

"More disappointed, really." Jack meandered aimlessly around the office, hands jammed into the back pockets of his jeans. He looked out the windows at the view, inspected the rows of herbs growing on the windowsill and the spines of books without— Gareth would have sworn to that—retaining a single image.

Gareth remembered nights like this, when they'd tried to make sense of arcane bits of intelligence Jack had turned up in his searches, and Jack had needed to move while his mind processed.

The appearance of a bowl of juggling balls on

Jack's desk hadn't surprised Gareth one bit, and he was ready to listen when Jack suddenly stopped walking.

"I'm bothered about all this suddenly becoming personal. That never ends well."

"I thought it was personal for you."

Jack shook his head. "Not like that. I don't want revenge or justice or whatever else Lisa is after."

"That's not what you said the night Lisa called us into Scotland Yard."

"I know."

Jack settled himself on the edge of Gareth's desk, close enough for Jack's jeans-clad thigh to touch Gareth's arm and for Gareth to feel the warmth emanating from Jack's body. Close enough for Gareth to hope that this search for contact was entirely deliberate.

"I was torn up about Ricky," Jack confided. "I needed someone to blame besides myself. So yes, right then I wanted a head to nail to the wall. Now, it's different."

"Could be Lisa's at the feeling guilty stage."

"It's not her fault Clive went into that club."

"You don't know that. They could have had a fight. You won't know why it's personal unless you ask her."

"Do you think she'll give me an answer?"

The Lisa Tyrrell Gareth knew was headstrong,

determined, and very, very sure of herself. She was also very loyal. "Probably not."

And just like that, Jack's shoulders relaxed, and the frown lines between his brows disappeared. "I'm gonna go see Nico and Daniel," he announced.

"What about…?" Gareth waved his hand around the room in an attempt to encompass the conversation they'd just tried to have.

Jack was already half out of the door, but he stopped at Gareth's words. "Don't worry. I'll make sure I watch my back."

Gareth sat, mug still in hand, staring past his avalanche of paperwork at the half-open door. He wondered what Jack's sudden appearance had really been all about. And he promised himself that Jack watching his own back was a thing of the past.

⬥ ⬥ ⬥

The cry was deafening in the dark, quiet room: a high, pain-filled wail dying away to a terrified whimper. Jack was up before the scream reached its peak, and he was wrapped around Nico before the boy's sobs started.

Just like Jack had all those years ago, Nico clung to his knife as if to a lifeline. But utterly unlike Jack, Nico allowed himself to be touched, to be pulled close enough to be comforted.

Jack had expected Nico's reaction. The evening had been too quiet and mundane for the teen to process. Nico's mind couldn't marry the recent horrors with teasing banter around the dinner table, with the boys washing dishes under Mrs. Flynn's careful gaze while Jack talked about chasing leaks and ribbed Skylar about his fashion sense and apparent fascination with purple eyeliner. There had been no mention of self-defence, the boys' daily knife practice, or the fact that Skylar had started to teach them when Jack was needed elsewhere.

Skylar Payne was quite the enigma: a highly paid, highly sought-after stylist and makeup artist who didn't look out of place next to his celebrity clients. Who, if the information Jack had found was even close to the truth, freelanced as an investigator and close protection specialist. And who put phenomenally lethal knife skills to use when needed.

Judging by the constant stream of insults, taunts, and bickering, Skylar and Raf Gallant had history, though Skylar was surprisingly innocent when compared to the rest of the safe house's occupants.

For that reason alone, Jack was grateful that Skylar wasn't close by when halting, strangled words emerged from between Nico's sobs.

The words froze Jack's blood and twisted his mind

into a wellspring of anguish, though nothing Nico revealed was unexpected. Not the imprisonment or the beatings, the abuse or depravities the boys had been forced to endure. Nico had paid attention, had caught and remembered names, recalled small details that made his tale harrowing in its vividness.

Jack didn't interrupt. He held the shaking, sobbing boy and rubbed calming hands over Nico's back and shoulders. He made soothing noises when Nico faltered, let him catch his breath and gather his courage to give voice to the horrors once more.

In those quiet moments, Jack wondered about the lack of sound and movement from the other side of the large double bed. Daniel slept so lightly that Nico's scream should have woken him. And yet, the blond boy lay curled on his side, unmoving and seemingly fast asleep.

The rest of the house was just as silent, poised on the edge of the abyss Nico's words created, the occupants holding their collective breaths while Nico sobbed out his anguish.

Jack focussed on Nico's weight in his arms, tried to tune out the boy's halting words or at least obscure their meaning in favour of hearing nothing but *sound*.

It worked as well as it ever had.

The words slipped through his defences like acid dripping into his soul, until Jack could smell stale beer and bitter aftershave and feel the bite of the lash on his back once more.

"Mrs. Flynn says that talking about bad stuff is your brain's way to get rid of it," Nico confided once the storm had passed, and only the occasional hiccup broke his voice.

"Hmm," Jack hummed. He'd been told that particular bit of wisdom too, and if it helped Nico, he was all for encouraging the teen to believe it.

Jack wasn't wired that way.

He had never shared the details of his imprisonment with anyone and had even learned—after Rio had explained to him what PTSD was and how it worked—to deal with the flashbacks on his own. Rio had offered to help, but Jack had never asked.

"When you were…." Nico's voice was little more than a hoarse whisper. "Did you ever think of killing yourself?"

"No, never." Not then, and never once since. "I was thinking of ways to get out," Jack explained. "I never considered suicide."

"I didn't either," Nico whispered, and Jack didn't need cat ears to hear the fear in Nico's voice. "Daniel does, though."

"Not anymore," Daniel said from the darkness, confirming Jack's suspicion that he had been awake all along. "Not anymore, Nico. I promise."

———◆◆◆———

"Shit, man, are you okay?" Raf waited in the hallway as Jack stepped from the master bedroom.

Jack had no idea how to respond to Raf's concern or to the quiet sympathy in Gareth's mother's eyes as she took his place in the boys' bedroom.

Nico had fallen asleep the moment Jack had tucked him in, exhausted from telling his story. Daniel had taken a while longer to relax. He'd clung to Jack and Nico, tears on his cheeks that he wouldn't wipe away, until sleep finally claimed him.

Jack had sat by their bedside for a while, needing space to breathe before he faced Raf and Skylar and people yelling demands into his ear. He needed the time to restore his defences, resurrect the detachment that most people took for cold-hearted professionalism, but that was his shield and armour.

Jack didn't believe in any higher powers to invoke in prayer. He knew that he couldn't promise complete safety. All he could do was go out and fight another day, make sure the rats were cleaned off the streets more often than not.

That was all anyone could ever do.

Which wasn't to say that accepting that fact was easy. Not in the face of Nico's anguish. Or in the face of Jack's own rage.

"Tell me you got all that," Jack begged Raf as he headed for the kitchen. He needed a drink. Just one, so he'd not get on the bike and go inflict damage in some club.

Raf nodded, the concern in the hazel eyes not lessening one iota. "We got it, annotated and witnessed. Skylar says it will clean up perfectly."

"Make sure Lisa and Clive get it. They need it most."

"You didn't need it at all, did you?" Raf muttered while Jack found the whisky in the kitchen cabinet and splashed a generous mouthful into a glass. "You were right when you said Nico would break."

"Nico *did not* break," Jack snarled. His professional facade could go right to hell. "He's one of the most courageous kids I've ever met. Most grown men wouldn't survive what he and Daniel have been through, so don't talk to me about breaking. Not after he's given you everything you need to nail Mitrovic to the fence!"

The whisky bottle thumped onto the kitchen counter, and Raf took a step out of the direct path of Jack's wrath, hands in loose fists up in front of his face. "Go ahead, blow off steam," he invited, "but keep in mind it's 2:00 am."

"Fucker." Jack drew a deep breath, not placated but recognising Raf's actions for what they were. He didn't need a mirror to know that he looked like an angry hurricane trying to keep a lid on a smouldering volcano. Precisely the reason he'd come down and gone for a bottle.

The whisky burned his throat, but it warmed and soothed as it went down. Jack relaxed his shoulders and took another sip, smaller this time, appreciating the flavour. He had a taste for Islay Malt, the soothing burn, the blend of soft and salty, the bite of peat behind the smoke. It did its job, easing the churning in his gut and taking the edge off the angry buzz in his mind.

"Where is everyone?" The quiet in the house suddenly seemed ominous, despite the late—or early—hour.

"Mrs. Flynn's traded off with you," Raf answered without hesitation. "Skylar is making the rounds outside. You should get some sleep."

Jack shook his head. "Not happening. You can go get some shut eye if you want. I'll keep watch."

"Nah, I'm good." Raf pulled another glass from the cupboard, picked up the bottle, and waved at Jack to precede him into the living room. "I'll keep you company. You look like you could use it."

Jack settled against the sofa cushions and cradled his drink, surprised to find that he was grateful for Raf's presence when, usually, he worked best alone. He kept his own counsel, made his own choices, and dealt with the consequences alone.

He wasn't used to people offering to watch his back or fight his battles, and he wasn't sure he liked the idea.

Fighting alone had advantages he didn't want to give up. For one, he never had to worry about anyone else getting hurt.

Right now, though, having company was good.

# Catch and Release

━━━━━◆◆◆━━━━━

**M**ornings where even the Gixxer's throaty rumble irritated Jack were rare. He rode faster than was safe in the dim light and pouring rain, just to make it to the quiet haven that was his desk.

Every winking traffic light intensified the snowstorm of pain behind his eyes.

Every squeal of tyre on wet asphalt or impatient blare of horn increased the tension in his back so that he welcomed the cool, empty darkness of Nancarrow Mining's underground garage with much more enthusiasm than it warranted.

Feeling like shit warmed over and with Nico's words still wreaking havoc in his mind, he sought his work as a condemned man seeks absolution.

The large open-plan office was dark and deserted as he dragged himself through the door. With luck, it would stay this way for at least another hour. By which time Jack hoped to have woken up enough to pass for human.

He hadn't fooled either Skylar or Raf at breakfast. And Gareth's mother had merely set a glass of water and a couple of Nurofen next to his plate and told him that Nico had slept peacefully for the rest of the night.

No need to guess where Gareth had learned to take care of people.

Settling at his desk, Jack glared at the tangle of coloured lines on his screen.

The image reminded him of leftover spaghetti and the taste of failure. While finding Mitrovic was his priority, he hated leaving the fraud case even temporarily unsolved. Maybe an hour of tracing data would grant him enlightenment. Or at least enough peace that he could face Gareth without his insides squirming with guilt.

Before he got started, though, he needed fuel. Nothing good would come of trying to do this without the presence of stimulants.

Jack started the coffee machine and waited with barely leashed patience through the minutes it took to brew a batch of chemical assistance. He added three spoonfuls of sugar to his mug before he gave it a cursory stir.

Minutes later he was deep in cyberspace and lost to his surroundings.

———————◆◆◆————————

"Hey, I've got it!"

Frazer blew into the office with a shout. His enthusiasm ruffled Jack's hair like a gust of fresh air and pulled him from his contemplation of spaghetti salad in four dimensions.

"You got what?" he asked, not taking his eyes from the screen or his fingers from the tattoo at his temple. He was still a long way from awake, and the familiar touch helped him stay focussed.

"A way to find out who is behind the leaks!"

The Scot bounced on the balls of his feet, making Jack feel a hundred years old. "You hit your head or something?" he grumbled. "Dial it down, it's early."

"Looking at you, it's before coffee." Frazer was irrepressible. "Come on, take a break. Get a caffeine fix."

"And listen to you yodel."

"I'll wait until you've finished your second mug…," Frazer wheedled.

Jack had already had three, and headache pills, but Frazer had clearly picked up on Jack's habits, and Jack felt he should encourage situational awareness, especially after the Gorish incident. He didn't relish scraping his colleagues from the carpet just because they didn't see the blow that took them out.

He rose without complaint and followed Frazer to the cafeteria, deciding to soak up the excess caffeine with a freshly baked custard danish.

"So you see, the trace should be able to tell us—"

"What?" Jack hadn't been paying any attention to Frazer's words, but a few of them registered almost by chance, and Jack's head snapped up in surprise.

"I said I could—"

"I heard you. When did you think of that?"

"This morning, why?"

"Because it's genius, that's why." Whether due to the caffeine or Frazer's idea, Jack was now wide awake and buzzing. "You thought of that *before* you had coffee?"

"Well… yeah…."

"You're never allowed coffee again. Come on, man, don't dawdle!" Jack was up and on the way back to his desk, not caring that Frazer had to run to keep up.

The spaghetti snarl was where he had left it, and Jack glared at the mess. He *loved* geometrics and used them every chance he got. The mess currently on his screen offended his sense of the aesthetic on multiple levels. "Pick one," he invited.

"What?"

"Pick a trace." Jack turned to Frazer. Interfering in any way with a hacker's data—even to offer assistance—wasn't considered polite, but the Scot had come up with a brilliant plan. Jack wanted him to know that. "Pick one," he repeated.

"Purple," Frazer said after a moment scrutinising Jack's screen. For the outcome of their experiment it hardly mattered which data set he picked, but his cheeks were pink with pleasure, and that was all Jack needed to know.

"Purple it is," he confirmed as he sat down. "Meet you on the other side."

———— ◆ ◆ ◆ ————

It took 127 minutes to locate the final destination of the leaked data. Jack's issue, once he'd found the first lead, had been one of too much data and a scarcity of time to chase down every lead he had until a pattern emerged. Frazer's idea had promised to take care of that.

Right now, the Scot sat at the end of his trace, IP address glowing brightly on his screen, waiting for Jack to reach the exit point of the spaghetti snarl.

"Wait," Jack cautioned when Frazer opened his mouth to speak. "Let's get this confirmed before... I'm almost...." He read out the IP address on his screen, not needing to hear Frazer's whoop to know they'd hit pay dirt. Frazer's idea had *felt* right, and Jack had a thing about trusting his gut.

"You're the man," he declared. Then he stuck two fingers in his mouth and whistled.

Gareth's door flew open at the sound, and both Gareth and Aidan Conrad came storming into the office.

"What?" Conrad asked as soon as he drew close. "You got the pimp?"

"Frazer's come up with a way to confirm the destination of the finance leak."

"Who?"

Jack had scribbled the name and IP address on a Post-it note. But rather than handing it to Gareth, he looked at Frazer until the Scot caught on.

"Donovan Nancarrow," Don Frazer informed them. "Julian's cousin."

––––––––––––– ✦ ✦ ✦ –––––––––––––

The rest of the day blurred into noise and frantic activity punctuated by mugs of hot, sweet coffee and headache pills. The corporate security office erupted into controlled mayhem as Frazer once more drafted in everyone present to help identify business-confidential information that had been compromised.

Jack watched as work groups formed and shifted, as evidence was secured and data shared across the room, as Frazer strategised and planned with a new, more overt confidence that looked good on him. Most of all, he watched Gareth Flynn, who stalked the office wrapped in a near-visible cloud of black anger.

Jack followed the remaining traffic to ensure all the data ended up at Donovan Nancarrow's IP address.

He took a call from Lisa and Clive, confirming how they'd obtained the information on the recording. The small conference room grew crowded with ghosts while he answered questions, and when it was finally over, he turned off the phone, closed his eyes, and rested his head on the table.

Just for a moment.

Gareth found him at some point and steered Jack to the sofa in his office. Jack went under so promptly he barely noticed Gareth removing his boots and draping a blanket over him.

He slept fitfully, Nico's words buzzing through his mind like a swarm of insects, stirring memories and fears he'd kept under lock and key for years, until Aidan Conrad's angry snarls interrupted the uneasy dreams.

The big man sat in the chair in front of Gareth's desk. His scowl matched the one on Gareth's face, and the bottle of Glenfiddich on the desk between them had a hefty chunk missing. Betrayal wasn't easy to swallow, not even with a mouthful of fine Scotch as a chaser.

"Sorry, kid, I didn't mean to wake you." The lawyer half turned in his chair when Jack sat up and rubbed his face.

"It's okay. I've slept long enough." Jack stood and stretched, assessing the two men. According to Donald Frazer, Aidan Conrad had recruited Tim Gorish to Nancarrow Mining, just as he'd recruited Gareth. If that was true, it was no wonder Aidan was sore about Gorish's betrayal.

"Did Gorish tell you why?" he asked and watched Aidan Conrad wince. "Money—really?"

"Yep," Gareth confirmed after another swallow of whisky. "Apparently all he was after was cash."

"I'm not usually vindictive, but I feel like changing my MO just for him," Aidan declared and held the bottle in Jack's direction.

Jack shook his head at the offer. He'd had his share last night. Besides, someone had to stay sober enough to drive the two men home, or at the very least stuff them into a taxi. "There's nothing wrong with being vindictive," he said, remembering all the times he'd taken out pimps or would-be molesters without feeling a shred of guilt for not going by the book. "They get the message much faster if you show that you're willing to break the rules."

All of a sudden, he had both men's full attention. It didn't feel good.

"What?" he queried.

"Interesting comment you made there."

"Yeah?"

"It was. Especially given that you're talking to a lawyer and a corporate security specialist."

"Because you two are so wedded to the rule book, of course," Jack quipped in a deliberately bored tone. "So what?"

"So what, indeed," Gareth murmured and reached for the whisky bottle to refill his glass, while Aidan Conrad stared at Jack.

"I know things," Jack said simply. "Fancy getting some food to soak up all that booze?"

Their dinner was excellent, and the idea to go out even better. Gareth stayed tense and quiet, but Aidan flirted with the waitress before he began quizzing Jack about the things he knew. Jack answered maybe two of the two dozen random questions the lawyer fired at him before he shook his head.

"Give it a rest, Conrad. You know how this works."

Aidan Conrad—six foot five and built like a brick

shed—actually pouted. "I want to know how you can find a suspect who's been on the run for five years in less than a week. When nobody else could."

"Maybe he's just that good," Gareth suggested.

"I *am* that good. And you better tell Raf Gallant that he's talking out of school."

"Not Gallant," Aidan disagreed. "Alex."

"Ah, crap!" More puzzle pieces slotted into place as Aidan's words confirmed another of Jack's suspicions. It had made sense, when he'd thought about it, that someone with Alexandra Marston's skill set would only move sideways. He just hadn't considered that she'd share what she knew, and now he had no idea what to say to Aidan Conrad.

"Ask her yourself," he finally settled on. "I'm not gonna get myself locked up for your entertainment."

Aidan's mien grew sober, and he nodded once. "I hear you," he said and returned his attention to his food and the conversation to the ongoing police investigation.

———◆◆◆———

It was barely nine when Jack parked the Range Rover outside Gareth's house. Gareth had said little during the drive, but his gaze was like a hot caress on Jack's skin, arousing and insistent. It didn't surprise Jack when Gareth was on him before the front door was properly shut.

Impatient hands pulled Jack's shirt up to reach skin, and Jack didn't fight when Gareth shoved him against the wall. He managed a single deep breath before Gareth's lips were sealed to his.

Jack shivered when Gareth's teeth caught his lower lip. He wound one leg around Gareth's thigh and pulled their bodies closer together, relishing the heat that shot through him as Gareth's hands caught skin and held tight enough to bruise while he practically devoured Jack.

That Jack had seen this coming, had waited for it ever since he'd woken on the couch in Gareth's office, didn't make it any less arousing.

Neither work nor alcohol or dinner had done anything to soothe Gareth's anger. The man was so tightly wound he almost clawed the ceiling. And Jack found that sexy as hell.

Their kiss grew into a messy, disordered onslaught of lips and teeth and tongues. Gareth's palms cupped his arse and rocked Jack's groin against his hip with every move, sending sparks through Jack's body, tiny shocks of pleasure that rose and spread until he saw stars from the corners of his eyes.

Jack's belt buckle clinked as Gareth yanked it open, and his hands reached for the buttons on Jack's 501s.

"Don't stop me, Jack, please…," Gareth growled as Jack pulled his hands from around Gareth's neck.

Why Gareth expected Jack to be any less enthusiastic about the impending explosion was a mystery Jack was too riled to explore. He ripped Gareth's shirt out of his waistband, not bothering with the buttons. He relished the sound of the fine fabric tearing, and then he had skin under his palms and Gareth's harsh breaths in his ear.

Denim scraped Jack's thighs as Gareth roughly yanked his jeans down to his knees. A calloused palm grabbed his cock and squeezed just hard enough to drag a moan from deep in his throat. Gareth's fingers dug into Jack's hip so hard he knew there would be bruises come morning.

Gareth's face was a study in heat and desire, and when he took a step back, reached for Jack's shoulder, and spun him around to face the wall, Jack wanted to howl in glee. Gareth's vaunted and often flaunted control wasn't worth shit right now.

Jack had fantasised about Gareth losing it, but seeing it live and in colour… that was better than anything his mind could have cooked up.

Gareth wrapped an arm around Jack's throat and pushed his chin up. The hold was tight, but it wasn't even close to a stranglehold, and Jack's memories stayed in their box.

His mind was full of white noise, and his body only took note of pleasure. Teeth scraped along the sensitive skin of his neck, and Gareth's fist was driving him insane with want.

"Gareth." The word sounded strangled, desperate, but Jack didn't care. "Please."

The fist disappeared from around his cock, the arm from around his neck, and Jack groaned his frustration.

Then the hands were back, both on his arse, kneading, massaging, spreading him. Even angry and riled Gareth wasn't heedless, and a tiny part of Jack's mind regretted that.

Gareth's chest met his back, and Jack found himself pressed to the wall. He registered the welcoming cool of the smooth plaster under his cheek before his world was ripped apart by white-hot pain and pleasure so searing he almost lost his mind.

"Fuck! Gareth, move!" Jack demanded, breathless and crazy and without regard for anything but the pressure building in his gut. His balls tightened, and his thigh muscles spasmed until he shook.

The pleasure was so intense it was almost painful, the pain so bright it was pure pleasure. Jack lost the ability to speak, to form coherent thoughts, to demand or even plead. All he could do was gasp at each hard thrust and slow retreat.

This… only this….

Gareth's fingers caught in Jack's hair and pulled his head back. Lips slanted down over his, touching messily between gasps and groans. The grip tightened, and Jack's whole body arched and tensed.

He almost stopped breathing as the tension grew like a wave, tall enough to swamp him.

A tight fist wrapped around him and squeezed… and Jack was done. His body jerked and shuddered with the savage release, and he heard Gareth's answering groan as Jack's orgasm pushed him over the edge a moment later.

Gareth's arms wrapped him up and held him so tight he feared for his ribs. Breath was hard to come by, as was logic, but Jack had just enough presence of mind to know what he needed to say.

He turned in Gareth's embrace, rested his cheek against the other man's, and smiled so widely that Gareth would feel it.

"Better?"

A deep sigh whooshed out of Gareth's chest, and he slumped sideways against the wall. "I'll tell you when my brain's working again," he murmured, breath warm on Jack's ear. "I'm sorry I—"

"Hey," Jack interrupted. "You don't get to apologise for something that awesome. You don't get to apologise for needing it, either. Not if we're partners."

He pulled Gareth close and smiled in triumph when Gareth let go, slumped against him, and let himself be held.

Raf's call came midmorning, when it was too late for breakfast and still too early for lunch.

Not that Jack had suffered a lack of breakfast or any other comfort that morning.

He'd woken to a blowjob that almost blew his head off, and Gareth hadn't stopped with that rather pointed display of affection. There'd been a long hot shower, more entertainment of the skin-on-skin variety, and then Gareth had made sure to provide more breakfast than even Jack could eat in one sitting.

Blissed out and overfed, it had taken Jack a while to remember his name. And a while longer to work out the reason for Gareth's excessive solicitude.

Once he *had* worked it out, had grasped that Gareth felt he owed apologies for the previous night's impassioned encounter and what he considered his loss of control, anger swiftly washed the last of the cobwebs from Jack's mind.

The resulting fight was short, loud, heavy on the profanities, and ended with Jack pinned to the kitchen door. Gareth's face, when he realised he'd lost it yet again, had been a study.

Jack cherished the laughter that followed. Gareth might remember a lot about their time serving together, but he'd forgotten a lot too. Some days Jack just had to remind him that he was stronger than Gareth thought. And much more stubborn than that.

⬥ ⬥ ⬥

"There's a board meeting at two today," Gareth informed him as they stepped into the buzzing office, only fifteen minutes later than usual. "You're presenting."

"In your dreams," Jack huffed, glad to note that nothing they'd done or said in the last two days made any difference to how they now worked together. So when Raf called to tell him that he'd put eyes into the building Mitrovic ran as an upscale dining club and wanted to discuss the previous night's results, Jack didn't hesitate.

"Are you anywhere you can conference?"

"I'm at the Yard. Lisa and Baxter are here."

"Let me get a room. I'll call you back in a minute."

Commandeering the small conference room at the far end of the corporate security office took moments. Gareth, Aidan, and Alex responded to his call and brief explanation with equal swiftness. Soon enough they sat around the big screen and watched Wednesday night at Goran Mitrovic's private members' dining club.

The clientele was a mix of professionals in their forties and fifties, smartly dressed and networking with the ease of long experience. Most enjoyed their food, many drank more than was perhaps advisable, and a few men were being handed what looked like a photo album along with their menus. Those men later entered the back of the club through a guarded door before returning to their tables half an hour to an hour later.

"It's too quick for gambling and too long for snorting a line," Baxter said, voice hopeful.

"None of them look the drug-taking kind, anyway."

"There's a theme night tonight."

Raf sounded so strange that the hair on the back of Jack's neck stood up. "What is it?" he asked, trepidation heating his gut.

"A fetish night."

Jack groaned. "Let me guess: school uniforms?"

"Leather and Lace. I've snagged a leaflet, and it shows pictures of boys in leather. According to the blurb almost anything goes." Raf held the A5 sheet in front of the camera so Jack could see and read it.

"Leaflets? Oh joy." Jack caught Gareth's concerned gaze and tried to muster a smile.

"Don't," Gareth admonished. "Do you think the boys are kept at the club?"

"Too risky. Clubs and restaurants are apt to be inspected at short notice. He'll bring them in for the night and move them come morning."

"Can we raid the club during theme night?"

"No. Too many unknowns."

To Jack's surprise Lisa backed him up. "Given our *little problem*"—her fingers drew quotes in the air beside her head—"he'll go to ground if he gets wind of any police activity. We're better off with an undercover attempt."

"Can we ask Daniel and Nico if they know about the dining club? If they've been there, maybe they can describe the car journey?"

"Yeah… no." Jack was adamant. Nico's halting words echoed in his ears, and in the back of his mind ran an endless loop of men in suits walking down a quiet corridor, returning after a time with satisfied grins on their faces.

Once more he heard the soft, flat sounds of footsteps on cheap carpet, the shiver-inducing scrape of a key turning in a lock, the menace of door hinges creaking softly. Every muscle in his body tensed, though the loop of memories rewound from there, as if his mind shied away from what had come next.

He would *not* force Daniel and Nico to relive those nights over and over. He would just find a way to—

"Jack, something's bothering you."

The conference room came back into focus around him. Six pairs of eyes watched him with concern, and Jack blinked once. He imagined his memories drifting through the room like smoke, to be blown into oblivion by the cool fresh air streaming down from the vents.

He focussed on the question he'd been asked and rested his chin on his folded hands. "I think he's recruiting," he said after a moment of watching Gareth's eyes change colour with the passage of clouds across the sky. It was a peaceful sight, at odds with the noise in his head. "It all fits: publicised, open event, Thursday night. The club's closed on Fridays, since very few regular members will be in town. Easy to open the place and have it back in working order by Sunday even if you add plentiful booze, pills, and backroom action. There'll be cameras all over the place, and the most likely candidates won't make it home come morning."

"Christ!" The bitten-off curse came from Aidan, and Jack saw his lips tighten in anger. "So what can we actually do?"

Jack kept it short and his language professional.

"Keep an eye on Mitrovic and follow him when he leaves. Take him somewhere quiet and find out where the boys are. Take him out before he authorises acquisitions."

"Have a few teams standing by to go get the boys out as soon as we have an address," Raf completed the thought. "I can see that."

"Don't get ahead of yourself," Lisa cautioned. "Not having a warrant works to our advantage with the security issues. But it means we're limited on manpower. You won't have teams all over the city ready to roll at a moment's notice."

"'S not much of an issue," Jack said confidently. "We just keep Mitrovic incommunicado until Raf has got the boys."

"Just?"

"Oh please!" Jack crossed his arms and tried to look as if need and rage weren't boiling in his gut like freshly extruded lava. He felt the touch of sweaty hands dragging on his skin, the sticky chill of saliva running down his neck, the....

Jack squeezed his eyes shut and ground his teeth until his jaw ached. He would go to that damn fetish night and find out where Goran Mitrovic was keeping the other boys prisoner. The courts could have the bastard if there was anything left after Jack was done.

"Hold up a sec," Aidan's deep voice cut in. "What

if he has some of the boys with him?"

"If he leaves with them, we follow him," Jack said tonelessly. "If he sends them home early, Raf can follow the boys, and I keep an eye on Mitrovic. If Raf's lucky we find the brothel without having to ask him."

And wouldn't that be a shame.

"What about backup for you?"

Of course, Gareth would ask. Jack cursed himself for trying to play by the book. If he'd taken Raf's call alone, Jack would already be well on the way to the fetish night. This wasn't Jack's first rodeo, and he neither needed nor wanted backup. More fingers in this pie only meant more noses to put out of joint.

"I'm good," he answered at the same time as Lisa said: "I'm going with you."

"What?"

"He's seen you twice," Lisa argued. "Best use me as a shield before he gets suspicious."

Jack stared at the large screen, willing Lisa to retract her words. She made sense, but she didn't know how Jack worked, didn't understand what she was getting herself into.

And Jack didn't want to explain.

Alex Marston was the only person here who might have an idea, but Alex stayed silent even when Jack shot her a look. Instead of dissuading Lisa, Alex returned Jack's look with a small smile. One that made a shiver run down Jack's back.

———◆◆◆———

"Hiding on the roof won't get you out of it," Gareth commented as he settled himself against the waist-high parapet. Jack had been tricky to find, and his posture—knees up against his chest and arms curled tight around them—telegraphed loudly how uncomfortable he felt.

"Fuck it, Flynn," Jack complained even as he accepted the mug of coffee—black, sweet—that Gareth held out to him. "I don't have anything to prove."

"No, you don't."

"Then why do you want me to stand up in front of the board of directors?"

"Maybe I want to show you off."

"Bullshit."

"Not," Gareth argued with a smile. Jack was adorable, all tied in knots. It made a welcome change from the uncommunicative, detached badass Jack was turning into before their eyes. Gareth understood that Jack needed the distance to deal with Mitrovic, but at least Jack *could* still change, *could* still gripe and mope. He hadn't withdrawn so far into himself that he was impossible to reach.

Jack had surprised all of them when he called them in to talk over their plans. Alex confided later that she had been prepared for Jack to vanish for a day or two and then resurface, shadows in his eyes and rescued kids in tow.

"Get Frazer to do it. He deserves it."

Jack's voice interrupted his musings and, as usual, what he said made sense. Frazer had picked up the threads that Jack had handed him and done an amazing job following where they led while Jack was tangled up chasing pimps and comforting children. Gareth had already authorised a hefty bonus, despite the uproar in the rest of the company.

Gareth leaned his head back, glad for a few moments of quiet. He approved of Jack's hiding place, liked the way the breeze stirred his hair and a barely discernible hint of brine diluted the scent of tar and exhaust fumes in the air. Even the noise of the nonstop traffic was muted up here. And thoughts of betrayal stung much less.

"Come on, boss," Jack wheedled as he finished his coffee. "All that upper level management crap isn't me."

Gareth turned his head and waited until he had Jack's full attention. "I want you to put the fear of God into them."

"And again… much more your style than mine," Jack began—and his eyes widened. "Shit! You think—
"

Gareth swallowed the rest of Jack's words in a bruising kiss, and Jack came along for the ride. He tasted of the coffee he'd just drunk, bitter and sweet, and Gareth could think of nothing better than to stay right there on the roof for the rest of the day, his tongue tangling with Jack's. His hand dropped down to cover Jack's crotch, and he squeezed once before starting to tap a strange broken rhythm across Jack's groin that had Jack fully hard in a breath and a heartbeat.

Jack wove his hands into Gareth's hair, and his body arched in search of more contact, but Gareth turned the kiss slow and sweet and undemanding. He wasn't going to send Jack into a board meeting looking as if he'd just rolled out of bed without getting any sleep. Ravished Jack—all kiss-swollen lips, flushed cheeks, and pupils blown black—was for his eyes only.

He stopped dancing his fingers across the black denim and cupped Jack's face instead. A mere brush of lips now, soft and promising, and Jack's eyes closed in resignation.

"Who?" he asked promptly when Gareth released him.

"Cecily Nancarrow and Graham Halston."

"Nonexecs, minor shareholders, one a second cousin to Julian, the other a consulting mining engineer," Jack rattled off, voice thoughtful.

"Cecily Nancarrow thinks she has power. Rather stupid if you ask me," Gareth passed judgment. "She's having a fling with Halston and might be trying to convince him to support Donovan in the next takeover bid."

"Would he make a good CEO?"

"No idea. Never met the man. Aidan thinks not."

"And Alex?"

Gareth blinked, surprised yet again. He really should have learned by now.

Jack pushed himself upright. "Frazer deserves a bonus," he said as he moved to the trap door at the far end of the roof.

"Already done."

<hr />

Only Gorish's seat remained empty at the long boardroom table when Jack was shown into the room. After the discussion on the roof, he had taken the time to make sure he looked the part Gareth wanted him to play, and Gareth had a hard time to stop himself drooling.

Jack wasn't wearing a suit. He had traded black denim for equally figure-hugging black leather and had changed into a fitted deep green shirt with gently twinkling cut stones for buttons. He'd left the top buttons undone, and the strip of leather showed against the hollow of his throat. Confidence and determination infused his every movement and for once, Jack Horwood actually looked his age.

He owned the boardroom from the moment he walked in, tablet in hand. He took a few heartbeats to take in the tableau—Julian at the head of the table, Gareth, Aidan, and Alex next to one another at the foot, the wide expanse of polished cherrywood between them and the nonexecutive directors—before his gaze flashed to Gareth, and he gave the tiniest of nods.

"Ladies and gentlemen, my name is Jack Horwood. I'm an IT security specialist." Jack was more than that, and his stance and his cocky smirk both said so. "Nancarrow Mining hired me to ensure our confidential information stays that way. In view of recent events"—he nodded towards the empty chair—"I would like to inform you that your private lives are now no longer private."

Shocked stares met total silence until Aidan Conrad huffed a laugh. "Why don't you tell it like it is, kid?" he asked. "Straight up."

Jack did just that. He outlined the betrayal and the investigation. He described how he had traced the leaked data and how the information had been hidden. He explained how they had found that Tim Gorish had been the source of the leak. And he showed, in vibrant colour, how tracing the leaked data had led them directly to Donovan Nancarrow.

Jack's words and demeanour struck just the right balance between professional dedication and quiet menace. Gareth watched Jack brace himself, shoulders square and legs slightly spread, as he explained how they would now examine bank balances and transaction details to determine if anyone else had accepted payments from Donovan Nancarrow in exchange for confidential information until Cecily Nancarrow was white as a sheet and tried to hide her trembling hands under the boardroom table. She certainly wasn't cut out for intrigue.

"Surely that's illegal?"

The querulous tone and high pitch of her voice grated on Gareth's nerves. Anything the woman did or said grated on his nerves. She tittered. She demanded favours. She expected to be treated with kid gloves just because of her family name. If she'd had a brain to go with the attitude, Gareth could have borne it better.

The question didn't affect Jack in any way. He

didn't even shrug. "So is theft, Ms. Nancarrow. And fraud," he said. "Tim Gorish's action could have wrecked Nancarrow Mining. Imagine how many people would be out of a job had he succeeded." Jack focussed all of his attention on Cecily Nancarrow, and Gareth knew how devastating Jack could be when he focussed.

"I don't condone theft, Ms. Nancarrow, and I've been trained to fight fire with fire. Yes, I will break the law to do my job if it is necessary. But I am perfectly prepared to suffer the consequences."

The unspoken *Are you?* hung in the boardroom. Gareth kept an eye on Graham Halston. The man would make a decent poker player. He'd taken all Jack's detailed explanations in stride, but Jack's threat to examine bank accounts had rattled him. So much so that he now seemed to contemplate a quick dash out the door.

He would be given exactly one more chance to remain on the board of Nancarrow Mining—Julian was a great believer in second chances—but Gareth had a close eye on the man now. As did Jack, who stood like an avenging angel before the wayward members of Julian's board.

"Stop drooling." A fist clipped Gareth around the back of his head, and he grinned up at Aidan, unrepentant. The army had taught him to take his pleasures where and when he found them. If that was in the middle of an emergency board meeting, so be it. And if Aidan had an issue with that he could just—

"In case you were wondering, Ms. Nancarrow," Aidan drawled with an enticing edge of threat to his voice. "Once we had evidence of fraud, we obtained a warrant to cover our investigation. We are—legally, you understand—examining everyone's accounts."

Gareth watched more colour leave the woman's face at Aidan's announcement and hoped that she had her fill of family intrigue. She was irritating enough to deal with on a good day. If Julian hadn't explained months ago that she was the best of a bad lot, Gareth wouldn't have understood why the man put up with her antics.

Jack's presentation prompted only a handful of questions from members of the board who genuinely supported the way Julian ran the company. Jack dealt easily with each, and Julian closed the meeting with a quiet word of thanks.

In the shuffle of everyone leaving, Jack stayed behind. He leaned against the wall beside the door, cataloguing and observing.

Gareth wondered what he saw to intrigue him and made a mental note to ask. Not right now. Not even today, since the hardest part of Jack's day was still in front of him.

"We're off home now to get Jack ready," he said so quietly that only Aidan and Alex could hear. "If you need anything, talk to Frazer, okay?"

Alex gave him a sympathetic smile. Aidan told him to stop fussing, and Jack, who couldn't have heard any of that exchange, surprised him. Again. He stayed motionless beside the door while board member after board member filed out of the room. Once Cecily had sidled past him, eyeing him as if Jack was a predator that might pounce if she took her eyes off him, he straightened and pushed away from the wall. A few long strides took him across the conference room to Aidan Conrad's side. His gaze slid from Gareth to the bulky lawyer and the petite woman beside him.

"Next time, just fucking ask," he demanded gruffly, before he spun on his heel and walked out.

# Plans and Preparations

<hr/>

"**I** had no idea you kept leather trousers at work." Gareth lay stretched out on Jack's bed, watching him select his gear for the fetish night. Jack's turning up to the board meeting in figure-hugging leather had been the kind of surprise Gareth appreciated.

"I keep a lot of stuff at work you don't know about."

The little shit bent over an open drawer as he said that, showing off that leather-clad arse just because he could. And while that was a truly beautiful sight, Gareth swallowed the next comment that made it to the tip of his tongue. Jack's mood was edgy verging on brittle and had been so ever since he'd stalked out of the boardroom.

"Wanna tell me what got you rattled?"

"No."

"Tell me anyway."

Jack rested his hands on his hips and glared. "I hate when people dig around in my past," he snapped. "There. Now tell me I'm a hypocrite."

"I won't tell you anything of the sort." Gareth sat up and swung his legs over the edge of the bed. "In case it matters to you, I found out after the fact," he said. "But the way Aidan tells it, Alex digs just enough so she's able to help when you need it." He watched Jack's shoulders relax a tiny fraction and pushed his advantage. "I understand if you have trouble believing that. After working where you did, I would too. But I've watched Alex for over a year now, and she looks out for people."

The minute shift in Jack's expression showed he disagreed. He didn't argue, though. He crossed the room, pushed Gareth back onto the bed and joined him on the covers. Gareth was okay with that. He wrapped Jack up in a hug and willed him to relax.

Relaxation wasn't on Jack's mind. He had his eyes closed, but he played with the buttons on Gareth's shirt until he'd undone every single one of them. His fingertips rubbed tiny circles over Gareth's chest and around the small golden hoop in Gareth's nipple before sliding down to his abs to trace the dips and grooves.

Jack's body lay tense against Gareth's, and as time passed, he grew more and more restless. His lips skimmed Gareth's neck, his teeth scraped Gareth's collarbones, and finally Jack slid lower on the bed until his cheek rested on Gareth's hip. His fingers traced the edge of skin along the top of Gareth's trousers, and Gareth relaxed into the touch, let his breathing grow ragged, and enjoyed the attention.

"Something you need there, brat?" he inquired when Jack shifted and slowly rubbed his cheek against Gareth's cloth-covered erection like a contented, overgrown cat.

"Gods, yes!" Jack didn't open his eyes, but the plea was so heartfelt that Gareth's body surged in response. He slid his fingers into Jack's dark hair and tugged.

"Get up here, then."

Jack was pressed up alongside Gareth in an instant. When Gareth leaned to meld their lips together, the kiss grew heated and hungry immediately. Desperation wasn't a good look on Jack, so Gareth curbed his inclination to tease and draw things out. "Tell me what you need," he demanded.

"You. Fucking me through the mattress. Now."

"Happy to oblige, hot stuff."

"I'm more than hot." Jack ground the evidence of his arousal against Gareth's hip. His breath was coming fast and uneven.

"Then strip. Now."

Jack almost fell off the bed in his haste to scramble

out of his clothes. Gareth had seldom seen anything so sexy, and it got better when Jack draped himself across the deep green quilt and watched Gareth shed his shirt and trousers with a look made from naked want.

Gareth leaned down for another kiss, and the sultry purr coming from Jack's throat poured fire into his blood. He snatched the lube from under the pillow and slid backwards off the bed, pulling Jack with him and arranging him at the edge of the mattress. His hands caressed Jack's hips and legs, thumbs digging into the soft, sensitive skin of Jack's inner thighs. The marks he'd left a week ago had faded.

"They were a good reminder," Jack said suddenly as if he knew where Gareth's thoughts had taken him. His eyes were wide and dark, but his gaze was clear. This wasn't something said in the heat of passion.

Gareth nuzzled the soft skin until he heard Jack's breath hitch. "Maybe you need reminding some more," he suggested and used lips and teeth to suck bruises into Jack's skin while slipping lubed fingers inside him.

Jack's breathing stutter-stepped, grew ragged and out of control, yet he remained silent. He had his lower lip between his teeth, stopping every sound. It looked six shades of hot, but it was far from what Gareth wanted.

He pulled his fingers free and made quick work of

the condom and lube. Then he hooked Jack's calves over his shoulders and braced his hands on either side of Jack's head.

"Look at me," Gareth demanded. He held himself totally still until Jack's lids fluttered, and his lashes rose. The green eyes were black now and blazing with heat.

"No hiding," Gareth ordered. He thumbed Jack's lower lip out from between his teeth and leaned to suck the abused piece of flesh between his lips, stroking gently with his tongue before he pulled back. "I want you here with me."

"I'm here," Jack breathed, and it sounded like a promise.

As Gareth started to move, and Jack lost himself in pleasure, he kept his eyes wide open. Moans, not curses, spilled from his throat at each hard thrust and there wasn't an ounce of fight in his frame. Gareth kept to his slow rhythm, his gaze riveted to Jack's, until Jack reached up and pulled Gareth's head down for a kiss that melded them together until they both came in a shuddering rush.

———◆◆◆———

"Why are you mad?"

Sprawled across Jack's bed in a sweaty heap,

working to regain breath and steady heartbeat, it had taken Gareth a while to notice. Now it was difficult not to. Gareth knew what loose and relaxed looked like on Jack. Right now, Jack's body was hard and tense, and he breathed through clenched teeth. Gareth rolled to his elbow and looked down at Jack's face. "Talk to me."

Jack shook his head, the jerky movement telegraphing frustration, not refusal. While Jack struggled to articulate what riled him, Gareth breathed. He had the patience of mountains when it was necessary. When it came to Jack, he needed it.

"I'm not sure why I'm letting myself…." Jack trailed off and said nothing else for the longest time.

"Lean? Ask for what you need?"

"That's just it. I've never been… needed… things. People. Especially not people. There was a time I would have killed anyone who touched my computer. Now I'd just get a new one. I travel light. Always have. I don't need… stuff. But you…."

"That's a bad thing?" The look in the green eyes made Gareth's chest hurt. Made him wish for something he'd never considered before. Something longer than a few weeks. The thought didn't even feel scary. "Is it a bad thing?"

"It's a new thing. I… don't know what to do with it."

"See where it leads?"

"What if I screw this up? What if you get hurt?" Jack's voice rose in agitation. "I'm telling you, I've never had this. I don't know if—"

"Jack," Gareth cut across the tirade, voice close to a whisper. "None of that matters. If you want to see where this goes, we'll sort it out. Question is: do you?"

If Gareth had tried to hold his breath waiting for Jack's answer he'd have expired right there. Jack lay back on the pillows and eyed the ceiling, brows drawn tight and the tattoo marching like an angry slash along his temple.

For the first time ever, Jack looked older than his years.

Much older.

The perfect facade had worn thin, and just the fact that Jack allowed the cracks to show told Gareth how far they'd come.

Not that it made waiting for Jack's answer any easier.

"Gareth?"

The gravel in Jack's voice went right to Gareth's gut. "Hm?"

"I've no idea what I'm doing, but I want…." Deep breath. "I want to see what this is. Why it feels so different."

The level of frustration in Jack's tone made sense.

Gareth didn't understand how they'd met again after seven years apart and seamlessly slipped into something that had never existed before, except in heated fantasies. If it confused him, then Jack, who had to analyse everything to death before dissecting the rotting corpse for further clues, had to be driven mad by his inability to rationalise what was happening and predict where this train was headed.

"We're in this together, you know." Gareth had gotten his breath back, though his heart was still beating up a storm. "I might have had a couple relationships that lasted longer than a weekend, but you're the first guy I've ever wanted to wake up next to. That sort of makes us even."

"Yeah? I think it just shows what you don't know," Jack snarked. He rolled over and pillowed his head on Gareth's shoulder. "Explain to me why this shit's in my head just before I'm supposed to go out and take down a pimp."

"Nerves?"

"Do I know what that's supposed to mean?"

"You're nervous?"

"Because of Jericho? Don't make me laugh."

"Who is Jericho?" The way Jack froze at the simple question was uncanny. Like a rabbit caught in headlights or however that cliché went. "Jack?"

"Shit." Jack sat up and rubbed his face. "I can't

believe I missed this." He leaned into his hands and breathed slowly in and out until his shoulders relaxed once more. "Don't ask," he said softly as he sat up. "Just… don't."

And with that he rolled off the bed and disappeared into the bathroom.

———————◆◆◆———————

The doorbell rang while Jack hid in the shower. Jack might have called it something else, but Gareth knew. He also knew that he couldn't call Jack on it. Not when Jack needed to get his head in the game. The doorbell was just another unnecessary distraction.

Gareth waited, hoping the caller would give up and disappear, but the ringing continued unabated until Gareth gave in and went to open the door.

He came face to face with a dark-skinned man, who wore attitude like the latest fashion accessory. Skinny jeans with strategic rips, orange hi-top Converse, and a psychedelically coloured Henley teamed with gleaming, shoulder-long dreadlocks to create what Gareth considered the perfect disguise. Nobody could look that authentic and not be undercover.

"Ah'm lookin' for Jack," the stranger drawled. He pronounced it *Jacques*, with even a hint of an *e* at the end. It sounded damned sexy.

"He's busy."

"He'll wan' this." Long flexible fingers dangled a keyring in front of Gareth's face. On it hung a tiny black memory stick.

Jack hadn't mentioned informants; neither had Lisa warned them of a delivery. The dreadlocked man would fit either category.

"Come in?" Gareth moved aside and pushed the door wider, and the man stepped through without hesitation.

"You're Gareth?" he asked once the front door was shut.

"Yes."

Coffee-coloured eyes traced from his head to his bare feet and back up to his face. The scrutiny was disconcerting, as if the man was checking the veracity of existing information.

"No' at all what I was expectin'," the stranger concluded.

He was older than Gareth had first supposed from the trim build and deep chocolate hair. Fine lines creased his forehead and the corners of his eyes. And those eyes had seen a lot.

Before Gareth could ask for clarification, the stranger's gaze slipped past him to the hallway door, were Jack stood in barely buttoned jeans and a knife in each fist. To Gareth's relief, the knives landed on the sofa as soon as Jack caught sight of their visitor.

"Rio."

The man crossed the room in three long strides and turned Jack bodily into the light to inspect the fading bruise on his ribcage. "Jesus! Didn' I teach you anythin'?"

Jack accepted the touch without protest. The corners of his lips quirked up. "Don't sound like Flynn. And for the record, you might have been teaching, but whether or not I listened is anyone's guess. What are you doing here?"

"Bearin' gifts."

"Gifts?" Jack's voice held a world of scepticism.

"Fine. I caught some rumours and did a little work on your target. He has a sideline smugglin' tobacco, which he keeps in a warehouse not too far from the dinin' club." Rio held out the USB key. "Blueprints, access codes… you know the drill. Ping me when you're ready to question him, and I'll arrange for a little trouble at the warehouse he'll wan' to go check out."

Jack was never more than a few steps away from a computer, so he simply took the key, plugged it into his laptop, and scanned the information, while Gareth watched both men with avid interest.

Rio had access to classified data and the resources

to propose and stage a diversion. And Jack was angry, but he trusted this man enough to ditch his weapons and turn his back on him. They had history of a sort, and Gareth would have loved to ask questions.

Matters grew more interesting when Jack stopped reading and raised his head, offering the dreadlocked man a terse nod.

"Thank you."

"You don' wanna know why?"

"Beyond the fact that you and Alex Marston are thick as thieves, and you told her my business? I recognise an apology when I see one, Rio."

"How'd you know?"

"You were the only person who knew about… Jericho." His eyes slid to Gareth. "Until recently. Now there are what? Two more? Four more?"

"You're pissed."

"It's my past, Rio. If I wanted MI-bloody-6 to know, I'd have told them."

"It's not like that."

"Sure. And Alex runs a knitting circle."

Jack's tone cut like a whip and his movements were short and sharp, like he was failing to leash his temper. That he allowed himself to show this much emotion told its own story. As did Rio's calm acceptance, the way he took the barbs and agitation in stride. He'd clearly dealt with a riled Jack before.

429

"She's tryin' to watch your back, Jack," he said, sounding like the voice of reason.

"Yeah. Hard to wrap my head around that, you know? She works for the crowd I just walked away from. As do you."

"Doesn' make us the enemy."

"No, it doesn't," Jack sighed, and his shoulders sagged. "I'm not stupid enough to turn down your help, either," he said and pointed over this shoulder at the blueprints on his laptop screen. "Provided these did come from you?"

It was telling that the Jamaican—Gareth had finally managed to place the accent—didn't even blink at the suspicion in Jack's tone. He merely held Jack's gaze and answered.

"Mine. I didn' alert them to anythin' I was doin', either. You give the word, you have a safe place to question the man."

Jack saw Rio to the door and didn't object when Rio curled an arm around his shoulders for a moment. Whatever he said to Jack was too low for Gareth to make out, but Jack nodded and straightened up as if a weight had lifted from his shoulders.

"I'll need it," he replied, voice firm.

The two shared a final gaze, then Rio was gone and Jack locked the door behind their guest.

"You're looking more cheerful," Gareth

commented as Jack came back into the living room and went straight to the laptop, once more reviewing the information that Rio had brought.

"I have reason."

"How so?"

"Didn't you hear what Rio said?"

Gareth shook his head, then realised that Jack couldn't see him. "No, I didn't."

"He told me that I've got a pass if I need it."

"He has the clout to offer that?"

"Oh yes."

Jack's answer came without hesitation, and Gareth found that more comforting than he could explain.

# ENDGAME

———◆◆◆———

J ack swallowed the tail end of an appreciative whistle as Lisa stepped from Baxter's car. Thigh-high black suede boots, schoolgirl plaits, and a black trilby combined for a damn sexy picture. The pleated leather miniskirt added allure, the simple grey jumper—engulfing her slim frame—the innocence.

As she stood in the orange glow from a streetlight, Lisa Tyrrell simply rocked the schoolgirl fantasy. And if Jack's memories of theme nights were true to life, she'd fit like icing on a wedding cake.

"Yep, I can see exactly why she caught your eye," Jack decided. Gareth loved facets and layers. He'd always been attracted to anything that wasn't what it appeared to be. And right then, Lisa Tyrrell fit that description to a T.

"What?"

"Don't even go there, Flynn. Don't try and deny it."

"Wasn't going to. It just occurred to me how scary you really are."

Jack flushed. "Not guilty," he defended himself. "I swear I've not been digging. Just… the way you two are around each other, it's obvious you have history. And not the kind you forge across a conference table."

"That's exactly what it is," Gareth said quietly. "History."

"It's okay," Jack assured him. "I don't mind." Maybe he did. A little.

"Nice look," Lisa complimented as she came across the street to stand beside them. "James Dean fan?"

"More Brando, but I couldn't find the hat," Jack grouched, plucking at the frayed hem of the white sleeveless tee he wore with leather trousers and motorcycle boots. He'd planned to team it with a chunky leather jacket, but it didn't look right without the hat, peaked cap, whatever. The snafu annoyed him since he had an inkling that the hat was gone, sacrificed to the greater good during one of his last missions. How had he forgotten that?

"Do you know he owns a gladiator skirt?" Gareth baited, as if he knew that Jack needed a distraction.

It had been entertaining to see Gareth go through his leather collection. For a brief moment, Jack had even considered wearing the gladiator outfit, but half the strips were suede, the other half raw leather, and getting blood out of either was a bitch. It was also obvious that Gareth had never tried to kick someone's arse wearing sandals.

"I also have a genuine tartan kilt in the wardrobe, but I didn't see you drool over that one."

"That's 'cause you were in the shower."

"Your tattoo is gone," Clive interrupted, leaning close to inspect Jack's temple. "Don't tell me that thing's not real."

"Fine. I won't tell you." Jack avoided the punch Baxter tried to throw. "Don't hurt yourself, there, Inspector," he admonished. "Doctors tend to get bitchy if you come in with ripped stitches."

"Don't remind me," Clive groaned, recalling the event Jack alluded to. "She was scary."

"Yep. But you had that coming."

Clive's smile died and his mien grew sober. "I wish I could go with you."

Jack didn't. He wanted to be alone when he questioned Mitrovic. He'd accepted that having her help in the club would be useful, but just the idea of Lisa close by when he made his move on the pimp made his gut clench and what-if scenarios rear their ugly heads. Jack worked alone for a reason.

He was grateful when Gareth drew him aside without spouting pointless reassurances or admonitions to be careful. As situations went—Gareth seeing Jack off—this was a new one. At least Jack thought so until his mind taunted him with the image of a cold, clear morning, of Gareth standing in a patch of sunlight and Jack walking away without a backwards glance.

No.

Jack kicked his wayward mind to the kerb and into a bucket of chemical waste for good measure. He focussed on the pattern of broken tiles on the pavement and breathed until there was nothing on his mind but the layout of the dining club, the location of cameras, and the man they were hunting.

His lips pulled up a little as he caught Gareth watching him. "Don't wait up."

"As if," Gareth huffed in mock annoyance, and the world was right again.

Gareth and Clive would be with Raf. With three cars between them, they'd be able to react to whatever transpired in the club. They could follow any of Goran's boys, if he moved them, or they could go check out whatever address Jack and Lisa obtained. All without alerting anyone on Mitrovic's payroll until it was well past useful.

The brief touch of Gareth's hand on Jack's nape was a promise. One that Jack acknowledged with a nod.

Lisa joined Jack under the streetlight as the others

got into their cars. She clinked softly as she moved, and Jack raised a brow in question. Smirking like the cat that got the cream, Lisa slipped her hand into the top of her boot and pulled out a pair of handcuffs.

"Nice."

"Girl's gotta be prepared." She tossed the plaits and struck a pose.

"And it stops them digging deeper."

"'Course."

Lisa's attitude made Jack laugh. They had their differences. He owed her a favour, and she could land him in a mountain of shit at a moment's notice. But despite all that, he found that he liked her.

"Let's get this done," he suggested, shoved balled hands into pockets, and found just the right level of swagger. Cocky, but still wet behind the ears. He sank into the persona and watched as Lisa did the same. It made her look even younger.

"I'll be fighting blokes off you all night," he groaned.

"That's the general idea, isn't it? You looked too damned memorable the night we met. Tonight, I'm taking the spotlight." Lisa's hand stopped him under a streetlamp. "Can I ask you something?"

Jack waited.

"What you used to cover the tattoo… does it last?"

"It's synthetic skin. Unless you take a knife to it, it's

fine."

"Why didn't you use it the other night when you went into the club?"

"No time. Clive only called me at six that evening and asked me to go in."

"Does he do that a lot?"

"Call me or give me no notice?" Jack saw the irritation in Lisa's gaze and waved. "Don't bother. And no to both. This was a special case. He'd gotten a sudden tip. He'd hadn't been able to get a handle on Mitrovic, and the rumours were... well, you've seen. So he called me."

Lisa considered that. "You haven't asked me why I'm doing this."

"Everyone has reasons."

"You don't want me here."

"No, I don't." Jack kept his eyes on Lisa's as he answered. "I'm not used to working with a partner. To having backup on standby. Or anyone ready to bail me out." He wasn't used to watching out for others, either. He wasn't sure he wanted the vulnerability or the responsibility that came with having a partner.

Lisa understood him anyway. Her teal green eyes glowed like chips of ice. "This isn't... it's personal."

"I know. That's why it bothers me."

The theme night at the dining club had drawn an impressive crowd of old and young, gay and straight, starched and kinky. It wasn't even eleven o'clock yet, but the place was heaving. Lisa Tyrrell hadn't expected to feel conservatively dressed, yet neither she nor Jack stood out among the leather and lace-clad clubgoers.

Vampire lookalikes in black suits, ruffled shirts and long cloaks were out in force. Capes swirled, lace bodices hugged nubile shapes and tried to contain voluptuous ones, and whips coiled and slithered over the parquet like a convention of snakes. Lengths of chain twinkled with every flash of the strobes, and if she'd been collecting, Lisa could have opened a leather cuffs and collars shop the following morning.

Inhibitions had gone right out the window with this crowd, and both alcohol and more hazardous means to relaxation were as freely available as Jack had predicted.

"He's here," Jack breathed into her ear while she contemplated the idiosyncrasies of spandex and acres of skin against the dark oak panelling of the formal dining room. *Weird* didn't even begin to describe the effect.

"Any sign of the boys?"

"He has two with him, for decoration only."

Jack's voice held a tone she'd not heard before, and Lisa turned to see his face. He stood with his back to her, seemingly relaxed and focussed on a trio of witches in minimalist clothing, but bands of muscles stood out hard and tight across his neck and back.

"Jack?" She wasn't sure if it was wise to touch him, decided against it, and knew she'd done right when he shook his head once and spoke loud enough to be heard without having to turn.

"Not now."

Moments later the crowd had swallowed him up.

Lisa, who'd only seen one grainy surveillance camera image of the pimp, managed to locate the man in the third room she explored.

He stood off to one side, watching the crowd with a speculative look in his eye that chilled Lisa to the bone. Clive's description of medium everything and bleach-blond hair wasn't doing the man justice, though his attire—smartly tailored black trousers and a maroon shirt—made him appear ordinary enough to be forgettable. Only the company he kept differentiated him from the rest of the crowd. No other patrons sported bodyguards or had their arms around two boys who looked too young to be out that late.

Lisa had wondered about that. She'd imagined that, if challenged, Goran Mitrovic would play the I-had-no-idea-the-boy-was-underage card. Not that it would work. Nobody who saw them would give the boys a year over fifteen, though Lisa had no idea how Jack had determined that they were nothing more than arm candy for the evening.

It was tempting to second-guess everything Jack did or said. The man was endlessly intriguing, and it would be a fun game to play, but Lisa knew that she couldn't afford the luxury. Jack had his skill set, she had hers, and if they wanted to get their hands on the pimp, she had to trust what he told her.

Goran's bodyguard steered the boys out of the melee and towards a marginally quieter corner. The one-blond-one-dark combination reminded her of Nico and Daniel, as did the eyes that never settled on anything. But while Nico and Daniel had clung to each other, these two boys were... too still. No fidgeting, no bopping to the trance and techno the DJ pumped out. They didn't even turn their heads to check out the more outlandish of the costumes that dotted the throng. It was eerie.

"Did he drug them?" she asked when Jack joined her again a while later. The man worked the club like a pro, never in the same place for long, watching, listening, and memorising, invisible in the crowd.

Jack shook his head at her question. "Don't think so." The strange tone—raw and subdued like a muted cry of anguish—was still in his voice.

"Then why are they so...?" Lisa had to stop herself

from staring at the two human statues beside the maroon-clad man as she might at a museum exhibit.

"I guess he's had them in solitary," Jack said and finally met her gaze. His eyes were shadowed with a mix of pain and rage. His fingers were like ice where she brushed across them, despite the heat in the room. "It's confusing when you first come out of solitary. Coming out into this…." He waved his hand to encompass the noise, the strobes, and the crazy press of bodies. "They're on overload."

As if he regretted giving her even that small glance, Jack's gaze shuttered, and he was gone again before Lisa could question him further. It was her turn to watch Goran and his boys, and she could soon attest to the fact that when you were not having fun, time didn't fly. It crawled.

Her concern for Jack wasn't helping matters. They touched base at intervals, and Lisa's dread grew despite the professional facade Jack hid behind.

*Something's wrong with Jack.*

She sent the text message during a bathroom break, and then stared in horrified disbelief at the answer on her phone's screen.

*Seriously fucked up case. He could be having flashbacks.*

Flashbacks. Jack Horwood struggled with flashbacks, and nobody had seen fit to even mention that? As soon as she got out of this club, Lisa Tyrrell was going to strangle Clive Baxter.

She returned to the crowded bar area where Jack kept watch over Mitrovic and his boys. He looked no different than he had before Lisa had read the text, and she wondered if Clive could be wrong. In Lisa's experience flashbacks temporarily disconnected a person from reality. While Jack was tense and something clearly bothered him, he was aware and focussed on their task.

They traded places, and Jack disappeared into the crowd.

Lisa watched the two statue-still boys, watched Mitrovic hold court, and wondered what had possessed her to volunteer for this op. Alex had tried to dissuade her as had Jack, and while she'd never worked prostitution or human trafficking cases, she'd spent enough time both undercover and on surveillance to know how such assignments went.

The reason had to be Jack, she decided when she spotted him working his way through the crowd towards her once more. Jack Horwood had looked like delicious jailbait the night she'd met him. Learning what he did—in his spare time, without jurisdiction or backup—had intrigued her. And maybe she had listened a little too long to the rumours about the man and his way of working until curiosity had prompted her to ask for a ringside seat.

"He's getting ready to move the boys."

Jack handed her a drink, which she promptly spilled to give herself an excuse to head once more towards the washrooms in the back of the club. Safely in a cubicle, she texted the update to Raf's phone, glad that something was happening.

*I can see them,* flashed up on her screen a few moments later, followed by a second confirmation. *On the move.*

An instant later Lisa was too.

⚬ ◆ ◆ ◆ ⚬

Keeping an eye on the pimp grew more difficult now that he had sent the two boys away and started to mingle. It was fortunate, then, that the club only had two exits. And that the layout of the rooms allowed them to keep both in sight.

Some of Jack's tension had eased as soon as the boys had left the club. He was more proactive shadowing both Mitrovic and the bodyguard the man schlepped around, more intent to get close enough to overhear conversations between Mitrovic and other guests.

Those guests were invariably older men, successful professionals in age and demeanour, and Jack seemed to burn their faces and voices into his mind, ready to find them again at short notice.

It was both chilling and satisfying to watch him work, knowing that many of those men who basked in their own power and importance were destined for a rude, unpleasant awakening at the hands of the law.

For that much Lisa Tyrrell had learned about Jack Horwood. The man would always be there when asked to help hunt a pimp. He would forgo sleep and home comforts to rescue the children. But his rage, and most of his considerable focus, were reserved for the men who used their money and position to buy what should never be for sale.

Lisa kept one eye on the exit and the other on the clock. She wondered how far Raf had followed the two boys, and she prayed that the next message on her phone would be the go-ahead to arrest Mitrovic.

It wasn't.

<hr />

The text that flashed up on her screen simply said, *Call me now.*

Lisa frowned, then stepped out into the night—phone already at her ear—and walked a short distance away from the entrance.

"It's Lisa," she said when Raf answered the call.

"Gone to shit," Raf's voice rasped in her ear. "Car took the kids to a private party. Shoot me later, but I found them in the middle of some seriously sick shit, and called it in. We've arrested the whole damn lot of them."

"Were the other boys there?"

"No," Raf sighed. "That's the problem. The two we have here have no idea where they're being held, only that it's a house with three floors and an attic. Gareth has been speaking to them, but they're—"

"I know." Lisa straightened her back and drew a deep breath. "So… we'll go get Mitrovic. Keep standing by."

"Will do. I just wish…." Raf broke off, and Lisa didn't need to ask. She flipped the phone closed without another word and returned to the club.

——————◆◆◆——————

She found Jack close to the club's back exit, looking as if he contemplated the benefits of a breath of fresh air or simply waited for a cab. The thin sleeveless tee clung damply to his torso, his shoulders slumped, and even his inky spikes drooped in apparent exhaustion. Jack Horwood looked all partied out, but the gaze he hid behind the long lashes was as sharp as it had been three hours earlier, and he even found a crooked grin for her when she drew near.

"Boys went to a private party," she whispered, wrapping her arms around his neck and leaning against him. Under the innocent look he'd perfected, Jack Horwood was all hard, solid muscle. He loosely draped an arm around her waist and turned them so others passing through the doorway wouldn't bump her while he listened to her relate Raf's news.

His stance didn't change while she spoke, and neither did his breathing or the strength of the hold he had on her waist. It made no sense unless…. "You knew?"

"It was an option," he answered, and the tone of his voice had changed to bleakest winter. "I triggered the warehouse alarm when I saw you come back in."

"Are you sure you can do this?" The question was out before Lisa could stop herself, and Jack's expression froze.

"Of course," he said icily, and they stood silent and still in what might have passed for a lover's embrace until Jack spotted movement in the club's parking lot.

"Aaaand… we're in business," Jack breathed into her hair when a black Jaguar eased out of its space and disappeared down the lane. "I hope you can run in these." Jack drew back and pointed to Lisa's boots with their four-inch heels.

"Try and catch me."

It wouldn't be quiet, not with a set of cuffs in each boot and metal caps on the heels, but it would be as quick as they needed it to be.

They'd discussed transport options earlier in the evening and had decided to go with simple. Cars left parked in this part of town often ended up on bricks. Taxis didn't follow any timetable, and Mitrovic or his men could spot a tail. Relying only on themselves, they could ensure they'd be at the warehouse when Mitrovic showed up. The place was less than a mile away.

A blind man could have followed their progress down the road. That early on a Saturday morning, the neighbourhood was so quiet their footfalls raised echoes. Jack's rubber-soled boots made little more than heavy scuffing sounds, but more than once Lisa elected to run along the grass verges bordering the road, just to muffle the staccato clack of her heels on the pavement.

She followed Jack down shortcuts and narrow alleyways and footpaths between houses, intent on her footing when the thin yellow glow of the streetlights petered out. When they reached the railway line and the entrance to the small industrial estate that backed up against it, they slowed and kept to the sliver of shadows beside the buildings.

A garage, a body shop, and a scrap metal dealer

lined one side of the estate. A self-storage space and four warehouses took up the other. The whole site was deserted but for a single man leaning against the middle warehouse's loading bay, only feet away from a black Jaguar. The glowing tip of a cigarette confirmed his location when clouds sped across the moon and took the light.

"Shit. He left the dog out front."

"Back door?" Lisa suggested.

"Doesn't have one."

They needed to be in the warehouse before Mitrovic had finished checking the fake disturbance. "Pretend you're out of it. I'll get us close," Lisa decided.

"Wait."

Jack pulled a knife from his boot and held it up against his wrist, ready to do damage.

"Don't kill him," Lisa ordered. "Source of information."

Jack grunted, whether in assent or argument Lisa didn't have the time to explore or worry over. He let her grab his wrist and pull his arm over her shoulder, slumping to even out some of the height difference between them. She wound her other arm around his waist and hooked her fingers into his belt loops before she stepped from cover and started to drag Jack down the street, weaving and cursing as she went.

They weren't quite in striking distance when the guard peeled himself from the warehouse wall and stepped into the street.

"Are you Dale?" Lisa called out before he could check them out.

"What?"

"Are you Dale?" she slurred. "My boyfrien's drunk an' t' man at the greashy shpoon said you c'n give ush a lift."

"What greasy spoon?" The man took a step closer, reached for Jack, and got a kick to the knee that took his balance and dropped him to the ground.

"What the fuck?"

He didn't get to comment any further. A kick to his ribs had the man trying to curl into a ball, and a kick to his jaw took him out. His head hit the road with an unhealthy crack, and Lisa had cuffs on him a moment later.

"Shit, he's out for good," she panted, dragging the guard's still form to lean against the wall while Jack punched the access code into the keypad by the door with unnecessary force. His body was coiled, his movements urgent, and he yanked on the handle as if he didn't believe the place had no other exit.

As soon as the lock disengaged and the door slid open, Jack was in the warehouse.

And Lisa was right behind him.

There was no sign of Mitrovic as Jack slipped through the door. Low-level lights outlined the loading bay and painted lanes along the floor, leaving the rest of the space suspended in gloom. A small partition separated the loading bay from the main body of the warehouse space. It blocked the sight of any merchandise, though the heavy scent of tobacco in the air was an easy clue. It hung around them, thick enough to catch in Jack's throat and sting his eyes.

Scuffing sounds from an area to their right had Jack move in that direction until the muted yellow glow of a light cautioned him to stop.

Lisa was close behind him, and Jack was unexpectedly grateful for her company.

The sight of the two boys—the blank faces and confused gazes as they stared at the mass of bodies writhing around them—had fucked with Jack's mind. More than Daniel's nightmare screams, and the sobbing words Nico had poured into his ears. Memories had boiled up from the tightly shuttered pit he kept them in, and Jack had been tempted to screw their plans and wring the pimp's neck right there and then.

The muted horror in Lisa's eyes while she watched the boys and listened to Jack's terse explanation had done more to pull Jack back from the edge than she would ever know.

The scuffing noise came again, followed by a metallic clank and a whirr.

"Safe?" Lisa's voice whispered in his ear.

Jack nodded, not really bothered one way or the other. He needed what was in Mitrovic's head, not his safe.

Three fast steps took him across the space.

He shoulder-charged Mitrovic into a stack of bales in plastic shrink-wrap, grabbed him by the front of his shirt, and yanked him off his feet.

Profanities rent the air as Jack's fist found its target once, twice, a third time. Mitrovic flailed, trying to get away from Jack.

The sounds he made could have been calls for his guard or incantations to the higher powers for all the difference they made. Jack clamped a fist around the pimp's throat and shoved him back against the bales. Lisa had cuffs around Mitrovic's wrists before he could regain his balance.

"We make a team," Jack decided.

"Agreed. Now what?"

"Now I need to string him up. And I'm told that…." Jack tipped his head back and tried to make out the tracks that ran the length of the ceiling above the rows of bales. He could just see the darker lines against the whitewashed background. They terminated by the sliding doors of the loading bay, only a few feet away from where they stood.

Jack looked for the controls for the chain hoist and found them right beside the safe.

Along with the switch for the overhead lights.

The hoist creaked to life when Jack pushed the buttons, and only moments later a large metal hook appeared right in Jack's line of sight.

"Perfect."

Positioning Mitrovic the way he wanted him was the work of moments. As was asking Lisa to keep an eye on the loading bay entrance.

With the seductive smile he'd practiced in the mirror until it was just this side of scary, Jack unwound the strap of the bullwhip from his waist and shook it out, not at all concerned when the pimp let out a high-pitched, gleeful cackle.

"You wanna whip me?" Goran's breathing sped at the sight of Jack holding the whip, and his eyes dilated at the prospect. "Go ahead man, I get off on pain."

"Yeah?" Jack reached into his boot and retrieved the knife he'd stowed on entering the warehouse. "Let me cut off your dick and feed it to you first, then. Let's see how much you *really* get off on pain."

"You can't do that."

"Says who?"

"The law." Goran didn't look nearly so excited when Jack offered him a close-lipped smile. "You're not allowed to torture prisoners. I know my rights."

"You don't have rights, arsehole. You're not a prisoner. And I'm not the law. Just someone who's been taking out men like you since he was old enough to hold a knife." Jack stroked his fingers along the pleats of the bullwhip, aware of Lisa's eyes on him and sure that he looked a sight with the whip in one hand and a knife in the other.

He cracked the whip, and the tip tore a broad gash into the nearest bale of smuggled nicotine. The tobacco scent got stronger, and flakes of mangled cigarettes snowed down around them in a lazy twirl.

He did it again, just to see Mitrovic flinch.

These days the bullwhip was an affectation. Once upon a time, it had seen a lot of use, mostly to lecture would-be molesters on the errors of their ways. The whip had been a good tool to deal with the ocean of anger inside him. Now it wasn't about anger anymore. And he had better tools at his disposal.

He stepped close to Mitrovic and ripped the maroon shirt open in one savage move, the silk-covered buttons popping and tearing. "Where are you keeping your boys?"

A sneer was all the answer he got.

The whip sang through the air, close enough to

Goran Mitrovic's flesh that the man flinched and swayed... towards the flick of the tightly woven leather cord, not away.

Son of a bitch really wanted to feel that whip on him.

Maybe it was going to be just that easy.

Jack sent the tip tearing into bales of fragrant tobacco until a snowstorm of dried leaves swirled around them.

"Where do you keep your boys?"

Mitrovic's eyes were dark with want. His tongue smoothed over the lip Jack's fist had split, worried at the cut. He didn't look frightened or cowed. He looked smug.

"You won't ever find them."

"Tell me where the boys are, and I'll give you what you want." The back of Jack's throat burned with bile as he offered the bargain, but he touched the whip to Goran's neck, dragged it over his nipples and down his crotch, not surprised to see a visible erection straining against the fine black wool of the man's tailored trousers.

This was all shades of fucked up. And he just couldn't do this.

Beat the shit out of the man? Sure.

Kick his arse into next week until he begged to talk? Sure.

Get him off? Hell no!

Jack thought of six boys locked into a living hell and raised the whip again. "You frequent a bevy of clubs, you run an escort service…."

"Jack!"

Lisa's voice stopped him midswing. She stood by the bales he'd shredded with the tip of the whip, peering intently at something beyond Jack's line of sight. Jack wound the whipcord around his hand and crossed the open space to stand beside her.

What he saw sent a hard, cold shiver through his frame, as if someone had stepped on his grave.

The bales of cigarettes he'd been decimating were nothing but a shell that surrounded a hollow space with a blanket at the bottom.

A space that was far too small to accommodate an adult.

Sounds dimmed and the warehouse blurred around Jack. The lights receded into distance until they resembled glowing baubles on a lopsided Christmas tree, and he heard his mother's voice tell him that he now belonged to Jericho.

Jack whirled around and returned to Mitrovic.

The first stab of the knife produced a shocked yelp. Then Mitrovic clamped his lips together and panted breath through his nose while his eyes dilated, and shivers washed over his skin.

Fucker hadn't been lying about liking pain. Not that Jack cared.

"Where. Are. The. Boys." Jack punctuated each word with a slice of the knife, not bothering to listen whether any of the resulting groans and grunts formed recognisable words.

He couldn't save the children who had cowered in those bales, scared and lost and alone.

He could save the ones he knew about.

He *would* save those boys.

"Where are the boys?"

"Fuck you!"

Blood pooled in the cuts, ran down Goran's torso, and soaked the waistband of expensive, tailored wool. It would stick and start to itch soon, and Jack hoped that he wouldn't still be here when that happened.

For now, he repeated the question like a grotesque mantra as the knife marks on Goran's torso grew more numerous.

They all started begging in the end.

Jack always prayed his targets broke before it got that far, so he could walk away, end the nightmare before it took over his mind, stop the voices before they crawled inside him, impossible to shift or erase.

It didn't happen often.

Men who thrived on inflicting violence against weaker opponents begged for their miserable lives long before they did anything useful.

Jack concentrated on producing neat, even slices so he didn't have to listen to the whimpered pleas of *No, don't!* and *Please, God!* and *Please, stop!* Words that never did anyone any good.

The past tunnelled his vision. Reality disappeared under memories of being held down, his face pushed into stained, threadbare sheets while his body fought for air, of cruel laughter when he begged and pleaded for his tormentors to stop, of pain so fierce he threw up, and of cold water waking him to new tortures when his body and mind had called a halt.

"Jack?"

His mind registered the concern in the simple query, and Jack swallowed bile. He fought through the haze, searching for something—anything—to ground himself.

The knife in his fist.

Sticky warmth on his skin.

The overwhelming scent of tobacco and the metallic tang of fresh blood catching in the back of his throat.

Finally, the excuse for a man right before his eyes, his chest decorated with neat rows of sluggishly bleeding cuts.

He looked over Goran's shoulder and found Lisa's eyes on him. The fierce teal gaze was muted, the woman's eyes brimming.

*Why is Lisa crying?*

The sight confused Jack enough that the memories released their hold and let him breathe.

Flashbacks as vivid as this one were rare. He tended to take down the pimps before he met the victims. This time there was Ricky. And Jack's failure to save him.

Jack didn't care if Lisa had guessed what was happening. He was glad for the distraction, glad that she'd called out to him when their objective got buried under an avalanche of memories. Without her intervention…. Jack had no illusions what the result would have been.

His focus returned to his task, to the man who still believed that he would get out of this situation with his life and his string of boys intact. It was time to crush that belief.

"You realise that I'm still being nice, right?"

Jack dragged the knife straight down Goran's abs. The cut would hurt like a bitch every time the man moved. He traced the blade through the blood that had collected along the waistband of Goran's trousers, then lower, let the edge bite through fabric to reach skin. He muffled his mind to the screams, nothing but grateful when Goran Mitrovic finally got the message.

Jack relayed the address, voice urgent. "You got that?"

"Got it." Raf was already moving. A few minutes later, a car door slammed, and Jack heard Clive and Gareth's voices in the background. It reassured him as much as Raf's next words. "Going in to check it out. Just hang in there, okay?"

The call disconnected and, as many times before, Jack wanted to be in two places at once. It rarely worked out that way, and his task here wasn't finished until Raf confirmed the information he'd extracted.

He couldn't relax, couldn't call Rio to tell him that his target smuggled more than tobacco, couldn't switch off while adrenaline kept him hot and twitchy.

Jack paced to the far side of the loading bay, away from the smell of blood and vomit, away from the rasping sounds of sobbing breaths.

He leaned his back against the wall close to the sliding doors where Lisa kept watch and tried to keep his body still, melt into the background as he'd been taught.

The phone in his fist was slick with sweat and blood. Jack had been in too much of a hurry to get the intel to Raf to make sure his hands were clean.

He'd have to get a new phone once he got home.

Gareth. Raf. Clive. Jack wondered how the three

got on. Clive knew what to expect. Raf might. Gareth.... Jack guessed that Gareth had never seen or even imagined what he thought the men would find in that house. His mind was right there with the three of them.

Then it wasn't.

He brooded over makes and models of phone.

Wondered how many boys they would find and whether they'd be alive.

Listened for the sounds of Mitrovic's ragged breaths in case the man had lied to him.

Dismissed the very idea.

Worried.

His mind ran itself ragged like a hamster on a wheel. And Jack didn't move a muscle where he leaned, plastered to the wall.

"We should call it in." Lisa's voice distracted him. She sounded cautious, as well she should. Jack was aware, but he wasn't ready to swear that he was all the way back. "At the very least, we should let your contact know that we're dealing with more than smuggled cigarettes."

"Not yet. As soon as they know, they'll swarm this place and won't give a hoot about anybody else's case."

"You think Mitrovic lied to you?"

"Wouldn't be the first one. If he thinks he can get

away with it. If he owes someone higher up the food chain. Or even if he runs more than one string of boys."

"You've seen all of that."

"Yes," Jack agreed. He didn't elaborate.

He wanted this over with.

Wanted out of this place where tobacco scent clung like an oily cloud of loathsome memories.

Wanted to wash the last few hours off his skin before taping his hands and hitting a bag until exhaustion forced his mind to shut up.

He wanted all of these with a passion so fierce it burned, but only professional detachment showed when he spoke: "Let's wait for Raf's call."

<hr/>

It took an hour before Raf called to confirm that it was over. They'd rescued four boys, bagged a couple of no-longer-so-eager customers, and had called social services and the local law to the scene to deal with the bureaucracy for the second time that night.

"Thank God for small mercies," Lisa breathed as she pushed the sliding doors of the loading bay just wide enough that she could slip out into the early morning.

The light was still thin and watery, but traffic noise

filtered into the estate, growing louder the longer she listened. The fine mist that had started earlier turned into a more serious drizzle, but Lisa stayed where she was.

She needed space and air.

Needed to hear something other than Goran Mitrovic's moans and laboured breathing.

Needed to see something other than a motionless, hollow-eyed Jack Horwood clinging to the wall.

She wrapped her arms tight around her torso, struggling to hold back a bone-deep shudder that had nothing to do with the early morning chill and everything to do with her mind accepting how scary Jack Horwood really was.

The man had been a tightly coiled bundle of energy all night, moving with focus, purpose, and more grace than should be allowed. Jack's experience shone through in the way he handled distractions, blended into the crowd, and never once lost sight of the target.

Lisa couldn't wait to find out what other information Jack had collected during those hours at the dining club. Rumours credited him with a photographic memory and mad skills in catching patterns before anyone else did.

When asked, Clive had told her to enjoy watching Jack work and prepare for making arrests from here to

Easter. Having seen Jack in action, she was more inclined to believe the hype.

Jack Horwood was all about control. He'd been running on adrenaline and rage, but he'd had himself in hand until she'd found the hiding space inside the tobacco bales. It was then that Jack had changed.

Lisa couldn't imagine what it took for Jack to withdraw so completely into himself that even his eyes looked lifeless. What it took for Jack to turn into someone who was prepared to torture to save a group of boys from more suffering. And do it outside of any capacity that could exonerate or even protect him.

Jack was a civilian. His actions, if misconstrued, would land him in jail for the rest of his life.

It was the most fucked up version of an eye for an eye that Lisa had ever witnessed. She should be revolted and yet….

"What you told him in there, is it true?" she asked in barely more than a whisper when Jack closed the sliding door and came to stand beside her in the street.

Jack looked steadily into her eyes as he nodded. "I am Ricky," he said, voice so calm it sent new shivers flashing across Lisa's skin. "I am Daniel and Nico and any boy those bastards have ever laid hands on. Only difference is, I stole a knife, and I got away. I was lucky, and I'm putting that luck to use."

"That's a job for the law," Lisa told him, voice quiet.

"Yes. Yes, it is."

"Then why—" Lisa didn't get far before Jack interrupted her.

"Because I made it out. Because I owe someone up there for that alone." He regarded her from the corner of his eye, considering, then went ahead with what he wanted to say anyway. "If you had arrested Mitrovic in the dining club as you wanted, we would have lost the boys. They would have disappeared into another hellhole, and we'd never have got them back."

"We could have kept the arrest quiet." That had been the one point of contention between them while they planned the takedown. She'd argued the matter hotly, but when Clive, Raf, Nell, and even Walshaw took Jack's side, she'd conceded and agreed to Jack's plan.

"You're deluded," Jack maintained, just as he had done before. "Men like Mitrovic keep ears everywhere. And I'm not the only hacker out there." He took a few steps away from her suddenly. Over his shoulder he said: "I work alone for a reason…."

"You regret that I saw you. You're sorry you had to torture Mitrovic."

Jack turned and stared at her, half twisted around. A smear of blood was drying on his cheek, and his T-shirt, hands and even his phone were streaked red. He looked like a barbarian warrior after a gruesome battle, but his eyes were clear and wide with disbelief. "I'm *what?*"

"You're sorry you—"

"I heard you the first time." Jack looked down at his blood-smeared hands. Held them out and turned them over this way and that as if he might read his answer in his palms. "You're so wrong, it's hilarious," he said, and his voice held the resonant silence Lisa associated with the white-tiled horror of the morgue. "This wasn't about the pimp. This is *never* about the pimp."

# DECOMPRESSION

<br>

❖ ❖ ❖

I f it hadn't been for the fleet of squad cars and the sea of flashing blue lights, Raf would have driven right past the small estate. The place was too nondescript to attract even a second glance from anyone passing.

His clearance let him drive close to the loading bay where Lisa leaned against the wall, the previous night's schoolgirl fantasy now a tired illusion. The grey jumper drooped off her shoulders, the fluffy wool turned limp by the soft drizzle, and the hat was missing. Strands of dark hair escaped from their plaits and spilled untidily around her, while a tartan blanket draped her shoulders and let her huddle into the warmth and shelter it provided.

Lisa was aware of Raf's approach, yet she never took her eyes from Jack Horwood.

Jack stood next to a police car, tablet in hand and eyes riveted on the small screen, ignoring the flashing

466

lights, milling officers, and the discomfort of drying blood all over him. He didn't appear hurt, but Raf thought it better to make sure.

"Any of that blood his?"

"No," Lisa got out before she flattened her lips into a tight line and breathed deep and slow.

Raf had wondered how Jack had extracted the brothel's location so quickly when they had failed to find the place by trailing the boys. Hard-as-nails Lisa Tyrrell looking faintly green next to a blood-spattered Jack Horwood answered that question.

"That bad, eh?" He pulled Lisa close and pushed her face against his shirt, letting her breathe the familiar scents of laundry detergent, aftershave, and leather until the nausea passed.

"I've never seen anything like it," she said, trying to keep her voice low enough that Jack wouldn't hear. "He didn't get angry. Not loud, I mean. It was strange. He was so detached… clinical…." She scrubbed a hand over her face. "Elsewhere."

"And that bothered you." It wasn't a question, and Lisa didn't treat it as one. She just nodded.

"Let's get you two out of here," Raf decided. He returned to the car and pulled a clean long-sleeved top from a bag on the passenger seat. "Horwood?"

Jack looked up from the tablet, and Raf waved the shirt at him. "You done?"

"Sure." Jack handed the tablet back to the officer in the car with a nod of thanks and stripped his bloody T-shirt off on the way to Raf's car, not bothered by the chill, the drizzle, or the audience. He found a relatively unstained corner of fabric to scrub at the drying blood on his face and hands before he pulled the clean shirt over his head.

"I need a shower."

"Hospital," Gallant instructed, not in the least surprised when Jack shook his head.

"No need."

"Hospital," he reiterated and backed Jack against the SUV, crowding him until Jack gave in and stopped arguing. *Elsewhere* was a good description of Jack Horwood right then. Raf wanted to make sure that was really all. And not just because Gareth Flynn had threatened him with any number of unpleasant fates should he fail to take care of Jack.

Jack buckled himself in and leaned his head back with a deep sigh. "Waste of time," he mumbled and closed his eyes. His breathing grew deep and even before the warehouse had disappeared out of Raf's rear-view mirror.

"He is unreal," Lisa said while Raf fought his way through London's morning rush-hour traffic, and Jack slept peacefully in the backseat, apparently unbothered by the night's events. "There's nothing in his file that even hints at… I underestimated him."

"You're not the first," Raf replied. "And you won't be the last. I've been talking to a few people, and they've all told me the same thing. If you're not ready to reap storm, don't call Jack Horwood. Not in a case that involves children."

⎯⎯◆◆◆⎯⎯

"Horwood. Wake up, we're here."

Raf's voice drew him from his nap. A hand touched his elbow, and Jack responded to the pressure. He moved until he had both feet on the concrete and blinked sleepily at the lights. A row of police cars was parked in his line of sight, and that didn't make much sense at all. Not that anything else did. He'd been in a nightclub… no, scratch that. Warehouse. He'd followed Mitrovic to the warehouse where the man kept his smuggled goods. Yes. And Lisa had—

"Jack!"

He flinched at the sudden shout, not prepared when arms wrapped around him, and he was engulfed in a hug forceful enough to threaten his ribs.

"Thank you. Thank you. Thank you."

*What the fuck?*

A scent like fresh water and freesias, unruly blonde

469

curls, and eyes like molten chocolate—it took time for Jack's tired mind to put the clues together.

"Don't, Gill." He tried to push the woman away. "I'm filthy."

"And?" Gillian Kent only hugged him harder. "Crap doesn't seem to bother you."

"Didn't get under my skin," Jack mumbled, still only half-awake and not filtering what he was saying. "Washes off."

"There you go," Gillian snorted. "Plenty of soap and water where I hang out. Now let me tell you what you did."

"Can I have coffee first?"

"How about a shower?" Raf interrupted.

"That too." Jack stretched, waking up enough to take notice of his surroundings, to recognise the underground parking garage of New Scotland Yard. "I thought you were dragging me off to St. Thom's?"

"You wanna go there?"

"Hell no."

"Good." Raf tossed him a duffel bag Jack recognised as his. "Let's go. Shower, then debrief."

Coffee, it seemed, had to wait.

The shower was welcome, though. After three rounds of soap, scrub, and rinse under a torrent of blissfully hot water, Jack's skin felt like his own again. Untainted by Mitrovic's filth. Shame he couldn't scrub his mind clean as easily.

Jack stretched under the water and closed his eyes. He had kinks in his back from falling asleep in the car after over twenty-four hours on his feet. Working each one out, slowly and methodically, helped him relax.

"You know she can run in those heels?" he asked randomly, convinced that Raf was close by. They had all looked at him as if he needed guarding. Jack scrubbed at the dried blood under his nails with a brush and conceded that, maybe, he did.

"She can kick arse wearing them too," Raf drawled back.

Jack's mind replayed the image of Lisa restraining the guard. "I know." Lisa Tyrrell could kick arse. She could also keep it together. He didn't dwell on the fact that she'd looked almost green in the early morning light. Instead he remembered her brief touch in the club and the intent teal gaze full of tears that had pulled him out of the worst flashback he'd had in years.

"She makes a damn fine partner," he decided once he was dressed and drying his hair.

"Well, colour me surprised. She's usually like you. Works alone." Rafael Gallant sprawled on the bench, long legs out in front of him and hands laced together behind his head. But for the shadows in his eyes he was a picture of ease.

And he didn't fool Jack for a moment.

"Give me the extras," Jack requested. Raf raised a brow, and Jack shrugged. "Whatever you're not going to mention in debriefing."

"What makes you think—"

"Gallant."

Raf looked sheepish. He reached into his pocket, pulled out a memory stick, and tossed it in Jack's direction. "Place had an office," he said in a voice so low that Jack almost had to read his lips. "I copied this while we were waiting for social services and the police to show."

"Customer data?"

"Maybe nothing. I didn't look."

"Baxter see you?"

"No. Neither did Flynn."

Jack shoved the tiny key into the front pocket of his jeans and waited for Raf to continue speaking. "And?" he prodded when nothing was forthcoming.

"Nothing."

Raf chewed on his lower lip and contemplated his feet until Jack let it go. He pulled on his boots and rummaged in his bag until he found a fleece top to wear over his long-sleeved tee. It would help ward off the shivers left over from the flashback and excess adrenaline.

"I've ordered a new phone," he said. "Someone will

bring it by. That a problem?"

"Nah. We'll swing by the front desk on our way up. You okay with debriefing over breakfast?"

"Anything that gets me out of here sooner."

———◆◆◆———

The main reception area was busy with both uniforms and civilians, allowing Jack to blend into the crowd without a problem.

His new phone—courtesy of Rio—was waiting for them when Rafael checked, and Jack dismantled the thing as soon as he'd sat down at the conference table, ignoring Baxter, Gillian Kent, Nell, and even Raf beyond a quick wave hello. Jack trusted Rio as much as he trusted anyone, but his leaving MI6 had changed many things, and Jack was taking no chances.

Coffee and breakfast appeared as he switched SIM cards, and he downed the first mug of black gold while he sent a check-in text to Gareth. He was working on the second mug along with a bacon sandwich when Lisa came in, showered and changed into tight jeans and warm wool.

Jack surprised himself when he got up and grabbed her into a tight hug. "Thanks," he said, voice low. "It was good to have you at my back."

"Don't make it a habit," she begged in an equally

low voice. "But call me if you need help, okay?"

Jack stared, stunned by the pronouncement. The events of the night were having unexpected results. Lisa knew it too, and for a moment, her eyes clouded with an emotion that was too quickly gone for Jack to read.

A shrug, a grin, and she was back to being Dr. Lisa Tyrrell, reaching for coffee, calling the meeting to order with her mouth full of apricot danish, and getting down to work.

———◆◆◆———

Jack was ready to head home when Rafael Gallant finally got around to saying what had been on his mind all morning. Right in the lobby, while shifts changed and uniforms milled around, while plainclothes officers waved and called to Raf, and his phone vibrated with call after call, Raf finally held Jack back.

"You're wasted as a corporate drone, Horwood," he said with a crooked grin.

"You recruiting for the Met now?"

"I'm… recruiting," Raf said. "If you ever need a job… hell, if you want some part-time excitement… look me up."

All of a sudden, Jack found it easy to smile. At

Raf's delivery that was far too deliberate to fool the spook Jack had been, at the man's unease, even at the time it had taken Raf to work up to making the offer. Tired and disconnected as he felt, it still amused Jack to wonder whose offer this really was. And why not knowing the answer cheered him in some small way.

He added a few watts to his smile and bumped Raf's shoulder with his fist as he walked past. "I hear you, Gallant. Thanks."

———————◆◆◆———————

Lisa called from the Yard, halfway through the morning. "Jack's okay, but I'm keeping him for debriefing."

Gareth leaned back into his chair and stretched his legs, contemplating the dark jeans and sturdy boots that had confused his team this morning. He'd had no time to make it home between securing the private party, rushing to the brothel site, waiting for police and social services for the second time that night, and facing rush-hour traffic. Given that he'd had the easier half of the job, he hadn't expected to see Jack at work.

"I know that he's fine. He texted me. Why did he need a new phone?"

"He got blood on his."

"Of course. Are you okay?" She didn't sound okay,

but it was safer to ask than guess.

"He's something else, you know?"

Lisa sighed, and Gareth knew then that his guess had been accurate, regardless. "That's true. But you didn't answer my question. Are you okay? Curiosity all sated?"

"I'm fine, Gareth. Thanks. Next time you need help…." Her voice trailed off, and Gareth held his breath. "Make sure you call me. Preferably before you let him loose and the shit hits the fan."

"Before *I* let him loose?" Gareth wished he had that much clout, but he didn't delude himself. Jack would do what he felt needed doing when it needed doing and worry about the consequences later. "Maybe you should tell him."

"I will, Gareth. I will." There was a smile in her voice now. "Clive promised I'd be knee-deep in warrants until Easter, and it looks as if he was right. So… I owe you."

"Call me when you're ready to fix your… internal problem," Gareth reminded her, pleased with the choices he'd made. "Or call me whenever."

⬤▬▬ ✦ ◆ ✦ ▬▬⬤

Baxter's call came almost three hours later, startling Gareth. In a hurried tone, tinged with unspoken apologies, the detective asked if he could drop Jack at Gareth's home.

"He took that bastard down," Clive explained haltingly. "He's finished debriefing, and there some…. And he's still…."

"Wired," Gareth supplied after a pause, imagining Baxter waving his hands aimlessly, trying to describe a clammed-up Jack, face blank and eyes distant.

Baxter's sigh was audible even through the background noise on the line. "Yes. I… I think he shouldn't be alone."

"You think correctly, Inspector. Please drop him off. He has a key."

"Thank you."

Unable to concentrate on his work, Gareth called it a day as soon as he finished the report he'd been working on. He wanted to call Jack, hear his voice, but stopped himself. Jack was too good at hiding, and Gareth needed to see for himself that Jack was okay.

After the horrors they'd encountered in Mitrovic's brothel and having had a glimpse of Jack's history, Gareth didn't believe that Jack would be fine. Not in a long while.

It made getting home and being there for Jack more important than ever. Traffic and speed limits be damned.

◆ ◆ ◆

Gareth could hear the bass before he'd unlocked the front door. The house vibrated on its foundations, rocked to each beat, and Gareth was grateful that his home occupied a corner plot, and the neighbours were some distance away. He didn't want to imagine Jack's reaction if someone came knocking on the door to complain about the noise.

Once inside with the front door safely bolted, Gareth followed the sound to the gym where he found Jack in jogging bottoms and an old army T-shirt with ragged tears where the sleeves used to be attached.

Jack's hands were taped, and he attacked the heavy bag in time to the beat. Sweat soaked his hair and his shirt, but the fluid, graceful way with which he moved sent a rush of warmth through Gareth's chest. Warmth that morphed into sheer gratitude when he saw that Jack's face and eyes were calm.

Gareth watched for a long while, enjoying the sight of rippling muscles and sinuous moves, wondering if Jack was aware of him standing in the doorway or if his mind was out to lunch. He got his answer a few minutes later when the music changed, and Jack stopped moving and looked over his shoulder.

"You're home early."

"You're here."

"And now, so are you."

Jack came so close that Gareth could smell him. Grapefruit shampoo, sweat, and musk, and damn him if the mix didn't turn him on. There was something about Jack's stance, though, that set off Gareth's warning bells.

The come-on lacked substance.

And wasn't it just like Jack to try to distract him?

"You need to talk about this, get it out of your system." Gareth took a step back, out of reach of the warm body before him.

Jack's eyes narrowed, but he didn't follow. He stayed where he was, hands on hips, and staring. "I'm not going to break, Gareth," he said, his voice rough. "Not over this. *Never* over taking down a fucking pimp."

Gareth didn't believe a word. "Then why that god-awful racket?"

"Oi, that's Wolfstone you're insulting, you heathen!" Jack shot back. "It's loud because I like it, and you weren't here." He pointed the remote at the stereo, and the sound in the room dropped to a level where Gareth could hear himself think.

The next song had a familiar intro, a simple guitar solo that reminded Gareth of the one quiet weekend they'd managed so far. Jack had gone home to pick up fresh clothes and had returned with a guitar case across his back. For the rest of that afternoon he'd lounged in the deep window seat of Gareth's kitchen, drinking red wine and plucking away at the strings while Gareth cooked. He'd played that very song, and as Jack picked up the lyrics, Gareth remembered its name: "Savin' Me."

Jack's voice was full of shadows, and Gareth's worry grew. His discerning eye spotted far too many knives in the room. Not to mention the bottle of Talisker Storm that had a good chunk of content missing.

"If you're not having a breakdown, then what…?" he asked as Jack's voice died away on the last chord.

Jack reached for the Talisker. He held the bottle up to the sky, brought it to his lips to take a swig, and then held it out to Gareth. "It's a wake," he explained. "Ricky's."

Gareth had no idea what to say. He hadn't forgotten the courageous youngster who had died from his injuries after offering to help Jack take down the pimp who had imprisoned him, but in the whirl of having Jack back in his life, hunting the man responsible for Ricky's death, caring for two traumatised teens, and all the troubles at work, Ricky hadn't been much on his mind. Now it appeared he'd been on Jack's. More than Gareth had realised.

He took the bottle Jack held out to him and

brought it to his lips. Sweetness and brine mingled on his tongue, morphed into heat that tempered to warmth as the malt slipped down his throat. When the burn had died to embers, Gareth slid his palm around the back of Jack's neck, drew him close, and sealed their lips together.

Jack didn't fight. He leaned and let himself be kissed.

"You've avenged him," Gareth said as Jack drew back.

"No." Jack's voice was rough with pain. He shook his head to emphasise his point. "I failed to save him." He took the Talisker from Gareth's hand and swallowed another mouthful before he set the bottle down and replaced the cap. "But maybe he'll sleep safely now."

━━◆◆◆━━

Jack's chuckle broke the stillness of the bedroom just as the first rays of sunlight reached the windowsill.

"What's amusing?" Fatigue dragged heavily on Gareth, and he battled to keep his eyes open.

Jack had been quiet after the end of his impromptu wake. He had showered and changed from his gym gear into ancient ripped jeans and a soft fleece-lined T-shirt, had watched Gareth cook and had eaten his

481

dinner in silence.

When Gareth suggested the hot tub in the garden, he had stared at Gareth for a moment but then followed him without comment. Under the soothing blanket of the jets, with nothing but Gareth and the stars for company, Jack's tight control began to ease.

He still hadn't talked much. He recounted small details he'd observed during the fetish night in the dining club, described one or two costumes, mentioned that Lisa could run in four-inch heels and kept handcuffs in the tops of her boots, all the while his body grew soft and pliant against Gareth's.

When Jack's breaths came deep and slow and even, Gareth had pulled him close and kissed him. Jack kissed back, eyes wide open, and they'd stayed like this for what seemed like hours just trading air and peace.

They'd retired inside around midnight.

Jack moved like a sleepwalker, semi-aware of his surroundings but not completely awake. Once in bed he settled against the headboard and contemplated the air in front of his face. Closing his eyes seemed too big a task for Jack, so Gareth wrapped himself around his lover, let kisses and soft touches remind Jack where he was and who he was with.

Jack didn't sleep, but neither did he pull away.

Now Gareth's arm curled around him, drawing Jack closer. Close enough to feel him huff another quiet laugh.

"So what's amusing?"

"Raf Gallant's crappy sense of timing," Jack replied. "Not sure why it needed saying today, but you should have seen it: Scotland Yard at lunchtime shift change, uniforms everywhere, people waving at him, his phone vibrating enough to rattle his teeth—and Rafael had nothing better to do than wonder if I might be looking for a job."

Gareth growled, not caring that he sounded like a possessive oaf. He tightened his hold on Jack's form until the younger man was stretched flush against him from shoulder to ankle. "I hope you told him where he could shove that offer," he said, deadly serious, and buried his nose in Jack's dark hair. "You're working for me now. With me. There'll be no more job hunts for you."

*Eight weeks later*

## EPILOGUE

————— ◆ ◆ ◆ —————

The décor was an exquisite blend of duck egg and white, from the stucco ceiling and delicate tracery around the windows to the tablecloths and Wedgwood china. Dark oak tables, chairs and sideboards contrasted the pale colours and turned the dining room from something frothy and feminine into an elegant, airy space that oozed sophistication.

The man who faced Lisa Tyrrell across the dinner table fit into the refined environs like the proverbial bull into a china shop. Square-jawed and olive-skinned with thick black hair and dark eyes, he looked like a bruiser rather than the political animal and expert manipulator he was.

"So you now have an ace hacker owing you a favour?" he asked when Lisa concluded her report. "I must say it: I am impressed."

"If there was ever a favour owing, sir, he's repaid it many times over," Lisa corrected, setting her silverware down to pick up her wineglass.

It was late. The venue was out of her way. Most of all, she hated the man's guts, but she never minded coming here.

The restaurant's menu was as exquisite as the décor of the private dining rooms. Despite it being only two weeks to Christmas, there was no turkey on the menu, no Christmas pudding and—thank the Lord for small favours!—nothing that required to be served in vol-au-vents.

Lisa had dined exceptionally well on smoked salmon and roast venison, and with the heavy claret warming her belly, she was ready to defend her sources with the fervour of a tigress. Only problem was, her dinner partner knew her too well.

"He'll think nothing of the sort, of course." He chuckled. "You forget that I've worked with Horwood. He's nothing if not accommodating, and I strongly suggest you keep him that way. Don't cash in whatever favour he thinks he owes. I want him as the ace up my sleeve. I'm sure there'll come a time in the not so distant future when a hacker of his calibre will come in handy."

"Yes, sir." Lisa kept her head down and her voice low, hiding her thoughts, even though she was seething. Jack had impressed her more than she could articulate, even to herself. He'd put himself on the line without a second thought to help rescue a string of boys, and Lisa couldn't conceive going to him to demand he use his skills to rig a party leadership election or something similarly mundane. She knew whom she was dining with, though. Appealing to her companion's morals was as pointless as praying for snow in June.

It was fortunate that he was as clueless as he was arrogant.

Lisa made it to the end of the meal without putting a foot wrong. She walked out of the club and called a cab. She curbed her impatience and waited until she was home and could use the phone she had stashed in the wall safe behind her bed. The one that couldn't be traced to her and that had only one single, equally untraceable number in its speed dial list. Even with those precautions, she stepped out onto her small balcony before she dialled.

"Yes?"

The voice in her ear was calm, soft, and female. Lisa breathed a sigh of relief and let her shoulders sag. Here was genuine power, someone who stood for the same things she held dear, who ignored political shenanigans and got things done instead.

"He's after Jack," she said quietly, the apology in

her tone almost too faint to hear.

"As you expected," Alexandra Marston replied. "Everybody knows he's gunning for the top job, but he's far too obvious to make a good leader. His scheming won't come to anything."

"I do hope you're right. And there's something else. He was late for our meeting. The club's steward knows me since we've met there before, so he was happy for me to wait in the lobby. The man he was meeting..." Lisa trailed off, unable to explain her misgivings, glad that Alexandra had enough patience to wait until she'd organised her thoughts. "At first, I thought he was meeting with your boss. But it definitely wasn't Julian, even though you might have thought so from a distance."

"Could have been Donovan. He looks a lot like Julian but has a burn scar beside his left eye."

"Yes, I saw the scar. Are they twins?"

"No. Really just cousins. Any idea what was under discussion?"

"No. But they were cosy together. Two-handed shakes cosy. And he said that Donovan could rely on him."

"That doesn't sound encouraging. Did you get the impression that Donovan was negotiating payback?"

"More like something up front. Why?"

"Because the man is becoming a nuisance. He

wants to take control of Nancarrow Mining from Julian. He's wanted it for years and never succeeded, but he never stops trying."

"And you let him?"

"So far, he's always been clumsy enough to trip himself," Alex admitted. "I've kept a watching brief, but most of the time Julian had a good enough grip on the situation. Maybe now, with Jack's help, we could settle the mess once and for all. Jack's damned good at digging up reasons."

"He is. But what if they were discussing protection for Donovan? Wouldn't Jack get into trouble digging?"

"We won't let that happen. We'll have Jack's back all the way. Don't worry."

The call disconnected.

Lisa's tiny sigh of relief turned into a well of anxiety a moment later. She didn't want to see Jack used by factions of power-hungry politicians and civil servants. The man didn't deserve that. But Jack's past and his skills made him a valuable commodity. And Lisa feared that in trying to protect him from evil, she'd just sold him into hell.

*Jack's story continues.*
*Read an excerpt from the second book in the Power of*
*Zero series:*

# GHOSTS

# SLEEPLESS

———— ◆ ◆ ◆ ————

The scents of cinnamon and vanilla swirled in the kitchen's warm air. They mixed with the enticing aromas of roasting meat and baking bread while the choir of King's College, Cambridge, sang tidings of comfort and joy. The whole atmosphere had a deeply peaceful tint… until strident guitar riffs tore through the soothing harmonies like a knife through a freshly baked loaf.

Gareth dropped the wooden spoon on a convenient plate and wiped his hands on the dishcloth he had slung over one shoulder. By the time he reached the ringing phone, X Japan's Toshi was wailing louder than the choir, and Gareth couldn't hold back a smile.

Leaving anything electronic in Jack's reach was risky.

Talking to people, reading e-mail, and sending the occasional text wasn't nearly enough functionality in a phone as far as Jack was concerned, and Gareth had long stopped wondering what his handset would do next. Jack fiddled with it daily and had probably programmed it to stop traffic, launch rockets into space, or order pharmaceuticals the moment Gareth sneezed.

Ringtones were his most recent obsession. They changed based on who was calling, the time of day, and even the location someone was calling from. When Gareth pointed out that he couldn't remember one ringtone for each person in his contact list, let alone three, Jack's face had gone blank in the same way it did when someone told him a joke he just didn't get.

Disinclined to mire himself in lengthy explanations, Gareth gave up arguing and simply answered the phone when it lit up and made noise, just as he'd done before Jack had started improving it. He didn't even ask why Jack had chosen X Japan's "Rusty Nail" as his personal ringtone. Or inquire why it was the only one that didn't change with time and tide. He simply memorised the sound of guitars and Toshi's voice and smiled every time he heard it.

If Jack had wanted a song that took Gareth far away from the spirit of Christmas, then he had succeeded.

"Jack?"

A background of traffic noise, metallic clangs and clatters, and the buzz of countless conversations made the younger man hard to understand. Borough Market was a hive on any normal day and on Christmas Eve it was bound to be mayhem. Add the misery of mobile phone reception in the city and Gareth was grateful the distinctive ringtone had told him who was calling.

"Vacuum-packed chestnuts are fine," he said, when he'd made sense of the wavering snatches of Jack's voice. "If you can find fresh ones, buy those too. What? Oh, half a dozen nets would be good. And don't forget the coffee," he reminded him, though hell would freeze over before Jack forgot to visit his favourite coffee shop to pick up a bag of freshly roasted Arabica beans to last through the Christmas period.

Gareth set the phone down and turned back to stir the Cumberland sauce simmering softly on the stove. The joys of Christmas were a long way from his mind despite the seasonal music and peaceful atmosphere.

Nancarrow Mining, where both he and Jack worked, closed over Christmas and New Year's, with only emergency personnel on standby. They'd finished work the previous Friday, and Gareth had been indulging his kitchen fetish for the last three days. By now he should have felt suitably mellow.

Instead, the cooking and baking spree had barely kept the lid on his unease. The bottle of wine he would usually have enjoyed as he cooked remained unopened in the well-stocked wine rack, and the frown that creased his brow didn't ease as he considered the results of his labours filling the large kitchen.

Pyramids of mince pies adorned one end of the kitchen counter, taking up space right beside a long row of jars.

Gareth loved relishes and chutneys, the jewel-bright colours and the muted ones, the sharp bite of the vinegar that cut the sweetness of pomegranates, mangoes, squash, and onion, the heady aroma of pickling spice and cinnamon and the hit of fiery chili. He made Christmas-themed relishes every year—to last throughout the season as much as to give away.

Two large hams sat beside the regiment of jars: boiled, studded with cloves, baked, and glazed to perfection, ready to feed the hungry while Gareth's favourite, his grandmother's famous venison pie—golden crust in elaborate pleats and thickly covered in sugar, cinnamon, and nutmeg—took pride of place, flanked by a lavishly decorated beef Wellington and a pork pie topped with cranberry compote.

He had no idea who, besides his mother, his sister, and their newest protégés, would choose to show up for Christmas dinner the next day. So he'd made sure there was plenty of food to go around, even if the wild hordes descended on Richmond.

Open house at Christmas was a tradition that Gareth had started while he served in the army and did not plan to give up now that he was a civilian. Initially intended for those of his men who had no families or whose families lived too far away for them to make it home, Gareth's Christmas dinners had turned into cheerful reunions over the years. And he loved it that way.

Jack had missed out on family occasions while growing up. Seeing how much he appreciated simple things like dinners at home, Gareth had expected Jack to love the idea of a big Christmas get-together. The almost-panic in his eucalyptus eyes and the bout of insomnia that had plagued him for most of the month had come as a shock. When the hint of panic had transformed into a shuttered gaze and forced cheer, Gareth had tried everything he could think of to draw him out.

But Jack wasn't talking.

He simply pretended that nothing was the matter, when a blind man could see that he was hurting.

At work, Gareth had watched Jack juggle for hours each day, unsure whether the vacant gaze masked thoughts of corporate network security or horrors long past.

He'd watched Jack's fingers, usually so sure and swift, stumble across the keyboard, their rhythm broken and uneven.

He'd watched him at home trying to make casual conversation when his mind was clearly spun into its own hell.

And he had no idea how to help.

"The mind has the ability to overcome many of the body's limitations," Alexandra Marston, Nancarrow Mining's resident psychologist, had told him when, cautious and reluctant and unsure, he'd gone to talk to her. "But you can make use of those limitations too. Push him far enough into physical exhaustion and his body *will* shut down to protect itself. And once he's slept, he should be able to think more clearly."

Like any former soldier, Gareth was familiar with the effects of sleep deprivation. He'd been taught how to deal with it too. Didn't mean he wasn't grateful for Alexandra's support.

Jack couldn't talk about his time working for MI6 except in the most general terms, making it difficult for Gareth to determine exactly what bothered his lover. Alexandra, an MI6 operative herself, didn't have that problem. She had heard every word that Gareth *hadn't* said—and she'd not even mentioned sleeping pills… or therapy. And while Gareth hated to push when he could not accurately predict the outcome, he had done as Marston had suggested. And then, two nights ago...

━━━━◆ ◆ ◆━━━━

"Does it still bother you?"

The soft touch woke Gareth from his doze. He lay as he'd fallen asleep, diagonally across the bed, a stack of pillows under his head. The lamp glowed on the bedside table, and outside the window inky blackness proclaimed the lateness of the hour. Jack was stretched out beside him on top of the quilt, head propped on a palm, while his fingertips traced the scar on Gareth's shoulder.

Jack's voice was as soft as the touch of his fingers. His gaze was so intent, Gareth could practically hear thoughts and memories chasing each other in his lover's head.

Despite training, work, and vigorous sex, the deep shadows under Jack's eyes still spoke more of sleepless nights than physical exhaustion, and Gareth wished Jack would just share what bothered him.

But sharing his troubles had never been Jack's way.

"It's been almost ten years," he said. "Plenty of time to forget about it."

"December 23," Jack replied, voice a mere breath.

"The last day of our tour."

Understanding lit Gareth's mind. Not so much at Jack's words, more at his tone of voice. "December 23," he mused. "Also the day you left the army. Why am I starting to think that was not a coincidence?"

Jack didn't answer, and that in itself was answer enough.

Gareth sighed and sat up. He didn't know why the idea of a big family Christmas, on top of everything else going on in Jack's life, had triggered such an intense bout of soul-searching. He only knew he had to do what he could to stop it. Jack walking out on his chosen career and family eight years ago had been a painful blow. Jack walking out on him—them—now would be worse.

*Please, don't let me fuck this up!* The silent prayer was a heartfelt plea, and Gareth took a moment to firm his resolve and let it steady him. He straightened his spine and drew a deep breath. "May I ask where you put it?"

"What?"

"Don't 'what' me, brat. Your letter of resignation."

Shock turned Jack's face perfectly white. His mouth opened and closed several times before brain and vocal chords connected into a stuttered "My what?"

"So you're not planning to walk out on me

tomorrow?"

"No!"

The horrified indignation in Jack's voice soothed Gareth's nerves. He reached out and closed a hand around Jack's bicep, pulling him up so their faces were level. "Then talk to me," he implored.

Jack's grey-green eyes were fringed with long, dark lashes. He could hide very effectively if he chose. Right then, he didn't flinch under Gareth's scrutiny. His gaze was steady, as was his voice. "I screwed up, and it almost cost you your life. I need to remember that."

"You also saved my life that day. You need to remember that too."

Jack's lashes swept down, and this time he was hiding. Well, Gareth was having none of that. He took a firm grip on Jack's chin and forced his head up.

"You're not hearing me, Jack," he growled. "You seem to believe that the truth is a one-way street when it's not. Every truth has at least two sides. So maybe you got too absorbed collecting that intel and I got shot. But you also saved my life. Both things are true, whether you like it or not."

"You're saying that failure can be redeemed?"

"I'm saying that it's pointless to fixate on endings and overlook that they're also new beginnings."

A deep breath shuddered out of Jack's throat. His

voice, when it came, was whisper-soft. "Always?"

"Always."

Tension bled from Jack's frame like air from a punctured balloon, and when Gareth stretched out and pulled him close, sleep claimed Jack in moments.

Never mind that Gareth wanted answers. That he wanted to shake his lover until he explained what the hell was going on. Jack was asleep, and Gareth— disinclined to wake him—could only gnash his teeth and possess himself in patience once more.

◆ ◆ ◆

Jack slept the rest of that night and most of the following day, the deep sleep of the totally exhausted. He barely stirred while Gareth moved through the house, cleaning, cooking, and preparing for the festivities— and Gareth considered this one of his biggest wins ever. He surfaced, ravenous as only Jack could be, in time for Gareth to feed him dinner and tuck him back into bed to sleep some more.

And now Jack was gone, ostensibly to visit Nico and Daniel, the two teenage boys they'd rescued from a pimp three months earlier, before he popped into their Strand office to make sure nothing untoward was happening at the company they both worked for.

He had to check in at Scotland Yard later too,

where Lisa Tyrrell and Clive Baxter were hard at work putting together the case against Mitrovic.

He had even offered to pick up the last of the shopping on the way back.

All totally innocent, acceptable activities, and yet Gareth cursed himself blue for ever agreeing to let Jack out of his sight. He still wasn't convinced that Jack would stick around. Not given the state of mind he'd been in the previous month.

A hiss from the stove reminded him that he had things to do, and Gareth rescued the Cumberland sauce before it burned, taking comfort in the fact that Jack had called.

If he'd really planned on bailing, chestnuts— fresh or otherwise—would surely not feature in Jack's thoughts.

The bowl of oranges caught Gareth's eye and his mind turned to the dinner he had planned for the two of them that night: a mix of rich, sophisticated flavours with a sprinkling of decadence. And if he wanted to have everything ready in time, he had better get started.

For someone who couldn't cook to save his life, Jack certainly loved to eat. He wasn't shy about experimenting with food and trying out new flavours, either.

Gareth appreciated that.

He reached for the largest of the oranges and started to cut long strips of peel, imagining the heady aromas of baking orange skin suffusing the kitchen. The scent took him right back to his childhood, and without him realising it, the comforting smells and cherished routine settled his mind.

Gareth spent the next hours chopping celeriac, peppers, and fennel for the most colourful of Christmas soups. He pounded bread, garlic, chili, and olive oil into a fiery paste and peeled potatoes for mash. He bathed a plucked goose in boiling water before popping it into the oven to roast and stewed red cabbage in a mix of red wine, sugar, vinegar, cloves, and cinnamon.

The kitchen smelled like an alchemist's idea of heaven and when Gareth selected the ripest of the six pineapples in his store and decapitated it with a mere flick of his wrist, he had almost convinced himself that his world was—and would remain—whole.

# ZERO RISING

When a homeless boy meets an ace hacker and learns that being called a zero is a compliment. One that comes with responsibilities.
The Zero Rising trilogy traces Jack's journey from a frightened, stubborn, homeless boy to a fiercely independent vigilante hacker.

**The Power of Zero**
**Two Divided by Zero**
**Zero Tolerance**

# THE POWER OF ZERO

Jack Horwood has not had a home since his mother sold him to a pimp, has not had a family since he walked out on his Army career. He spends his days chasing secrets for MI6 and his nights chasing pimps and men who buy children for sex, seemingly content until Gareth Flynn, his former Army CO and the man he fell for when he was seventeen, walks back into his life. Suddenly endings turn into new beginnings, two scared, abused boys need his help, and his past won't let him go even as he tries to make a new life for himself.

**Job Hunt**
**Ghosts**
**House Hunt**
**Swings & Roundabouts**
**A Simple Mistake**

# MEET JACKIE

Jackie Keswick was born behind the Iron Curtain with itchy feet, a bent for rocks, and a recurring dream of stepping off a bus in the middle of nowhere to go home. She's worked in a hospital and as the only girl with 52 men on an oil rig, spent a winter in Moscow and a summer in Iceland and finally settled in the country of her dreams with her dream team: a husband, a cat, a tandem, and a laptop.

Jackie writes a mix of suspense, action adventure, fantasy, and history, and loves stories with layers, plots with twists and characters with hidden depths. She adores friends to lovers stories, and tales of unexpected reunions, second chances, and men who write their own rules. She blogs about English history and food, has a thing for green eyes, and is a great believer in making up soundtracks for everything, including her characters and the cat.

And she still hasn't found the place where the bus stops.

To chat with Jackie about books, boys and food, join her in her Facebook readers group *Jackie's Kitchen*, or find her in all the usual places.

Printed in Great Britain
by Amazon